Enduring

· The Dominion Saga: Book Three ·

S.J. WEST

LIST OF BOOKS IN THE WATCHER SERIES

The Watchers Trilogy

Cursed

Blessed

Forgiven

The Watcher Chronicles

Broken

Kindred

Oblivion

Ascension

Caylin's Story

Timeless

Devoted

Aiden's Story

The Alternate Earth Series

Cataclysm

Uprising

Judgment

S. J. West

The Redemption Series

Malcolm

Anna

Lucifer

Redemption

The Dominion Series

Awakening

Reckoning

Enduring

OTHER BOOKS BY S. J. WEST

The Harvester of Light Trilogy

Harvester

Hope

Dawn

The Vankara Saga

Vankara

Dragon Alliance

War of Atonement

Enduring

CHAPTER ONE

(Helena's Point of View)

Hell seems empty now that Anna and her children are no longer in it. As I look around the room I designed for them to stay in, I can't help but feel a hollowness that their presence once filled. Oh well. I won't be alone for much longer since Cade agreed to relinquish his freedom in order to save Anna's daughter. I know his unconditional devotion to Anna and her children will ensure his quick return to my side. He isn't someone who would ever choose to help himself over others. I, on the other hand, will always choose whatever serves my own selfish interests first.

As I await Cade's return, I walk over to the dining table and tidy up the mess of dirty dishes and leftover food that was left there. It isn't something I would typically fuss over. Normally I would just snap my fingers and send the clutter elsewhere, but I want to maintain the illusion of being a considerate ruler to those who reside within my cloud city. The 'Empress of Nimbo' would bring back what she borrowed.

Just as I'm about to place the empty containers back into the basket I used to bring the food in, I notice something propped up against one of its inner walls that I neglected to give to Anna while she was here. I set the containers back on the table and reach in to pull out the framed photograph of Lucifer and Amalie. Right before Hale gave the order to blow up the propulsion system keeping Cirrus in the sky, I took the picture from Anna's chambers. I had intended to use it as a segue to inform my sister about the demise of her beloved cloud city, but even the best laid plans don't always pan out the way you expect.

I begin to feel my anger towards Lucifer twist my stomach into a tight knot as I look at his happy face. If anyone in the history of the universe deserved to remain a miserable wretch, it was my father. I toss the picture over onto the four-poster bed behind me and return to my task. After I have the basket repacked, I make a quick trip to Nimbo to return it to the kitchen staff there. As I expected, the servants are impressed that I would personally take the time to return the items to them.

"Are you hurt, Empress Helena?" one of the cooks asks me with a great deal of concern over my welfare as she looks pointedly at my dress.

I glance down and notice the splotches of blood dotting the white outfit I got while on alternate Earth. I knew the birthing process would be a messy affair, but I wasn't prepared for all the blood Anna lost. When I held Liana in my arms, some of it obviously transferred to my clothing. This is a prime example of why I prefer to wear red. I don't know what I was thinking when I allowed Lucas to pick out my dress.

"Oh, it's nothing," I assure the woman with a carefree wave of my hand. "I cut my finger somehow and didn't realize it until it was all over my dress. Thank you for pointing it out, though. I should probably go change before anyone else becomes alarmed by my appearance."

Without waiting for a reply—because, frankly, I don't need anyone's permission to leave—I teleport up to my room in the palace to change clothes. I choose to don a simple maroon dress to welcome Cade back to my home. As I study my reflection in the full-length mirror in my bedroom, I begin to wonder what he'll think of my choice of attire. He seems like someone who would prefer a more brightly colored dress, like a pale yellow or even a peach. Maybe I should rethink the red I always wear...

Wait.

Why am I even contemplating such a thing?

Why should I change something I like just to please him?

First, it will be the color of my clothing. The next thing you know, I'll be changing who I am to meet some idyllic expectation he has for his 'perfect' soul mate. And for what purpose? Just to make him happy?

Ludicrous.

I will not change the color scheme of my clothing, and I definitely won't change anything about myself just to please him. He'll have to learn to accept me for who and what I am. It's not as if I expect him to turn into a bad boy for me. Why should I be expected to turn into a goody-two-shoes for him?

In fact, I quite like what we have. I've often heard it said that opposites attract, and in our case, I would have to agree. Cade and I couldn't be more different from one another if we tried, yet there's an undeniable connection between us that keeps drawing us together. It's the proverbial moth to flame scenario. In this case, he's the moth and I'm the flame. I just hope he doesn't end up flying too close, because we all know how tragically that will end.

I can't seem to put a stop to my desire to have him around more, and he obviously can't prevent himself from caring about me. If he could have squelched his feelings for me, I'm sure he would have by now. I mean, I'm not exactly the kind of woman you want to take home to meet your family. I'm the kind of woman you want to hide your family from for their own safety.

Before I phase to my bedroom in Hell, I take one last look at myself in the mirror and tuck a few wayward strands of hair behind my left ear. When I became corporeal, I soon learned how much maintenance a real body requires. It's very tiring to keep myself looking perfectly coiffed all the time. My sister makes it look so effortless with her natural beauty and regal grace. Though, she *has* had years to perfect the intricacies of dwelling on Earth.

When I phase back to Hell I find Cade sitting on the side of the bed in Anna's room, his shoulders slightly slouched. I notice he's holding the framed photograph of Lucifer and Amalie that I left on the bed. The brooding expression on his face makes me wonder what he's thinking as he looks at the pair in the picture.

"Was my sister happy to have her baby back?" I ask pithily, breaking his contemplative mood. I suspect I already know the answer to my question, but I feel the need to ask it in order to break the silence in the room.

He looks over at me and stands from his seat on the bed. Before giving me his answer, he sets the picture on the nightstand.

"Yes. She was very happy," he tells me, turning to face me fully. "They all were."

Cade's voice doesn't hold an ounce of joy in it, and I find his expression disappointingly unenthusiastic.

"And are you having second thoughts about agreeing to our bargain?" I ask curtly.

"You didn't give me much of a choice, Helena," he replies just as testily. "You knew I would do anything to get Liana back for Anna and Malcolm. I'm not going to stand here and lie that I'm happy about this arrangement."

"Is that your subtle way of saying you don't want to be with me?" I ask, feeling my temper about to flare at his blatant insubordination.

"No, that's not what I'm saying," he replies, openly frustrated. "I'm saying that I would have liked the option to choose. You gave me no other option. There was only one choice to make."

"Do you feel like I'm punishing you by making you stay?"

"Honestly," Cade says with a little more warmth, visibly relaxing his shoulders as he accepts his fate, "I think you made the deal because you're lonely."

"That's rather presumptuous of you," I scoff. "I'm the ruler of Hell, and a whole cloud city full of people who would love nothing more than to spend time with their new empress. I don't *need* you to keep me company. I have others who can perform that function."

"Then why keep me here if it isn't to ease your loneliness?"

9

S. J. West

I don't answer because I don't want to admit that he's right. I've cornered myself into an argument that can't possibly end favorably for me. Considering the confidence in Cade's expression, he knows I'm trapped too.

"I was fairly certain you would come back," I say instead, "but I did wonder if you would consider reneging on our bargain."

"Why would I do that?" Cade asks, looking confused. It's apparent such deceit never even crossed his mind. Good grief. Did the man ever have a selfish, self-serving thought?

"Considering the fact that I absconded with Anna's first-born, I thought you might be too upset with me to return here on your own."

"I always keep my word," he states proudly, lifting his chin a notch, "but I would like to know the reason you took Liana from Anna."

"My purpose is none of your concern, dear heart," I reply, being purposely vague with my answer.

Cade remains silent as he waits for me to expand upon my reply of my own volition. When I don't, he sighs heavily in disappointment.

"Why can't you leave Anna and her family alone?" he asks wearily. "Will you always try to spoil their happiness?"

"I don't owe you any explanations about why I do certain things," I tell him bluntly.

"No, you don't," he agrees, continuing to look at me with disappointment, "but I wish you would. Maybe I can help you accomplish whatever it is you want to do without involving Anna and her family in your schemes. If you're not willing to tell me why you took Liana, would you be willing to tell me why you gave her back so easily?"

"I only needed her for a short amount of time to do what needed to be done," I reply, "and that's all you're going to get from me on the subject."

"And who does it benefit?" he asks, narrowing his eyes as he looks at me with barefaced suspicion. "You or her?"

"If there is one thing you should know with absolute certainty, it's the fact that I always do whatever benefits me the most. Thinking about what's good for others has never motivated my actions."

We stare at each other for a moment, neither of us seeming to know exactly what to say or do next. I don't intend to assuage his curiosity any further about my plans for Liana, and he seems smart enough to recognize that fact without asking any further questions.

Now that he's here, I have absolutely no idea what to do with him. Our range of activities is limited in Hell. I doubt he would appreciate a tour of my torture chambers. Although, there is one place within my domain that he's sure to consider beautiful.

"Would you like to see something extraordinary?" I ask him.

Cade continues to stare at me for a little while before saying, "I already am."

Involuntarily, I smile.

"You should do that more often," he tells me with a small, appreciative grin. His blue eyes twinkle with amusement as he continues to watch my reaction to his compliment.

"I smile all the time," I profess, hoping he can't see how flushed my face has become with his lingering gaze.

"No, you smirk," he gently corrects. "There's a difference. I guess I'll just have to figure out ways to see a real smile on your face from time to time. It's a much better look on you."

"You can try to pull off such a miracle," I challenge playfully, "but I rarely find the urge to feel happy about anything."

"I suppose I'll have to fix that." Cade's smile broadens as mine begins to fade. A normal woman would find his statement flattering, but I immediately feel offended by it. His tone makes it sound like his real intentions are to 'fix' me, when I'm not broken. I'm perfectly happy with the way I am, yet I decide not to say these words to him, at least not yet. It would only lead to an argument, and that isn't what I want right now.

"Let me put my original question to you a different way then," I say, swiftly changing the subject before my pride gets the best of me, and I end up ruining the moment. "Would you like to see something that you've never seen before?"

"I've lived a very long time." He looks dubious about my proposal. "There aren't many things I haven't seen."

"I can assure you, dear heart, that you have never seen what I'm about to show you."

"Well, now you have me intrigued. Then, yes, please show me this wonder that you believe will interest me. Is it here or on Earth?"

"Here." I walk over to Cade and wrap one of my arms around his. "It's guarded by the leviathans, so don't say anything after we phase into their chamber. I would rather not have to destroy them for trying to harm you."

"Should I feel flattered by your offer to kill them to defend my life?" He asks, his eyes filled with mirth at such a notion.

"They're my favorite creatures here, so yes, you should feel very flattered that I would kill them to protect you."

I teleport us to the center of the leviathan chamber. As I look out across the great expanse of honeycomb structures sheltering my slumbering creations, I can't help but feel an immense sense of pride in their existence. When I glance down at the section of rock we're standing on, I see the inscription Lucifer carved into it. I'm not sure why he felt the need to chisel it for all to see, but since it's written in archangel script only a few of us are able to read it.

As we stand in the circle of words, I take hold of Cade's hand to make sure he doesn't let go before I say the magical phrase.

"Em hunc numdim entrovit et hoc."

A loose translation of the code words would be '*From here I enter into worlds.*'

The rock beneath our feet disappears, and we begin to freefall into total darkness.

I hear him gasp in surprise and he involuntarily tightens his grip on my hand. I'm pleased he has enough self-discipline not to shout out his alarm, like most people would in this situation. He remains silent as he entrusts me with his life.

Our descent gradually begins to slow as we reach a pocket of warm air near our destination. A soft white light slowly seeps up from below us, allowing me to see him in half- shadows. I take advantage of our continued weightlessness while it lasts and turn my body in the air until I'm positioned directly in front of Cade. He silently watches me as if he's intrigued to learn what I'll do next. I would hate to disappoint him with inaction.

I reach up with my free hand and gently slide it around to the back of his neck. My lips part of their own accord as I fill my lungs with a tremulous breath and feel the core of my being tense in excited anticipation. I close my eyes as I lean forward to press my mouth against his. He isn't exactly resistant to my kiss, but he doesn't respond very enthusiastically either. I sense that he's still mad at me for taking Anna's little girl away from her. It's not as though I didn't give her back, for goodness' sake!

I pull away from him and say, "You're not being very much fun."

Cade's eyes darken with resentment as he stares back at me. "I'm not your personal plaything, Helena. I won't kiss you on command. Do you really need to be reminded that you just kidnapped Anna's child? You're lucky I'm even standing here."

"You make yourself sound like some sort of prize I should feel fortunate to have in my life," I reply scornfully, dropping my hand away from his neck but keeping hold of his hand. "I'll have you know that I was much happier when I didn't have to deal with all these…*emotions* I have when I'm around you. You're a complication that I'm doing my best to deal with."

"I'm sorry I've *complicated* things for you. Having you thrust into my life isn't exactly something I had planned on either."

I sigh in disappointment. It seems like every conversation Cade and I have ends up in an argument, no matter how pleasant we may start out. It's tiring and not what I want from this little excursion of ours. For once, I'm trying to do something that is only meant to give him pleasure, yet he's trying to ruin it by shoving my shortcomings in my face. I take a steadying breath and exhale slowly, forcing myself to let go of the burning anger building within my soul.

As we continue to float down to our destination, the warmth of a million worlds envelops us in a soft glow. Cade is the first one to break our eye contact as he looks around the cavernous space in pure wonder, our argument forgotten for the moment. I step away from him as he turns to take in the spectacle of the universe literally laid open before his eyes. Every inhabitable celestial body ever created by God is represented here in miniaturized form. Some stars are brighter than others, and some planets sparkle a bright shade of blue-green like the Earth. They all contain sentient life and the promise of new souls to harvest for my domain. Even though there are millions of worlds in the universe, nothing compares to the energy derived from the souls on Earth. They hold the greatest power for a couple of reasons. For one, Earth was the first planet to be populated with humanity. Secondly, the veil separating Heaven from Earth is at its thinnest, passively imbuing the humans who live on that planet with Heaven's energy. It's the main reason Lucifer focused the majority of his time and attention on the humans there. The conversion of one Earthly soul was worth thousands of souls from any other planet.

"What is this place?" Cade asks as he continues to look around, completely mesmerized by what he sees.

"Lucifer named it the Nexus," I tell him as I watch his reaction to what I say next. "From here, you can travel to a vast majority of the worlds in our reality with a single touch. God took him to almost every planet He made when it was just the two of them in Heaven. After his fall, Lucifer traveled back to the planets and left permanent phase trails open to the ones that he visited."

"Why would he want to keep them open?"

"He used to send some of his little minions to other planets on missions. It was more for his convenience than anything else. He didn't want to have to come down here every time he ordered them to go somewhere for him. The silly fool tried to use it to find the other princes of Hell when God scattered them throughout the universe. He soon figured out that his father wouldn't let him find them until the time was right and that they would only be returned through the Tear."

"Have you gone to any of these worlds?"

I shake my head. "Not yet. I've been a bit preoccupied with things on Earth, but I have a little free time now and thought you might like to go with me to look at some of them."

He turns his attention away from the Nexus to look back at me.

"Are you asking me out on a date?" he teases with a roguish grin.

"If you want to think of it in such a provincial way, I suppose it could be termed that. I would rather call it an adventure." I walk up and hold my hand out to him. "Will you travel through the universe with me, Cade?"

Without hesitation, he places his hand into mine.

"Do we have to journey back through Lucifer's phase trail to leave the planets, or can we just phase back here?" he asks.

"We can just phase ourselves back here, and after we visit a world we'll always have a phase point there."

"Phase back to this spot in the Nexus?" he asks, looking confused. "Then, why did we come here through the entrance if you could have just phased us directly here?"

"I thought you might like the drama of it all," I say with a small shrug. "Anyway, where should we go first?"

"You choose," he tells me excitedly. "I'm sure you know a little something about each of them from Lucifer's memories. You can probably make a better choice than I can."

Cade's newfound eagerness and enthusiasm to roam distant worlds with me is infectious. I feel another genuine smile threaten to reveal itself, but I stifle it before it has a chance to take root. I don't want Cade to get too cocky about his ability to make me happy. The last thing I need is for him to think he can influence my emotions so easily.

This little adventure of ours is something I've been meaning to do for quite some time now. In fact, ever since I became corporeal I've wanted to trek through the universe and see in person the places Lucifer could only share with me through his memories. I know why I resisted the urge to make this trip: I didn't want to go to these different worlds alone. I wanted someone to share them with, and now that I have Cade by my side I feel as though it's time to traipse through the cosmos to see what else it has to offer me.

I look around at the multitude of worlds we can travel to, and faintly wonder if Cade would be so eager to use the Nexus if he knew that the energy required to keep Lucifer's old phase trails open came from the torture of souls in my domain.

I'm sure his enthusiasm would wane if he were privy to that piece of information, which is exactly why I decide to keep it to myself.

I tighten my grip on his hand and reach out towards a lavender-hued planet a few solar systems away from our own.

"Here we go," I warn, lightly touching the planet with the tip of my index finger.

We're instantly transported to a world with a purple-hued sky and puffy grey storm clouds. Streaks of white lightning illuminate the atmosphere with flashes of their brilliance. The sun for this world can be seen on the horizon, but its footprint in the firmament is far less than that of the Earth's sun. I assume its distance from this world is the primary contributing factor to the chill in the air and less-than-hospitable barren terrain. I see no visible signs of sentient life or vegetation.

"Is this world unpopulated?" Cade asks me as he studies the rocky terrain we're standing on.

"Not all life lives on the surface of each planet," I explain. "I thought you would know that already."

"I do," he replies, meeting my gaze with his, looking a bit perplexed. "I guess I just assumed you would take us to a planet that was a little more hospitable for our first date."

"Taking you to a world halfway across the galaxy isn't impressive enough for you? What were you expecting? That I would wine and dine you in some fancy off-world restaurant?" I ask, finding his expectations for our first date amusing. Cade shivers slightly as a brisk gust of wind rushes past us. Since he's still shirtless and only dressed in his black leather pants and boots, I can literally see how the cold is affecting his body.

"Frankly," he says, briefly glancing away from me, surveying our surroundings with a critical eye before giving his answer, "I thought you would choose something that was at least more scenic. I mean, I understand that you've never been to these worlds

17

before, but surely Lucifer shared his memories of them with you. Isn't there at least one with more beauty in it than this?"

I quickly phase us back to the Nexus to erase Cade's disappointment in the first planet I chose.

"Follow me," I tell him as I begin to walk towards a world I remember quite well from Lucifer's travels.

The planet looks more brown than green from this godly perspective, due to the number of mountains crisscrossing its landscape. From what I can remember of this world, each city is built within a lush green valley surrounded by snow-capped mountains. The physical barrier helps protect each city-state against foreign sovereignties. The percentage of its surface covered in water is about half that found on Earth. After I touch the planet, Cade and I are instantly transported to its surface.

We find ourselves standing on a gravel path located on the side of a hill. Lush green grass borders each side of the trail, which overlooks the city built within the valley of this particular mountain set. The metropolis laid out before us contrasts greatly against the natural backdrop of the snow-capped mountains.

"What planet is this?" Cade asks, taking in the sight of the city and surrounding mountain range with a great deal of interest.

"They call it Sierra," I inform him. "I suppose because fifty percent of its surface is composed of mountains."

"Does the city have a name?"

"If memory serves me correctly, I believe this one is named Arcas. Would you like to go down and take a closer look at it?"

"Absolutely," he says eagerly.

When he looks away from the city and back at me, my heart involuntarily skips an entire beat. It's amazing how an emotion can change the aura of a person so instantly. Cade practically glows with joy, making me wonder what it must feel like to experience true happiness. The closest I've ever come to that emotion was the first time I left Hell and walked across the Earth's surface. I felt like the shackles of what I am were finally loosened, allowing me the freedom to find out who I want to become. I'm still working towards figuring out that riddle, but I feel as though I'm getting closer to discovering my true destiny.

"Come on," I tell him, tightening my grip on his hand. "I think I might actually know a person who can help us have a good time here."

Cade peers at me quizzically. "I thought you said you hadn't been to any of the planets yet."

"I haven't," I confirm as we begin to walk down the path towards the city. "Lucifer sent some rebellion angels here a very long time ago to gain a foothold on this planet. I know where at least one of them is because she came to Hell when she heard Lucifer was allowed back into Heaven. I suppose she didn't believe the rumor and had to see for herself that he was gone. She certainly wasn't very happy about that. Not many of them were."

"Don't they realize that if Lucifer can earn redemption it means that they can too?"

I let out a small derisive laugh. "Most of them have given up on the possibility of such a miracle for themselves. It's a bit funny really. Out of all of them, Lucifer was the only one who kept his hope of returning to Heaven alive. He never would have admitted that fact to any of the others, but his thoughts were always an open book to me. I can't say I blame him. Heaven *is* quite nice. He was a fool to give it up so readily."

Cade comes to a complete standstill, forcing me to stop walking as well.

"You said that like you've been to Heaven and experienced it for yourself," he says, looking at me in complete confusion. "Or are you just going by what you've seen in other's memories?"

"Ohhh," I say, smiling as I realize something. "That's right. You don't know what happened in that alternate reality. Your father extended an invitation to me to enter into His hallowed realm while I was there. Apparently, He wanted to have a little heart to heart with me."

"And how did that go?" Cade asks, looking skeptical that such a meeting of the minds would end on a friendly note.

"About as well as you would expect," I reply, not intending to tell him what God showed me while I was there. The possibility of Cade and me having a happy life and a child together is a completely ludicrous notion. I don't want to get his hopes up by telling him what God showed me. He doesn't need to know, and I have no intention of blindly believing that the fantasy world God concocted could actually come to fruition. "I would rather not talk about that part of my trip, but I will tell you what else transpired there."

As we continue to walk hand in hand to Arcas, I fill Cade in on everything that occurred during my time on alternate Earth. I can tell by the look in his eyes that he wants a better description from me about my experience in Heaven, but I wisely choose to ignore his sideways glances and deftly steer the subject towards Lucas. I have to admit, the kid amused me more than once with his blunt honesty. I truly hope he keeps that trait as he matures. Humans have a tendency to rein in their true thoughts and feelings about others due to their need to appear kind and accepting. Sometimes, the better course of action is just to say exactly what's on your mind. Who knows, the person you're talking to might just take the time to look in the mirror and choose to become better than they are.

By the time we reach the bustling city streets of Arcas, Cade's attention becomes absorbed by the sights, sounds, and smells of this strange new world I've brought him to.

Sierra isn't as far along as Earth in its technological advancements. If I had to place it within Earth's timeline, I would say it is somewhere between the years 2050 and 2100 in comparison. The city is filled with geometrically-shaped skyscrapers made out of glass, steel, and stone, and the paved streets are filled with sleek, colorful automobiles. There doesn't seem to be a consensus among the populous as far as fashion is concerned. People simply wear whatever they want to, even if that means eating from a sidewalk food vendor in a couture gown or getting married in shorts and a crop top. Instead of dressing the way society expects them to, each person here has their own sense of style and stays true to that no matter where they go.

As we pass a sidewalk hotdog vendor, I can't prevent the deep rumble that emanates from my stomach when I smell the delectable scent of slow-roasted meat. Surprisingly, even through the sounds of the city, Cade hears my body's cry for sustenance.

"I don't suppose you have any money for food?" he questions me, looking doubtful I will give him a positive answer.

"No," I admit disappointedly. "I don't have any currency on me, but we don't need it."

Cade narrows his eyes and asks, "Are you planning to steal some food?"

"No," I say unequivocally, "we won't have to stoop to that level. As I said earlier, I know someone here who can provide us with what we need. Just follow me. Her establishment isn't too far away."

Cade remains by my side as I walk him through the city towards our destination.

"Who is this rebellion angel we're going to see anyway?" he asks as we walk. "Do I know her?"

"In Heaven her name was Jaoel, but here she's known as Evelyn."

"I don't remember her," he admits with a frown.

"Of course you don't. It's not as if you had time to ask every rebellion angel's name during a battle. You were made to kill them, not befriend them," I reason.

I hear Cade sigh deeply as his gaze lowers to the cement street we're walking down.

"You have nothing to feel guilty about," I declare, knowing his code of ethics is warring with the purpose he was made for. "God made you to kill and win the war. You did your job. Feel proud of that fact."

Cade turns his head and looks at me. "You should never feel prideful about anything, much less killing."

"Death is just a part of life," I say dismissively, wishing for the hundredth time he would get over his own guilt complex and move on already. "Besides, you didn't kill by choice. It's what you were created to do. You were just a weapon used by God to make sure Lucifer never had a chance of winning. If you want to lay the blame for what you did on anyone, it should be your father."

Cade sighs heavily again and says, "Can we change the subject? I would rather not talk about this with you, not right now at least. From what I've been told, you're supposed to have a good time on dates."

I shrug one shoulder. "Whatever you want. I would much rather have a good time, too, which is exactly why I'm taking you to Evelyn's establishment."

"Why type of place does she operate here?"

"It's right over there," I say, turning my head slightly to look down and across the street at one of the few black stone buildings in the city. From what I remember from Lucifer's memories, the building was once a courthouse in this world before Evelyn bought it and transformed the interior into her nightclub. Its austere façade gives the place a sense of grandeur, telling those who are allowed entry that they are special.

"The Grace House is an upscale nightclub," I tell him. "Evelyn has kept her roster of clientele very exclusive to ensure that it stays at the top of everyone's list of places they have to visit when in Arcas."

"Are you sure she'll even let us in then?" Cade asks jokingly, with a note of seriousness.

"Absolutely," I reply confidently. "Evelyn always does what's in her best interest, and making me mad would not bode well for her."

We walk across the street and approach the front of the nightclub, which already has a long line of people attempting to gain entrance. Two guards dressed in dark suits stand in front of the black metal double doors that lead into the interior. I notice one of them recognize me instantly. His eyes widen in shock, and his mouth hangs open slightly as he watches us walk up the stone steps towards him.

"Hello, Enis," I say to the rebellion angel, who has been Evelyn's faithful friend since they were wee little angels together in Heaven. For whatever reason, they considered themselves true siblings. I never quite got it, but whatever floated their boats, I suppose. "Is Evelyn around?"

"She's inside," Enis answers guardedly, eyeing Cade with a great deal of misgiving. His puzzled gaze lingers on our joined hands. It isn't hard to tell such intimacy is confusing his small mind.

"We would like to go inside and have a bite to eat," I inform him. "I'm sure Evelyn won't mind entertaining us while we're here."

"And... why *are* you here?" Enis asks cautiously, with open apprehension over my sudden appearance on his world.

"That's really none of your business," I retort. "But if it will ease your mind, we're just here for something to eat unless you want to turn it into more than that. I would be more than happy to oblige, if that is your wish."

Enis hesitates before slowly shaking his head, causing his short, curly brown hair to bounce slightly. "No. I have no desire to do that, Helena."

Without another word, he turns around and places his hand on the glossy surface of the black metal door behind him. There's a faint blue glow underneath his hand as the door reads his palm print. A second later, the double doors slide open. Enis takes a step back from the entrance and extends his arm towards the interior.

"After you," he says, indicating we should proceed within.

Still holding Cade's hand, we walk side by side into The Grace House. I sincerely hope the proprietor doesn't give us any trouble. I would hate to burn such a nice establishment to the ground because of poor service.

But I would.

In less than a heartbeat…

CHAPTER TWO

The entrance turns out to be a long dark hallway with only a row of soft white spotlights shining down from the high ceiling to light the way. At the other end of the hall are another set of black steel doors. When we make it halfway down, a holographic image of Evelyn appears in front of the doors. She's dressed in an elegantly tailored white suit made to accentuate her feminine form and a matching fedora tilted down slightly to mask half her face in shadow. Her long blonde hair is tucked into a tear-drop bun at the nape of her neck.

"Welcome to The Grace House," the hologram says. "My name is Evelyn Grace, and I want to personally congratulate you for making it onto our exclusive guest list. Please think of this place as your own personal sanctuary for the evening. Dance, eat, and enjoy your time with us. My home is yours…at least for tonight."

The image disappears just as we come to stand in front of the doors leading into the heart of the nightclub. Enis walks over to the other side of Cade and places his hand on this door, too. After the perfunctory security scan of his palm, the doors slide open to reveal the true interior. Pulsating music fills the air as we come face to face with the real Evelyn Grace. Her hair is styled in long, loose curls, and she's dressed in an alligator textured black leather dress with a gold zipper holding the front together. If I had to guess, I would place the age of the body Evelyn is inhabiting to be around fifty-five years old.

"What the hell are you doing here, Helena?" she asks rather obnoxiously, hands on hips.

"As ancient as you are, I thought you would have better manners when welcoming your guests, Evelyn," I say in response. "It's a wonder you're still in business."

"I didn't invite you," she replies, crossing her arms defensively against her waist. "So, technically, you're not my guest."

"I'm sorry, Evie," Enis says, walking over to stand beside her. "I wasn't sure what to do with her. She said all she wants to do is get something to eat."

Evelyn's stern expression softens when she looks over at Enis.

"It's not your fault," she reassures him with a much kinder tone than she's used with me thus far. "You did the right thing by letting her in." Evelyn looks back at me with what I can only term as loathing in her eyes. "I just don't like surprises."

"I'm learning that life is full of them," I tell her with a tight-lipped grin. "Get used to it."

Evelyn sighs in resignation. "So after you eat, you'll be leaving and never coming back?"

"We'll see," I say, attempting for Cade's sake to tolerate Evelyn's outspoken disdain. I doubt he would appreciate me killing our host for the evening right in front of him, but this particular rebellion angel is testing the limits of what little patience I have cultivated over the years.

Evelyn looks Cade up and down with a great deal of interest and a possible criticism on the tip of her tongue.

"Are you here with her of your own free will, War Angel?" she questions skeptically.

"Yes," Cade replies without hesitation, even though it's not quite the truth. If it weren't for our bargain, I seriously doubt a spot by my side would be his first choice. More than likely he would be with Anna and her family instead. They were his home, not me.

"Why would you willingly torture yourself by being with her?" Evelyn asks, clearly dumbfounded by his answer.

"She's my soul mate," he informs her, surprising not only the two rebellion angels staring at us but me as well. I'm not sure if it was his words that surprised Evelyn and Enis, or his willingness to state such a fact so bluntly for all to hear. For me, it was the ease with which he admitted to the connection between us, like it was the most natural thing in the world to do.

Evelyn's eyebrows rise, openly showing her surprise. "Well, now I've heard everything. I didn't even know someone as cold-hearted as her could have a soul, much less someone who would admit to being a perfect match to it."

"If I were you, I would think very carefully about what you say to Cade next," I warn Evelyn in a low, threatening voice. It's one I reserve for those foolish enough to cross me. If she doesn't tread carefully, I may just snap her head from her spine, even with Cade watching.

Evelyn drags her gaze away from Cade and looks at me like I'm a stranger to her. It seems my threat has opened her eyes to a new side of me. Honestly, I'm not sure how I feel about that or the fact that I do indeed feel protective of Cade.

"Get them whatever they want," Evelyn tells Enis as she continues to consider me with open curiosity. "All I ask is that you not harm the other people who are here, Helena. All they want to do is have a good time."

"And that's the only reason we're here," I assure her. "But you're doing a piss poor job of making that happen. I'm surprised this place of yours does so much business if this is the way you treat all of your customers."

Evelyn's gaze drifts back to Cade, pointedly settling on his bare chest. "We have a strictly enforced dress code here," she informs him, but not unkindly. "I'll have someone bring a shirt to your table that you can wear while you're here."

"Thank you," Cade says, nodding his head in her direction to show his appreciation of her kindness.

"Take them to one of the corner booths so they can have some privacy," Evelyn tells Enis. Although, I suspect the booth is to ensure the safety of her patrons more than seeing to our comfort. "Make sure they get anything they want."

Evelyn turns and walks away from us, towards the bar that takes up most of the wall to our right.

"Please follow me," Enis says to us.

As we walk through the nightclub, I have to admit I'm a bit impressed with the way Evelyn has maintained a balance between old-world charm and modern technology. A white marble dance floor is the focal point for the large room. Hanging directly above the crowd of people dancing are five large crystal chandeliers. White, sheer drapes hang from black poles on either side of the dance floor, casting an illusion of intimacy and romance. Near the wall at the north end of the room is a raised stage where the DJ is located. Laser lights shine down from the ceiling, bringing a festive air to the crowded affair.

The booth Enis escorts us to is located in a far corner of the room. It's upholstered with maroon velvet fabric and is in the shape of a semi-circle with a round, black-clothed table in the center.

Being a consummate gentleman, Cade allows me to position myself in the booth first before he takes his place by my side.

"I'll bring some menus over for you to look at. In the meantime, is there anything I can get you to drink?" Enis asks us.

"Do you have sweet tea here?" Cade asks.

"Yes, we have that." Enis looks over at me questioningly.

"A glass of your best red wine," I tell him.

"I'll be right back with some menus and your drinks," Enis says, bowing slightly to us before he walks off.

Almost as soon as he leaves, a young woman walks over to our table with a long-sleeve white dress shirt in her hands.

"Ms. Grace asked that I bring this to you, sir," the blond girl says, openly ogling Cade's bare-chested state. I feel like tearing her eyes out of their sockets, but I refrain from acting on natural instinct and allow her to keep her sight, for now.

Cade accepts the shirt graciously, bestowing the girl with a grin and quiet, "Thank you."

The girl smiles back at him, but quickly wipes it from her face when she happens to look in my direction. I suppose whatever she sees in my expression scares her witless. She ends up scurrying off as if her hair suddenly caught on fire. She doesn't even take time to spare Cade a second glance in her hasty retreat.

Cade quickly dons the shirt he was given, leaving the top two buttons undone. As he's buttoning the cuffs on the sleeves, he notices me watching him.

"What?" he asks as a self-conscious smile tugs at the corners of his mouth. "Haven't you ever seen a man put on a shirt before?"

"Of course I have," I say, as if his question is a rhetorical one, "but I was just thinking that you look just as handsome with clothes on as you do without them."

Cade's smile grows into a full one as he finishes buttoning the last cuff.

"You're getting better at flirting," he says, as if it's a praise.

"I'm not flirting. I'm simply stating a fact."

He chuckles. "I'll take the compliment whichever way it's meant."

"So," I say, drawing the word out while I tap the tips of the fingers on my left hand against the table, "what exactly do people do on a first date?"

Cade turns slightly in his seat to face me. "I think we're supposed to get to know one another better."

"I'm not sure there's much I can tell you about myself that you don't already know," I say. "My life isn't exactly a mystery. Plus, I've already been through your memories. I know almost everything there is to know about you."

"Do you know what my favorite color is?" he asks.

I have to pause to think about that one. Finally, I admit, "No. I can't say I paid attention to any reference to that fact."

"I love the color red," he tells me with a broad smile as he looks pointedly down at the dress I'm wearing.

I let out a small laugh and have to ask, "And when exactly did red reach such a high status in your opinion?"

"The first time I saw you," he states, never glancing away from my gaze. I know his answer is an honest one because Cade has never told a lie in his entire existence.

"And what was your favorite color before you met me?"

"Yellow-orange."

"Not too much of a stretch to red then."

"No, not too much."

I consider Cade for a moment and have to ask, "What exactly do you see happening between us? Do you have some fanciful future planned where we're living happily ever after?"

"Honestly?" he tilts his head, looking lost for an answer. "I don't know what the future holds for us. I can't think much past this date of ours. I know who and what you are, and I also know that you're someone set in your ways. I think the real question here is what do *you* see happening between us."

I have to look away from Cade's earnest expression. I know what he wants. He wants me to give him some hope that we can have a future where we're both happy, but I don't see that as a possibility. One of us will have to bend to the other's will, and I know I will never bend to anyone.

The illusion God placed me in while I was in Heaven haunts my thoughts. Building a life with Cade where we're happy and have a child together is so far out of my reach I know it's an impossibility. Even if I could have that sort of life, would I really want it? I won't lie to myself. I know a part of me does, but there is also a stronger, more fortified part of me that finds the whole notion repulsive. I've survived on the pain of others for so long, I simply can't imagine living any other way. Yet, what if I did become more than what Lucifer made me to be? Is it time for me to step out of the shadow of what I was created for and make myself into someone who lives for more than death and destruction? I don't feel ready for that, and there are too many wheels in motion right now for me to even contemplate such a thing. No, if this relationship with Cade is going to work he'll have to be the one who changes, not me.

"I don't see us buying a home and raising a family like normal people do," I tell him truthfully. When I look back at him, I don't see disappointment on his face. I think he knew the moment we met that such a conventional relationship wasn't something we could ever have. "Right now, all I'm interested in is dealing with the feelings I have for you."

"And what do you feel for me, Helena," he whispers with a patient look on his face as he awaits my answer.

If I tell him that he makes my heart ache every time he looks at me, or that just the sound of his voice brings me comfort, I know I'll lose control over the situation.

Instead of confessing such an intimate account of how he actually affects me, all I can force myself to say is, "Different. I feel different when I'm around you."

"I hope I make you feel *different* in a good way."

"Maybe the more important question here is how I make *you* feel."

"Confused," he readily admits, looking the part. "I know what you are. I know what you've done, yet I can't stop this burning need I have to be with you."

"And if you could stop feeling the way you do about me, would you?"

As I wait for his answer, I become aware that I'm holding in my breath, anticipating his reply. A part of me wants him to say that he wishes we weren't soul mates. It would make both of our lives so much easier, but there is also a part of me wanting to hear him say he can't imagine his life any other way.

"It would certainly make both of our lives easier," he says, unknowingly voicing my own thoughts just before reaching out to grasp my right hand underneath the table, "but now that I know what having a soul mate feels like, I can honestly tell you no. I wouldn't want things any other way."

I slowly breathe out a sigh of relief, but keep my expression closed off so he doesn't have an inkling how his answer has affected me. All I need is for him to think he has the upper hand in this relationship.

Enis approaches the table with two menus in his hands. As he gives us each one of the small black leather-bound booklets, he says, "Please feel free to order anything. I'll be back in a few minutes to see what you want."

Enis walks away to stand by the bar while we peruse the menu.

It doesn't take me long to figure out what I want to eat, and I'm glad to see Cade quickly decides what he wants as well.

Enis must have been watching us because he promptly returns to the table after we set our menus down.

"And what can I get you both this evening?" he asks.

"You go first," I tell Cade.

"I'll have the seared filet mignon with roasted new potatoes," he tells Enis.

Enis turns his attention to me. "And for you?"

"The same," I reply, finding it strange that Cade and I would order identical dishes.

"I will have them out to you shortly," Enis says before turning to walk towards a door that I presume leads to the kitchen.

"How much do you want to bet they have our meals prepared in less than ten minutes?" I ask Cade.

"I'm sure they want to see us gone as quickly as possible."

"The story of my life," I say more to myself than Cade.

"I don't want you gone," he says, retaking my hand underneath the table and squeezing it gently.

"Not yet," I reply with a wan smile. "Give it time. Eventually, everyone wants to leave me."

Lucifer's face flashes in my mind, but I quickly squelch it. All I need to do is confess my daddy issues to Cade. That's a surefire way to make him want to turn his back on me and run away as far as he can get. The ironic thing is that I would do the same thing if our positions were reversed.

"I don't think Lucifer asked for forgiveness to get away from you." Cade's ability to understand where my thoughts have wandered surprises me. It's almost as if he just read them. I could deny I was referring to Lucifer, but what would be the point? Cade simply deduced that I was speaking of my father because, out of all those who have resided in Hell, he was the only one who had the option of leaving it.

"Maybe not," I concede, "but it was at least a happy bonus for him. He detests me, and there's nothing I can do about that even if I wanted to."

"I think I know what you need right now," Cade says, keeping a hold of my hand as he begins to scoot out of the booth. "Come on. Let's dance."

"Uh, I don't dance," I declare, yanking my hand out of his grasp before he has a chance to pull me with him.

"Yes, you do. I've seen you dance."

"At balls and such. Not that." I nod my head towards the horde of undulating bodies on the dance floor. To be honest, it looks more like they're having a clothed orgy in syncopation to the thumping music. "I do *not* dance like *that*."

"Are you that scared of letting yourself go for even a moment?" he asks, attempting to goad me into doing what he wants.

"I let myself go all the time when I torture people," I reply curtly, "but I have a feeling you don't want to hear about that part of my life."

My words seem to have the desired effect on Cade, and he sits back down in the booth. However, he doesn't scoot over to sit right next to me this time. He maintains a certain distance between us, and his face becomes drawn with contemplation as he considers the weight of my statement.

"Sometimes," he begins, looking down at the table and not meeting my eyes, "I forget what you are."

"I don't understand how you can," I scoff bitterly, finding his admission an insult to the very core of who I am. "Are you hoping that some miracle will happen and I'll change?"

Almost reluctantly he looks over at me, shaking his head. "No. I know you can't. It's not in your nature to be nurturing and kind to others. But I've also come to realize that what you do serves a higher purpose. You're the darkness that hides in the corner of every human's sin. Those who believe in Heaven and Hell know you exist, and either refrain from committing a depravity that will doom them to your tender care or forge ahead and lose their souls to you forever. I can't say I like what you do to those who end up in your domain, but whether you want to admit it or not you serve a function in the grand scheme of things."

"Let me get this straight, you've been able to justify what I am and certain things that I do to make them almost noble in your eyes," I say working through his rationale. "Just to satisfy my curiosity, how have you justified the deaths I caused in Cirrus by sending in my hellspawn? Or the death of Anna's maid, who I murdered with my own two hands? Was I serving some higher calling by orchestrating all of that?"

"I'm fully aware that you can be beyond cruel, and that you will most likely continue to do things I don't like, but I'm not deluded enough to believe that I can force you to change." He pauses, seemingly to collect his thoughts as I patiently wait for him to continue. "All I ask," he finally says, his words measured as if to make sure I hear his next ones clearly, "is that you don't hurt any of my friends."

"So are you giving me your permission to hurt everyone else in the world except those you care about?" I ask, amused by his request.

"That's not what I said, Helena." Cade's tone is low, almost admonishing. "Obviously, I don't want you to hurt people, but I also know I can't protect the world from you. All I do know, without a shadow of a doubt, is that if you hurt the people I consider to be my family, I won't be able to forgive you no matter how much I might

35

want to. I won't be able to continue whatever this is growing between us because I won't be able to look at you anymore. Can you understand that?"

"Yes," I say, not liking his ultimatum but also grasping his need to warn me about the ramifications of my actions. "I can't promise you that none of the people you care about won't be hurt by my plans. Things will happen that aren't completely under my control, but I can tell you that I have no intention of physically harming Anna or any member of her family. As for your War Angel brothers, they know the risks involved in protecting what Anna holds dear. You should tell them to stand down when the time comes because that's the only way I can promise they won't be hurt."

"You know they won't. War Angels don't run away from fights. We run towards them."

I shrug. "Then there's nothing I can do beyond what I've already promised, dear heart. You'll have to decide for yourself whether or not you can live with the things I have to do."

"What are you planning to do, Helena?" he whispers desperately.

"It's not something you need to worry about. There's nothing you can do to stop what's already been set into motion. The most you can do is help Anna with the fall-out when the time comes."

"I thought you said you weren't going to hurt her or her family."

"By that, I meant I wouldn't purposely set out to kill any of them. Really, Cade, for someone who just said they understood they can't change me, you seem bound and determined to see such a miracle transpire."

Cade looks away from me and stares at the people on the dance floor as he contemplates my words. With his profile to me, I have a chance to just look at him. Even brooding, he's the most handsome man I've ever seen. It takes every ounce of willpower I possess not to stretch my arm out and trace the side of his face with the tips of my

36

Enduring

fingers. Before I lose control of my actions, I avert my gaze away from him and focus on the dancers. They look so foolish jumping around against one another. I have to wonder what enjoyment they're actually obtaining by acting so wildly. Control is everything to me. It's something I can never give up.

Neither of us has to break the silence that's formed like a brick barricade between us. Enis does it by bringing over our plates of food and a complimentary basket of buttered bread.

"Please let me know if you need anything else, and feel free to leave once you're done," he adds.

Enis walks away before I can make a pithy comeback to his unsubtle suggestion.

"Well, Evelyn definitely needs to work on the hospitality of her employees around here," I comment dryly as I pick up my fork.

Cade doesn't say anything. He simply begins to eat his steak, not bothering to attempt a breach over the wall of silence that continues to separate us.

Whatever. He can ruminate over what I've said for a while. My body is famished for sustenance, so I begin to eat as well.

By the time we're both finished with our meals, I'm ready to go back home. I thought traveling to different worlds with Cade would be fun, but his surly attitude has tarnished what was supposed to be a memorable adventure for the both of us. I might have to reconsider this whole soul mate thing.

"Have you been to many places on Earth?" Cade asks me, finally shattering his silence as he lays his fork down on his empty plate.

"I can't say that I have," I admit, taking a last sip of wine from my glass. "Why do you ask?"

37

"I did a lot of traveling after we arrived there. I thought since you showed me a world I've never seen before I would do the same for you. There are a multitude of wonders on Earth. You don't have to travel halfway across the galaxy to see something new."

His statement sounds a bit like a complaint, but I decide to forgo my usual snarky retort. However, he seems a bit ungrateful about my effort to do something fun with him.

"I'm not sure I'm properly outfitted to go globetrotting around Earth," I say, briefly looking down at my red dress. "I'll need to return home to change. Why don't you have Enis bring us something for dessert while I'm gone? I'll be back in a moment."

Without waiting for a reply, I phase back to my bedroom in Hell directly in front of the wooden wardrobe there. It doesn't take me long to find something to wear since I have very few outfits which aren't dresses. I pick a red jumpsuit with a wraparound waist and wide legs. I snatch up a pair of flat black sandals to complete the ensemble. After I lay out everything on my bed, I begin to unzip the back of my dress. I suddenly get the strange sensation that I'm being watched. My first thought is that Cade is in the room and playing the role of a voyeur, yet such a lascivious act seems to go against his boy-next-door nature.

I look over my shoulder and stare at the person standing a few feet behind me.

At first, I seriously consider the possibility that I've gone completely mad.

"No, you haven't exactly lost your mind," the illusion says, promptly clearing up that mystery for me. "And I'm not exactly an illusion. Just a manifestation of the logical part of yourself that you seem to be missing right now."

I lower my arms to my sides and turn to face a figure that looks exactly like me in every possible way. She's even wearing the same clothes as me.

"I don't understand what you are," I confess as I stare at her.

"I'm the part of you that will always remain here," she tells me, lifting her hands slightly in the air to indicate she's talking about Hell. "Your soul may have a corporeal form to reside in, but this place is who you are. Why are you pretending that you can have anything resembling a real life?"

"Because I'm *real* now," I argue.

"You'll never be like Anna," my alter ego taunts. "I know that's what you really want, but that's never going to happen. You can never escape who and what you are. The sooner you admit that fact, the better off everyone will be, including Cade."

"He cares about me."

"Perhaps, but your feelings for him will end up destroying who he is. Do you really want that to happen?"

"He simply intrigues me," I argue, "and I'm curious to see where all of this will lead."

"You can't lie to me, Helena. I am you. I know exactly what you feel and think. Stop this before you ruin what we have planned. If you stay focused on our goal, you can have dominion over both Hell and Earth. That's what you really want. Don't let Cade pull you away from what you've been working so hard towards."

"I'm not," I defend. "Everything is going as planned."

"Then why haven't you sent Silas and the others to Earth yet? You know that has to be done in order to take the next step. Strike now while Anna is preoccupied with the babies. You're missing a prime opportunity to take her down once and for all."

"I'll send them when I'm ready."

"You need to send them now!"

"I said I'll do it when I'm ready!" As I yell, I realize I'm only arguing with a manifestation of my id. A part of me knows she's right, but I hate to admit when I'm wrong, even to myself. "Fine. I'll do it now, if that will make you go away and never return."

"I am you. It's not exactly like I can go anywhere."

"Then just don't materialize in front of me like this again," I say, waving a hand in her direction to indicate what I mean.

"I'm only here because you needed me to remind you what needs to be done."

"I'll take care of it! Now just go!"

The illusion of me vanishes, making me wonder if I'm losing my grasp on reality.

I snap my fingers in the air and bring Silas, Jered's son, to me. He looks momentarily startled by my abrupt summons, but he quickly recovers.

"Is it time?" he asks me eagerly. It's apparent he's been impatiently waiting for me to send him back to Earth.

"Yes," I tell him. "Anna is vulnerable at the moment. She won't see what we have planned coming, and what you and the others will do should work to our advantage. Very soon, the people of the world will want Anna's head served on a platter. Unfortunately, they're too civilized for that sort of action. At the very least, she'll lose her throne and the respect of everyone on Earth. Just make sure you follow the plans I gave you. Don't miss a step along the way in your rush to show your father you don't need him anymore."

"I don't," Silas states stubbornly. "I thought I've proven that to you by now."

"Emotions, especially where loved ones are concerned, can be tricky to deal with. Just remember that I'm the one who is giving you this opportunity to leave Hell. I can bring you back just as easily."

"That isn't really a threat to me. You know I consider this place more of a home than I do Earth."

"You say that now because it's been so long since you've been back. I just don't want you to believe you're safe from me there. Your soul belongs to me. I can pull you back here anytime I want. Don't forget that, Silas."

Silas bends at the waist in supplication. "I am yours to command for now and for always, Helena. My loyalty is to you alone."

"Very well. As long as we understand one another. Now, I assume you and the others you have chosen are ready to go?"

"Yes. We've been ready for quite some time."

"Good. Let me get dressed and I'll take you where you need to go first."

I snap my fingers and transport Silas back to where he was before I brought him to me. I quickly change my clothes and check my reflection in the mirror to make sure everything is in place.

I feel a slight flutter in my heart, but I'm not sure if it's because I'm setting Silas and his men in place for their mission or because I'll be spending more time with Cade. I turn away from the mirror, deciding it doesn't matter what the reason is exactly.

I'm going to have a wonderful time either way.

CHAPTER THREE

(Anna's Point of View)

"Anna..." Malcolm sweetly whispers in my ear, lovingly tugging its lobe with his teeth as he practically begs, "Open your eyes, Anna. I need you."

I was so tired after Malcolm and I cleaned the babies that we placed all the children in bed with us to cuddle. I know the babies and Lucas are sandwiched in between Malcolm and me in a safe cocoon of domestic bliss. I tried my best to stay awake and continue to marvel at the miracle that is my family but exhaustion overcame me, dragging me underneath the veil of dreams.

"Anna..." I hear Malcolm whisper again, a note of throaty desperation in his voice. "You're dreaming, my love. Open your eyes for me."

The combination of his gentle plead for my company combined with the warm trail of maddening kisses his lips are making along my neck prompts me to open my eyes. When I do, the first thing I see are the waves of a blue-green ocean sweeping over a great expanse of pristine white sand. The baby-blue sky overhead is filled with the wispy white clouds my city is named after. We're lying on a four-poster wooden bed with white and peach colored sheer fabric tied to the posts to make a canopy, shielding us from the rays of the sun, but allowing its heat to penetrate through just enough to warm my skin. It's been so long since I was allowed to share a dream with Malcolm. The seals prevented me from doing it, but now that the twins have been born it looks as though that particular connection with Malcolm has been restored, along with my natural brown hair and eye color.

As I lay on my side, I feel the heat of Malcolm's naked form behind me. It's only then that I realize I'm nude, too. With one arm loosely encircling my waist, he continues the gentle assault of his lips against my flesh, causing certain parts of my body to cry out for the same ardent attention.

I turn my body until I'm lying flat on my back and able to see the beauty of my husband's face. His long black hair flows freely in the sea's light breeze. As I stare up at Malcolm, the love I feel for him fills every cell in my body to bursting. The muscles of my heart tighten to a point I fear it might stop beating all together.

"Is this a dream?" I ask breathlessly. "Or are you real?"

"Both." When he smiles down at me, all I can do is stare at his full lips and wonder why he isn't kissing me with them. Never one to act shy around him, I show Malcolm exactly what I want. I lift my arms and wrap them around his neck, promptly solving the dilemma of him not kissing me.

Meeting absolutely no resistance, Malcolm lowers his head until our lips finally touch. The warm pressure of his mouth teasing mine causes an involuntary groan of pleasure to issue forth from my throat. I feel him slide one large hand across the naked flesh of my stomach until it gently cups the side of a breast. Along with a gentle squeeze, he begins to tease my nipple with the pad of his thumb in a rhythmic, circular motion that sends the tiny nerve endings there into a pleasurable frenzy.

I know we're inside one of Malcolm's dream worlds, but every touch and gentle tease feels as if it's real. Usually, the physical contact we share in his dream worlds always feels like a faint shadow of the real thing. I'm not sure what's different, and in this moment I really don't care. All I know is that I want to feel Malcolm inside me. I want everything my husband has to offer me and more.

I know Malcolm is fully aware of the difference, too, considering how a certain part of his anatomy is reacting to our foreplay. When he lifts his hand away from my breast, I automatically whimper at the loss of the contact until I feel him slowly slide it between my thighs to give another feature of my body some overdue attention. As I feel his fingers play with the most sensitive part of my core, I have to break our kiss long enough to take in a deep, shuddering breath. While I'm reminding my body how to breathe, Malcolm doesn't miss a beat and begins to kiss the side of my face until his mouth reaches my ear.

"I've missed you," he whispers, causing my body to tremble even more as his breath warms the inside of my ear. "I've missed this."

The quickening of his fingers against my flesh causes me to gasp in pleasure, driving me to the breaking point and beyond. As I close my eyes and give voice to the joy Malcolm is selflessly giving me, I feel the heat of his body leave my side for a brief moment. When I feel the warmth of his hands again, this time on my thighs, I open my eyes just long enough to watch him lower his head as his mouth deftly takes over the job his fingers were performing. I lose count of the number of times my husband shatters the center of my being as he works his magic again and again.

At one point, I grab a handful of his long dark locks and yank his head up before saying, "Stop. I need more."

Never one to question what I want from him in bed, Malcolm crawls across the mattress on his hands and knees above me until we're face to face again. I lift my legs to wrap them around his waist as he lowers his hips to comply with my urgent plea. I hear Malcolm gasp as our bodies finally connect, allowing himself to experience pleasure. The first thrust of his hips causes me to cry out and beg him not to stop.

Malcolm does as I demand, his groans growing more guttural with each thrusts. Not wanting to be selfish, I say, "Don't hold back."

As the movement of him inside me reaches a fever pitch, I can't prevent the tears that slide from the corners of my eyes as we lose ourselves in one another. After we're both sated and pleasantly exhausted, I wrap my arms around Malcolm's neck, pulling him down until the entire length of his body is lying on top of me. The sensation of his warm skin against mine makes me feel safe and protected. While we both try to steady our breathing, I quietly continue to cry until it turns into an uncontrollable sob.

Malcolm lifts his head and looks down at me. Even through the blur of my tears I can see his worry over my outburst, but I still can't stop myself from crying.

"We're all alive," Malcolm reminds me, knowing without having to ask why I'm so emotional. "The babies are safe. Lucas wasn't harmed, and you're all back home with me. We're together again, Anna. That's all that matters."

"I just…" I begin, but the intensity of my feelings doesn't allow me to go on any further before another sob breaks free.

Malcolm continues to hold me close as he says, "Let it all out, Anna. Just let it out. I'm here for you."

And I do just that. I tried to stay strong while Lucas and I were with Helena, but now that that ordeal is over my emotions are a jumbled mess. I'm worried about the seal Helena gave Liana and what it might mean to my daughter's future. I have no doubt whatsoever that Helena has more misfortune planned for my family, and I'm certain none of her schemes will leave us totally unscathed. Her hatred for humanity and her jealousy over the relationship Lucifer and I have is bound to make her seek even more vengeance than she already has. What worries me most is the fact that I'm not certain I can stop her. Ever since she introduced herself to the world as the Empress of Nimbo she's been controlling things without anyone, besides us, being cognizant of the way she's manipulating things to her advantage.

Eventually, my tears stop flowing and my heart feels bereft of hope for the future. How can Malcolm and I possibly live a happy life with Helena shadowing our every step? Are we doomed to live out the remainder of our lives with the specter of her miserable existence haunting us?

"She won't win," Malcolm tells me confidently, after I voice my concerns to him about the fate of our family and the world. "We won't let her."

"But that's the problem, Malcolm. I don't know if it's even possible for us to stop her."

"Anna," he says in a deadly serious tone while holding my gaze with his to make sure I hear what he says next, "you need to believe that everything will work out the way it's supposed to. I have a hard time believing my father would allow Helena to rule the Earth. There has to be a way for us to get rid of her."

An image of the sword Xavier gave me on alternate Earth flashes through my mind.

"You might be right."

I go on to tell Malcolm everything that happened on alternate Earth. My bringing the sword back from there is definitely a surprise to him, but when I tell him I killed the Lucifer of that reality he looks completely floored by the drastic measures I had to take to ensure the safety of not only my own life but also the lives of our children.

"I wish I could say I'm sorry you had to kill him, but I'm not," Malcolm states flatly. "He deserved what he got. I'm just sorry you're the one who had to do it."

"No one else could," I remind him. "I'm the only one who can kill an archangel. Besides, he forced my hand. I didn't have any other choice."

"Helena might be able to kill archangels with the power she gained from the seals, but the verdict is still out on that one. Until she tries to use it on one of the princes, we won't know for sure if she's that powerful."

"Supernatural abilities or not, she's proven herself to be quite adept at manipulating things in the political arena. If it wasn't for her, I wouldn't have to worry about winning the election against Catherine."

My eyes well up with tears again as I remember there might not even be a Cirrus for Auggie's mother to take control of anymore.

"Helena told me Cirrus was destroyed," I say, clearly remembering that I didn't see it in the sky above New York City. After traveling back from alternate Earth, Helena and I were deposited there. I searched the sky for my cloud city until Helena informed me of its fate. "Is that true or was she lying to me?"

"It hasn't been destroyed," Malcolm is quick to reassure me, "but it was sitting at the bottom of the ocean the last time I was inside it."

I quickly sit up on the bed, causing Malcolm to follow my action.

"It's what?" I exclaim, feeling my heart beat so hard inside my chest that it's causing me to feel physically ill. "Then how can you say it's not destroyed?"

"The force field around it never gave way. It protected the city when it plunged into the ocean and prevented it from being flooded. I promise you that it's perfectly fine. In fact, it's probably back in the air already. I'm sure the others have taken care of it for us."

"What about the hellspawn in it? Are they still there?"

"No. When you and the others went to alternate Earth, the fissures to Hell closed. The War Angels were able to kill the ones that were inside the city. All we need to do is repair a few buildings and do a little clean-up before our citizens can return to their homes."

"Helena told me that the rebellion angels were the ones who tried to destroy it. Do you know exactly what they did?"

"Apparently, they blew the propulsion system. We were able to repair it, though. Like I said, we just need to spruce things up a little before people can return to their homes."

"If we can get people back into the city, I might just have a chance to win the election against Catherine."

"You need to stop doubting how much the people of Cirrus respect you, Anna," Malcolm admonishes lightly. "I think you've shown them enough during the months you've been in power and certainly in the past few days that you're more than capable of running a cloud city. Considering the fact that Catherine ran off to Nimbo to live in comfort at the palace, I don't see how people can view her as anything more than a ruler who still puts her own selfish needs first."

I sigh heavily and lay back down on the bed. Malcolm lies on his side beside me as I stare up at the sheer material above us. I remain silent for a while as I watch the fabric billow in and out in the imaginary breeze from the illusory ocean.

"What are you thinking about?" Malcolm asks. He has one arm bent to prop his head on as he watches me.

I look over at him and say, "I'm trying not to think because, if I do, I might start crying again."

I feel his free hand rest against the flesh of my stomach and begin to make feather-light circular motions.

"How is it that everything feels so real here?" I ask him as the warmth of his caress brings me comfort. "Normally, things don't feel like this when we're inside one of your dreams."

"I have no idea, my love," he replies as a slow, appreciative grin spreads his generous lips while his eyes drink in my nakedness. "But I'm certainly not going to complain about the change. I like playing with you far too much to question my good fortune. Maybe my father had something to do with it."

I giggle at Malcolm's absurd suggestion. "I would think God has more important matters to deal with than to ensure that we can make love in your dreams like we would in reality."

Malcolm lifts a dubious eyebrow, as if he doesn't quite agree with my assessment of God's priorities. "Normally, I would agree with you."

"But you don't?" I ask, finding Malcolm's answer curious. "Why?"

"The last time I saw Him, He was... helpful."

"In what way?"

"He told us you were on alternate Earth after we couldn't find you in Hell. He even took us all to Cirrus so we could fix the propulsion system while you were away. To be honest, I haven't seen Him be that accommodating in eons. Maybe He's decided that we've been through enough, and that we're due a little cooperation from Him."

"Or He's providing us with a gentle lull before the storm," I warn, trying to be pragmatic about the situation.

"I would rather think of it as a reward for what's already transpired."

"Maybe that's true, but you know as well as I do that Helena isn't finished with us. She's up to something. We just need to figure out what before she has a chance to implement her next scheme."

"Well, I for one would just like to enjoy a little quiet time with you and the kids. I think we've earned that, don't you? Besides, Helena will probably be preoccupied for a while with Cade."

"I wish we could do something for him." I say worriedly.

"Even if Helena hadn't forced him to trade in his freedom before releasing Liana, I think Cade would have found a reason to spend more time with her. You know better than anyone else how all-consuming the attraction between soul mates can be. It was only a matter of time before he went to her. This way, it doesn't make him look like he's choosing to spend time with her instead of us. He needs to figure out if he has a future with her or not, and I think the sooner they both decide that the better."

"He isn't safe with her," I state, knowing in my heart that Helena will only bring Cade misery.

"Perhaps the same can be said about her with him," Malcolm suggests.

"I know you think it's possible that he might be able to change her, but she's so set in her ways, Malcolm. Even if he does attempt to perform such a miracle, I have a feeling Helena will rebel against it happening."

"Well, there's really nothing we can do to help Cade until he asks us to," Malcolm reasons. "I suggest we concentrate on us for the time being."

Malcolm leans over and begins to plant warm kisses in the valley between my breasts, causing me to close my eyes and simply allow myself to enjoy his adoring ministrations.

"We should probably wake up and see to the children," I weakly argue.

"They're still asleep," Malcolm informs me, as though he has a window into reality. "I told Vala to watch them while we all slept. She'll wake me up if we're needed back in the real world."

"That was very good thinking," I praise as Malcolm lifts his head from my breast to look into my eyes. He smiles at me, breaking my heart all over again with the love he holds for me in his expression.

"I've been known to have a good idea from time to time."

"So have I." I deftly roll Malcolm onto his back until I'm straddling his hips. "Right now, I believe we should take advantage of this little piece of nirvana. Besides, you're not the only one who can come up with good ideas."

"I always enjoy learning more about your ideas," he tells me with a pleased smile at my forwardness. "Please, show me what you have in mind."

"As you wish," I say before showing my husband exactly what I want to do to him.

I'm not sure how long we stay in our dream world, but at one point while we're lying in each other's arms just talking, Malcolm lets out a grunt of pain. He wiggles his left foot up from beneath the sheet we're under to inspect it, as if he believes he'll see some sort of injury there.

"I think it's time to wake up," he regretfully informs me. "I told Vala to bite me on the foot as soon as the kids woke up."

I lean up to kiss Malcolm deeply once more, not wanting to face the outside world just yet.

After I force myself to pull away, I tell him, "Maybe we can find time to do this in the real world, too."

Malcolm smiles, but he doesn't look convinced such an event will happen anytime soon. "I believe our children will be keeping us busy when we're not out trying to save the world from Helena. Plus, your real body needs time to heal from the trauma it sustained from the pregnancy and birth. Modern medicine can only heal you to a certain extent."

"Then I'm glad we have this," I say, kissing his mouth thoroughly before willingly relinquishing our fantasy world.

When we do wake up, I hear Lucas' sweet voice singing a song. I turn my head on the pillow to look over at my son. I find him sitting in front of the babies, softly serenading them. When I glance over in Malcolm's direction I find him watching our son, too, with a proud grin on his face. Neither of us says a word or moves until Lucas is through with his song.

"That was beautiful, sweetie," I say as both Malcolm and I sit up in bed.

"Aww, man," Lucas says, looking slightly disappointed that we're awake. "I was hoping to give you and Dad a little more time to sleep. Did I wake you up with my singing?"

I look at Vala, who is sitting slightly behind Lucas but next to Malcolm's foot that she just bit to ensure we woke up.

"Absolutely not," I reassure him. "It was just time for us to get up. Besides, I need to feed the babies."

"Are you hungry, Anna?" Vala asks. "Lucas and I can go get you something to eat if you are."

It's only then that I realize it's been a very long time since I last ate. In fact, I haven't really eaten anything since I was on alternate Earth.

"I'm famished actually. I would love something to eat."

"Come along, Lucas," Vala says, hopping down from the bed and heading for the door. "Let's give your mother and father some privacy while they tend to your brother and sister. We'll go downstairs and ask someone to prepare them some food for us to bring back up. I'm sure neither of them has eaten very much in the past couple of days."

Lucas opens the door for Vala as she leads the way out. Luna follows Vala out into the hallway. Before he leaves, Lucas turns to us and asks, "Do you want anything in particular, Mommy?"

"Anything will do," I tell him.

"Okay. Be right back!"

After Lucas and the dogs leave, I pick Liam and Liana up in each of my arms while Malcolm nestles double stacked pillows on either side of me. Liana tries to wiggle out of my hold for some reason. When I don't let her go, she begins to cry in frustration.

Finally, I'm able to lay the babies down on the pillows. Liana stops crying, but her little body still jerks as if she's agitated by something.

I unbutton the front of my nightgown to expose my breasts. Liam attaches to my nipple right away. The sensation is an odd one and slightly painful, but I know the milk I'm able to provide from my body is nutritious and exactly what they need right now. With Liam steadily eating his fill I attempt to feed Liana, but every time I try to place my nipple against her mouth she turns her face to the side, refusing to accept it.

"I don't understand," I say to Malcolm in worry. "Liam attached right away. Why is she being so fussy?"

"Maybe she isn't hungry?" Malcolm suggests, even though I can hear the doubt of such a thing in his voice.

"Maybe," I reply, but I'm certain that isn't the actual problem. Liana's obstinate refusal to suckle feels more like a personal rejection of me. On my third attempt to coax her into taking my nipple into her mouth, she begins to wail as if she's in some sort of physical pain.

From his seat next to me on the bed, Malcolm quickly reaches for the top drawer of the nightstand, pulling it out to retrieve the silver rattle Lilly gave me as a wedding present. According to her, it had the power to calm any baby. He places it above Liana's head and begins to rattle it, drawing her attention and instantly quieting her cries. She begins to gurgle in delight at the soft chiming noise the rattle makes, and I see an opportunity to try to feed her once more while Malcolm keeps her distracted. This time, Liana doesn't refuse me and automatically latches onto my breast.

"Ouch," I complain softly as Liana begins feeding in gusto.

"Are you all right?" Malcolm asks in concern, continuing to use the rattle to keep Liana calm while she nurses.

I quickly nod. "Yes. I'm fine. I'm just relieved she's finally eating. I wasn't sure what we would do if she didn't."

"Well, we would have just tried a bottle," Malcolm reasons.

"I don't understand why she wasn't attaching. From the way she's eating now, she had to have been starving."

Malcolm remains silent as he peers at Liana with a look of worry and confusion.

"What are you thinking?" I ask him, feeling my own bubble of worry rise to the surface. "Do you think something's wrong with her? Do you think it has something to do with the seal Helena gave her? Is it making her hate me?"

"Anna, no," Malcolm protests, ceasing to move the rattle. "Liana's just a baby. She doesn't even know what love and hate mean yet."

"That might be true about regular babies, but you and I both know that the twins aren't normal newborns. They understand things that they shouldn't at their age, and we don't even know why."

Our conversation is interrupted by a light knock on the door. Malcolm stands and walks over to see who our unexpected visitor is.

After he opens the door I catch a glimpse of a handsome man with shoulder-length, curly black hair standing in the hallway.

I've never met him before, but I know who he is even before a surprised Malcolm asks, "Aiden?"

CHAPTER FOUR

"Hey, Malcolm," Aiden replies, smiling at my husband with unreserved happiness. Malcolm steps over the threshold to give Aiden a brief hug in greeting.

"What in the world are you doing here?" Malcolm asks as he steps away from Caylin's husband.

"Our father thinks it's the right time for me to explain a couple of things to you and Anna." Aiden briefly looks in my direction and sees that I'm in the middle of breastfeeding the babies. "I can wait, though. It looks like you're busy."

"Why don't you go downstairs?" Malcolm suggests. "The others should be down there somewhere. You might try the kitchen first. Lucas is supposed to be making us something to eat. Just ask them to lay the food out on the kitchen table instead of bringing it up here. That way you can tell us all why you're here, unless what you have to say is only meant for Anna and me to hear."

"No," Aiden says with a small shake of his head. "It's not supposed to be a secret. The others are welcome to hear it, too."

"Great. Then give us a few minutes and we'll be right down."

Malcolm closes the door and returns to his spot beside me on the edge of the bed.

"Why do you think God sent Aiden here instead of just coming to us Himself?" I ask, finding God's logic hard to understand sometimes.

Malcolm shrugs. "I have no idea, but He must have thought Aiden was the best person to relay this information personally. At least he's here to give us answers and not just more questions."

"I suppose what you told me earlier might be true," I muse. "Maybe God *has* decided to be more helpful."

"Well, don't get used to His cooperation," Malcolm replies with a small chuckle before leaning forward to kiss my lips. "I'll go find you something to wear for when you're ready to go downstairs."

"Just get one of my maternity dresses," I instruct as he saunters over to the walk-in closet. "Until I get that miracle cream Desmond told me about a few months ago, this stretched out belly of mine isn't going anywhere anytime soon."

Malcolm steps out of the closet a few second later with a sleeveless white chiffon gown that has a plunging neckline. The material of the skirt has a concealed slit in the front that isn't visible until you walk in it. The dress displayed two of my best assets when I was pregnant, while working the miracle of making me feel beautiful…even with my stomach extended out to the size of a house.

"Do you think we can have this dress taken in after you lose the baby weight?" Malcolm asks, laying the gown out on the end of the bed almost reverently. "I love how easily accessible certain parts of your body are in it."

"Malcolm," I chastise, briefly looking down at the babies, "we're not alone, you know. The babies can hear you."

"Well, it's not like I said which parts the dress let me fondle," he counters playfully. "I doubt they know what we're saying anyway."

"We don't know that for sure," I remind him. "As we've discussed before, they seem to understand more than they should."

"I shall attempt to refrain from displaying my never-ending lust for your luscious curves while we are in the presence of the wonder twins."

I can't prevent a giggle at Malcolm's nickname for the babies, but they were indeed a wonder to behold.

As I gaze at Liam, I'm instantly filled with an overwhelming sense of mutual acceptance that doesn't need to be verbalized. With my son, I feel the light of love ignite my soul every time I look at him. It's the same way I feel when I'm around Lucas.

When I turn my gaze to Liana, I'm disappointed that the same cannot be said. There's a disconnect between my daughter and me that I can't quite understand. Her previous reaction to me was disheartening, to say the least. I'm not sure if her response is a natural animosity towards me or if it's being caused by the seal Helena gave her. Was that Helena's goal all along? To make one of my children despise me? The more I think about it, the more I doubt that is the case. Her real purpose will more than likely serve some particular need she has. Liana's rejection of me could simply be an unforeseen side effect from having the seal.

As Liana maintains a steady gaze on me with her bluer than blue eyes, I know that she's only feeding from my breast because she has to in order to survive. I have no doubt that if she was given an alternative means of gaining sustenance, she wouldn't hesitate to take it. The chasm separating us seems almost impossible to traverse, but I silently make a vow to her that we will find a way to overcome it. She's my daughter, after all, and no matter what she might feel for me or how she treats me in the future I will always love her. I just need to make sure she understands that interminable fact.

"You never did ask me which of the seals Helena gave her," I say to Malcolm. "Do you want to know?"

"I have to admit that I was curious, but I didn't want to upset you any more than you already were at the time."

"It's Lucifer's old seal," I reveal. "Silence. Do you think that's significant?"

"It could just be Helena's way of rubbing Lucifer's nose in his own failings," Malcolm reasons. "You know how much she hates him. What better way to get back at him than to give his granddaughter his seal?"

"Maybe," I reply, having a bad feeling it means so much more.

Thirty minutes pass before we're ready to make our descent downstairs. After the babies drink their fill of milk, they both promptly go back to sleep. I ask Malcolm to carry Liana down while I cradle Liam in my arms. I worry that if I hold Liana she might begin to cry again, and I don't want her to wake Liam. Besides, my son seems completely content in my arms. The cherubic little smile on his sleeping face seems to indicate that he loves having me hold him. I'm not sure the same can be said about Liana at this point. As Malcolm walks in front of me, down the stairs from the second floor, I can hear him speaking to Liana in a hushed tone. I don't think he intends for me to hear what he's saying, but I do.

"I need you to do me a favor," he whispers to our daughter. "Be nice to your mommy. She literally went to Hell and back with you kids. She also suffered through a lot of pain to bring you and your brother into the world. If you're as smart as we think you are, show her how much she means to you because she means the world to me, little girl. She's my life, and I can't live without her. So, I would really appreciate it if you were nicer to her."

I secretly hope Malcolm's words have some effect on Liana's disposition towards me, but I'm not counting on it.

When we reach the kitchen, we find Aiden helping Lucas make pancakes on the gas stove. Luna, our resident hellhound, is sitting patiently a foot away from Lucas with an eager look of expectation on her face as she waits for him to drop a pancake, either intentionally or unintentionally. Most of my War Angels are present as well. Zane and Xander are sitting on stools at the kitchen island, while most of the others are sitting at the large wooden dining table in the room. Only Gideon is missing from my contingent. I also notice that Lucifer, Jess, Mason, and my papa are nowhere to be seen.

Ethan, the commander of the War Angels, sees us enter the room before anyone else does. When he stands from his seat at the table, the others notice our entry and also rise to show their respect.

"We're all glad to see you looking so well, Anna," Ethan says, walking away from his chair to come stand in front of Malcolm and me. Funnily enough, when Ethan peers down at Liam and Liana, his expression turns to one of extreme apprehension. I have to say that he almost looks scared by them, which amuses me. I've never seen Ethan look nervous about anything.

"Have you never seen a baby before?" I ask Ethan, unable to come up with another reasonable explanation for his reaction to my children.

"I've seen them," he says slowly, keeping a wary eye on the babies like they might jump out of our arms and attack him, "but I can't say I've ever been this close to one, or two in this case, before."

"Hold your arm out," Malcolm practically orders as he tries to hand Liana to Ethan.

To my great amusement, Ethan actually retreats from us, taking a step backwards.

"I don't think that would be wise," Ethan protests. "What if I drop it?"

Malcolm raises his eyebrows at Ethan in obvious annoyance. "I would appreciate it if you refrained from calling my daughter an 'it', Ethan. Just bend your arm like mine is and you won't drop her."

Without giving him any other recourse, Malcolm forces Ethan to either take Liana in his arms or risk her being dropped in mid-air.

A very reluctant Ethan accepts Liana's small form, cradling her gently against his chest. I watch as she opens her eyes and looks up at my War Angel commander, as if silently questioning who he is to her.

"Hello," Ethan says, obviously not having anything else better to say to a baby.

I hear Xander snicker from his seat at the kitchen island. When he looks at me, I give him a withering glare that quickly wipes the smirk over Ethan's awkwardness off his face. With Xander looking properly contrite, I return my attention to how Liana reacts to Ethan. She doesn't make a sound as she continues to look up at him questioningly. After a few seconds, she must deem Ethan as safe because she closes her eyes again to go back to sleep.

Without saying a word, Ethan hands Liana back to Malcolm, who readily accepts her.

"Uh, thanks for letting me hold her," Ethan says, not sounding thankful at all, before making a hasty retreat back to his seat at the table.

"The pancakes are almost ready," Lucas informs us as he lifts one out of the pan in front of him and gingerly places it onto a white china platter that must contain at least forty of them already. "Go ahead and sit down. Aiden and I will bring them to you."

With the table already set with plates, utensils, and glasses, Malcolm and I sit side by side at the head of the table.

Lucas hops down from the stool he was standing on and grabs the platter of pancakes to bring over to us.

"Those look delicious," I croon as the intoxicating scent of freshly made pancakes fills the air around me.

Lucas smiles proudly as he sets the platter on the table in front of us.

"Aiden showed me a little trick with them," Lucas tells me. "We added in a little bit of vanilla and cinnamon."

"No wonder they smell so delectable," I praise, causing Lucas' smile to grow even wider with delight.

"How many do you want, Mommy?"

"I'll take two please."

"Anna," I hear Aiden say as he comes to stand beside me and slightly behind Lucas, "why don't you let me hold Liam for you while you eat?"

"Are you sure?" I ask, not wanting to bother my great-grandfather many times over with such a task.

"It would be my honor," he replies. Aiden's expression is one of reserved happiness as he gazes down at my son. It's almost as if holding Liam will bring him joy and sadness at the same time. I don't quite understand it, but it doesn't give me any reservations about handing my son over to him either.

I hold Liam out for Aiden to take, which he does readily. Aiden's brows lower slightly as he studies my son's face with baffling intensity.

"Hello, Liam," Aiden says, caressing the side of my baby's face with the tips of his fingers. I'm suddenly overcome by the odd sensation that this isn't the first time Aiden and Liam have met. It feels more like a reunion between two souls than a first meeting. I don't comment on it because Lucas draws my attention away from them as he begins to fork a pile of pancakes onto my plate.

"I'm pretty sure I said I only wanted two, sweetie," I tell him, trying to keep my tone from sounding ungrateful for his apparent need to feed me.

"You're breastfeeding, right?" Lucas asks, catching me off guard with his knowledge of such a thing at his age. "I read that you need to eat at least an extra 500 calories a day when you're breastfeeding, and since you've got twins it has to be closer to 1000 calories."

I lean towards Malcolm and whisper, "I thought you were going to start keeping an eye on what he reads."

"We've been a little busy," Malcolm whispers back as his excuse.

"Don't worry," Lucas assures me. "Cade only read the helpful stuff to me from the book about babies. He never let me look at the pictures it had."

The mention of Cade's name tugs at a corner of my heart, making me realize just how much I already miss his presence among us. My War Angel guard doesn't seem complete without him.

"Speaking of Cade," Ethan says from his seat at the other end of the table beside Roan, "where did he get off to? The last time we saw him was in the living room when he brought Liana back."

It's only then that I realize Cade's brothers are in the dark about the bargain he made with Helena to secure Liana's release from Hell.

"He's with Helena," Malcolm informs them, saving me from the discomfort of having to explain things.

All the War Angels immediately erupt with questions. Malcolm has to raise his free hand and say, "Calm down and let me explain the situation."

My husband goes on to tell them why Cade is with our arch nemesis.

"It figures that *thing* would hold a child's well-being over Cade's head to make him do what she wants," Xander grouses, unable to conceal his disgust over Helena's ultimatum.

"How long does he have to stay with her?" Alex asks, looking more concerned over Cade's welfare than mad at Helena.

"He didn't know," I reply. "I don't think they put a time limit on it."

"This might be for the best anyway," Ethan ruminates as he leans back in his chair with a reflective expression on his face. He looks down the table at me and says, "Maybe spending more time with her will finally break any notion he has that he can change her."

"Well, we don't know that he can't," I half-heartedly argue.

"Don't we?" Ethan counters, looking steadfast in his opinion about the situation. "She may have a physical form, Anna, but she's still Hell itself walking on two legs. It would be like asking Heaven to change. I don't think it can be done and the sooner Cade realizes that, the better off he'll be."

I decide not to debate the point with Ethan. I still have hope, if only a sliver, that Helena can become more than she was made to be. I can see from the looks on the other War Angels' faces that my optimism for her reform is not shared by any of them. The only mutual point of fact is worry over Cade's safety, but I'm confident he won't allow Helena to manipulate him into doing anything that he doesn't want to do. Yes, she did coerce him into spending more time with her but, as my husband pointed out earlier, Cade probably would have ended up doing that anyway.

I see Roan hold up his hand as he says, "I have a question."

"I can't promise we'll have an answer," I tell him. "What's your question?"

"It seems strange to me that Helena would go through all the trouble of kidnapping Liana only to give her back so readily," he points out. "Do you know why she did that?"

I look over at Malcolm, not sure if we should tell them about the seal. He meets my gaze and nods at my unasked question.

I look back down the table at Roan. "She gave Liana one of her seals."

Again, the War Angels erupt with a dozen questions.

"I'm sorry," I say over the bedlam in an attempt to quiet them, "we don't know what it means. We have no idea why Helena would willingly give up a seal like that, but I think we can all agree that she did it to benefit herself in some way. The only thing we can do now is wait to see what she's up to."

Atticus looks over at Aiden, who's still holding Liam in his arms.

"Do you know what Helena's planning, Aiden?" Atticus asks him. "Is that why you were sent back here?"

I look over at Aiden beside me and watch as he shakes his head at Atticus.

"I'm sorry," he replies. "I don't know what Helena has planned. That isn't why God sent me back."

"Why are you here?" Malcolm asks hesitantly. "You said God thought it was time you told us something important. What is it?"

"I'm here to tell you more about your children," Aiden answers. "And to inform you that I've been assigned to be Liam's guardian like Will is Liana's guardian."

"Why does he need one?" I ask nervously. "What are you protecting him from?"

"Whatever might come," Aiden replies. "All I know is that God came to me and asked if I wanted the job. It's a duty I gladly accepted, especially when He told me who Liam really is."

I feel my forehead involuntarily crinkle, showing my confusion. "What do you mean by that?"

"Is he a reincarnation of someone?" Malcolm asks. It was a logical question. Since Lucas was the re-embodiment of Gabe, Malcolm's inquiry made perfect sense.

"Not exactly," Aiden says tentatively. "Do you remember God telling you that the seals became Liam and Liana's souls?"

"Yes," I say. "We've known that almost since they were conceived."

"The energy from the seals that was used to generate their souls was also attached to something else," Aiden tells us, watching our reaction closely before he continues. "I know you've been wondering why the babies have been acting like they know what's going on around them."

"And this something else that their souls are attached to is what caused that?" Malcolm questions, attempting to work through what Aiden is trying to tell us.

"Yes. Malcolm, do you remember who God asked to protect the seals before the princes stole them from Heaven?"

"Of course. Seven of the Guardians of the Guf."

Aiden looks at Malcolm meaningfully, as if indicating that he just answered his own question.

"Are you saying," Malcolm says slowly, making the connection, "that the souls of the guardians the seals once belonged to are now inside our children?"

"Yes," Aiden answers, looking down at Liam with a faint smile. "And Liam has the soul of the guardian who made me inside him. God knew I would want to be the one assigned to protect Andel and your son."

Silence reigns supreme in the room after Aiden's revelation as we all try to digest the information he's just revealed to us.

"Wait a minute," Ethan chimes in. "I thought the guardians died when the princes took their seals."

"I did, too," Aiden admits, "but God explained to me that the bond between the Guardians' souls and the seals is so strong that one can't be separated from the other."

"Does that mean the souls of the Guardians are the souls of our children?" I have to ask.

"No," Aiden answers with a small shake of his head. "They each have their own soul, but their soul is now permanently tethered to the soul of their respective Guardian. It's very similar to how all the vessels were connected to their archangels. Liam and Liana will have their own thoughts and emotions, but they will also always have their Guardian with them in the back of their minds."

"So it was the Guardians who were controlling things while the twins were still inside my womb?" I ask, finally making sense of the babies' actions.

"Yes. I suppose they knew what needed to be done and did it."

"So the seals Helena still has contain the souls of their respective Guardians, too, right?" I ask.

"Yes. God told me that while the seals were inside the princes, the souls of the Guardians were in a dormant state, but when you," he says, looking at me, "took the seals from them they awoke. Apparently, the Guardians feared you wouldn't survive carrying all seven of the seals at once. So, when you became pregnant, they saw an opportunity to transform the energy of the seals into souls."

"That actually makes a lot of sense," Malcolm says. "They are Guardians, after all. That's what they were made to do, make souls."

"If Andel is inside Liam," I say, "which Guardian does Liana carry?"

"A Guardian by the name of Arel," Aiden tells us.

"Are the Guardians still controlling what the babies do?" I have to ask.

"No," Aiden says with certainty. "Like I said, your children have the same opportunities as anyone else to grow up and become who they want to be. Andel and Arel will simply remain in the background, unless your children want them to play a greater role in their lives."

I have to admit I'm a little disappointed by Aiden's answer. If I could have laid the blame of Liana's reactions to me on the Guardian inside her, then it wouldn't have been my own daughter rejecting me. Feeling on the verge of tears, I lay the blame of my sensitive emotional state on having just given birth, but I know the root of the matter goes a lot deeper than that. With this new information, I feel as though I've doomed my children to a state of being that they never would have had to overcome if it weren't for me. If I hadn't conceived them while I was still on my mission to retrieve the seals from the princes, they wouldn't have to be sharing their bodies with Andel and Arel. Once they become old enough to understand everything, will they both end up hating me for making them live with this burden?

"Are you okay, Mommy?" Lucas asks with concern, placing his small hand on my shoulder to show his support. "You look really sad and you shouldn't be. What's wrong?"

"It's nothing, sweetie," I try to reassure him. "I think I'm just tired and a little overwhelmed learning all of this."

"You need to eat," Lucas proclaims, as if his pancakes will solve all of my problems.

"You both need to eat, I think," Zane says, standing from his stool at the kitchen island and walking over to Malcolm's side. "Let me take Liana for a while. I promise not to drop her."

Malcolm chuckles at Zane's gentle gibe at Ethan's earlier worry.

To my surprise, Liana actually gurgles with joy when Zane takes her into his arms.

"She likes you," I say despondently, wondering if my daughter will ever greet me with unbridled joy like that one day.

"She's just mesmerized by my dazzling good looks," Zane jokes with a wink in my direction.

"No doubt," I agree, forcing a smile I don't actually feel.

Lucas quickly darts away from my side to grab something off the kitchen island, but returns within seconds to his spot beside my chair.

"You need lots of maple syrup," he declares, drizzling the sticky goodness on top of the mound of pancakes he stacked on my plate. After placing just enough over my pancakes, Lucas walks over to Malcolm to hand him the now half-empty bottle. "Take this, Dad. I'm going to get Mommy some milk."

As I watch Lucas perform his thoughtful task, a sense of being loved by him fills my heart. If Lucas loves me, surely Liana will, too, given enough time. It could be that I'm just over- reacting anyway. She's just a baby after all. At this point in her life, her only concerns are being fed, held, and kept in a clean diaper. Perhaps I'm over-thinking things.

At least, that's my hope.

CHAPTER FIVE

After Lucas brings me my milk, I finally satisfy the growling beast grumbling inside my belly and begin to eat the fluffy pancakes on my plate.

"Where's Gideon gotten off to?" Malcolm asks as he makes the first cut of his own pancakes with his fork.

"Jered took him to see Bai so she can give him a tattoo," Ethan tells us as the rest of the War Angels pass around the platter of pancakes amongst themselves at the table.

Since Bai is JoJo reincarnated, her tattoos have the ability to protect my angels from the remaining princes of Hell. Those who have one are immune to the effects of an archangel's power to kill them. Cade was the first to get one from Bai, and tested its effectiveness by enraging Levi until that particular prince unleashed his power. Thankfully, the tattoo worked or Cade would be a pile of black ash right now.

"And where are Lucifer, Jess, and Mason?" I ask in between bites. "They haven't returned to Heaven yet, have they?"

"Do you really think they would leave before seeing the babies or you?" Ethan replies with a hint of admonishment.

"No. I suppose not." I end up feeling a little silly for even thinking such a thing. The trio had traveled all the way from Heaven to help us when we needed them the most. Of course they wouldn't leave without saying goodbye first.

"Andre took them to see a rebellion angel named Christopher," Ethan says, supplying me with the missing information I really wanted to know. "From what Andre told us, he's been hiding out in Montana since Lucifer's redemption."

I remember Christopher quite well. He was the rebellion angel Lucifer set into place within Catherine's personal guard to watch over me. Unfortunately my last memory of Christopher is one I've tried to expunge from my memory, even though I know it will haunt me until the day I die. He was given the unpleasant task of bringing me Millie's severed head in a box. It was Levi's demented gift to me in his vain attempt to break my will. If Malcolm and Lucifer hadn't rescued me from my own blind rage that night in Hell, I would have murdered Levi and doomed my soul forever.

I feel a sudden pang of guilt for not thinking about Christopher after Lucifer's redemption. I briefly wonder if he's sided with the rebellion angels who seem determined to make me suffer for my father's return to Heaven. Then again, he had watched me grow up and kept me safe in Lucifer's stead. Surely he cared for me in some small way.

"Do you know why they went to see him?" I ask.

"They didn't say," Ethan answers. "I'm afraid you'll have to ask them when they return."

As we eat, I begin to wonder what Lucifer is up to and if he is trying to recruit Christopher to help me with my rebellion angel problem. Apparently, ever since Lucifer returned to Heaven, many of the rebellion angels he left behind on Earth decided the best way to get back at my father was to take their aggression out on me and my family. Helena has kept them at bay for as long as she can, but even she doesn't seem to be able to control all of their actions. Of course, she could just kill them all if she wanted to, but it's obvious she has other plans for them and has no desire to do something so rash.

In all honesty, I don't want them dead either. If they die in their current unforgiven state, they would be relegated to live in Hell with Helena for all eternity. I made a promise to Lucifer that I would try to help them repair their bond with God, but it's obvious they would rather kill me than accept any guidance from the daughter of the man they believe betrayed them.

At the end of our meal, Gideon and Jered phase into the kitchen by the kitchen island.

"Did I miss the pancakes?" Gideon asks, looking distressed by the possibility.

"I saved both of you some," Lucas reassures him, hopping out of his seat by my side to run over to the oven. He pulls out two plates with four pancakes on each. He hands one to Jered and one to a rather excited Gideon.

"Is it my turn now?" Xander asks as he turns on his stool at the kitchen island to look at Jered.

"Yes," Jered tells him. "Bai and her mother are expecting you."

"Finally," Xander mutters, but I see a faint smile of eagerness on his face before he phases to Brutus' house where Bai's family is staying.

Gideon sits on Xander's now-deserted stool while Jered walks over to the table to sit in the chair closest to Malcolm. Finished with his meal, Lucas picks up Luna's ball to play a game of fetch with her off to the side of the table.

"So how is everyone over there?" I ask Jered, eager to hear how my friends are faring.

"Kyna wants to come over, but I wasn't sure if you were ready for guests just yet," Jered tells me as he reaches for the almost-empty bottle of syrup on the table. "Linn and her children are doing well, especially since Brutus' servants are able to help her with the older kids so she can concentrate on the baby. She asked me to send her best regards to both of you on the birth of the twins."

In a different time and under better circumstances, Linn wouldn't have sent her well wishes through an intermediary. She would have come in person because she wouldn't have been able to keep herself away from seeing the newest additions to our family.

"That was nice of her," I say, turning my gaze away from Jered so he doesn't see the sadness in my eyes over Linn's message.

"Just let me know when you're ready for Kyna and Brutus to come over," Jered says, swiftly changing the subject to something he knows will cheer me up. "I think she would have returned with me if Brutus hadn't advised her to wait to see what you wanted."

"I would love for them to come over," I reply with a feeling of being loved by two of my favorite people in the world. The union of Brutus and Kyna is a match made in Heaven, literally, and having them around always makes me feel happier. "But I also think we need a day to get some rest, if we can."

"That's what I thought," Jered says with a wink. "She'll understand."

Just then, Lucifer phases into the kitchen with my papa in tow. Shortly after they appear, Mason phases in with Jess and Christopher.

"I smell pancakes," Jess says excitedly, sniffing the air like a hound dog on the hunt for its favorite bone. She quickly scans the table in search of the elusive objects of her desire, but quickly discovers that there are no more pancakes to be had.

"I'll make you some, Jess," Lucas quickly declares, setting Luna's ball on the floor before heading over to the stove. "Anyone else want some?"

"Well, I won't say no to that offer," Mason tells my son with a kind smile.

In the depths of my ancestor's eyes, I see the love Mason harbors for Lucas even though they haven't been able to spend much time together. It's obvious from the loving way Jess and Mason look at my son that his reincarnated form is invoking memories of Gabe. Thankfully, Lucas doesn't remember anything about his previous life, and I sincerely hope we can keep it that way.

I know their current state as heavenly travelers won't last for much longer, but I'm eternally grateful for their willingness to leave Heaven in order to help Malcolm and me in our time of need. It's then I realize the truth in what Malcolm said earlier about God being more helpful lately. I'm not sure why He's assisting us so much, but I'm not about to question His motivation.

"I'll help you, Lucas," Aiden says as he walks over to Jess with Liam in his arms. "I'm sure Jess won't mind looking after Liam for a little while."

"Are you kidding me? You better give me that baby so I can smell him," Jess says rather impatiently.

"Smell him?" Ethan asks, looking completely lost by Jess' statement.

"Babies have a one of a kind smell," Jess declares as she readily accepts Liam from Aiden. As she cradles him in her arms, she leans over and inhales deeply. "I didn't realize how much I've missed that smell until right now."

From the corner of my eye I see Zane, who is still holding Liana, dip his head slightly to give my daughter a sniff. The action brings a smile to my face, making me realize something.

"I think it would be a good idea for all of you to take turns looking after the babies," I announce to the War Angels in the room. "It's one of the reasons God sent you to Earth, after all."

"We were sent here to babysit your kids?" Atticus asks, looking dubious about my reasoning skills.

"No, you were sent here to have children of your own," I remind him. "Remember? You're supposed to start the next evolutionary step between humans and angels."

"Oh yeah, that," Atticus says, averting his gaze from mine and not sounding too enthusiastic about the undertaking.

As I look around the room at the other War Angels present, I notice that none of them seem particularly excited about the second part of their mission here on Earth.

"Don't you want to have children?" I ask, watching their reactions to my question.

"It's just odd to be *expected* to produce offspring," Ethan answers for himself. "I think we all want to find someone we can love like you and Malcolm love each other. But, during the time we've been here, we've all learned just how rare that kind of love is to find. It makes committing to someone that much harder to do because none of us wants to settle just to satisfy our father's agenda. We all want to honor His wishes, but we also don't want to throw away our only opportunity to meet someone we can truly love."

"And you shouldn't settle," I reply, looking at them all. I become acutely aware of a growing sense of shared guilt among them for their personal desire and realize that it needs to be squelched as quickly as possible. "I think God sent you here to experience everything an Earth- bound life has to offer, and that includes falling in love. You shouldn't feel any guilt over wanting that for yourselves. I want that for you, too. No one should ever rush into a relationship when it comes to spending the rest of your life with that person."

"That's pretty much what we've all decided," Ethan says, sounding relieved that I agree with them. "We may not be able to stay on our father's timetable but, like you said, we don't want to waste this opportunity either."

"Did God give you a deadline?" Malcolm asks, looking confused by such a possibility.

"No," Ethan is quick to say. "He didn't specifically tell us that we needed to find wives within a specific timeframe, but we all assume He wishes us to start families as soon as possible."

"Where He's concerned, I wouldn't assume anything," Lucifer chimes in. "I would advise you to do what you feel is right."

With Lucifer making his encouraging statement my attention is drawn to Christopher, who is standing by his side.

"Hello, Christopher," I say.

"It's good to see you again, Anna," Christopher replies, looking uncertain about being in my presence again.

I turn a questioning glance in Lucifer's direction, hoping my father will explain why he brought Christopher into my home.

"I asked him to come with us so we're all on the same page," Lucifer clarifies. "We've talked, and he's offered to help with your rebellion angel problem."

Malcolm leans back in his chair and crosses his arms over his chest.

"Help us in what way exactly?" he asks in a cautious tone.

"You need someone on the inside of the group so you know what their plans are," Lucifer begins to explain.

"But Levi knows he worked for you," I remind Lucifer, "and Helena certainly knows where Christopher's loyalties lie."

"That's one reason I've been staying out of sight since Lucifer's departure," Christopher admits to me. "I'm certainly not welcome among the others."

"So how exactly is he going to be able to help us?" I ask Lucifer.

"He will act as a go-between to relay messages from someone within the group we just recruited to help you," Lucifer informs me.

I wait for my father to expand upon his explanation and tell us the name of this mystery ally, but he doesn't.

"And who is it within the rebellion angels' ranks that you've asked to help us?" I ask, seeking an answer to a question that seems unnecessary.

"I think it would be better if you didn't know who it is," Lucifer responds. "That's the whole point of having Christopher help out."

"But why can't we know this person's identity?"

"We have no way of knowing if any of you will have to go back to Hell," Lucifer reasons. "If you do that, Helena can simply look into your memories and discover who is helping you. If all you know is that Christopher is your go-between, then she won't receive any information that will endanger your operative within the group."

I look at Christopher. "And you're all right with becoming Helena's target of interest if she learns you're assisting us?"

"I'm not scared of her," Christopher says without a shred of fear. "She can't do anything but kill me, and I'm prepared for that. I've asked my father for His forgiveness, and my soul is prepared to meet any punishment Helena might deem worthy for me."

Christopher's revelation knocks me slightly off guard.

"I didn't realize you had asked for God's forgiveness," I admit.

"A few of us have," Christopher reveals. "And, hopefully, more of them will when they realize what they're doing is only damaging their souls further."

Lucifer clears this throat as if he's uncertain he should give voice to his thoughts.

"I've asked our operative to contact me if an opportunity presents itself when I can speak to all the rebellion angels at once," Lucifer reveals.

"To what end?" I have to ask.

"I plan to tell them how wrong I was to go against God and allow my pride to fuel my anger. I'm not going to shirk my responsibility to them. I know I'm the reason they were all cast out of Heaven, and I think they need to hear me own up to that fact. I'm not sure how many of them I can reach by admitting to my own faults, but I hope my words will influence at least some of them. Vengeance isn't what they should be seeking right now. There isn't a single doubt in my mind that they all want to return to Heaven, even if they profess that they don't. I probably won't be able to convince all of them to seek redemption, but I can at least plant a seed of hope inside the souls of some of them. Perhaps it'll be enough to turn the tide of this fight in your favor. If enough of them come to our side, it might be just enough to stop the others from trying to kill you. I believe I have at least a fifty-fifty shot at making it work. They all followed me once in a war we were doomed to lose. I'm hoping I can convince at least a portion of them to follow me one more time and allow the light of His love for them to fill their souls again."

"I think if they're willing to listen to you, that will happen," I say. "How long does your operative think it will take before you're able to speak to them?"

"I don't believe it will be too much longer. Apparently Helena is planning something big soon, at least that's what our informant said."

"Does this person know what it is?"

Lucifer shakes his head. "No, but all of the rebellion angels predict it's coming soon. If I know Helena at all, she'll act as swiftly as possible. It's the perfect time to make a move against you since you're distracted by the babies. I would certainly take advantage of your split focus."

"It makes sense," Malcolm says, looking worried. "If she's going to do anything, she'll do it now. Ethan, we need you to inform every War Angel to keep their eyes open for anything out of the ordinary. We don't know where Helena will strike next or when, so they need to stay vigilant until the threat is over."

"If it's ever over," I mutter under my breath, but Malcolm hears it.

"We'll find a way to stop her from interfering with our lives," my husband promises me. "You have to keep believing that, Anna."

I do my best not to look worried, but I can tell from the look in his eyes that Malcolm knows exactly how scared I am of what Helena might try to do to our family now and in the future.

"So where are Cade and Xander?" Mason asks, noticing their absence from the room.

"Xander is getting his tattoo from Bai," I answer. I want to tell them where Cade is, but the words simply won't come out.

"Cade's with Helena," Malcolm says for me.

"Uh, why?" Jess questions, looking flummoxed.

Malcolm takes the lead and tells them exactly why Cade is with her instead of us.

"Why did she give Liana up so readily after going through so much to get her in the first place?" Lucifer asks, never one to be shy about getting to the heart of the matter.

We've already told the others in the room what Helena did. There's no point in hiding the fact from the rest of them, and Lucifer might actually have a theory to help explain her action.

"Helena gave Liana one of her seals," I tell them.

Lucifer immediately walks over to Zane, who is still holding a slumbering Liana.

"Let me see her," he orders brusquely.

Without hesitation, Zane hands my daughter to her grandfather. Almost as soon as she's in his arms, Liana begins to wail as if she was suddenly dropped into a vat of boiling oil. I immediately stand and go to her. Before I'm even halfway to them, I realize I'm not the best person to bring comfort to my daughter.

"Give her back to Zane," I tell my father.

Lucifer does as I ask, and Liana immediately quiets once she's back in Zane's arms.

I stop beside Lucifer as we both look at Liana safely cradled against Zane's chest.

Lucifer looks over at me with a troubled frown marring his otherwise-handsome face.

"This isn't good, Anna," he says gravely, "I assume she has the same reaction to you?"

"Not quite as violent," I reply, finding small relief in that fact, "but she definitely doesn't care for me very much. Is it the seal that's causing her to react this way to us?"

"I'm sure it's playing a part, but I think more than that is going on here."

"Then what's wrong with her?" I practically beg. "I can't live with my own daughter hating me, Dad. It's breaking my heart."

"Could that be why Helena gave her the seal?" Zane asks, gently rocking Liana as he holds her. I feel a moment of jealousy that she's allowing him to do something I myself desperately want to do. "Is she trying to cause Anna distress by making Liana dislike her?"

"I don't think so," Lucifer says, mulling over the possibilities. "That's probably just a bonus side-effect to the real reason."

Lucifer peers at Liana, but she has her eyes shut as her breathing levels out. She begins to suckle on a closed fist as she turns her head towards Zane's chest and appears to fall back to sleep.

I sigh in relief that she was so easily quieted, but the pain of rejection still stings my heart.

"Can Anna take the seal away from Liana like she did the princes?" Jess asks, attempting to find a solution to our problem.

"She could if she wanted to risk killing her own daughter," Lucifer says rather condescendingly, but Jess doesn't seem to take offense. I think she realizes my father is simply concerned over the latest obstacle Helena has placed in our lives. "None of us has any way of knowing how tight the connection is between Liana's soul and the seal. It's possible Liana can give Anna the seal when she gets older and understands the consequences, but for now I don't think it's wise to just take it away from her."

As I study my father's expression, I can tell he's trying to figure out what Helena's end game is by giving Liana a seal. After all, it's the energy she derived from taking the seals away from me that allowed her to finally break the shackles keeping her trapped in Hell. Obviously, she doesn't need all five seals to maintain her corporeal state, but it seems odd for her to risk it just to transfer a seal to Liana. From my experience with carrying the seals in my own body, I fully understand the pull of the power they bestow on their holder. Why would Helena willingly make my daughter stronger? What does she hope to gain from such an action?

I have to find the answers to those questions quickly; not only for my daughter's well-being, but also for the sake of my own sanity.

"I'll help you figure it out before I leave," Lucifer promises me. The earnest expression on his face tells me that he will keep his word, and I immediately feel a sense of comfort in his love for me and my children.

"Wait," I say, suddenly realizing something. "Aiden told us that each seal contains the soul of the Guardian who was protecting it. Did you know that?"

"Yes," Lucifer reveals, "but they weren't awake. They were in a dormant state."

"Well, what's the name of the Guardian who had your seal, and is that Guardian awake in Liana now? Aiden told us that the Guardians awoke when I absorbed the seals. They're the ones who transformed the energy from the seals into souls for the twins."

"Hmm," Lucifer says, "interesting. To answer your question, the Guardian in charge of my seal was named Jequn. It's more than likely that he's awake. It's also possible that Jequn will do what the other two Guardians did and make a soul for Liana's first-born child. If that's the case, marry her off early so she can get rid of it as quickly as possible."

"I will let her choose who she marries and when," I say. "I refuse to push her into a loveless marriage."

"Uh, Anna," Zane says, drawing my attention to him.

When I look back at him, I see a look of near terror on Zane's face.

My heart skips a beat in worry. As I walk over to him and Liana, I ask, "What's wrong?"

It only takes me a couple of steps before I know exactly what the problem is and feel relief wash over me as realization sets in.

"That can't be a natural smell," Zane professes as he peers down at Liana in disgust.

"I'm afraid It's completely natural," I assure him with a sympathetic smile. "She needs to have her diaper changed."

"Good grief," Gideon says from his seat next to Zane as he pushes his half-eaten plate of pancakes away from him. "That unholy stench certainly curbed my appetite. I've smelled better things in Hell."

Zane lifts his arms in an attempt to hand the burden of my stinky child over to me.

I hold my hands up in the air. "I can't take her. She'll just fuss if I try to do it. Besides, I think this is a wonderful opportunity for you to learn how to take care of a baby's needs, Zane. This way, you'll know what to do when you have one of your own."

Zane looks less than confident that he's up for the challenge, but he lowers his arm and cradles Liana to his chest again.

"If you say so," he says hesitantly. "Where are the supplies I need to use to clean her up?"

Malcolm stands from his seat at the table. "I'll be right back with them."

My husband phases, but returns less than a minute later with a black bag filled with supplies for such an occasion. He walks over to the kitchen island Zane is still sitting at and sets the bag down on top of it. He opens the flap and pulls out a slim foldable white pad, laying it out in front of Zane.

"Lay her down on it," Malcolm orders.

Zane does as instructed, treating Liana like a porcelain doll he's afraid he'll break.

"Wouldn't you rather do this?" Zane asks Malcolm hopefully. "I would hate to deprive you of such a thing."

"Trust me, I've changed more diapers in my life than I want to admit to," Malcolm says. "Buck up, War Angel. If you can handle fighting a horde of rebellion angels and hell-spawn, you'll survive changing a diaper."

Zane doesn't look convinced by Malcolm's words of encouragement as he begins to unfold the blanket swaddling Liana. The aroma of my daughter's little present fills the air in the room, causing a few of the War Angels to cover their noses in a vain attempt to temper the flow of the unpleasant smell into their lungs.

"I agree with Zane," Roan says with a pinched face and slight cough. "That smell can't be natural."

"Oh, put your hands down," I admonish them. "In fact, I think you should all come closer and watch Zane so you know what to do when your turn comes."

"I don't think it's safe," Atticus protests.

"I would rather go pick a fight with a prince of Hell," Roan mumbles.

Ethan stands from his seat at the table.

"Anna gave us a command," he tells his men. "No matter how much we might fear for our own lives right now, we have to do what she tells us."

I hear Malcolm snicker, drawing my attention back to him. He looks mightily amused by my War Angels' predicament. I refrain from admonishing him because my angels all stand from their respective seats and walk over to the kitchen island to have their first lesson in diaper- changing. He's already taught me how to do it, so I see no need to take up space unnecessarily around the tutorial. I leave them as Malcolm begins to give Zane step-by-step instructions on how to perform the task.

"Here you go, Grandpa," I hear Jess say as she hands Liam to Lucifer. "I know you're itching to hold him."

I witness what has to be a rarity in the universe. As Lucifer cradles Liam in his arms, he smiles.

"Hello, Liam," Lucifer says as he marvels at my son's perfection. "It's a pleasure to finally meet you."

I glance at Aiden, who is involved in a conversation with Jered at the table, and see him briefly look up while his charge is meeting his grandfather for the very first time. He grins at the introduction and quickly returns his attention to Jered to continue their conversation. I wasn't sure what his reaction would be, since Lucifer's return to Heaven only happened a short while ago. After all the animosity my father had built up over the years with almost everyone in the room, I have to say I'm somewhat surprised by how welcoming they've all been towards him.

As I watch Lucifer with Liam, I have to wonder if he ever held and looked at me the same way when I was a baby. Millie once told me that Lucifer would come to Cirrus once a year to visit me on my birthday. Supposedly, I was asleep during his visits, but surely he held or touched me while he was there. The sight of him with my son makes me even more determined to find a way to connect with Liana. Being held and loved by your parent is such an important part of growing up.

I search the room and find my papa leaned up against the counter nearest the stove. He's supervising Lucas as he makes more pancakes and listening to something Vala just said to him. I was so lucky to have had Andre Greco raise me as his own daughter. He didn't play a role in my conception, but since the day I was born, he accepted the responsibility of being my father. No child in the history of the world could have ever asked for a more loving and compassionate parent.

I feel a well of love threaten to spill over for my papa as a deluge of happy memories from my childhood plays through my mind. I walk over to him because, of anyone else in the room, he has earned the right to be called grandfather by my children. I know he'll give them the same unreserved love he has always lavished on me because that's just the kind of man he is. In all my years with him, I have rarely seen my papa say a harsh word to anyone unless it was well- deserved.

"Papa," I say as I walk up to him, "why don't you come see your grandchildren?"

I notice him briefly glance in Lucifer's direction before settling his gaze on me again.

"I didn't want to intrude," he tells me, looking uncertain about his role in the gathering.

"I don't want you to ever think your presence is an intrusion," I tell him in earnest. "You're my father, too. Don't forget that, because I never will."

My papa smiles. "Okay. I won't."

I loop an arm through one of his. "Now come with me. I want Liam and Liana to meet the first man I ever loved."

My papa follows me across the room without putting up a protest.

The world I live in is filled with uncertainties at the moment, but even through all the chaos there's one truth I know I can always hold on to during the difficult times. I have a family who loves me unreservedly, and together we can face whatever tries to tear us apart.

CHAPTER SIX

(Helena's Point of View)

After I give Silas and his men my instructions and deposit them where they need to be, I return to Grace House on the planet Sierra. When I phase back there, I find Cade still sitting in our cozy little booth, but I don't find him alone pining for my return. Evelyn Grace is sitting across from him, wearing a sympathetic expression on her face as she gazes at Cade. I suspect she cornered him while I was gone inorder to better understand why Cade wasn't trying to make his great escape from my company during my absence.

"Wonderful, her royal pain in my ass is back," Evelyn says less than enthusiastically when she spies me.

My first instinct is to obliterate Evelyn from existence for her open defiance, but since I don't want to ruin my first date with Cade with homicidal rage and subsequent murder, I say, "Did you have any doubt that I would be returning?"

"No, but sometimes I can't prevent myself from being an eternal optimist."

"I hope you find yourself witty, Evelyn, because I certainly do not."

"For some reason, I don't have a hard time believing that," she replies caustically. "You actually have to have a sense of humor to find my sarcastic repartee amusing."

Before I can make my retort, I hear Enis say behind me, "Evie, you have a visitor."

Evelyn's attention is instantly diverted away from me to Enis.

"Where is she?" Evelyn asks, quickly standing from her seat at the table. As she smooths the wrinkles from her dress, I notice her scan the throng of people in Grace House in search of this mysterious guest.

"She's sitting at the bar having a drink," Enis informs her. For some reason, he doesn't sound particularly pleased about this person imbibing alcohol.

"Damn it, Enis!" Evelyn says irately, snapping her gaze back at her best friend. "Why would you let her do that?"

Evelyn quickly turns on her heels and heads toward the bar area, Enis following closely behind her.

"You know how she is," he tries to argue. "She does whatever she damn well pleases. She may call me Uncle Enis, but the respect that's usually associated with such a title has been sorely lacking in her attitude of late."

I hear Evelyn growl in frustration as she continues to make her way across the room to the bar built against the far wall. Curiosity gets the better of me, and I watch as Evelyn approaches an attractive blond sitting on a stool at the bar. Once she reaches her, Evelyn reaches out and grabs the woman's right shoulder, deftly spinning her around until they're face to face. Considering the striking resemblance between the two women, I instantly know the identity of Evelyn's mystery guest.

"Who is that?" I hear Cade ask as he vacates his seat in the booth to stand by my side.

"Evelyn's daughter," I answer as I watch the two women have a rather heated argument.

"Daughter? But Evelyn is a rebellion angel. She can't have children."

"I didn't say she gave birth to her."

"I'm afraid you've lost me."

I force myself to stop watching the quarrel to return my attention to Cade.

"Evelyn Grace isn't the first name this particular rebellion angel has had on this planet, but it's the one she's kept for the longest time. The real Evelyn Grace was on the verge of death right after she gave birth to her daughter, Julia." I turn my head slightly and nod it in the direction of Evelyn and Julia before looking back at Cade. "Instead of leaving Julia an orphan, the rebellion angel took over Evelyn's body and has been living as her ever since."

"Does Julia know that her real mother is dead?"

"I really don't know or care," I say honestly, already becoming bored with the subject. "It's none of my business, and I would rather not become involved in a domestic squabble. I have enough disputes with my own family to deal with."

"If you would stop antagonizing her," Cade begins, "Anna would probably be willing to call a truce to the fight the two of you are embroiled in."

"I'm perfectly aware of that," I say testily. "Though, why you think that's something I want is rather mind-boggling. Have I ever given you the impression that I'm someone who's interested in peace? What would that gain me? Nothing. Pain and hopelessness are the only things I care about because they feed me and make me stronger. If there is one immutable truth I learned during my visit to alternate Earth, it's that peace can only lead to my destruction. Is that what you want, Cade? For me to become weak and useless?"

"You're twisting my words, Helena," Cade replies defensively. "That isn't what I said and you know it."

I stare at Cade for a few seconds before allowing myself to smile at him. The confused look on his face at my reaction only makes my lips stretch even more.

"Can I ask why you're smiling?" Cade asks cautiously.

"There aren't a lot of people in this world who would have the audacity to stand up to me like you do," I tell him. "I like it. I wouldn't want to be with someone who didn't fight for what he believes in. Don't lose that quality, dear heart. Otherwise, you may not survive this little adventure into the unknown that you and I are embarking on."

Cade seems to accept my answer, and holds his right hand out to me.

"Then let's keep going," he suggests. "Let me be your guide to an Earth you haven't explored yet."

I accept his offer by placing my hand into his.

Cade phases us to a spot within Cirrus territory that I recognize straightaway. We're standing on a plateau that overlooks a grand expanse of colorful, layered rock formations. The pale beige sandstone layers act as a stark contrast to the red limestone ones, causing them to be the most prominent to catch the eye.

"The Grand Canyon?" I ask in a tone that does nothing to hide my disappointment in Cade's first location choice.

A warm breeze flows through and over the gorge, forcing me to lift a hand to shield my eyes from the dirt it kicks up. I end up coughing slightly as some of the dust makes its way into my lungs.

"Why on Earth would you bring me here?" I ask incredulously. "It's just a big hole in the ground!"

"It's more than that," Cade tells me in an even, calm tone. He doesn't seem in the least bit offended by my less than enthusiastic attitude. "It's a testament to Earth's history and how much has happened here through the ages."

I look out across the grand vista once more, trying to appreciate Cade's point of view. Unfortunately, it doesn't work.

"All I see is a gigantic, lifeless pit," I say, unable to perceive the beauty of such a place like he apparently does.

I hear him sigh. Presumably he's disappointed in my lack of enthusiasm over the sight, but I'm not about to lie to him just to assuage his misguided attempt at romance. If he wants to impress me, he'll have to step up his game and do better.

He tightens his hold on my hand and phases us to yet another location that is just as unimpressive to me. I almost begin to feel sorry for Cade and his clichéd notions of what I will find romantic or even remotely interesting. As my ears are assaulted by the roar of crashing ocean waves, I look down at my feet and see that they are now buried in sugar-white sand. With a growl born from frustration, I yank my hand out of Cade's to quickly slip off my strappy black leather sandals before they're completely ruined by the sand or an overzealous saltwater wave.

"I take it you don't like it here either," Cade surmises with an amused lilt in his voice.

"No," I reply tersely as I clap the bottoms of my sandals together to get rid of the sand clinging to them. "My shoes are probably ruined thanks to all this sand, and the stench of that saltwater will be impossible to get out of my clothes now."

"O-kay," he says, sounding hesitant to take me anywhere else since I've heartily disliked his choice of locales thus far. "Should I even attempt to take you anywhere else, or are you becoming too annoyed to go any further with me?"

When I look up at Cade, I can tell he desperately wants to find a place on Earth that we both view the same way. Unexpectedly, I feel a sense of guilt wash over me for stridently voicing my displeasure in his failure to show me something I find even remotely beautiful on this planet. Yet, I don't like seeing him so dejected and have to wonder if he realizes one very important fact regarding the two of us.

"We're very different people, Cade," I patiently explain. "It's going to be almost impossible to find a place that we can both find beauty in."

"I'm acutely aware of the fact that we view things differently," he replies, "but I also believe there's a way for us to find some common ground. There just has to be."

I tilt my head slightly as I consider the almost desperate look on his face.

"Why is this so important to you?" I have to ask.

"I need to know there's more to us than just being soul mates," he replies like a confession.

I feel slightly taken aback by his answer. "Isn't being soul mates enough of a connection for you? What more do we really need?"

"So much more," he says as his gaze trails away from mine. He stares across the ocean to the red-orange sunset. I remain silent, allowing him time to place his thoughts in order before he speaks again.

Finally, he says, "I know you probably don't want to hear me compare us to Anna and Malcolm…"

"And you would assume right," I interrupt brusquely. "I have no intention of being as sappy as my sister is in her own love life. If that's the sort of lover you need, then I am not the one for you."

Cade returns his gaze to me. "You're the only one for me, Helena, and you know that better than anyone else. I'm fully aware that we can never be the way Malcolm and Anna are together. The all-consuming love they share only comes once in a generation. I'm not deluded enough to believe we'll have a life like theirs."

"Then I'm confused," I admit. "What is it that you want?"

"Right now, all I want is for us to find a place that we both like. If we can do that one simple thing, then maybe we can build on that and figure out other things that we both like. After watching Anna and Malcolm together, I know that a lasting relationship needs to be built on more than just love and sex."

"Well," I say, unable to hold back a smile at his use of the three-letter word I've been waiting for him to bring up, "why don't we start with sex and build from there? I'm quite positive we would both enjoy that little activity."

Cade shakes his head at me as if silently chastising me for my thoughts concerning sex, but I notice he's helpless to prevent the glint of desire I see flare in the depths of his eyes.

"Sex is nothing to build a relationship on, Helena," he admonishes. "If all I wanted was sex from a woman, I could have gone to the Ladies in Waiting in Cirrus months ago. I want a deeper connection to the woman I make love to for the first time."

"I have no doubt you could connect with me on a very deep level," I say huskily while taking a small step forward until my breasts are barely brushing against Cade's chest. "Let's not forget that I've held what you have to offer so don't sell your attribute short, because it's anything but."

Cade stares at me as if he's considering my words, but I can already tell by the steely determination in his blue-grey eyes that he isn't going to take me up on my generous offer.

"Why are you being so stubborn?" I ask agitatedly, taking a step back from him. "As I've said before, we will end up in a bed together at some point in our lives. Why prolong the inevitable?"

"Because I want our first time together to mean something more than just satisfying a physical urge for you, Helena. I want you to feel it in here," he says, placing his right hand over my heart.

"And how do you know I can feel anything there besides hate?" I ask in a whisper, because even I don't know the answer to my question.

"If you can hate with all your heart, then you can love just as fiercely," Cade declares. "Hate is only a feeling, just like love. I think you've simply been programmed to hate for so long you don't realize you're capable of more than that. You've never really had a reason to love anyone or anything, but now you do. Let me show you a world where love can be a permanent part of your life. I would pledge my love and my life to you, Helena, if you would only do the same."

"Are you asking me to marry you?" I ask flabbergasted. "If you are, the answer is a resounding no!"

"Of course I'm not proposing to you, Helena," Cade replies, looking frustrated by my response to his heartfelt sentiments. "If I ever decide to do that, you'll know it. What I'm asking is that you open your heart to me and allow for the possibility that you can love me back."

"And if I at least 'allow for the possibility', as you say, will that make you happy?"

"Yes, if you really mean it. If you're just planning to tell me you will without actually meaning it, then don't say it. I don't particularly want to be lied to by you."

"How will you know the difference?" I challenge. "I could just pretend to go along with what you want from me in order to ease your mind and make you more pliable to my will."

"Do you honestly think I wouldn't be able to tell the difference? Have you forgotten that I can tell a truth from a lie?"

"Actually, I had forgotten about that annoying little trait of yours," I confess. "Oh well, I guess I'll just have to tell the truth then. I will *allow* for the possibility that my heart can be opened by you and that it *might* be able to learn how to love. However, I want it noted that I don't believe such a miracle will occur, but I will allow for the possibility if it will put an end to this conversation."

Cade grins, looking quite satisfied with himself. "That's all I want from you, Helena. As long as you don't purposely try to lock me out of your heart, we have a chance to find happiness."

"Would you be at all insulted if I told you I thought you were deluding yourself?"

"No," he replies with a shake of his head, "I'm not insulted. I don't particularly concern myself with what others think of me. As long as I keep true to my own beliefs, whatever anyone else thinks of me is simply their opinion."

"I'm sure your brother War Angels consider you delusional as well," I say with certainty. "If they haven't said it to your face, they're definitely thinking it behind your back."

"Are you always so cynical?" he asks, looking at me with a great deal of annoyance.

"Can you honestly stand there and tell me that any of them are pleased that I'm your soul mate?"

Cade remains silent for a moment before answering, "No. I can't say that they're happy about the situation. I normally see pity in their eyes whenever the subject is brought up."

"They *should* pity you. You're stuck with the one person in the universe who has a numb heart where the subject of love is concerned. Even I pity you to a certain extent, Cade."

"Well, don't waste a lot of time feeling sorry for me just yet," he says, walking up to me and placing his hand on my left shoulder. "I still have a chance to make you realize you feel something for me, even if you don't want to admit it."

Cade phases us again in his stubborn attempt to find a place on Earth that we can both at least agree to like.

I find myself standing next to a large mangled heap of iron. I have an intimate knowledge of this place since Lucifer visited it religiously at least once a year.

"And why would someone with a sunny disposition such as yourself find the remnants of the Eiffel Tower beautiful?" I have to ask. "You do realize most humans consider it a gloomy reminder of what happened during the Great War, don't you?"

93

"I know that," Cade replies as he looks up at the mammoth pile of twisted metal. "But there's still beauty in what it once represented."

"And what is that exactly?"

"Love," he states simply. "Thousands of lovers declared their feelings to one another on this exact spot. There aren't many places in the world where that can be said."

"I have to admit that this site could almost pass as a place I don't detest," I acknowledge. "Unfortunately, Lucifer and Jess tainted this particular wonder of the world for me."

"How so?"

"Don't you remember that intimate little scene I showed everyone starring Jess and Lucifer?" I ask. "Lucifer always brought Jess here on her birthdays while she was alive. Even after she died, he continued to come here on her birthdays to pay tribute to his memories of her. If it weren't for those detestable facts, you would have found a place we could call our own."

Cade looks troubled by this news. I'm sure he thought the destructive force the Eiffel Tower represented would be attractive to me, while the romantic legends surrounding it appealed to his foolish, idealistic heart.

"You had the right idea," I tell him to ease the blow of his disappointment. "You shouldn't feel bad that you didn't remember the connection it has for me to Lucifer."

"Give me a minute," Cade says as he takes a seat on a flat spot of the tower. "I know I can think of a place we can both enjoy."

I sit down beside him to slip my sandals back on my feet. When I stand back up, I grimace at the feel of sand between my toes. I know no amount of brushing will get the sand off my skin. I'll need to take a bath in order to rid myself of the grit.

Cade stands from his seat and immediately twines the fingers of one hand with mine.

"I know where to go," he declares proudly. "And if this place is a bust, too, then I'll give up. I promise that I won't force you to go anywhere else with me."

"You would give up on your quest that readily?" I ask, feeling a sense of displeasure that he would cease this endeavor so easily.

"No. I'm not giving up exactly. I'm just confident that you'll like the next place I take you to."

"Well then," I say, feeling more satisfied with his cockiness, "show me this wonder on Earth that you believe I will at least like."

Cade smiles and phases us to our next location.

CHAPTER SEVEN

Thick grey storm clouds cover the sky and a rumble of thunder vibrates the green grass beneath my feet, causing them to tingle slightly from its might. As I survey the corner of the world Cade has phased us to, all I see is a variety of tombstones dotting the landscape for as far as my sight will allow. It's a tapestry stitched by death himself in its most blatant form.

"A graveyard?" I ask, slightly bemused by his choice of locale.

"Do you find anything disagreeable here?" he asks, expectantly awaiting my response.

I stand stock-still, allowing myself to be filled with the unique aura of the place. Obviously I knew about the existence of cemeteries, but I have to admit this is the first time I've actually stood in one. There is a unique calm amidst the silence of the dead. Ever since coming to Earth, I've felt bombarded by the hustle and bustle of humanity's constant need to get ahead in life. It seemed as though they were always doing something and being exceedingly noisy about it. However, this place holds a tranquility I haven't experienced on Earth before now.

"Well?" Cade prods as another roar of thunder shakes the ground, a little harder this time.

"Congratulations. You actually *did* find a place that I can tolerate on this planet," I answer, feeling proud of him for succeeding in a task I thought impossible. It makes me wonder what else he might be able to succeed at that I previously labelled as being unachievable.

A triumphant smile graces Cade's face, involuntarily causing my heart to skip a beat. I quickly avert my gaze because I feel sure that's the only way to break the spell he seems to have cast over me. I feel his hand reach underneath my chin as he gently lifts and turns my head back towards him.

"Why are you looking away?" he whispers, a raspy quality to his voice. The once-proud smile that graced his lips only seconds ago is gone now, but there is a lingering twinkle of happiness in his eyes that affects me just the same. I don't feel in complete control of my feelings, and that is something I do not like.

I take a slow step away from Cade to put some distance between us, turning my back to him as I begin to walk through the cemetery.

"Tell me," I say, eager to change the subject so he understands that an answer to his question will not be forthcoming, "why would this be a place that you like to visit? It's not exactly happy or beautiful. You've already proven that you prefer colorful locales. This seems a bit gloomy for you."

"It might sound strange, but I like walking through cemeteries from time to time."

I come to a complete stop and turn around to look at Cade.

"Whatever for?" I have to ask.

Cade looks around as if he's searching for something in particular. Presumably he finds it, because a pleased grin stretches his lips as he looks back at me and holds out a hand for me to take.

"Come with me," he beckons, "and I'll show you exactly why I like walking through them."

I give him my hand to hold and he gently tugs me forward to follow him past rows of tombstones. We finally come to a stop in front of a rather sad excuse for a grave marker. It's a large plank of wood that someone painted on for the inscription.

Here lies Howard Abernathy

Beloved Husband and Father

Bring us, O Lord God, at our last awakening into the house and gate of heaven

"Such elegant wording should be on a more impressive tombstone," I comment dryly, not understanding why Cade purposely picked this particular grave marker to point out to me.

"I don't think Howard Abernathy really cares that his family didn't have the money to buy him a fancy headstone. I'm sure he's happy just to be remembered so fondly by the people he loved most in this world."

"That bottom phrase sounds familiar to me. Why is that?"

"It's part of an Anglican prayer by a man named John Donne. It's possible Lucifer either heard or read it at some point in time and passed the knowledge onto you through one of his memories."

"Yes, that's probably why." I begin to walk down the row of graves we're on and notice a theme to the tombstones we pass. "It seems as though everyone here was loved by at least one person during their lives."

"Yes," Cade replies as he follows behind me. "That's the reason I like to come here. I'm sure some of these people weren't the nicest in life, yet those they left behind choose to memorialize the love they once shared. I think that says a lot about humanity."

"What? That they're forgetful?" I scoff with a derisive snort.

"No," he says patiently. "That they can forgive almost anything, given enough time. I think that's a quality worth admiring, don't you?"

"If you want my honest opinion, I would have to say no. I find it rather pathetic. If someone was cruel to others, why should they be remembered in a favorable way?"

"How would you want to be remembered?"

"I can't die, so your question is moot," I quip.

"But let's say that you could die; how would you want the world to remember you?"

"As someone who took charge and never let anything get in her way."

"Wouldn't you want someone to call you 'beloved' on your tombstone?"

"I guess it depends if they meant the sentiment or if they simply put it there to make them feel better about themselves. Have you ever considered the possibility that these people simply put what was expected of them by others on the grave markers of their dearly departed? Human society seems more concerned about the way things appear than how they actually are. If you ask me, they're just a bunch of hypocrites who allow themselves to become slaves to what the social order dictates."

"That's an extremely cynical way to view the world, Helena."

I shrug, unaffected by his words. "What can I say? I'm a glass-half-empty kind of person."

Cade remains silent after my declaration. I think the reality of his self-imposed task to reform me is finally sinking into his psyche. I slow my gait quite a bit until he's walking by my side. Without giving it much fanfare, I reach out and grab hold of his hand as we continue to walk through the cemetery.

As we're walking down our third row of graves, a light rain begins to fall.

"I guess we should probably go," Cade says, sounding unsure about where to take me next. "Do you want to go back to Hell?"

"No," I say, continuing to walk as the rain gradually begins to pick up in intensity. "You said you wanted me to experience new things, and walking in the rain is something I've never done before. Let's just enjoy it while we can. My clothes are basically ruined anyway."

Cade doesn't make a verbal reply. He simply tightens his hold on my hand and continues to walk in the steady pace we've set for ourselves. It doesn't take long before we're both drenched to the bone. A strong gust of wind begins to lash the raindrops against our skin, and I involuntarily shiver from the cold. Before I'm even given the opportunity to make a protest, Cade phases us out of the graveyard and into a living room I've never been to before. The home we're in is filled with an old-world charm. The walls are painted a warm white and the sandstone-colored beams in the ceiling are exposed, adding a sense of rustic simplicity. The upholstered furniture in the room is arranged around a white driftwood coffee table with an oval-shaped glass top. The furnishings and knick-knacks scattered around all follow a general color scheme, ranging from white to a sea-foam blue. As I turn to look around the room, I see a large panel of glass on an outside wall, facing an ocean.

"Where are we?" I ask as I continue to take note of the open floor plan of the space, which includes a kitchen opposite the living room.

"This is my down-world home in Cirrus," Cade informs me as he watches my initial reaction to his house. "Do you like it?"

"It's very…you," I reply as I look away from the room and back at him.

"Very me," he says, mulling over my words. "Is that a good thing or a bad one in your opinion?"

"Neither," I say candidly. "It's simply a statement of fact. Now, why exactly are we here?"

"I thought you might like to get out of your wet clothes."

Intrigued by his suggestion, I raise a questioning eyebrow and ask, "And will you be helping me out of them, dear heart?"

Cade looks embarrassed by my teasing and looks away, unable to meet my gaze.

"That wasn't my intention," he mutters before chancing a glance back in my direction. "At least not yet."

I have to smile at his cheekiness. "Well, just for the record, I anxiously await the time when it is your intention."

Cade lifts his right hand to softly cup the left side of my face. He holds my gaze with his and I feel a sexual tension develop between us that even he can't deny. The pad of his thumb slowly follows the contour of my cheekbone. When he takes a small step forward, I patiently wait for him to follow through with what should naturally come next, a kiss.

To my great disappointment, he phases me to a bathroom in his home. It's large with a slate-tiled walk-in shower, separate bathtub, toilet, and vanity.

"A shower should help warm you up," he says, dropping his hand away from my face and back to his side. He turns around and walks over to the vanity. Once there, he bends down to open the cabinet underneath the sink and pulls out a fluffy white towel. He then proceeds to walk back and hold the towel out for me to take.

"I think I can find you something to wear in my closet."

I almost suggest that it might be easier if I just phase to my room in Nimbo and retrieve some of my own clothes, but I decide against it. For one thing, I don't want to run the risk of seeing Levi. The other reason is that being clothed by Cade in his own garments might help hasten the connection we're building with one another. Wearing your potential lover's clothing is a rather intimate act. Maybe if he sees me completely undone, sans makeup and perfectly coiffed hair, I'll seem more approachable. I honestly don't know what he's waiting to happen before he finally deems it's time for us to have sex. I know he wants me; of that I have no doubt. I just need to figure out how to make him realize we could be enjoying each other's bodies instead of denying ourselves a great deal of pleasure.

"Thank you," I tell him, accepting the towel. "I would appreciate some fresh clothing."

"I'll leave them by the sink," he tells me before phasing to what looks like his bedroom, considering the fact I can see a bed through his phase trail.

If I thought I could be successful in my seduction of him, I would follow Cade's trail and throw caution to the wind. However, I know the gesture would be a futile one. No. I'll simply be patient and wait for him to decide when the time is right. I shake my head in dismay. Patience has never been one of my strong suits. Yet, where Cade is concerned I seem to have an abundance of it.

After I strip off my wet clothing and step into the glass-enclosed shower, the warm spray of water from the showerhead instantly melts away the tension in my muscles. Even though I want to, I don't linger in the water for very long. I have more important matters to attend to with Cade.

When I step out of the shower and begin to dry off with my towel, I notice a folded white t-shirt and a pair of black drawstring shorts sitting on top of the vanity. I dry my hair as well as I can before dressing in the clothes Cade left for me. The V-neck t-shirt is long and hangs to mid-thigh. I consider just wearing the shirt and nothing else but decide against it. If I had some clean underwear I might do it, but I don't think he would appreciate me sitting bare-bottomed on his furniture. The shorts are, of course, too big, but after wrapping the drawstring around my slim waist twice, I'm able to keep them from falling off.

I scrutinize my appearance in the mirror above the sink and like what I see. My cheeks and lips are a rosy red from the warmth of the water, and my hair looks tousled enough to give the illusion of natural, stretched-out curls. I flip my hair to the side and begin to fluff it up a bit by scrunching it with my fingers.

I immediately stop the motion of my hand as I stare at my reflection in the mirror.

What in the world am I doing?

I'm primping for someone who should feel fortunate to have me want him in my bed. If anyone should be making an added effort here, it should be Cade! Why am I acting like some simpering lovesick girl trying to attract the attention of her beau?

Ludicrous. I immediately use both of my hands to ruffle my hair, completely messing it up. If Cade wants me, he should be the one doing all the work to have me, not the other way around.

I stomp out of the bathroom, feeling rather superior about my stance. The room I step into turns out to be a bedroom. Following the general beach theme of the house, the large bed in the room is covered with an ocean-blue comforter trimmed in white with a coral motif embroidered into the fabric. Standard pillows stacked three-deep and a grouping of matching throw pillows add a feel of hominess to the ensemble. The room is mostly white with splashes of blue to add contrast.

When I walk out of the bedroom, I find myself back in the living room. I don't see Cade anywhere, but I do spy that the front door is wide open, allowing the sound of the ocean to breach the general silence of the house. After I step over the threshold, I soon discover the large front porch attached to Cade's home.

"Do you feel better?" I hear him ask from the right of me.

I turn my head and find him lying on a large swing bed, that is hanging from the porch ceiling by four thick chains with nautical rope twisted around them. The bed itself looks rather comfy with bolster pillows on each end and a mound of decorative ones stacked against the back. Cade's naked torso is propped up by a few pillows, and he's lying with one leg stretched out while the other one is bent at the knee. Unfortunately, he's still wearing his pants or the scene would be perfect. He has one arm crooked at the elbow and resting behind his head. Since it's summertime, twilight can last for hours at the end of the day instead of mere minutes like it does during the winter. I have to admit that the scene is a quaint picture of seaside tranquility.

Without changing his position, Cade stretches out his arm and holds his hand open to me.

"Come here, Helena," he beckons, but not in a demanding way. His words aren't laced with the intent of it being an order. He's simply making a request for my company.

"I'm not sure there's enough room for both of us on there," I tell him as I walk over.

Cade sits up and systematically begins to toss the decorative pillows onto the porch behind the swing. Once I reach him, he scoots over and lies on his side to make room for me.

"There's plenty of space," he tells me, grinning as he pats the empty spot beside him as if to prove his point.

"I suppose there is," I reply, wondering where all of this will lead. Without questioning my good fortune, I sit on the bed and lift my legs to lie down on it with Cade.

As if it were the most natural thing to do Cade brings me into his arms, allowing me to rest my head against his chest. The warmth of his body next to mine and the rhythmic rise and fall of his chest with every breath he takes lulls my senses. I begin to feel something that's a rarity for me. It's an emotion I've only ever felt while inside my own domain: peace. I give myself permission to ride the wave of serenity for as long as it will allow me. I start to understand why people like to be by the ocean so much. If you allow it, the crashing of the waves against the shore can soothe your senses with their rhythm.

"Sometimes I look at you and I can't believe how beautiful you are," I hear him whisper.

I open my eyes, not having realized that I had even closed them, and tilt my head up to look into his face. The passion in his gaze captures me, rendering me speechless. I patiently wait to see where all of this will lead.

"You're one of the most stunning women I've ever seen," he tells me as he tilts his body in such a way that my head slides off his chest to rest against his arm like it's a pillow. With him completely on his side, he uses the fingers of his free hand to trace the contours of my jawline. When he reaches my chin, he begins to explore the softness of my lips, which part of their own accord in anticipation of what might come next. I glance up to meet his gaze and see the heat of pent-up desire there. It's a look I feel sure is mirrored in my own eyes.

Once gaining their fill of my lips, Cade glides his fingers down the curve at the front of my neck until they arrive at the tender flesh between my breasts exposed by the cut of the shirt's V-shaped neckline. I hold my breath, excitedly waiting to see if he's brave enough to study that portion of my body any further. Instead of exploring the contours of my breasts, he leans his head down and gently begins to tease my lips with his own. His kiss is feather-light at first, undemanding and unassuming. I begin to feel an urgency build inside me, silently begging Cade to discover everything I have to offer him even deeper and more thoroughly. When I feel the first flick of his tongue against my upper lip, I sigh in sweet anticipation of what will surely come next. I open my mouth wider, inviting him to delve deeper. Without missing a beat, he gently coaxes my tongue into a playful dance with his own that only excites the growing needs of my body. I immediately feel physical proof against the side of my thigh that his desire is rising in intensity as well.

Cade's mouth briefly leaves mine as he repositions his body over me. His knees are bent on either side of my body to carry the brunt of his weight. He slides both of his arms underneath my shoulders and cradles my head in his hands as leans back down to continue his gentle assault of my mouth. By leaning down his hips brush against my own, and the proof of his desire for me begins to steadily stroke against the most sensitive part of my sex. I have, of course, experimented with self-pleasuring the little nub between my legs, but having Cade rub himself against that sweet spot causes me to lose what little control I have over my body. Without even having to think about it, my pelvis begins to lift slightly off the bed to meet each of his thrusts. I soon discover that the faster I move the more pleasure I gain, until I feel as though my whole world is splitting in two.

As I float down on a cloud of sexual bliss, Cade's lips leave mine, forcing me to open my eyes to figure out why he isn't kissing me anymore.

"What's wrong?" I ask breathlessly. The movement of his hips ceases, but I still feel the proof of his desire against the juncture of my thighs. "Why are you stopping?"

His eyes seem to search my own for some unknown answer to an unasked question.

"Cade…" I breathe out as a soft plea, lifting my hips slightly to prod him to finish what he's started. "Don't stop. Not now."

His lips stretch into a small grin, but it's laced with a melancholia I can't quite understand.He leans his head back down until our foreheads touch, and closes his eyes.

"I can't yet," he tells me, the words coming out like an apology. "You're not ready."

"I seriously beg to differ," I reply, feeling rather perturbed by his answer. "I've been ready since the moment we met."

With his eyes still closed, Cade grins again. This time it's a much happier one.

"So you've wanted me to do this," he says, tilting his hips to thrust himself against me once more, "since you first saw me?"

"Of course I have. Haven't you?"

He lifts his head from mine to capture my gaze with his once more.

"Yes," he admits. "But the time isn't right yet, Helena. Like I said, you're not ready."

"Then get off me," I order, roughly pushing him so hard he ends up flying off the bed and onto the planks of the porch. I stand and walk over him to re-enter the house. Once inside, I slam the front door shut behind me and storm into his bedroom, slamming that door too for good measure.

With a growl borne of sexual frustration, I begin to angrily toss the decorative pillows on his bed onto the floor before crawling underneath the covers.

"Why is he so stupid?" I ask the empty room, punching the one pillow I left on the bed to rest my head on. "Stupid, stupid, stupid!" I rant, punctuating each word with a strike of my fist into the pillow.

I'm not sure how long I toss and turn in bed, at least an hour or more. I eventually calm down and decide to raid Cade's kitchen to search for something to eat. When I venture outside the room, I find him sitting shirtless in one of the chairs at the kitchen island. He hears me come out of the room and turns slightly to look in my direction.

"I thought you fell asleep," he says. "Or did I wake you by making the tea?"

"I wasn't sleeping," I inform him brusquely as I walk over to him.

Set before him I see what looks like a scone on a small white dish, and a cup of tea.

"Do you have any more of those?" I ask, looking pointedly at the scone.

"Yes. Would you like one?"

I nod and sit down in the chair next to his. Cade leaves his seat just long enough to pour me a cup of tea from a kettle on his stove and grabs a brown paper bag from off the counter.

"Here," he says, handing me the bag while setting the cup down in front of me, "you can have your pick. There are vanilla and chocolate ones in there."

I open the bag and pull out the triangular biscuit-like cake in a chocolate flavor. Cade brings me a small plate to rest it on.

As I'm nibbling on my snack, he says, "I didn't mean to make you mad, Helena. That wasn't my intention at all."

"Why don't you enlighten me and explain exactly what your intention was," I say, on the verge of being incensed by his words all over again.

"I know you've been frustrated with me putting off making love to you, so I thought if I at least gave you pleasure it would satisfy your needs until the time is right."

"So tell me this," I say, placing my scone on its plate while I give Cade my full attention. "Why is it that you get to decide when the time will be right for us to have sex? If you care for me as much as you say, doesn't what I want factor into your decision making at all?"

"Of course it does," he says, looking taken aback by my questions. "But would you really want me to make love to you before the time is right?"

"But when will the time be right?" I ask irately. "You still haven't told me that yet!"

"Please, Helena, don't be mad at me for wanting to make our first time together special. I want you so badly right now the ferocity of it would probably bring this house down around us."

"Then I don't understand what's holding you back," I say, at a total loss.

"And I can't tell you without ruining everything."

I huff in aggravation, but the earnest way Cade is looking at me stops me from slapping him senseless.

"Fine," I say, seeing that this is a battle I'm doomed to lose anyway. "I won't keep questioning you about this as long as you promise me that we'll at least have sex sometime this century."

"I can't promise you that," he replies, sounding increasingly unsure as to when the union of our bodies will ultimately take place. "However, I *can* tell you that I hope it doesn't take that long."

I pick up my scone again and begin eating it. It's so delicious I end up taking a second one out of the bag after I finish the first one.

"These are quite good," I tell Cade. "Where did you get them?"

"There's a small bakery in New York that I go to from time to time…" his words trail off as if his thought isn't completely finished but he's unsure whether to tell me the rest.

"What aren't you saying?" I ask, not ever being one to beat around the bush about things.

"I was wondering if I could go see Lucas tomorrow morning," he says, casting a furtive glance in my direction.

"And why would you want to do that?"

"His birthday is tomorrow," Cade reveals. "With everything that's been going on, I'm not sure if Malcolm and Anna remember that. One of his favorite things is cupcakes from this particular bakery, and I would like to take him some and wish him a happy birthday in person. I know we haven't exactly discussed the terms of our bargain, but I was hoping you would allow me to go to him on his special day."

I take a moment to consider his request. It would be so easy for me to squash his hopes and tell him that he can't go see Lucas. I have every right to deny his request since our bargain is open-ended. Yet, for some reason, I want Cade to wish his friend a happy birthday. There are definitely things that I don't like about Lucas, particularly his ability to see into the future, but I have to admit that I like the kid's spunk. His unique sense of self is refreshing. I would never admit it to anyone, but I like Lucas. He amuses me, and that is something not many people can do.

"You can go long enough to deliver your present to him and wish him well on his birthday," I tell Cade. "I have some matters to attend to in the morning anyway. Once I'm done, I'll meet you back here. How does that sound?"

"Extremely reasonable," he says, sounding surprised by my acquiescence.

"Don't look so shocked," I tell him, finding his surprise annoying for some reason. "I'm not a complete ogre, no matter what other people might think about me."

"I'm sorry," he says in a properly contrite voice. "I just expected you to put up more of a fight. Thank you, Helena. It means a great deal to me that you're not trying to talk me out of going."

I give a slight shrug. "It's the kid's birthday. From what I understand about human behavior, some of them consider it a big deal, especially when they're as young as Lucas. I sincerely hope Malcolm and Anna haven't forgotten about it."

"I'm sure they haven't," Cade says with his words, but the tone with which he says them doesn't sound so convinced. "Can I ask what it is that you have planned for tomorrow?"

"Of course you can ask, but that doesn't mean I will tell you."

He seems to take the hint and leaves the issue alone.

After I finish eating the second scone, I drink my cup of tea and stand from my seat.

"Come lay with me in your bed," I order, holding out a hand to him. "I would like to go to sleep."

"Not that I'm complaining," he replies, taking my hand and standing from his chair, "but why do you want me in there with you?"

"Because if you stay out here or go sleep in another bed, I'll end up wondering what you're doing. If you're in bed with me, I'll be able to go to sleep that much faster."

Cade silently follows me as I lead him back to his bedroom. He has to grab a pillow for himself from the floor before climbing underneath the covers with me. He lies flat on his back and I end up curling up against his side with my head resting on his chest.

Even though we're in the back of the small house, I can still hear the faint crashing of the waves outside. Considering the fact it was a noise that greatly annoyed me only a few hours ago, it seems odd that I should now find a sense of comfort in it. I begin to wonder what happened to change my mind about the sound.

I fall asleep still pondering the difference in my mood, without ever coming up with sufficient answer to my dilemma.

CHAPTER EIGHT

(Anna's Point of View)

Having my family around me is a blessing unlike any other in my life. As I sit beside Malcolm and observe the individuals in the room, an overwhelming wellspring of love bubbles up inside my chest and I begin to wonder what I did during my time here on Earth to earn the devotion and unyielding support of so many good people. I'm grateful beyond words to be able to bestow such a powerful support system upon my children. I grew up only having my papa, Millie, and Auggie to lean on for encouragement. Liam and Liana will have a host of people they can go to at any time during their lives. Considering the dangers we have to face on a daily basis, I know they'll need all the help they can get.

"So," Jered whispers to us as he crosses his arms on the table in front of him and leans towards us to ask, "what's the plan for Lucas' birthday tomorrow?"

I feel my heart stop and hear myself gasp.

"Damn it," Malcolm curses under his breath. "With everything that's been going on, I completely forgot about his birthday."

"It's understandable," Jered sympathizes. "You've both been through a lot lately."

"So have you, but you didn't forget," Malcolm says, not allowing for excuses where we're concerned.

I've known for months that Lucas' birthday would be close to the due date for the twins. I should have remembered my own son's birthday without having to be reminded.

"Listen," Jered continues to whisper in a conspiratorial tone, "why don't you let me and Andre handle it? We can arrange to have a surprise party for him in Cirrus."

"Is it back in the air?" Malcolm asks anxiously. "I felt Anna call to me before we could test the repairs to the propulsion system."

"Desmond is there now, working on getting it into the sky," Jered tells us. "He recruited a few War Angels stationed in Nacreous to help him."

"Speaking of War Angels," Aiden says from his seat beside Jered, "do you know where Manakel is? He was Arel's War Angel. Since Liana and Arel now share a connection like Liam and Andel, I think you should tell him. He deserves to know what's going on before word spreads and he hears it in passing."

"Wasn't Manakel stationed in Nacreous?" Malcolm asks Jered.

"Yes. He goes by the name of Marcus now," Jered replies. "Let me go to Cirrus first and see if he's with the group helping Desmond. If he isn't, I'll go to Nacreous and track him down there."

"Are you sure you have time to do so much for us?" I ask Jered, worried he might be trying to do more than he should in an attempt to forget what happened between him and his son in Hell.

Seeing your own child doomed to an eternity of servitude to Helena had to have been devastating. If that ever happened to one of my children, I'm not sure if I could remain sane. However, Jered has had a thousand years to prepare himself for the truth about his son. He had to have known Silas would end up in Hell when he died, but knowing something is true and actually having to come face to face with that fact are two very separate things.

"Don't worry, Empress," Jered says with a confident smile. "I can handle things. Tracking Marcus down shouldn't be hard, especially if he's already in Cirrus with Desmond." He stands from his seat and says, "I'll be back shortly with him. Then I'll return and begin coordinating tomorrow's activities with Andre."

"Eh, coordinate what activities exactly?" my papa asks from his spot as the center of attention among Jess, Mason, and Lucifer as he holds Liam in his arms.

"I'll tell you after we get to Cirrus," Jered replies, waving my papa over to him. "Come on. We've got some work to do."

My papa hands Liam over to Lucifer, who readily accepts my son, before walking over to Jered.

"Wait!" I hear Jess call out from across the room from her spot between Mason and Lucifer. "I want to go to Cirrus, too. I keep hearing about these cloud cities. I want to see one for myself."

"Come on then," Jered says, waving her closer to him as well.

"Well if she's going I'm coming, too," Mason declares.

"Does anyone else want to go to Cirrus?" Jered asks the others in the room.

"I want to go!" Lucas says, holding up his hand as if he needs to in order to be seen.

Jered looks a little crestfallen that Lucas wants to join the group, but it's also obvious he's not about to say no to the birthday boy.

"Can I go, too?" Vala asks. "I would like to check on my office to see how much damage was done."

"Come on, you two," Jered says, waving them both closer.

Lucas rushes over and grabs his hand quickly, as if he's concerned Jered might change his mind if he isn't fast enough. Luna walks over to stand by Lucas, because wherever he goes she goes, too.

After Jered phases everyone to Cirrus, Aiden stands from his chair.

"I should be leaving, too," he tells us. "Our father allowed me to stay here a little longer than I'm really supposed to."

"So I presume we won't see you again unless Liam is on the verge of death?" Malcolm asks in a resigned voice, standing from his seat to shake hands with Aiden before his departure.

"Unfortunately, that's the rule both Will and I have to follow," Aiden states, sounding disappointed about the restrictions placed on his visits to Earth.

I notice Lucifer walk over to the table towards Aiden.

"You can't leave without saying goodbye to him," my father states, handing Liam over to his guardian angel.

Aiden smiles, gladly accepting my son back into his arms. Seeing the love Aiden has for Liam in his eyes eases a worry I wasn't even aware that I had for my son. I know that no matter what happens, Aiden will always watch over Liam. Even when Malcolm and I are no longer on Earth, our children will have their guardian angels looking out for them.

Aiden bends down and kisses Liam on the forehead.

"You take care of your big sister," I hear Aiden whisper to him. "The two of you will need each other in the years to come."

"Well, that sounded rather ominous," Malcolm comments, looking even more worried than he already was. "Are you privy to something we should be made aware of?"

"Nothing more than the fact that our father deemed it necessary to give them both guardian angels," Aiden tells us. "You know He doesn't share anything before we're supposed to know it."

Malcolm sighs heavily. "Yes. I'm acutely aware of His penchant for driving us crazy."

Aiden smiles. "Everything will turn out the way it should, Malcolm. It always has, and it always will. We just have to maintain our faith that He knows what's best."

"Oh, faith I have plenty of," Malcolm assures Aiden. "I'm quite confident that, even if I ask Him why Helena gave Liana a seal, He won't tell us."

"I meant to ask," Aiden says, "which seal does she have?"

Before I can answer, we hear Lucifer say, "She has the one I carried. Silence."

"How did you know that?" I ask him, finding it odd that he would know the answer before even seeing the seal on her back. "Malcolm is the only person I've shared that information with."

"I know Helena," Lucifer answers. "She'll do whatever she can to hurt me, and giving my granddaughter my seal was probably the icing on the cake for her. The irony of it all was just too tempting for her."

"Besides hurting you, do you think Helena has another reason for giving Liana that particular seal?" I ask, curious to hear his take on the matter.

"Undoubtedly," he replies, looking at my husband. "I'm surprised you haven't guessed the reason yet, Malcolm. You know as well as I what happened on alternate Earth when Ravan opened the seventh seal."

"Liana isn't Ravan," Malcolm says defensively. "She would never do that."

"Do what exactly?" I have to ask, becoming more worried with every passing second that Helena has purposefully harmed my daughter in some way. Malcolm never liked to talk about his time on alternate Earth, so I have no idea what either of them is remembering. "What are the two of you talking about? What happened when Ravan opened the seal?"

Lucifer raises a questioning eyebrow at Malcolm. "Do you want to tell her, or shall I?"

"You do it," Malcolm replies, sounding disgusted by the whole conversation. "I don't think I have the stomach to think about the implications."

116

Malcolm sits back down heavily in his chair next to me, as if the weight of the world has suddenly landed firmly on his shoulders. I'm faintly aware that everyone else in the room has stopped their conversations also and are all focused on listening to Lucifer's next words. My body involuntarily tenses up as if bracing itself to hear my father's explanation.

"Ravan phased to Heaven and opened the seal there," Lucifer tells me.

"And what did that do?" I ask, understanding that such an event could only lead to disaster, but I'm not sure what kind exactly.

"It sealed Heaven off from that reality. The souls of those who died between the time the seventh seal was opened and Heaven was accessible again either wandered the Earth aimlessly or found their way to Hell and became trapped there forever."

"So you think that's why Helena gave Liana your seal? She plans to use Liana like the Lucifer on alternate Earth used Ravan?"

"I think it's a possibility that you have to consider," my father says, looking much calmer about the situation than I feel. He probably doesn't want to add to my alarm by showing his own worry, but I can see it in his eyes and so much more. "This is all my fault, Anna. If I hadn't taken the seals out of Heaven in the first place, this never would have happened. If you want to lay the blame of this fiasco on anyone, it should be me. I'm not sure if I'll ever be able to forgive myself if something happens to your daughter because of something I did."

With his words, I suddenly realize something very important.

"I think you may have just uncovered another reason Helena gave Liana your seal, Dad," I tell him. "She knows the guilt you'll feel if she's ever able to coerce Liana into opening the seal in Heaven. What better way to exact her revenge on us both than to turn my daughter into her pawn? It's the perfect plan, if you think about it."

"Our daughter will *never* do what Helena wants," Malcolm declares, leaving no room for argument. "I won't allow it to happen. *Ever.*"

I, unlike my husband, am plagued with doubt about our daughter's future. Considering how much Liana seems to detest me and Lucifer, is it beyond the realm of possibility that she will grow in Helena's shadow and come to hate humanity just as fiercely as my sister does? Will she one day become the harbinger of Hell and doom millions upon millions of souls to an eternity in Helena's domain?

None of the War Angels left in the room has said a word, but I can see some of them begin to fidget in their seats as if confirming to me that they have the same doubts as I do concerning my daughter's fate.

"Dad," I say, looking to Lucifer for more answers about what Helena has done to my baby girl, "do you have a theory as to why Liana seems to hate us so much?"

"Yes," he says, looking more troubled about this answer than the one he just gave us explaining why Helena transferred his old seal to Liana.

"What are you thinking?" I prompt, bracing myself yet again for what I'm about to hear.

"I have no idea if it's true or not, of course," he says, "but I've often wondered if Helena was able to cross over to the Earthly realm because of her connection to you, Anna."

"Me?" I ask, feeling confused. "How did I help her escape Hell?"

Lucifer studies me for a moment, taking in the return of my brown hair and eyes.

"She was able to form a connection to you when you had the seals, correct?" he asks.

I nod. "Yes."

"And after you had the babies, that connection was obviously broken."

"Oh no," I say, quickly standing up from my chair and rushing over to Zane, who is still holding a slumbering Liana in his arms. "No, no, no, no, no…." I repeat, as if saying the word enough times will change what's happened.

I'm faintly aware of Malcolm following behind me as we go to our daughter. As I stand next to Zane, I reach out and trace the side of Liana's face with my index finger. Almost instantly her eyelids fly open, and she stares at me with her bluer than blue eyes. I shake my head, denying to myself what should have been blatantly obvious to me. As tears of despair and guilt cloud my vision, I pull my hand away from my daughter's face and stare at the few strands of hair on her head. There isn't much, which is probably why I didn't notice it before now. When I saw the healed skin of Liana's belly button, I should have realized then what happened. Helena healed me once too, right after she took the seals from me. She said she was able to do it because of our connection to one another.

"Her hair is white," I say in a breathless whisper to Malcolm as my world begins to shatter around me.

"You don't know that for sure," Malcolm argues. "She barely has enough to even be called hair. It's more like peach fuzz."

I vigorously shake my head as I turn to face my husband. "Stop denying it, Malcolm! Look at her! The sooner you accept that she's connected to Helena, the sooner we can figure out a way to help her through it."

"Our daughter is *not* connected to that monster, Anna. I refuse to believe that!"

"Then you're just being foolish," Lucifer chastises my husband. "Why else would a newborn show her mother so much loathing? Of all the people in this world, Helena despises both Anna and me the most, and now your daughter has a direct connection to her wrath. Listen to your wife, Malcolm, and prove to me that you aren't the idiot I always took you as being. Face up to the facts of the situation and be strong for your family. Burying your head in the sand over this will do no one any good."

Malcolm's shoulders sag as he slowly forces himself to accept the truth of what my father just said. He takes me into his arms and holds me tighter than he ever has before. It's only then that I realize I'm sobbing. I'm not even sure when I started to cry. As warm tears of despair continue to stream down my face uncontrollably, I cling to Malcolm as if my sanity depends on him continuing to hold me.

"We'll figure something out, Anna," Malcolm says with conviction. I feel him kiss the top of my head as he continues to murmur words of encouragement to me. "She'll grow up knowing that we love her more than anything in this world. No matter how much influence Helena might have on her, we'll fight her every step of the way. We can do this. I know we can."

I try to take encouragement from his words, but hopelessness threatens to consume me from the inside out. If we have any hope of saving our daughter's soul from Helena's clutches, she'll need to form a strong, everlasting bond with the people around her. Only the love of family and friends will be able to pull her back from the darkness Helena is sure to force upon her.

I pull back from Malcolm enough to look into his eyes.

"You have to be her rock," I tell him, clutching his shirt with my hands as if such an action will make him listen to me more than he already is.

"We'll both be there for her," Malcolm replies, sounding unsure as to why I only included him in my statement.

I shake my head vigorously, because he doesn't understand the full impact of what I'm trying to say.

"We have to face the fact that she may never be able to love me," I'm barely able to say. I'm weeping so hard from a feeling of loss that I can barely take in a full breath. Just the thought of my little girl hating me as much as Helena does fills me with a hopelessness that makes the future seem bleak and nothing more than an endless sequence of heartbreaking moments. "You have to be there for her when she needs someone to guide her. She has to know that she can come to you for anything."

"I promise I'll be there for her," Malcolm says as he attempts to wipe my tears away with his fingers, but it's no use. As soon as he wipes away one trail of tears, another set takes their place. "But we'll both be there for her, Anna. She'll know she's loved unconditionally by both her parents."

"You have to be her *friend*," I tell him, taking a shaky breath. "And I have to be her *parent*."

Malcolm looks slightly confused by my emphasis on the two separate roles we need to play in our daughter's life.

"You know as well as I do that she's going to be a handful," I say, unclenching my hands and releasing my grip on Malcolm's shirt. I take a step back and clear the tears away from my eyes because I know what my part in my daughter's life has to be. "She'll have to be disciplined, and you can't be the one who does it. The responsibility has to fall to me. She already hates me. She'll just hate me a little bit more for being the one who punishes her."

"Anna…" Malcolm begins with a tone that tells me he thinks I'm making a hasty, emotional decision.

"That's the way things have to be, Malcolm," I say resolutely. "You have to be her friend, and I have to be the disciplinarian. Tell me you understand that. I need you to go along with this because it's the only way I can think of to save her."

I begin to sob again, even harder this time as realization sets in that I've lost the love of my daughter before I even had a chance to earn it. Malcolm brings me back into his arms and simply holds me. He doesn't try to convince me that I'm making the wrong decision. All he says is the one thing I need to hear in that moment.

"We'll do whatever you think is best, Anna. I will support any decision you make as long as you always listen to my opinion about it. Can you promise me at least that much?"

I nod my head and sniff as I try to bring my grief under control.

"Um, I'm sorry. Have we come at a bad time?" I hear Jered say in the room.

I pull away from Malcolm to look in the direction of Jered's voice.

I see that he was successful in the mission we sent him on, because standing by his side is the War Angel he was sent to find. Marcus.

I haven't spent much time with Marcus, but I did remember meeting him on a few occasions since the War Angels came to Earth. He is tall with short, cropped hair the color of milk chocolate and piercing hazel eyes that always seem to catch the light just right to make them glow. He stands before us, dressed in the black War Angel uniform they all wear when they're on duty. Marcus has always struck me as slightly cocky in his opinion about himself, but whenever he speaks to me, he tempers that attitude and shows me the respect I deserve as his commander on Earth.

"Hello, Marcus," I say, wiping away the last of my tears. I've allowed myself the indulgence of mourning the loss of my daughter's love. Now, we have things that need to be done, and I can't afford to waste any more time by being weak. "Has Jered told you why we wanted you to come here?" I ask.

Marcus nods slowly. "Yes. He explained everything to me." I notice Marcus look between Liam and Liana. "Which one is she?"

"This is Liana," Zane tells him, lifting the arm he's using to cradle Liana slightly to indicate which baby is the one he seeks.

"Do you mind?" Marcus asks me, lifting his right hand to signify he wishes to approach Liana.

"Come see her," I tell him. "That's why we asked Jered to bring you here. Aiden thought it was important for you to meet her since she carries Arel's soul."

"I thought Arel was lost to us forever," Marcus says as he makes his way over to Zane.

"Would you like to hold her?" Zane asks.

Marcus looks to me, silently asking for permission. I nod and watch to see what Liana's reaction will be to him.

Marcus gently takes her from Zane. As soon as my daughter is in his arms, she seems to wake up. Marcus simply stares at her, looking unsure of what to say or do next.

After a few seconds of awkward silence, Marcus clears his throat and states, "My name is Marcus, Liana. Arel created me during the war in Heaven, and I was her personal War Angel. She named me Manakel, but I chose the name Marcus before God sent us here to help your mother." He clears his throat again, briefly glancing in my direction before continuing. "I want you to know that I will always be here for you and your family. If you ever need me to do something for you, I will do it."

I see one of Liana's little hands reach out towards Marcus' face. He bends his neck down until she can reach him. She ends up grabbing his bottom lip and playing with it, which causes Marcus to laugh.

As I watch Liana's reaction to Marcus, I feel jealousy seep into my heart and spread like wildfire. I don't want to close my heart off to my daughter, but it might be the only way I can protect myself from a pain so great it could cripple me in time. What other option do I have left open to me if I want to remain sane?

"You look tired, my love," Malcolm says to me, not even attempting to hide his worry. "I think you should get some more rest. It's been an eventful evening."

"I agree," Lucifer chimes in. "Why don't you take her upstairs, Malcolm? We can watch over the babies for you."

"Make sure you bring them up if they look like they're getting hungry," I tell Zane and Lucifer.

"I promise we will," my dad says.

Without wasting any time, Malcolm takes my hand and phases us up to our bedroom.

"Would you like me to run you a bath?" Malcolm asks, gently rubbing his hands up and down my bare arms in a soothing manner.

"No," I say dejectedly, turning towards the bed and walking over to it. "I just want to go to sleep."

Malcolm phases to my side of the bed even before I'm able to reach it, and pulls down the covers for me.

"Would you like to put on a fresh nightgown?"

I shake my head and sit on the edge of the mattress to slip the shoes off my feet.

"I just want to go to sleep, Malcolm."

After I climb into bed, my ever-loving husband pulls the covers over me and leans down to give me a kiss.

"Do you want me to leave you alone tonight so you can have your own dreams?" he asks.

"No." I reach my right hand up to cup the side of his face, desperately needing the physical contact to ease my broken heart. "Build me a beautiful world where I can forget about things for a while. I don't want to be alone, Malcolm. Not now."

He leans down and lightly brushes his lips against mine. "All right, my love."

My husband quickly sheds his clothes before climbing into bed with me. He takes me into his arms, and I'm instantly lulled to sleep by the warmth of his body, his eternal unquestionable love, and a heart that beats only for me.

CHAPTER NINE

When I enter into Malcolm's dream world, I find myself standing in the study he had in his Lakewood home. The house no longer exists, of course. Levi burned it to the ground right after he found Malcolm and me in the small workshop on the property.

"I miss this house," I tell Malcolm, who is dressed exactly like he was the night of our first kiss.

"I've been thinking about rebuilding it," he tells me as he loops his arms around my waist. "What do you think?"

"You should," I say, laying my head against his chest and breathing in the scent of him. I wrap my arms around his waist, trying to hold back the sorrow I feel threatening to consume me, but it's a losing battle.

As I begin to sob over the loss of my daughter's love to Helena's madness, Malcolm tightens his hold on me.

"Oh, Anna," he says, his voice an echo of my pain.

I know he can feel my heart breaking because of our bond with one another. I wish I could prevent him from having to endure the depths of my sorrow, but the connection between soul mates can't be turned off on a whim. We are one, and when either of us has our heart broken, the other will always feel it. It's both a blessing and a curse.

"I wish..." I try to say between sobs, attempting to take in enough air to finish my thought. "I wish I could hold her just once and see her smile up at me."

Malcolm remains silent for a while as I continue to cry. Then he says, "Anna, I could make that happen for you if you really want."

I sniff before lifting my head from the wet spot I've made on his shirt.

"How?" I ask, wondering how my husband can work such a miracle for me.

"I could do that here," he tells me, closely watching for my reaction to his suggestion.

I know what he means. He could conjure a figment of Liana in his dream world. One I could hold who wouldn't automatically start to cry. It wouldn't be real, but it might be the closest I can ever get to the real thing.

"Do it," I say, taking a step back from him.

I immediately hear the happy gurgle of a baby. When I look to my left, I see a white bassinet sitting in the room now. I don't move. I just listen to the sounds of the imaginary infant. Malcolm takes my hand and urges me with a small tug to walk over to the bassinet with him. When I look inside it, I can almost believe it's really Liana lying underneath the white baby blanket. I stare at her for a long time, trying to work up the courage to lift her into my arms. Even though I know she isn't real I still feel hesitant to touch her, in fear I'll be rejected all over again.

"Go ahead," Malcolm encourages, letting go of my hand. "Pick her up, Anna."

I look over at him and see a sad smile on his face as he watches me.

"Do it, my love. Maybe it will help you in some small way."

I work up my courage and reach inside the bassinet to lift the baby into my arms.

Again, I'm amazed by how tangible things feel inside Malcolm's dream world. Liana feels so solid in my hands. When I bring her closer and cradle her against my chest, I can almost imagine that I'm back in the real world, and that Liana is allowing me to hold and love her the way I so desperately want to. As I study her face our eyes meet, and I see that Malcolm has given his version of Liana eyes the same brown as mine. Liana's little lips stretch as she smiles up at me, gifting me with her acceptance and unconditional love.

But I know this isn't real. This isn't my baby. This isn't my Liana.

As I continue to hold Malcolm's perfect rendering of our daughter, various moments in the not-so-distant future begin to play through my mind. When the real Liana takes her first steps and refuses to come to me, will I have Malcolm recreate the moment in his dream world so I can experience it the way I want to? When Liana scrapes her knee for the first time in the real world and refuses to let me comfort her, will I beg Malcolm to conjure a close facsimile of the event just so I can relive it the way I imagine?

Will I end up wanting to live out a perfect life with my daughter in a world that doesn't actually exist just because I can't handle the reality of our relationship?

As hot tears of grief begin to stream down my face again, I place the dream world Liana back into the bassinet and run out of the room, a desperate Malcolm calling after me.

I'm not sure where I'm going, but all I know is that I need to get away. It was stupid of me to believe holding a fake baby would make me feel better. If anything, it's made me feel even worse. It gave me a taste of what I could have had if Helena hadn't interfered. She stole my daughter's love away from me before I even had a chance to earn it. It's something I'm not sure I can ever forgive her for doing to me.

I end up running out into the backyard and towards the workshop where Malcolm and I shared our first kiss. I throw the door open and run inside, collapsing in a helpless, sobbing heap on top of the worktable. Seconds later, I feel Malcolm's warm hand rest on the small of my back.

"I'm sorry," he says. "I thought it would help, not make you feel worse. Forgive me, my love."

"It's not your fault," I tell him, forcing myself to stand up straight. I turn to face my husband and allow him to pull me into his arms. I know he needs to be comforted just as much as I do.

"There has to be something I can do," I tell him, wracking my brain for a solution to the problem. "I don't want to give up on finding a way to gain Liana's love, but what can I do to change how she feels about me?"

"Maybe she's not the one you need to work on," Malcolm says.

"What do you mean?"

"If she's feeling Helena's hatred for you, maybe Helena is the one you need to make amends with."

I pull away from Malcolm to look up at him. I'm about to ask him if he's serious, but I can see for myself that he's dead serious.

"Do you think that would work?" I ask, considering his suggestion. In times of desperation a mother will do anything for her child, and right now I'm willing to do whatever it takes, even if that means making Hell herself my best friend.

"I think it's at least worth trying," he replies. "If you can find a way to make her stop hating you maybe that will be enough to change the way Liana reacts to you."

I wipe my tears away because my husband has opened a door of opportunity for me that I hadn't considered before.

"I can try," I say as I cling to the only hope I have of saving my baby girl. "I mean, I don't know if it'll work but I can try."

"It won't be easy," he cautions.

"I know that," I assure him, "but it's better than doing nothing or not having any hope at all that there's a solution to the problem. I have to try, Malcolm, and I'll need your support. I know how much you hate Helena, but you're going to have to temper your dislike for her for a while."

"I'll do my best," he promises, and that's all I really need from him.

Filled with a new sense of optimism, I throw my arms around Malcolm's neck.

"Thank you," I whisper to him as I feel his arms wrap around me and hold me close. "Thank you for thinking of something."

"Anytime, my love," he says in relief. "Just remember that you can do anything you set your mind to, and I will always stand by your side. You don't have to go through this alone. I promise you that we won't let our daughter be taken over by Helena's hate without a fight."

The ache in my heart is less painful now. It's strange how the tiniest ray of hope can transform your emotions almost instantly. I refuse to sit back and watch my daughter's soul languish in the pool of Helena's hate. She deserves to live a life where she can make up her own mind about things, and I will fight with everything I have at my disposal to make sure that happens.

"Now that we have a plan, what would you like to do for the rest of the time we're here?" Malcolm asks.

"I think I'll let you decide that. I trust your brilliance."

The next thing I know we're standing back inside Malcolm's study, but this time we're both dressed in layer upon layer of clothes plus a coat and knit caps with earflaps. I step back from Malcolm and have to ask, "Why are we dressed like this?"

"Are you questioning my brilliance already?" he asks with a roguish grin.

"Just curious," I admit.

Malcolm points to a chessboard set up in front of the fireplace in the room.

"I thought we would play a game of strip chess."

I can't help but bust out in a laugh.

"Only you could turn playing chess into foreplay," I tease as I walk over to sit down in the chair on the right side of the board. I readjust the hat on my head and clap my gloved hands together. "Come on! Let's get this game started!"

"So eager to see me naked?" he asks with a throaty, pleased chuckle.

After Malcolm takes the seat across from me, I move one of my pawns forward to begin the game.

"Always, my love," I say truthfully. "Who wouldn't want to see you naked?"

"That's very true," he replies without the least bit of modesty. "I could probably name at least a hundred women off the top of my head who would love to have the pleasure of seeing me nude."

"Luckily for you, there will only ever be one woman who will ever see you naked again."

"It's sad in a way," he sighs. "Denying all the women in the world the delight of seeing me in the buff. It's almost a crime against humanity."

"I can't say it makes me sad at all," I tell him. "If you haven't realized this already, I don't particularly like to share you with too many people. Call me selfish, but I like having you all to myself most of the time."

Malcolm looks at me and shakes his head, as if the motion itself is a chastisement of my unapologetic selfishness.

"Think of all those poor people you are relegating to a life without at least one naked vision of me, my love. How can you be so cruel?"

I have to giggle at his jest. It feels good to laugh after all the crying I've done.

Malcolm smiles at me, and I know he's happy because he's been able to lift my spirits with newfound hope and a moment of pure silliness.

"You should know," I say, sacrificing one of my pieces to his on the chessboard, "that I intend to lose this game in record time."

"And here I thought you loved me for the way my mind works," Malcolm teases, moving his piece to capture mine easily.

I immediately pull the knit cap off my head and toss it onto the floor.

"I do love your mind," I assure him, moving another piece for him to capture. "But that doesn't mean that I don't enjoy lavishing other parts of you with my adoration."

Malcolm stares at me for a moment as if he's thoughtfully considering what I just said. Before I can take another breath, the scene around us changes to the one I woke up to earlier. We're lying naked, side-by-side in the bed on the beach again.

"What happened to the strip chess foreplay?" I ask jokingly as Malcolm rolls me over on top of him in one swift motion.

"I decided I would much rather have you lavish other parts of me with your love," he says with a cheeky grin. "Are you complaining?"

"Absolutely not," I reply, leaning down until our breaths begin to mingle. "You're simply showing me just how brilliant you are by not wasting what precious little time we have here."

"Then get to adoring me, woman!" he says, playfully slapping me on the backside. "I refuse to wake up until my every carnal desire has been satisfied."

"Oh, really?" I ask. "And what about my needs? Will they be satisfied as well?"

"Very well," he promises. "I don't believe I've ever left you wanting, have I?"

"Never," I agree, kissing him on the lips before sliding down his body to show him just how much I truly adore him.

Eventually, we are woken up from our dream world by a knock on the door. I'm reluctant to leave our seaside paradise, but I know the only reason we're being disturbed is because the babies need to be fed. Malcolm and I both awaken, and he tells the interlopers into our fun to enter the room. Zane and Xander walk in, holding Liana and Liam.

"Were they any trouble?" I ask my War Angels.

"None at all," Zane assures me.

Malcolm arranges the pillows around me like he did before and takes our children from the others' hands.

"Do you want us to wait outside so we can take them back downstairs with us?" Zane asks.

I shake my head. "No. You can leave them up here. I'm sure they'll probably just go straight to sleep afterwards."

"Cool," Xander says. "Jered needs some more help preparing Lucas' birthday party. If you need us, we'll be in Cirrus."

"How is the city?" Malcolm asks. "Has anything changed?"

"It's in good shape considering everything it's been through," Xander says. "Some of the buildings need to be repaired, but you saw that damage when you were last there. As long as nothing else happens that requires our attention, it shouldn't take very long to make the place inhabitable again."

"Then let's all start praying that nothing else goes wrong," I say.

"So show us the tattoo you got from Bai," Malcolm says to Xander. The last time we saw him, he was heading to Brutus' home so Bai could grant him protection from an archangel's power to end a regular angel's life.

Xander turns around so his back is facing us and uses both of his hands to scrunch up the back of his shirt up to his shoulders to reveal his tattoo.

I have to smile when I see a large pair of black angel wings.

"Very appropriate," I tell him.

Xander lets go of his shirt and turns back around to face us.

"I thought so," he replies with a small shrug. "Ok, well, like I said, we'll be in Cirrus. If you need us back here, just send word."

Both Xander and Zane phase to Cirrus.

"I can't wait to go back home," I tell Malcolm as I look through their phase trails with a sense of longing. Unfortunately, all I see is a blank stone wall. "It feels like it's been forever since we were in the castle."

"It hasn't really been all that long."

"I know, but it's been longer than it should have been. We shouldn't have had to leave at all. If Helena hadn't…"

"My love," Malcolm interrupts with a note of caution, "remember what we talked about. Remember what you need to try to do."

I sigh heavily as I look down at Liana, lying on her pillow next to me. I quickly slip my breast from the top of my dress. Liam begins to suckle on my nipple right away. Liana takes some coaxing, but hunger seems to help her overcome her dislike of me. Liam is gentle in taking what he needs from my body. Liana, not so much. She clamps down harder than she needs to, but I don't complain. At least she's allowing me to feed her. That's all I can ask from her right now.

"Only for you," I whisper to Liana, "would I try to befriend my worst enemy."

"We can do this, Anna," Malcolm says in an attempt to boost my morale. "We have to."

I nod but don't make a reply. In order for me to truly attempt to bond with Helena, I know I have to let go of my resentment of her for causing this problem in the first place. I know she's a selfish creature who only does what generates more power for her domain. Helena may be the mistress of Hell, but I fear her ambitions reach much farther than that. Until she has complete dominion over the Earthly realm, too, she'll never be completely satisfied. She will do whatever it takes to advance her own cause no matter who gets hurt in the process.

"Maybe Cade can help us," I say, clinging to hope, however small, that her soul mate can change Helena.

"Do you think we should even tell him?" Malcolm asks. "He did caution us about revealing anything important to him because Helena can read his thoughts when they're in Hell."

"I think we might have to take the chance. We need him to find reasons for the two of them to be around us more. That's the only way this is going to work. I can't exactly befriend Helena if she's never around us."

"I think it would look suspicious if we tried to track Cade down, though. We may just have to wait for him to come to us."

"Patience may be the key, for now. I'm sure an opportunity will present itself soon."

As soon as the babies are fed, we lay them down in the bed with us and they both fall asleep within a matter of minutes. Malcolm suggests we do the same and return to his dream world to pick up where we left off. I heartily agree. I do love my husband with all my being and the physical contact we share, whether it be in his dream world or the real one, always helps ease my worries.

The next morning Malcolm and I get up early so we can make Lucas breakfast to start his seventh birthday off right.

When we go downstairs, we're surprised to find Cade in the kitchen arranging a dozen colorful cupcakes on a white platter at the kitchen island. He's talking and laughing with Ethan, who is the only other person in the room.

His presence feels like a sign from God that our plan is destined to work. My mood is instantly lifted by his unexpected visit.

"Just the man we were hoping to see," Malcolm says to him.

Cade looks up and smiles. He appears happier than I thought he would be after spending so much time with Helena. Perhaps I was wasting my energy worrying about him while he was around her. It obviously isn't changing him for anything but the better.

"I hope you don't mind that I brought cupcakes for Lucas. I know how much he likes them, and every little boy should be spoiled on his birthday."

Malcolm and I had both forgotten about Lucas' birthday until Jered brought it up yesterday, but Cade remembered without having to be reminded by anyone.

"I know he'll love them," I tell Cade. "We're having a party for him in Cirrus later today if you would like to come."

"That's what Ethan was just telling me."

"We've got everything ready," Ethan reports, "and people have been invited to join us there this afternoon."

"Who have you invited?" I ask.

"Just family and friends," Ethan assures me.

"So it will be a small affair?"

"Well, not exactly. We did invite all the War Angels to come."

"Ahh, so two thousand War Angels will be attending."

"Hopefully," Ethan confirms, looking pointedly at Cade before continuing, "*all* two thousand of us will be there."

Cade suddenly looks uncomfortable and I assume I know the reason why.

"Will Helena let you come?" I inquire.

"I can ask," Cade replies. "She might. She seems to have a soft spot where Lucas is concerned. It's why she let me come over here this morning to wish him a happy birthday."

"A soft spot?" I ask, remembering quite clearly how violently she reacted to him when he showed her a possible future with his visions. Lucas told me at the time that he saw Helena crying in the prophecy, but he didn't know why she was so upset. "I thought she hated him."

Cade shrugs. "Apparently not. I guess the time they spent together on alternate Earth changed her mind about him."

"Well, if that's the case," I say, seeing an opportunity present itself, "why don't you tell Helena she's invited to come to the party with you."

Malcolm isn't very surprised by my offer, but Ethan has definitely been thrown for a loop.

"Why would you invited that *thing* to spend time with us, Anna?" Ethan asks.

"She isn't a thing," Cade is quick to remind him. "She's a person, and if you're just going to be rude to her we definitely won't be attending."

"Please, Cade," I say, taking a step forward. "I can promise you that no one will be rude to her there. You have my word on that."

S. J. West

Cade looks at me in total confusion. "You're not planning to do something to her, are you, Anna?"

I feel rather insulted that he would imply such a thing, but his question is a valid one.

I may indeed have the means by which to harm Helena.

While on alternate Earth, Malcolm's double there, Xavier, gave me the sword Jess once recovered from that reality's Garden of Eden. He said he felt as though it was part of his destiny to wait for my arrival so he could give me the weapon. At the time, I assumed God meant for me to retrieve it and use it against Helena. I still think that, but I don't believe using it now will advance my quest to build a relationship with her and, by proxy, end my daughter's hatred of me.

"You have my word that no one will harm her there," I vow.

Cade considers my offer before saying, "I'll ask her, but I wouldn't count on us being there."

"I understand. Just make sure she knows I'm the one who invited her and that I would really like it if she came."

Cade nods, still looking unsure about my reason for inviting Helena to what's normally a friends-and-family-only event. I would tell him the truth, but I fear if Helena discovers my real motive she'll think I'm only using her as a means to an end. I can't deny that's true. I fully intend to use her to help my daughter, but I'm also leaving myself open to the possibility that Helena and I can actually build something of a sisterly relationship with one another.

Malcolm was right in what he said earlier. I will have to let go of what has happened between Helena and me if my plan has any chance of succeeding. For my daughter's sake, I will attempt the impossible. I can't fail her. I have to try.

"Cade!"

Lucas rushes past Malcolm and me and practically leaps into Cade's arms.

"Are you back?" Lucas asks excitedly as Cade picks him up. "Did you find a way to escape from Helena?"

Cade chuckles and shakes his head slightly. "No. I haven't escaped. She said I could come here to wish you a happy birthday and bring you those."

Cade looks pointedly at the platter full of cupcakes on the kitchen island.

"Are they from that bakery in New York?" Lucas asks excitedly as he practically begins to salivate.

"Yes, they are. I know how much you love them."

"You're the best," Lucas says, wrapping his arms around Cade's neck and hugging him tightly.

Cade closes his eyes and smiles, basking in the love my son has for him.

When Lucas finally lets go of Cade he looks over at Malcolm and me to ask, "Can I have a cupcake for breakfast? You know it's my birthday."

"That's fine," Malcolm says in a tone that tells Lucas he's only getting his way because it *is* his birthday. "But at least drink a glass of milk with it."

Cade sets Lucas back down on his feet so he can get himself the required glass of milk to drink with his sweet birthday indulgence.

"What time is the thing?" Cade asks Ethan, purposely not saying the word party in front of Lucas.

"The party starts around noon I think," Lucas answers, having already deduced what 'thing' Cade is referring to in such a roundabout way.

"How do you know that?" Ethan asks, flabbergasted. "We made sure we didn't say a word about it while you were around."

Lucas shrugs like it's no big deal that he already knows about the party.

"I had a vision about it," he replies. "And Cade, tell Helena I saw her there, too, so she has to come with you."

Now I'm the one who feels shocked. The decision to invite Helena was only made by me a few minutes ago. Yet Lucas knew she would be coming even before I extended the offer.

"I'll be sure to let her know," Cade says, looking just as surprised as I feel. Although, I'm not sure if he's startled by Lucas' foreknowledge or the fact that Helena seems destined to attend the gathering. The latter would be my guess.

"I should probably be getting back to her," Cade says. "She had to go do something in Nimbo this morning, and I told her I would be back before she returned."

"I guess we'll be seeing you later then," Ethan says, looking concerned about the addition of Hell incarnate to the festivities.

"It'll be all right," Cade assures him. "She'll be on her best behavior, Ethan. If she's not, I'll make sure she leaves before things get out of hand."

Ethan nods, accepting Cade's promise to keep Helena in check.

"Until this afternoon," Cade says to us just before he phases.

From his trail, I see that he's gone to the beach house he built not far from our own. I knew it was his personal sanctuary, and find it strange that he would go there to meet Helena. Perhaps he thought surrounding her with everything he holds dear would soften her heart towards him. I sincerely hope that it has because, in order for my plan to be successful, I need her to be pliable to forming a friendship with me.

I don't know if it will work, but right now it's my only hope.

CHAPTER TEN

(Helena's Point of View)

Every time I leave Cade, I feel an aggravating ache build up inside my chest like a part of me is missing. It's an odd sensation, and I detest feeling as though I need him in my life. Being dependent on someone else for my own happiness seems like a deplorable way to live, yet existing without him would be an even worse fate. If I hadn't arranged a meeting with Hale and Silas this morning, I never would have returned to Nimbo. Instead, I would have stayed with Cade in his little beachside home and seen how the day would have unfolded for us. Considering the way he clutched me to him before I left his side this morning, I'm confident he would have preferred that I stayed as well.

It simply wasn't possible, though. I've set certain plans into motion that I need to get an update on. If things proceed as they should, almost every person in the world will hate Anna as much as I do by this afternoon. I'll finally be able to end her rule of Cirrus and place one of my own puppets on the throne. Catherine Amador may believe she's the ruler of Cirrus once I win her crown back for her, but it's just that type of idiocy and arrogance I'm counting on. Humans are so easily manipulated after you stroke their egos. If you let them believe they're in control of their own fate, you can lead them almost anywhere you want them to go. I wonder if this is the way God feels. Even though He gave his creations free will, He still seems to know exactly what will happen. Perhaps He and I aren't that different after all.

"And just where have you been all this time?" I hear the irritating voice of Levi question me, as if he deserves to know my whereabouts when I'm out of his sight.

I turn away from the large window that overlooks Nimbo from my suite in the palace. I find Levi sitting on one of the couches in the center of the room.

"What I do and where I go is none of your business," I retort hotly.

"And what am I supposed to tell people when they ask me where you are? If you want us to maintain the illusion of a happily married couple, you need to at least let me know what I should be telling others when they can't find you."

"I realize thinking for yourself isn't exactly your strong suit, Levi, but I thought even someone with your limited intellect would be able to come up with an excuse for my absence. If I need to hold your hand every step of the way, you become more of a liability to me than an asset. Prove to me that you're worth keeping by my side and maybe I'll let you live. Otherwise, I'll chop you into bite-size morsels to feed to my hellhounds and rule Nimbo all by myself."

"All I want to know is what you expect me to tell people so that our stories match up. There's no reason to get so nasty, Helena."

"I really don't care what you tell people. Just handle it and don't bother me with idiotic problems even a child should be able to solve on his own!"

"What's put you in such a foul mood anyway?" he asks, unable to keep himself from sounding annoyed by my scolding. "Or dare I even ask?"

"I was perfectly fine until you showed up to bombard me with inane questions," I gripe. "Actually, just looking at you is enough to irritate me most of the time."

"Why is it that you hate me so much, Helena? I've done everything that you've asked of me, yet you continue to act vile. I have to say it's rather frustrating."

"It's because you repulse me on a variety of levels, you ignoramus. Now, why don't you just sit there quietly and look pretty? You might as well stay to learn the next phase of my plans for Anna. I'll need your help soon to finally remove her from the Cirrus throne."

Levi sits up straighter and eagerly leans forward in his seat.

"Do tell," he says excitedly. "And how to do you plan to work such a miracle, or am I not allowed to ask such a question?"

"You'll learn my plan soon enough. We're just waiting on two more people to arrive. They should be here soon."

"How long has this plan of yours been in place? Did you ever actually intend for there to be an election to put Catherine back on the throne?"

"The election was just a way to bring Catherine back from obscurity and place her in the forefront of everyone's minds when the time came to choose Anna's successor. My plan has always been to force Anna off her throne in disgrace."

Levi smiles, obviously pleased with my scheme even before he hears the specifics of it.

Thankfully, I don't have to be alone with him any longer than I have to because Hale phases into the room with Silas.

"You're late," I chastise them. "You both know that I don't like to be kept waiting."

"I'm sorry, Helena," Silas is quick to apologize, kneeling on one knee in front of me in total submission. With his head bowed, he says, "Please forgive us. Our tardiness wasn't an intentional slight. We had a little trouble moving the package to its location. Neither of us wanted to come here without first accomplishing the task you gave us to complete."

"So it's done?" I ask.

Silas raises his gaze from the floor to look up at me. "Yes. Everything is set to go on your command. All we need to know is when you want us to follow through with your instructions."

"Let's see. It should be done early enough for the other cloud cities to hear about it, but late enough for there to be a light show for any spectators lucky enough to witness the event," I say. "So, wait six more hours before initializing the first phase of my plan.

I'll be otherwise occupied when the time comes, but I'll be back tomorrow morning to deal with the aftermath."

"As you wish," Silas says with a small nod of his head.

"Are you sure this will be enough to force Anna to abdicate her crown?" Hale asks, looking exceedingly eager for my sister's public disgrace to occur.

"With a little prodding by me, yes."

"Excuse me," Levi says, holding up his hand like a student wanting to ask a question to his teacher. "What exactly is supposed to happen?"

I briefly tell Levi what Silas and Hale have been up to. Once I'm through he busts out in laughter, unable to contain his jubilation over Anna's imminent humiliation.

"That's just classic!" Levi howls with joy. "I wish I could be in the same room as Anna when she hears the news. Can you imagine her reaction?"

"Yes, I can," I say irritably. "Now please, do shut up while the grownups are talking."

Just as I turn my head to return my attention to Hale and Silas, I see Levi raise his hand again.

"What?" I snap, looking at him sharply.

"It seems to me that it would solidify our position if other royal families besides us demand that Anna relinquish her crown. If you want me to, I can go to Stratus and speak with Lorcan Halloran, or Abaddon. I never really know what to call him these days. I'm sure it won't take much to convince him to side with us. He hates Anna just as much as we do after she humiliated him in that duel for Kyna's freedom. Mammon's support is a given. The only one I'm not so sure about is Baal. Ever since he fell in love with Bianca Rossi he's been unreliable, to say the least. He may not be so willing to go against one of Bianca's best friends."

"Tell him that if he wants his precious Bianca to remain alive, he had better do as we say. His love for her should be the only leverage we need to obtain his support. Now, why don't you scamper along like a good little minion and make sure Lorcan and Baal know what I expect from them. I was going to let it be a surprise, but you can tell Lorcan that his cloud city will also be playing a role in today's events. He'll find out in what capacity soon enough."

Levi stands, looking none too pleased by my belittling of him in front of the others.

"And will you be here when I return?" he asks.

"No," I reply curtly. "I won't be back until in the morning. I've already said this, Levi. Once Silas' broadcast is seen by all the cloud cities, I will need you to begin organizing the meeting of the other royals on Mars for tomorrow. We'll need to act fast before Anna has a chance to mount a defense. The quicker we strike, the better the outcome for us. I'm not even sure Anna's closest allies will be willing to argue on her behalf after today."

"Then I guess I'll see you in the morning," Levi says, sounding almost disappointed that I won't be returning until then. If I didn't know any better, I would say he was jealous. I'm sure he's deduced that I'm spending time with Cade. Who else would distract me at such a crucial time in my plot to finally take Anna down?

After he phases to Stratus, I return my attention to Hale and Silas. Silas is still kneeling on the floor before me.

"Stand, Silas. You've done well. I'm very pleased with what you've been able to accomplish during your return."

"I'm only here to do your bidding," Silas says like a good little soldier.

I turn my attention to Hale. The leader of the group of rebellion angels who wish to see my sister dead doesn't look as happy as I thought he would, considering what is about to happen.

"What's wrong, Hale? You don't look satisfied by my plan."

"I'm not," he says bluntly. "Don't get me wrong. It's definitely a step in the right direction, but most of my brothers and sisters would rather see Anna's head on a pike."

I study Hale for a moment because I want to gauge his reaction to what I'm about to tell him next.

"Lucifer is back on Earth," I inform him.

Hale's eyes grow wide and his mouth slack. To say he is surprised to hear my news is an understatement.

"Why is he here?" he asks in a low voice. It's almost as if he's afraid Lucifer might hear his question.

"Why do you think? Come on, Hale. You're smarter than this. Did you honestly believe he wouldn't come back to help Anna if given the opportunity? He wants to find a way to stop your vendetta against his precious daughter and her family."

Hale lifts his head defiantly. "Well, he won't find a way unless he intends to kill her for us. We know that the babies have been born. Making sure that they lived was your only restriction against us killing Anna. Now that she no longer carries them inside her, do you give us your blessing to end her life without any repercussions from you?"

Hale's question makes me wish I hadn't already promised Cade that Anna and her family would remain unharmed. I know Hale will be upset by my answer, but there's no helping that. He'll just have to learn how to live with disappointment.

"For now," I say, doing my best to assuage his anger beforehand, "Anna and her family are still under my protection, and tell your cronies that if any of them even touch a hair on her head that I will personally skin them alive and feed them to one of my leviathans. I'm doing this for your own good, Hale. Not only is Lucifer back, but so are Jess and Mason. Even if you could get through Anna's War Angels, I seriously doubt you would be able to cut those three down before they ended your life."

"Don't underestimate how powerful our hatred is," Hale tells me. "When you're properly motivated, it's amazing what you can accomplish. As things stand now, we'll be watching to see what happens later today. Hopefully your plan will succeed, but sometimes even the best plans don't always work out the way you think they will."

"Oh, I have every confidence that mine will," I assure him. "Now, if the two of you don't mind, I have somewhere else I need to be right now. I assume the two of you have things to do to prepare for this afternoon."

Hale doesn't show me the respect he should, and simply phases himself and Silas out of the room and back to complete their mission.

Once they're both gone, I walk into my bedroom and check my reflection in the mirror. I couldn't very well attend the meeting that morning wearing Cade's t-shirt and shorts. As soon as I returned to Nimbo, I changed into a rather attractive one-shoulder red dress that was more an asymmetric piece of artwork than clothing. It's a little dressy if Cade simply intends for us to stay at his beach house for the remainder of the day, though. I turn around and pick up Cade's clothing from my bed just in case I need them again. For good measure, I also grab some undergarments from my wardrobe to take with me.

When I phase back to Cade's home, I immediately know he isn't there. Homes lacking the presence of a second entity inside them tend to feel empty. I never noticed the effect that another life can have on a physical space before I became corporeal. I suppose you have to be a living creature in order to feel the energy of another one. As I look around the living room in my soul mate's home, a longing to have him near settles over me. I've noticed that the more I'm around Cade the more I want to be around him. He's become my soul's addiction, and I'm not exactly certain how I feel about that.

"Stop being stupid," I berate myself as I place the clothing in my hands on the glass top of the driftwood coffee table. "He'll be back soon."

When I look up from the table, I notice something that I hadn't before now. The inner wall separating the living room from the master bedroom is made up of a series of ten horizontal shelves that are evenly spaced between the floor and the ceiling. Set along each shelf is a multitude of seashells of various sizes, shapes, and colors, and a host of starfish. I walk over to the display to discern if there is a pattern to the randomness. Scattered here and there near the edge of the shelves are small rectangular pieces of metal with dates engraved on them. Only five out of the ten shelves are decorated and the last date to be engraved was only a couple of weeks ago.

Even before he speaks, I feel Cade phase into the room behind me.

"Do you like them?" I hear him ask.

"Some of them are pretty," I answer with honesty as I pick up a quarter piece of a sand dollar and turn around. I hold it up and ask, "But why keep a broken one? Why not just keep the perfect ones and throw something like this in the trash?"

"Even something that's broken can be beautiful," Cade tells me, looking at the small piece of shell I'm holding. "I can remember exactly how excited Lucas was when he found that on the beach, so now it holds that memory for me, and that's the real treasure."

"So all of these," I say, waving a hand at the display, "are shells you and Lucas have found together?"

"Yes."

I turn around and place the broken sand dollar back in its spot on the shelf.

"And the date plates are the exact days you found them?" I ask.

"Yes."

I shake my head. "You're more of a sentimental fool than I thought you were."

Cade walks around the couch that separates us to come stand by my side.

"I don't think it's foolish to hold onto keepsakes if they mean something to you. One day, I hope I can do something like this with a child of my own so we can always remember the times we were able to spend together."

I look over at Cade and ask, "And who do you plan to have this imaginary child with?"

"I hoped we could adopt one in a few years," Cade tells me, watching my reaction closely.

I don't make a reply because I would hate to obliterate the beautiful fantasy he has of us having a happy, normal family. It's almost as if he still doesn't realize we can never have a life like other people. Even though I remain mute on the possibility of fulfilling Cade's dream sometime in the future, I can tell by the dimming of happiness in his eyes that he already understands what my thoughts are on the subject.

"We can have whatever life we choose," he tells me. "All we have to do is work towards it."

Still, I don't say anything. If I choose to deny his words, he'll simply argue his position on the matter that much harder. If I choose to support his fantasy, he'll expect more from me than I'm willing to give.

Besides, everything we have or might have in the future could be destroyed by the events about to take place this afternoon. Once my plan is set into motion, Cade may hate me so much he won't be able to look at me again much less want to plan a life with me.

Perhaps I should hide him away in Hell for a while so he remains ignorant of what I'm about to do to Anna. Otherwise, I fear I might lose him forever.

"Did you have any plans for us today?" I ask him, already devising one of my own to get him safely away from the Earthly realm until I'm ready for him to return.

"Actually," he begins, sounding hesitant to bring up his next subject, "we've been invited to a party."

My head tilts of its own accord. "A party? What kind of party and given by whom?"

"Anna has invited us both to Lucas' birthday party," he reveals.

To say that I'm flabbergasted by what he just said is an understatement. It takes me a moment to gather my thoughts.

"Why in the world would my sister want me at her son's party? I thought she would hate me because of what I did to Liana."

Cade's eyes narrow on me. "What did you do to Liana?"

"Anna didn't tell you?" I ask, unable to hide my surprise.

"No. She didn't, but I think you should."

"It seems strange that she wouldn't tell you," I muse, pondering the reason Anna wouldn't take advantage of the situation and portray me as a villain in his eyes. Is it possible she hasn't noticed what I've done yet? No, that would be virtually impossible. Then why not use it to tarnish Cade's growing feelings for me? I have absolutely no idea and fear I'll never understand the way my sister thinks.

"Helena," Cade says sharply, pulling me out of my reverie, "tell me what you did to Liana!"

"Don't yell at me, Cade," I warn coldly. "I am *not* someone you raise your voice to."

"I need to know," he begs, looking worried over Liana's welfare.

"It's nothing that will harm her," I reassure him. "I simply gave her one of my seals."

Cade instantly looks confounded by my answer. "Why would you do that? I thought it was the power from the seals that made it possible for you to leave Hell."

"I took a calculated risk giving it to her," I say with a nonchalant shrug. "It seems to have worked out, though."

"But why would you risk your freedom like that?" he asks, still looking baffled by my decision.

"It's possible that I could have been placing my ability to travel between realms at risk," I acknowledge. "It's also possible that I did the one thing I needed to in order to save it."

"How so?"

"When Anna first began collecting the seals, I could feel a connection develop between us. All of the hate and anger that the seals absorbed through the years began to change her and strengthen her tie with me. It was like we were connected by an ethereal cord that allowed an exchange of energy between us. Somehow, as the power of our connection to one another became more solid it also began to alter her physical appearance. After I absorbed five of the seals from her the connection between us lessened, but it remained, just in a weakened form. I'm not sure if I would have been able to traverse the veil between Hell and Earth if I hadn't still been bound to her through her children. I assumed that once her children were born my bond with Anna would disappear. Did you notice anything different about Anna when you last saw her? About her physical appearance?"

"Yes," Cade verifies. "Her hair and eyes are brown now."

"That's just what I suspected would happen."

"But if you're connected to the children anyway, why give Liana a seal?"

"Call it an insurance policy," I say. "I needed to make sure my bond with at least one of the children is so strong it's practically unbreakable."

"Which seal did you give her?"

"Her grandfather's seal of silence," I say, gaining a small amount of pleasure in the fact. I'm sure Lucifer has seen his granddaughter by now. How ironic that she now carries the seal that he once did. He's probably even guessed why I decided to give her that particular seal. With her ability to phase into Heaven, she can act as a harbinger of eternal damnation to millions of trapped souls just like Ravan Draeke did on alternate Earth.

"Is there a reason you gave her that one and not one of the others?" Cade asks. "Or did you do it just to hurt your father?"

"Both," I freely admit. "More one than the other, though, if I'm being truthful."

"What is it that you hope to gain by giving her that seal, Helena?" he asks warily.

"Nothing, for the moment. If I were you, I wouldn't concern myself with why I do certain things. I *can* promise you that she won't be hurt by having the seal. It won't kill her."

"Will being connected directly to you change who she is destined to become?"

I shrug. "How am I supposed to know the answer to that question? I might be extremely powerful, but even I can't see into the future."

"What's to prevent her from taking the seal to Heaven when she gets older and returning it there?"

"She could," I say cautiously, not wanting to delve too deeply into this subject. "But that would simply break the seal open and cause its destructive forces to be unleashed. That's exactly why Anna had to wait until she had all seven seals before returning them to Heaven. If she had tried to take them back one by one, they simply would have broken open. Once they were bound together inside her, she could have returned them because their collective energy was strong enough to keep them intact. It would have been a good plan, but it was doomed to fail once she became pregnant."

"What do you mean?"

"Two of the seals were transformed into the twins' souls. If I had allowed her to phase back to Heaven, she would have automatically released the seals she had left because of the pain they were causing her. Those seals would have broken open and caused all kinds of havoc."

I pause in my explanation because I finally realize a great truth that I had been blind to before now.

"He played me like a fiddle," I mutter to myself, unable to believe how easily I had been manipulated.

"He who?" Cade asks, looking puzzled by my self-admonishment.

"Your father, that's who," I tell him, shaking my head. "I can't believe I did exactly what He wanted me to without even realizing it until now. Here I thought I was being clever when all I did was follow His plan from the start."

"Oh," Cade says as realization finally dawns on him, too. "You believe God wanted you to take the five seals Anna had left because He knew if she tried to return them to Heaven they would open there."

"Yes. Clever old fool. Well... I guess it's I who turned out to be the pawn. I ended up doing exactly what He wanted."

"So, you believe God always planned for you to walk the Earth? Not to sound ungrateful that you're here, but why would He want that to happen?"

"Why don't you ask Him?" I ask irritably. "He's the one who seems to have all the answers. Apparently, I'm being used by Him just like the rest of you. At least you knew it, though. I didn't have a clue, which just makes my stupidity even more unforgivable."

"You're not stupid, Helena," Cade says, attempting to console me. "You're one of the smartest people I've ever met."

I look at Cade and sigh. "If only you were just saying that to get me into bed, but you're actually being sincere."

He chuckles. "Do I need to take you to bed and ravish your body just so you'll stop obsessing over it?"

"Yes, please!" I say eagerly, feeling my mood instantly perk up with the possibility of a little morning delight with Cade…in his bed…naked on top of me. Or vice versa. I'm not opposed to doing all the work.

Cade holds my gaze with his own for a long time. Again, he looks deeply into my eyes as if he's searching for something in particular.

"If you told me what it is you're waiting to see in my eyes," I say, "I'm sure I could make it appear."

He breaks the intensity of his stare and smiles. "I'm afraid it doesn't work like that. You're not ready yet anyway."

"That excuse is getting a little old," I tell him, feeling annoyed. "What's to stop me from just taking what I want from you?"

The smile on his face instantly vanishes, making me wish I could take back my words.

"Would you really rape me just to satisfy your own needs?" he questions. "Could you be that cruel to me?"

"That's not what I said."

"That's exactly what you said. If you took what you wanted from me by force, that's what the humans call rape, Helena."

"I wouldn't do that to you," I say, feeling a strange sensation form inside my chest. I think it might be a form of guilt for even suggesting I would harm Cade in such a vicious way. Since I've never really felt it before, I'm simply making an educated guess. "You have to know by now that I wouldn't intentionally hurt you."

"Where you're concerned, everything is questionable."

His words wound me more than I'm willing to admit, so I remain quiet on the issue and quickly decide to change the course of our conversation to something less serious.

"So are we going to Lucas' party?" I ask. "Or are you too ashamed to be seen with me in public?"

"I would like for us to attend it. Would you be willing to go?"

"Yes, if for nothing else than to see everyone's faces when I walk into the room. Who else will be there?"

"Anna and Malcolm's family, the other Watchers, and all my brothers."

"Are you certain this was an invitation to a party and not an ambush?" I have to ask, considering the number of War Angels who will be present.

"Anna promised me that no harm would come to you while you're there."

"And, of course, you would have known if she lied to you."

"Yes. I would have, but Anna would never lie to me anyway."

It only takes me a moment to make a decision.

"Do I need to bring a present?" I ask. "Isn't that part of the tradition for these events?"

"You can, but I don't think anyone expects you to bring anything."

"What are you taking?"

"My brothers and I had something specially made for Lucas."

I wait for Cade to provide more details about his gift, but when he doesn't I have to ask, "So what is it? Or are you going to make me wait until Lucas opens it at the party?"

"Well, I was thinking about showing it to you, but making you wait to see it sounds like a lot more fun."

"Can't you just tell me what it is?" I ask, finding myself uncharacteristically curious to find out what a group of War Angels would give a seven-year-old boy.

"Of course I could, but what would be the point in that?"

"I can't believe you're teasing me so unmercifully!"

"And I can't believe you're getting upset about a birthday present that isn't even yours," Cade laughs, finding my aggravation amusing.

"Whatever," I say deciding to drop the subject. "What should I buy him? You're his best friend. What's something he would enjoy?"

"Hmm, that's hard to say. He has so much. Finding something that he doesn't already own might be difficult. He does enjoy eating candy, though. Maybe we could put together a basket of different candies for him to share with the other children who will be there."

"Who makes the best candy on Earth?"

"I've heard there's a candy store in Virga that has the best chocolate in the world," Cade tells me. "We can go there and check it out. We have a few hours to kill before the party is scheduled to start anyway."

"I wouldn't mind seeing Virga, actually. I haven't been there yet and who knows if I'll ever have a chance to visit it again. Do you know what part of the city the store is in?"

"I'm sure it won't be too hard to find," he tells me, holding out his hand for me to take. "Are you ready to go?"

I place my hand into his. "Do you think I'm overdressed for the party? Should I change before we go to it?"

Cade looks me up and down appreciatively. From the slow smile that blossoms on his face, I already know what his answer is before he even says it.

"The dress is prefect," he tells me, bringing me closer to him for something more than just phasing.

As he bends his head to kiss me, I take a quick, deep breath and allow myself to melt into him. It's then that I decide I'll need to whisk Cade away from the party before Silas and Hale enact the first stage of my plan. If he finds out what I've coordinated behind his back, I think I'll lose what ground I've gained in our relationship. No, I need to keep him in the dark about the details. He may care for me, but he'll end up seeing me as a monster if he finds out what I'm about to do. I can't let that happen.

He'll simply have to remain in Hell for the time being.

There's no other option.

CHAPTER ELEVEN

(Anna's Point of View)

I ask Malcolm to take me to Cirrus a couple of hours before Lucas' party is scheduled to begin. I need to see the destruction that my cloud city has endured with my own two eyes. Jess and Mason offer to look after Liana and Liam for us, while Vala asks to tag along. I think she understands I need someone who loves Cirrus as much as I do to be with me. That's not to say that Malcolm is indifferent to the damage our city has suffered, but Vala has been my constant companion since childhood. We both grew up there and only someone you share memories of a place with can fully grasp how such devastation affects you.

"Thankfully, the palace was built incredibly well," Vala reports as she, Malcolm, and I stand out on the veranda connected to our suite of rooms in the palace. "When I came here yesterday with the others, we only found a few cracks in some of the walls and ceilings, but overall the structure is sound and safe enough for us all to move back into when we're ready."

As I look out across the great expanse of my once-beautiful city, I see that quite a few buildings weren't made as well as the palace and now exist as piles of rubble littering the streets around them. So many lives will be altered by the events that have taken place here in the past few days, and so many of my citizens will have to adjust to the new reality of their existence. Those without homes to go back to will need to be relocated until new buildings can be constructed. The extent of the damage makes me realize that hundreds of decisions will need to be made in a very short amount of time if we want to move people back to Cirrus within the next few weeks.

"I don't see how we can have the election, considering the amount of work that needs to be done here first," I tell them both.

"Don't worry about the election, my love," Malcolm says. "Your father spoke with Olivia Ravensdale while we were in Hell. Supposedly, she asked for an official delay and had the election pushed back until Cirrus is back to normal. Catherine will just have to cool her heels for a little while. I think we have enough to worry about without adding her unfounded attempt to usurp your throne to the list."

"I still can't believe she thinks I murdered Auggie just to rule Cirrus," I say, feeling my temper almost get the better of me over Catherine's hurtful accusation. "If she knew one thing about me, she should have known that I loved her son like my own brother."

"Helena and Levi have poisoned her mind against you. She lost her only son and control over her cloud city within a very short timeframe. It was bound to cause a psychosis, and the two of them took advantage of her state of mind."

"Befriending Helena seems almost impossible when I think about the things she's done to cause me pain." A feeling of hopelessness threatens to consume me when I consider the impossible task I've set for myself. How am I ever going to make peace with Helena if she continues her attempts to ruin the life I'm trying to build with my family?

"You have never failed at anything you set out to accomplish," Vala reminds me, sounding proud of the strength she sees in me. "Look at the miracles you've worked with Malcolm and Lucifer. They're two of the most bullheaded men who have ever walked the Earth. Yet you finally made Malcolm realize he can't live without you, and you showed Lucifer how strong the love between a parent and a child can be. Who else in the world can claim those two things? No one but you."

"She has a point," Malcolm agrees. "If anyone has a chance of becoming friends with Helena, it's you."

"You'll need to make an effort not to hate her so much, too," I remind him.

"I'll do my best," he grumbles, "but I'm not even on good terms with Lucifer."

"Then you and Helena have something to bond over: your mutual dislike of my father."

Malcolm chuckles. "True enough, my love."

I twine an arm around one of Malcolm's and wave Vala closer to my side until I can place the palm of my hand on her head.

"I want to go to my papa's house," I tell Malcolm. "I would like to see if it survived Cirrus' plunge into the ocean's depths."

Malcolm phases us to the home where I was raised.

Thankfully, we find the Greco household mostly intact. The structure itself has withstood any major damage. However, the furnishings and such inside are a jumbled mess, but that was to be expected. I'm just grateful that my childhood home is still standing. We all walk up the grand staircase to my suite of rooms in the house. As soon as I step through the doorway of the front room, a plethora of memories suddenly comes rushing back to me all at once. Most of them involve the woman who was a constant source of love and encouragement in my life and the closest thing I had to a mother on Earth. Millie.

No child could have asked for a better surrogate mother than Millie. She was always kind and loving, and never shied away from telling me exactly what she thought, especially if she believed I was doing something wrong. I miss her council on the day-to-day events in my life. I know I could go to Heaven and visit with her if I wanted to, but it just isn't the same. Sporadic visits with loved ones are a far cry from having them by your side every single day.

As I look around the room, I notice the glass doors leading from the living room to the large terrace are shattered. It isn't an unexpected sight. Most of the glass in the city will have to be replaced. I walk over to the wrought-iron doors and swing them open to look out at my city from this vantage point.

There's an unnatural quiet surrounding my home. Cirrus feels like a city of the dead instead of a thriving metropolis. The sooner we get its residents back into their homes and businesses the better.

I feel Malcolm come up behind me and wrap his arms around my still-swollen waist. I make a mental note to ask Desmond about that miracle cream that will help shrink my abdomen in a shorter amount of time than nature would normally allow.

"Do you remember what happened on this balcony?" he asks, pressing his warm, full lips against the crook of my neck, tenderly sucking on the sensitive flesh there.

"You held me for the first time," I reply, leaning back into his arms as I begin to remember that fateful night. "I didn't know who you were, but I did know your touch helped ease the pain I was feeling from absorbing the first seal."

"And you knew that you loved me," Malcolm reminds me, trailing his lips up my neck to gently tug on my earlobe with the edge of his teeth.

"And that I loved you," I agree, finding immense joy in the feel of my husband's touch.

"Uh-hmm," I hear Vala say, "should I make myself scarce for a while? The two of you look like you might need some alone time to get matches."

Malcolm stops kissing me to look over at Vala, who is standing beside us. "And how in the world do you know about getting matches?"

"If you stay around Jess and Mason for any length of time," she replies, "you inevitably learn more than you ever wanted to know about matches and marshmallows. They were teasing each other about going to Nacreous for some reason. There was some talk about finally getting matches on every continent."

I can't help but giggle at what Vala overheard my ancestors discussing. Malcolm informed me all about matches and marshmallows a long time ago. Envisioning Vala listening in on a conversation between Jess and Mason discussing the subject is just too good of a visual not to have a hearty laugh over.

"Unfortunately," I tell her as I turn around to face my husband and rest my hands on the back of his neck, "I don't believe Malcolm and I have time to get matches. I still want to see the rest of the city before we're supposed to meet with the others in the palace. You did make sure to send word to everyone that they should be here early, right?"

"Yes. I sent out a message to everyone."

"How do you think they're going to react when I tell them Helena will be attending the party?" I ask worriedly, anticipating a very bad reaction from some of them, most notably Lucifer.

Malcolm shrugs his shoulders. "It doesn't really matter, does it? It's a fact they're going to have to deal with whether they want to or not."

"Lucifer isn't going to like it," I sigh. "I don't see him staying long enough to see her arrive."

"That might be for the best, actually," Malcolm replies, sounding relieved if that is indeed the outcome. "If we have any chance of making things work with Helena, today needs to be as stress-free as possible. We need to make her feel welcome in our home, and I'm not sure we can do that with Lucifer present."

"You may be right," I concede, "but I also don't want him to feel unwelcome."

"I don't think you'll have to worry about asking him to leave. As you just said, he probably won't even stick around once he hears she's coming. I say we focus on Helena and forging a relationship with her for Liana's sake. Our children take top priority, Anna. We can't worry about hurting other people's feelings, especially when your own are in such turmoil. If we just handle one thing at a time, we'll make it through this. I promise."

I lift myself onto my toes and wrap my arms around Malcolm's neck, resting my head on his shoulder.

"I'm not sure what I would do without you in my life," I whisper, taking comfort in the fact that I have a man like him to stand beside me no matter what happens.

"That's the one thing you don't have to worry about, my love," he murmurs. "I will always be in your life."

I allow myself the indulgence of just holding my husband and relishing the love we have for one another. Our love has already seen me through some of the darkest days of my life. I wish I could say that I'll never have to face times like that again, but I fear the previous ones were just a prelude to even darker times to come.

I pull back from Malcolm and kiss him full on the lips. The idea of getting matches is tempting, especially in moments like this, but I am still the Empress of Cirrus. That title comes with certain obligations, and I know my subjects will want an update on the state of their home soon.

Even though I don't want to, I break the kiss.

"Show me the rest of the city," I tell him, trying my best to ignore his smoldering look of carnal need. His stare is practically begging me to give into my own desires and throw caution to the wind just this once.

Reluctantly I pull away from him and say, "I need to see the remainder of the damage before we meet with the others."

Malcolm nods his understanding. I know I don't have to worry about his feelings being hurt because he understands how much I want him, too. Unfortunately, we have more important matters to attend to right now.

We continue to survey the destruction right up until it's time for us to meet with the others in the ballroom of the palace. When we phase there, we find everyone present except for Jess and Mason. We asked them to stay in Malcolm's New Orleans home to take care of the babies while the party was taking place. I didn't want the children anywhere near Helena. She's already turned one of my kids against me. I can't risk her poisoning Liam towards me, too. Plus, I'm not confident she's through interfering with Liana's life. The more distance I keep between them the better.

As I look out at the faces of my friends, family, and War Angels, I take a deep breath and say, "Thank you all for coming here today. I know Lucas appreciates each of you taking time out of your busy schedules to celebrate his seventh birthday with us." I take another deep breath before continuing. "I feel as though I should warn you all that Helena will be joining us later."

"What?" I hear Lucifer say sharply from his spot in the front of the crowd. He looks confused and angry, which is just what I expected from him. "Why is that thing coming to your son's birthday party?"

"I invited her," I tell him, holding my head up despite his obvious anger.

"Why?" he in turn asks, looking even more perplexed.

"Malcolm and I decided that befriending Helena may help Liana in the long run. If we end the hatred between us, maybe Liana's reaction towards me will soften. Please understand that I need to try this, Dad. I need to find a way to help my child deal with what's been done to her. I can't undo what Helena did, but maybe I can find a way to give Liana a portion of her life back."

"This isn't going to work," Lucifer says flat-out. "You can't make friends with a creature that never should have existed in the first place. She may look human, Anna, but she isn't. If you insist on going through with this, you need to remember that fact. She doesn't make friends. She can't love. That isn't what I created her to do."

"She's a sentient being," I remind him. "She has the capability to think for herself now. You may not have created her to feel anything except hate, but she's grown beyond what she was initially made to be. You need to stop hating her so much, Dad. Whether you like it or not, she's a part of you just like I am."

Lucifer's face is a mask of control. Even though I can feel his anger, his expression remains placid.

"I can't stay here if she's coming," he tells me. "I won't pretend that I accept her, and I fear my presence would simply hinder what you're trying to attempt. All I ask is that you not trust her, Anna. You're right. Liana is being affected by the way Helena feels about you, and that should tell you something. She hates you. She despises the fact that you even exist. You shouldn't trust anyone who abhors you that much, least of all her."

"I know." I tell him. "I'm not going into this blind, but I have to try everything I can think of to help my baby, no matter how objectionable it might be to others."

"I understand that, and I wish you the best of luck in what you're attempting to do for your child. I'll return to Malcolm's home in New Orleans and wait there for you with Jess and Mason."

Right after Lucifer phases out of the room, Jered pipes up and says, "I'm afraid I need to leave, too, Anna."

"Why?" I immediately ask him, finding his departure an unexpected one.

"Basically for the same reason as Lucifer," he tells me regrettably. "If I stay, I'll only get in the way of your purpose for inviting her here. I would probably end up confronting her about her plans for Silas, and that would only lead to a heated argument. I understand your need to find a way to help Liana because I have the same desire to help my son. He may be too far gone now to be saved, but if I don't at least try to find a way to help him I'll feel like I've failed him all over again. I truly want you to succeed here today, Anna, but I'm certain my presence wouldn't help your cause."

"Jered," Lucas says from his spot beside our friend as he tugs on his shirtsleeve, "do you really have to leave? You did so much work putting the party together."

Jered kneels down on one knee in front of Lucas and brings my son into his arms for a hug.

"I wish I could stay," Jered says apologetically, "but I think it would be better if I go. After she leaves, I promise to come back. Okay?"

Lucas nods his head but doesn't make a reply.

Jered lets Lucas go and stands back up.

"I'll come and get you when she leaves," Desmond promises him.

"Thank you," Jered says before phasing.

I look out at the rest of my family and friends. I begin to wonder if I've made a terrible mistake by asking Helena to the party. It was supposed to be a happy time for Lucas. What if I've ruined it by trying to rush things with her?

"Does anyone else feel like they need to leave before she arrives?" I ask them.

No one says a word. I breathe a sigh of relief that I haven't completely ruined Lucas' birthday celebration.

"I'm not leaving you unprotected while that thing is here," Xander proclaims, looking at his brother War Angels. "We were sent to Earth to protect you from all harm, and we can't do that if we leave. You don't have to worry about us, Anna. We're here for you no matter what."

"Thank you, Xander," I say, smiling with pride that, out of all my War Angels, he was the one who made the declaration.

I know going to Hell was hard for him, but it seems as if revealing his long-kept secret to the others has finally helped him accept what happened in Heaven. He seems changed for the better, and I hope this means I don't ever have to venture into the Ladies in Waiting again to fetch him.

Suddenly, Barlow and Travis Stokes transport into the room. I can't help but smile at our genius friend, Travis, because he's decked himself out for the party. However, his idea of party- wear seems a bit strange. He's wearing his signature roller skates, which isn't unexpected, but he's also wearing an odd yellow plastic helmet on his head with a golden horn attached to the top of it. In his hands, he holds a large plastic box that is almost overflowing with what looks like parts to build some sort of mechanical contraption.

"Are we late?" Barlow asks, seeing that most everyone else who was invited to attend is already present. "I could have sworn we were on time."

"You're not late," I reassure the brothers. "We just needed to have a small meeting to discuss something."

Travis looks at the crowd and states, "It must have been something important. You all look so serious."

"Don't worry, Travis," Lucas says, walking over to his friend. "Hell's coming to my party, and my mom wanted to warn everyone about it first."

"Hell?" Travis asks, looking as perplexed as he sounds.

"Don't worry about it," Lucas says with a wave of his hand. "My mom's War Angels won't let anything happen to you while you're here. What's in the box?"

Travis still looks confused, but he leans over and holds the box of parts down so Lucas can look inside.

"I thought I would help you and your friends make matchbox robots. Kind of like a party favor they can take home afterwards."

"That's awesome!" Lucas says excitedly. If there was one thing my son loved doing, it was making things that actually served a function. Travis couldn't have given him a better birthday gift.

Lucas turns his head to look at me and asks, "When are Bai and her brothers coming over?"

"I'll go get them," Desmond offers. "Brutus has had his hands full lately dealing with the Cirrus refugees. I told him I would bring Kyna and the kids up here for the party so he didn't have to worry about it."

"Make sure Kyna knows Helena is coming," I tell Desmond. "I don't want her to be surprised, and tell her if she can't make it we understand."

"Oh, don't worry about her, lass. Even Hell itself won't keep her away. She's been dying to talk to you since the babies were born."

Desmond phases to Brutus' house in the down-world to bring up the rest of our friends.

Everyone else begins to relax and mingle, giving me my first real opportunity to look at the room and all the work Jered and the others did to prepare it for the party.

Small round tables with white tablecloths have been decorated with floating bouquets of balloons. Each arrangement is composed of a large silver star on top with a mixture of pearly white and blue balloons underneath it. They're tethered to the center of the tables by trails of silver and blue ribbons. Each of the small tables has four blue chairs. In the center of the room is a larger table that holds the birthday cake and snacks. The cake has four round layers, each one smaller than the one underneath it. The layers are covered with dark blue fondant and have a trail of white glittery stars of various sizes that wind around the cake from top to bottom. Sitting on top layer of the cake is a white wolf that looks just like Luna, flaming fur and all.

I see Olivia Ravensdale walk out from amongst the crowd of War Angels, with my papa by her side.

"I didn't realize you were coming," I tell Olivia as she draws closer and kisses me on the cheek.

"I hope you don't mind me being here," she replies, glancing at my papa, "but when Andre invited me I jumped at the opportunity to see you again. How are you, my dear?"

"Just trying to hold it together," I tell her truthfully, attempting to smile but not really feeling it.

"Well, you look lovely. Motherhood suits you well."

"Anna!"

I look over and see Kyna shuffling towards me. For someone so plump with pregnancy, my friend can waddle faster than anyone I've ever seen. Kyna has me enveloped in her arms before I can even say, "It's so good to see you."

"As big as I am, it's kind of hard not to see me coming a mile away," she playfully complains. "So I'm guessing the babies aren't here since Helena is supposed to make an appearance."

"No, they're not," I tell her regrettably.

"That *is* a pity," Olivia sighs in disappointment. "I was hoping to see them, too."

"Well, why don't the both of you come home with us when the party is over?" I suggest. "I swear they're two of the most precious and perfect babies ever, but I know I'm totally biased in that opinion."

"Well, of course you are," Olivia says in complete understanding. "Every mother believes her children are the most picture-perfect creatures on Earth. It's completely natural."

"So," Kyna says, eyeing the display of food by the cake, "are we waiting for something to happen before we eat or can we just serve ourselves?"

"Feel free to eat all you want," I tell my friend, remembering the hunger of pregnancy quite well.

"Please allow me to escort you," my papa tells Kyna, holding out a bent arm for her to take. "Brutus would kill me if I didn't make sure you were fed properly."

"Thank you for being such a gallant enabler," Kyna giggles, readily taking my papa's offered arm. I'm silently thankful he plans to assist her to the table. In her present condition, I could see her toppling over on her quest for sustenance.

"I wouldn't mind eating a small snack either," Oliva says.

"Thankfully, I have two arms," Papa informs her, holding out his other arm for her to take.

Olivia smiles and slips her arm through his as if they've done it hundreds of times before in their lives.

Malcolm told me that my papa was in love with Olivia, and it's plain to see that she has feelings for him, too. I can't think of anyone else in the world I would rather see my papa fall in love with than the Empress of Nacreous. Olivia is one of the best women I know, and I would be honored to have her as a stepmother, if their relationship progresses that far.

While everyone is enjoying themselves, I feel as though I'm sitting on pins and needles waiting for Helena to show up. I realize Lucas' vision may not come to pass. His visions were possible futures, not ones set in stone, but something deep down inside me is confident she'll show up.

"Stop worrying so much," Malcolm whispers to me as we watch Lucas, Bai, and her brothers work on the robots Travis is helping them build. The table they're all sitting around is strewn with various parts and gadgets. To me it all looks a bit chaotic, but Travis and Lucas seem to know where everything they need is located.

"I can't help but worry," I say as I cross my arms in front of me and begin nervously tapping the index finger of my left hand against my right arm. "I'm worried about her coming, and I'm worried that she won't show up. No matter the actual outcome, I'm worried."

"Well you can stop worrying that she won't come, because there she is with Cade."

CHAPTER TWELVE

I follow Malcolm's gaze to the bottom of the grand staircase in the ballroom. As always, Helena looks impeccable as she stands proudly by Cade's side in a very fashionable red dress. Her right arm is looped through a medium-sized basket crafted out of silver wire. Nestled inside it is a variety of candies anyone with a healthy sweet tooth would salivate over appreciatively. I notice Cade is carrying a rather large box wrapped with gold foil paper and topped with a red ribbon.

A heavy silence settles over the room as people become aware of their presence. Most everyone turns to give them their full attention. I feel more than see my War Angels become more attuned to their surroundings, as if they expect an attack to take place at any second. I suppose anything is possible where Helena is concerned but I take comfort in the fact that Cade is with her, looking more relaxed than I've seen him in quite a while. I know that if Helena tried to harm anyone present at the party, Cade would never be able to forgive her. She may not have much of a heart, but whatever does exist inside her chest belongs to Cade.

I know my moment has at long last arrived, and if I want my plan to work it's either act on it now or let the opportunity pass me by forever.

I take a step forward, and then another until I'm standing in front of the couple who has brought our gathering to a standstill.

"Welcome," I say as I look between them. "I'm glad to see that you decided to accept my invitation, Helena."

Helena raises a questioning eyebrow in my direction. "To be quite frank, I was surprised to receive one from you, Anna. Considering how things stand between us…"

"Well, I can't honestly say that I'm pleased that you gave my daughter one of your seals," I tell her, attempting to talk about the elephant in the room before things get out of hand, "but I also assume this means she's under your protection now. If nothing else, you're not one to rush into something without having it planned out to a T, and I seriously doubt you would waste time doing something just to have it ruined by a wayward rebellion angel seeking vengeance."

"Yes. She is under my protection. You don't have to worry about her safety around me or anyone else under my command."

"Then I suppose there's a small silver lining to something that can't be undone."

Helena tilts her head as she considers my rather calm attitude about the situation.

"What are you up to?" she asks, her eyes narrowing on me suspiciously. "It's not like you to want to bury the hatchet so readily, especially when it concerns one of your own children. What's really going on here, Anna?"

"I'm tired," I tell her truthfully. "I'm tired of us always bickering with one another. You keep calling me your sister, yet you never treat me as if you really believe that. I'm tired of the hate that's built up between us, Helena. I'm ready for a little peace in my life, and finding a way for you and I to coexist with one another is the only way I see that happening."

"So what are you offering me? Your friendship?" she asks skeptically.

"My offer is to stop hating you if you're willing to do the same."

Helena remains quiet on the issue as she continues to keep a wary eye on me. I'm not sure if she believes I'm trying to play a trick on her or if she believes I'm sincere in my offer. Her expression gives nothing of her true feelings away.

Finally, she mutters, "I'll think about it."

I sigh in relief because I know it's the best possible outcome I could have hoped for from this first attempt at forming a bond with her.

"Is that for me?" I hear Lucas ask eagerly as he comes to stand by my side.

Instinctively, I place a protective hand on his shoulder.

"Why, yes, it is," Helena tells him as she hands the basket of candy to him. "Cade and I spent quite a lot of time traipsing around Virga this morning to find you the best candy they had to offer."

"Awesome!" Lucas says excitedly, greedily accepting the basket from Helena's hand.

A flash of Helena poisoning the candy enters my mind, but I quickly squelch it before fear has a chance to take hold. Cade would never allow such a thing to happen. Plus, I know Helena would by no means risk losing him over such a petty act of cruelty to a child.

"Can I share it with the others?" Lucas asks me.

"You can each have one piece of candy," I tell him sternly. As he scampers back to the worktable with his treasure trove of sweet delights, I call out, "One piece, Lucas! So choose wisely!"

When I turn back to Helena and Cade, I suddenly realize that I have absolutely nothing to say to them. How am I supposed to start a conversation with Helena and keep it centered around an inconsequential subject after everything that's happened between us? Most of our discussions have always involved life and death matters. How do you start a normal, polite conversation with someone like her?

"Good to see you again, Cade," Malcolm says, coming to my rescue and making the situation a little less awkward. As my husband shakes Cade's hand, I suddenly feel my years of training to entertain as an empress kick into gear.

"That's a very lovely dress, Helena," I say. "I don't think I've ever told you before, but you have exquisite taste in clothing. Do you use one designer in Nimbo exclusively?"

"No. I have a few that I go to," she replies. Her stiff demeanor tells me that she's still uneasy with me acting so nice to her. I have to admit that it does feel rather unnatural, but I have to forge ahead for Liana's sake. If I'm ever going to have a chance at a normal relationship with my daughter, I have to make this work.

I continue to make polite conversation with her about the various clothiers I buy from in Cirrus. This leads to a conversation about how each cloud city has adopted their own style for both traditional and casual clothing. I slowly see Helena's posture begin to relax, which makes me feel like I've accomplished something.

"Cade, is that Lucas' present from all of us?" I hear Gideon ask as he walks up, sucking on a lollipop.

"Hey, Gideon," Cade says with an easy smile. "Yes, it's his present."

"Can I open it now?" Lucas asks from his place beside Bai over at the worktable.

Gideon snatches the present out from under Cade's arm. "You bet, little buddy!"

"What did you all get him?" I whisper to Cade. "Gideon is so excited you would think the gift is for him, if you didn't know any better."

"You'll see," Cade says cryptically as he watches his brother War Angel take the box over to Lucas.

Gideon places it on a table next to the one the kids are working at and takes a step back so we can watch Lucas remove the lid of the box. I see what looks like a mound of white fabric, but I quickly realize the cloth is simply covering something else within the box.

Carefully, Lucas lifts the white material up and to the side. He lets out a gasp of surprise as he peers at the contents. I watch as he reaches in and pulls out a black and white feathered cape, just like the one the War Angels came to Earth wearing.

S. J. West

"We all donated a feather from our own capes to make that for you," Cade calls out. "We had enough to make one you can wear now and a larger one you can wear when you get older."

"It's…it's…" Lucas stammers, staring at the cape in his hands with wide eyes, "it's awesome! Look, Bai!"

Lucas quickly turns to Bai, still clutching the cape in his hands as if he fears it might disappear forever if he lets go of it.

"Put it on, Lucas!" Bai encourages excitedly.

Lucas doesn't need any more encouragement than that to do such a thing. He quickly tosses it onto his shoulders but seems to have a little trouble with the silver clasp at the neck. Gideon kneels down in front of him and fastens it.

"There you go, little buddy," Gideon says with a smile. "Now you're an honorary War Angel."

Lucas turns around as the other War Angels in the room comment about how good he looks in his new attire. I feel myself truly smile for the first time in a while as my son models for his War Angel admirers.

"That was a very thoughtful gift."

I turn my head to look at Helena, surprised to hear those words come from her mouth.

She must feel my gaze on her because she looks directly at me and says, "Don't look so surprised, Anna. I may not practice it, but I can recognize kindness when I see it."

"Mommy," I hear Lucas say as he taps me on the arm to pull my attention away from Helena.

I look down at him and ask, "Yes, sweetie?"

"Can we have some music?" he whispers. When I see him give a furtive glance in Bai's direction, who has resumed working on her matchbox robot, I understand exactly why Lucas wants the music.

"Let me see what I can do," I whisper back, with a wink for good measure.

After Lucas returns to his seat beside Bai, I turn to Malcolm and ask, "Do you know how to turn on the sound system for this room? I'm sure there has to be some pre-recorded music available."

"I think I might know where it is," he says, "but whether or not it's functional is another matter entirely. Let me grab Travis and take him with me. If it needs to be repaired, he'll know what to do."

"Thank you," I say.

Malcolm walks off to fetch Travis.

"I could play something for Lucas while we wait," Cade offers unexpectedly.

"I didn't realize you played an instrument," I confess, instantly feeling ashamed that I didn't know that about him.

"I taught myself how to play the guitar when we first arrived here," he informs me.

"If you don't mind doing it, I think Lucas would really enjoy having you play something for him. Thank you, Cade."

"I'll be right back," he says to me before looking at Helena. "Will you be all right staying here by yourself for a few minutes? I just need to phase home and get my guitar and picks."

"I'll be fine," Helena reassures him. "I doubt Anna will let anyone attack me while you're gone."

"No one here wants to hurt you," I tell her.

Helena lets out a derisive snicker. "If you truly believe that, Sister, then you're more delusional than I thought. Everyone here, besides maybe the children, would rather see me trapped back in Hell than roaming the Earth freely, and if you didn't have your own hidden agenda, you would want the same thing. Of that, I have no doubt whatsoever."

"I'll admit that things would be easier if you were still trapped there," I say, seeing no reason to lie to her about that. If I did, she would see right through it. "But you're here now and I think we need to try to make the best out of an awkward situation. I would much rather have you as an ally than a constant adversary."

"I'll be right back," Cade tells Helena, leaning over and kissing her lightly on the cheek.

Cade phases to his beach house, leaving Helena and me standing together in uncomfortable silence.

"I had no idea he played the guitar," I say to her. "Has he played for you yet?"

Helena shakes her head. "No. He hasn't, but I can't say that I'm surprised he taught himself how to play. He seems like the type who would do such a thing."

"So, how are things progressing between the two of you?" I ask, seeing an opening into Helena's inner thoughts. It's a topic that most women would discuss with each other, especially if one of them is falling in love for the first time.

Helena purses her lips, looking reluctant to share such personal information with me about her relationship with Cade.

"If you don't want to tell me, that's fine," I assure her. "I just thought you might like to have another woman's perspective on the situation. I know when Malcolm and I first started spending a lot of time together it was a confusing period in my life, but I had people around who gave me a lot of good advice."

Helena continues to look at me as if she can't quite decide if I'm being sincere in my offer or if I'm simply digging for information.

"He aggravates me," she finally confides. "He stoutly refuses to have sex."

Well…I can't honestly say that's where I saw the conversation starting off, but I guess it's as good a place to begin as any. At least she's talking to me.

"Has he told you his reasons why?" I ask.

"No," Helena huffs in aggravation. "He just keeps looking at me and saying that I'm not ready yet, but I'm more than ready!"

Helena's outburst causes quite a few eyes to turn our way. I smile at them all, reassuring them that everything is fine.

When I return my attention to her, I say, "Well, I think it's important to remember that he's an angel, Helena, and he's waited a very long time to have a chance to live on Earth. He probably just doesn't want the two of you to rush into things and miss all the small moments before sex becomes an issue."

"But we're soul mates! It's not as if I'm likely to find another one of those lying around to help me satisfy my physical needs. I'm a very willing partner. What else does he want?"

"I'm not sure," I say with a shrug. "Maybe he's waiting for a perfect moment before the two of you are together physically. I do understand your frustration, though. Malcolm drove me nuts about making love. I thought I was going to go crazy before it finally happened."

"What had to happen to make him give in?"

"I had to marry him."

Helena grunts her irritation. "Well, if that's what Cade is waiting on, we're never going to have sex."

"You wouldn't even consider marrying him?" I ask, finding her reaction strange.

"*Holy* matrimony?" Helena asks incredulously, looking at me like I may have lost my mind. "Do you honestly believe that God Himself would bless a union between Hell and one of His perfect little War Angels?"

"The War Angels aren't perfect," I tell her. "I thought you would have realized that while they were in Hell with you. None of God's creations are completely flawless, Helena. We've all made mistakes, and we'll all continue to make them for the rest of our lives. God doesn't only love us when we're perfect. He loves our imperfections, too."

"It must be nice to view the world so idyllically," Helena says, almost sounding envious of me. "To think you can be loved by just being yourself."

"Are you capable of loving anyone?" I ask her pointblank. Malcolm and I have had discussions concerning Helena's ability to love, but neither of us knows the truth. All we've been able to do is speculate on the possibility. But if Cade is truly Helena's soul mate, surely that means she has the capacity to feel such an emotion for someone.

Helena remains silent, but I can tell she's seriously considering my question.

"I don't know if I am or not," she states truthfully. It's then that I remember that my ability to know when someone is lying to me has returned.

Helena honestly doesn't know if she can love someone or not.

"Have you ever tried to love someone?" I have to ask.

"No one has ever given me a reason to care about them, much less love them."

"You know that Cade is in love with you, right?"

Helena gives a little shake of her head as she says, "He has no reason to love me except for this soul mate business."

"You should just accept his love and not question it, Helena. I think you want to love, but that you're afraid to let your walls down, even for him. Cade would never intentionally hurt you. That's not the type of person he is."

"I know that," Helena snaps as she looks away from me, but I can tell she's seriously contemplating my advice to her. I just hope she takes it.

Cade phases back in beside us, grinning from ear to ear as he holds his guitar in his right hand.

"Sorry it took me so long," he apologizes. "I hid my stash of picks from myself. It took me a while to remember where they were."

"It's fine, Cade," I say. "We were just having a little talk while we waited for you."

Helena looks in Cade's direction but not directly at him. Instead, she rests her gaze on the guitar he's holding.

"So you can really play that thing?" she questions, sounding intrigued by the possibility.

"Pretty well actually," Cade replies, grinning at her. "Let me show you."

Cade sets off towards the table the kids are sitting around. When Lucas sees the guitar in Cade's hands, he seems to know exactly what's about to happen. My son pulls out the chair he was using and instructs Cade to sit down on it.

I can't help but smile as I watch Lucas walk over to Bai, lean his head down next to hers, and whisper something in her ear. Bai lifts her hands to her mouth to hide an embarrassed giggle, but when Lucas holds his hand out to her, she readily accepts it and stands from her chair. Lucas leads her over to the front of the room and onto the dance floor. He places one hand on the side of her waist and lifts their still conjoined hands up to assume a proper stance for dancing. He looks over at Cade and nods his head, indicating that he's ready for the music to commence.

Cade strums the strings of his guitar before he begins to play a piece of music I've never heard before. It's a slow tune, filled with hope that acts as an unexpected balm on my aching heart.

I chance a glance in Helena's direction and notice her watching Cade with an intensity that makes me wonder what she's thinking in that moment. I have more hope now than I did at the beginning of the day that my plan will work. During our conversation about Cade, I felt Helena open up to me in a way she never has before. Perhaps being around him has made her realize that she can have a life away from her domain that isn't filled with so much hate and pain. I have to believe that there's a part of her that wants to have a normal life filled with the love and kindness of a good man.

Just as I'm about to look away to leave her with her thoughts, I watch in horror as everything I've worked so hard for that day is shattered to a point where I'm not sure it can ever be repaired.

Seemingly out of nowhere, Lucifer rushes Helena, grabs her by the upper arms, and pushes her until her back slams against the wall behind us with a distinct thud.

Cade's music abruptly stops, as does my hope for peace with Helena.

CHAPTER THIRTEEN

(Helena's Point of View)

"What are you planning?" Lucifer yells at me, his eyes wild with madness. "I know you're up to something!" He pulls me forward just enough to slam me back up against the wall again, this time even harder. "Tell me what you're about to do to Anna!"

I smile at Lucifer because I catch a glimpse of the old bastard in him resurfacing. Nothing would make me happier than to see him revert to the man who brought humanity to the brink of extinction with the Great War.

"Wouldn't you like to know," I mock with a low, throaty laugh.

There was a time when this sort of tactic from him might have made me bow to his will and obey him…but not any longer.

"You don't control me anymore, old man," I taunt haughtily. "I'm not even sure you ever truly did."

"Tell me what you're going to do!" he demands again.

I feel him pull me forward, presumably to slam me up against the wall again, but he never gets the chance to complete the action.

Like my knight in shining armor, I watch as Cade grabs Lucifer by the shoulders and pulls him off me.

"Stay away from her, Lucifer!" Cade warns as he comes to stand between me and my father like a protective barrier. "This is not the time or the place for you to attack her!"

"We're out of time, you fool!" Lucifer rails. "And what kind of War Angel are you to take up for that thing? You know what she's capable of, don't you? She's a creature that thrives on the misery of others. If you think she can love you, you're deluding yourself with a romantic fantasy that will *never* happen. All she cares about is herself and destroying humanity any way she can. Has she even told you that she's given Liana one of her seals?"

"Yes, she did," Cade answers.

"You know what she's done to the one God sent you to defend, yet you still want to protect the one person who is a threat to her? I thought you cared about Anna more than that, Cade. How can you love someone who has made Liana hate her own mother?"

I see Cade's shoulders stiffen after Lucifer's revelation. I have to admit that I'm clueless about what he's referring to.

And then... everything falls into place.

When I look over Cade's shoulder at Anna, our eyes meet, and I can see the depth of her pain. I didn't know it would happen. I didn't know Liana would be able to channel how I felt about her mother through our new bond, but I consider it an unexpected gift.

"Why would Liana hate Anna?" Cade asks, still unable to comprehend the connection. Sometimes, he's just too naïve to fathom the strength of my hate for Anna.

"You're an idiot," Lucifer spits out as if he's talking to a dog. "They're connected to one another by the seal, you fool! Not only has Helena taken the love of her only daughter away from Anna, but she's planning something that will take her crown away from her, too!"

As I keep my gaze fixed on Anna, I see her wince as if Lucifer's words have caused her physical pain.

All that talk about wanting to forge a peace between us makes sense now. I knew she was up to something and now I know what. Anna couldn't care less about me, but in order to win the love of her daughter back she had to lower her moral standards and attempt to befriend me. Too bad Lucifer just ruined her plan. Now I know nothing she says can be taken seriously. It wasn't as if I had planned for us to become bosom buddies anyway. After the events of this afternoon play out, she'll return to hating me again. It was foolish of her to think there could ever be an everlasting peace between us. Our relationship with one another can never be a tranquil one.

"How can you stand there and defend a creature who does nothing but cause pain and misery to the people you're supposed to be protecting?" Lucifer demands of Cade.

"Maybe a better question is, how can you stand there and blame her for what she is," Cade counters caustically. "You made her yet you refuse to accept the fact that she's your daughter, too! Perhaps if you had been a better father to her, she wouldn't be as broken as she is now!"

"That *thing* is *not* my child. I only have one daughter and that's Anna!" Lucifer stridently declares.

"It's no use, Cade," I tell him. "He'll never see me as anything but the worst part of himself he would rather forget about."

I push myself off the wall and walk up to Cade, touching him gently on the arm.

"Let's go," I say. "I think we've disturbed Lucas' party quite enough."

Without waiting for his consent, I phase Cade to my bedroom in Hell and seal it off so Lucifer can't follow. All I need right now is for him to come down here and continue to prattle on about the virtues of my saintly sister.

Cade turns around to face me.

"What was he talking about?" he asks, anger tinging each of his words. "Are you planning to hurt Anna? You promised me you wouldn't."

"I have no intentions of causing her any physical harm," I declare in exasperation. "I do have a plan that may cause her to lose her crown, but you've known for a while now that I'm the one who organized Catherine Amador's comeback to retake the Cirrus throne. That has never been a secret."

"Considering how violently Lucifer attacked you, he seems to believe you're about to do something else to help your plan along. Is that true?"

"Yes, but it's nothing that concerns you, dear heart. Political games are played this way. You have to do certain things to cause a response. You shouldn't worry about it. No one you care about will be hurt. I can promise you that much."

"But you've already hurt Anna," he points out angrily. "Liana hates her mother now because she's connected to you. It has to be tearing Anna's heart to pieces."

"There's nothing I can do about that," I quip.

"Did you know it would happen?"

"I had no idea!" I profess honestly. "But I'm also not going to stand here and tell you that I'm unhappy about it. Granted it's a side-effect I didn't see coming, but I'm not about to lie and say I'm sorry it's happened."

"Where does all of your hate for Anna stem from? Is it because Lucifer loves her and not you?"

Cade's question brings me up short. I pause to think about my answer. I should automatically deny that I need or desire Lucifer's acceptance and love but would that be a lie, even to myself? Why *do* I hate Anna so much? She's never done anything to me to warrant my hatred. I've always been the aggressor in our relationship. The only time she's ever truly tried to kill me was that night in Cirrus when I unleashed my hell-spawn in her city. Even then she had to know stabbing me with her sword, even attempting to use her powers on me, wouldn't end my life. It was a sad attempt by a desperate woman.

Maybe Cade has hit upon a truth with his question. I'm not completely sure.

"That's probably part of the reason," I admit. "When you live with someone for as long as I did Lucifer, you tend to feel a bit territorial about their relationships with others."

"Can't you see that you're just punishing Anna because you feel slighted by Lucifer? She reached out to you today…"

"Only because she's trying to find a way to make her daughter not hate her as much," I interrupt. "She doesn't want to be my friend because she likes me."

"It may be her motivation, but I think it should prove to you that she's willing to give you a chance."

"Give me a chance," I scoff with a roll of my eyes. "I'm not sure why you think having Anna as a friend is even important to me."

"Because I believe you want friends. I think you want people in your life you can count on, but you're too scared to admit it. Lucifer's rejection has damaged you more than you might want to acknowledge, Helena." Cade takes a step forward. "But I'm not rejecting you. I know who and what you are, and I accept the fact that there are things about you that I don't like. I also accept the fact that you may never change."

"Even if I wanted to change," I tell him, "I don't think I can."

"And I accept that fact," he says. "All I ask is that you think about how what you do affects me, too."

"Think about you?" I ask, confused by his request. "What is that supposed to mean?"

"When you scheme against those I care about," he says, "I want you to consider how it will make me feel."

"And why should I care about how my actions affect you?"

"Because I think you want what we have growing between us to work out as much as I do."

"Stop listening to the idiot. He just wants to change us into something he can love without feeling guilty about it."

I look over Cade's shoulder and see the mirror image of myself standing a few feet away.

"Go away," I tell her.

Cade glances over his shoulder to look for the person I'm addressing.

He looks back at me and asks, "Who are you talking to?"

It's only then that I realize the other me is simply a figment of my imagination.

"I'm not a figment," she tells me irritably, crossing her arms over her chest as she stares at me with an air of disapproval. "I'm just the sensible part of you that comes out when you're about to do something stupid. You need to throw this guy out of your life and concentrate on what's about to happen."

"Helena?" Cade asks. "What is it? What's wrong?"

I shake my head. "Nothing. Come on." I take hold his hand and quickly phase us out of Hell.

I transport us to a spot I know no one else will think to search for us. Our cemetery.

I feel my body instantly relax as we stand amongst the graves. The quiet of the place calms my nerves and brings a sense of peace to my heart.

"Walk with me," I practically order, tugging him along to stay by my side.

We walk for a long time without talking. Occasionally I stop to read a headstone, but I never linger for more than a minute. Thirty minutes go by and still Cade doesn't say a word. He simply allows me some time to think about what he said to me.

I begin to wonder if I should stop my plan and find another way to disgrace Anna. Even if I wanted to put an end to it, I'm not sure there's time. Silas and his men have probably already started the countdown and found a safe place to lay low until it's time for him to make his broadcast and have the rebellion angels enact the second part of our plan. I have no idea where they are right now or how to contact them. I glance over at Cade as we walk, wondering how he'll react when he finds out what I've done. I know he won't be pleased, but will he see me as a monster he no longer wants to be around once he learns the truth?

I really can't take that chance.

I stop walking and turn to him. "I need you to do something for me."

"What?"

"I want you to stay in Hell for the next couple of days. Will you do that for me?"

"Why?" he asks, obviously suspicious of my motives.

"I can't tell you that right now. I promise I will but, if you care about me like you say you do, I need you to do this for me. Will you?"

Cade studies me with a critical eye for a moment before saying, "Either you're hiding me from something or you're hiding something from me. Which is it? If you answer that question truthfully, I'll do as you ask."

"I'm hiding something from you," I confess, but it's the truth and he's already promised to do what I want as long as I didn't lie to him.

"And how mad will I be when I discover what you're hiding from me?"

"I'm guessing very mad," I say confidently. "Otherwise, I wouldn't be trying to hide it."

"Who are you hurting this time?" he questions in a low voice that tells me he wants to know the answer and yet he doesn't.

"No one you know personally," I promise.

Cade sighs heavily and looks away from me. I'm not certain if he just can't bring himself to look at me or if he needs a moment to collect his thoughts. It's probably a little bit of both.

When he does look back at me, he says, "Will I be there alone or will you be staying with me?"

"Most of the time I'll be with you, but tomorrow morning I have an appointment that I have to keep. I'll need to leave you alone for an hour, maybe two at the most."

"I don't like being there," he tells me candidly. "It makes me feel uncomfortable."

To be honest, I don't particularly want to stay in Hell right now either. My stubborn subconscious has more control over my mind while I'm there than I like. The only advantage to keeping Cade in Hell is that no one can enter into my domain unless I allow them to, and he can't leave without my permission.

"If I let you stay somewhere else," I say thinking of a compromise, "do you promise not to leave?"

"Where else would we go?"

"Back to planet Sierra," I say. "I'm sure Evelyn has a place we can use while we're there."

"I would much rather stay there than Hell," Cade replies in relief. "Are you sure she won't mind putting us up for a while?"

"Of course she won't," I say, secretly thinking that even if she did it wouldn't matter. She'll do what I want or face the consequences of defying me.

"In fact, we should go there now and get you …"

I suddenly drop to my knees, clutching my chest with both hands.

"Helena!" Cade yells in dismay as he kneels down beside me, grasping my arms to prevent me from toppling over onto the ground and landing onto my face. "What's wrong?"

I take in a large gulp of air, unable to answer his question as I begin to absorb a cascade of new energy. I let out a cry that's a mixture of both pain and ecstasy. I know exactly what's happening. Silas and the others have set the first part of my plan into motion, and now I'm reaping the rewards from their effort: an infusion of new souls has just entered Hell.

CHAPTER FOURTEEN

(Anna's Point of View)

As soon as Cade and Helena phase out of the room, we decide to leave Cirrus and continue Lucas' party in our New Orleans home. It doesn't feel safe to stay in my cloud city, considering the fact that it's been the main target of both Helena and the rebellion angels twice now. If what Lucifer has been told is true, we need to brace ourselves for whatever is coming next. I knew Helena would probably take advantage of our split attention since the babies were born, but I suppose I hoped that by trying to befriend her we could move beyond her vendetta against me.

Now, Helena knows I was only being friendly to her because I was trying to help Liana. No, that's not exactly true. If I'm being completely honest, I was trying to help myself. I wanted to make Helena stop hating me enough to give me a chance to form a relationship with my child. I don't see that as a possibility now. Not unless Helena has an unexpected revelation that makes her more amenable to a truce between us.

Once we have the party set up in the dining room Lucifer pulls Malcolm and me aside, asking us to follow him down to the kitchen.

"There's someone you need to talk to," my father tells me. "Andre and Jered have been keeping an eye on him until you could go speak with him yourself."

Lucifer phases to the kitchen, giving us no other option but to phase to follow him.

Once there, I'm surprised to find Baal present. When I first met Baal, he inhabited the body of Rafael Rossi, former Emperor of Alto and Bianca's husband. Rafael's corpse was found in the rubble of Alto, after Baal and Mammon tried to destroy it. Baal then assumed the body of Ryo Mori who was recently elected Emperor of Cirro, which is the cloud city that controls all of Asia.

"Why the hell are you in my house?" Malcolm asks him coarsely.

Enduring

Baal rises from his chair at the table, hands raised as if to prove he comes in peace.

"I only came here to give you the warning about Helena's plans," he says. "That's all. I swear. Like I told Lucifer, all I know is that she has something big arranged for later today and that it's supposed to force Anna to abdicate the throne of Cirrus."

"She didn't give you any details?" I ask.

"I never met with Helena personally. She sent Levi to tell me to be ready to back them up tomorrow."

"Tomorrow?" I ask in confusion. "I thought whatever she has planned was supposed to happen today."

"It is," Baal verifies, "but after it happens the Empress and Emperor of Nimbo will send invitations out to all the cloud city leaders to attend a special meeting in the Mars pavilion tomorrow morning. Presumably, they're going to ask you to step down and hand over control of Cirrus to Catherine."

"Well, that's never going to happen," Malcolm grumbles. "But I still don't understand why you're here telling us this. Why risk betraying Helena?"

"She threatened Bianca's life if I don't cooperate with their plan," Baal tells us. "I didn't like it, but I'm not strong enough to fight and win against her. Your wife is the only one I know of who might be able to take her down before she becomes even more powerful."

"So you genuinely care that much about Bianca?" I ask him, unable to hide my misgivings about such an occurrence being true. "Enough to risk your own life to give us this information?"

"I know I'm a bastard," Baal freely admits with a nonchalant shrug, "and I don't deserve someone like Bianca, but I also can't help the way I feel when I'm around her. Do I love her? I'm not sure. I think I do. All I know is that I've placed her life in danger by caring about her, and I need your help to ensure she stays alive. I know you and

193

S. J. West

Bianca are friends. All I ask is that you help me protect her from Helena. I'll do whatever you want as long as you can guarantee that you'll keep Bianca safe."

"I can't make a promise like that," I tell him, "but I can assure you that she'll be under my protection until this war with Helena is over."

"I've never heard you call it a war before," Malcolm says to me.

"She's threatening our family and my city," I reply. "I don't see how we can think of it any other way now."

I look at Lucifer. "Have you heard anything from our contact within the rebellion angels about this?"

"You probably won't," Baal tells us before Lucifer has a chance to answer. "Helena is keeping those in the know to a very small number. Levi wasn't even told what's going to happen today until right before he came to see me. I could tell he wanted to fill me in on the details, but he fears Helena as much as or more than any of us. He kept his mouth shut because he doesn't want to get on her bad side any more than he already is."

"Our contact hasn't reached out to us," Lucifer tells me, answering my initial question.

There's a moment of silence before Baal asks, "I don't suppose Gabe has had a vision of what will happen?"

"That isn't his name now," I say tersely. "And don't ever call him by that name again or, so help me God, I will tear your tongue from your mouth. I refuse to have him learn about his past life through you. His name is Lucas and, no, he hasn't mentioned having a new vision recently."

"You know, I owe… the other version of Lucas…a debt of gratitude," Baal says. "He showed me my death once. It was supposed to be by your hands, Anna."

194

"There's still time for that prophecy to be fulfilled," I threaten.

"No," Baal replies, with a small shake of his head. "I'm certain I've changed my fate. I'm sure you've been told that not every vision he has is destined to come to pass. That's where freewill comes into play. There are parts of our destiny that we can alter if we're willing to change ourselves enough to do it."

"And you think you've changed?" I scoff, not seeing a difference in him yet. "Have you already forgotten that you colluded with Mammon and Levi to kill me not so long ago?"

"No. I haven't forgotten," Baal says with a note of regret. "It was a last-ditch effort on my part and one I couldn't refuse to take a role in at the time. I thought if I could kill you first that maybe, just maybe, I could save myself that way."

"And now you believe you're going to prevent your death by becoming my ally?"

"Yes," Baal says bluntly. "You're not someone who kills for joy like Helena does. You actually have a moral code that you live by. Look, I'm not a good person. I freely admit that, but for Bianca's sake I'm willing to become the man she needs."

"Does Bianca know this yet?" I ask apprehensively. The thought of Baal desiring a relationship with one of the few people I call a friend doesn't sit well with me. Yet he seems so earnest in his feelings for her. Do I have a right to keep them apart if it's what Bianca wants? Who am I to decide what her fate should be?

"I've been writing to her since I took the Cirro throne," Baal tells me.

"Love letters?" I ask in surprise.

"No. I didn't want to scare her off. I've mostly been asking questions about how she's implementing your initiative to share cloud city technology with the down-world. It's a topic she feels as passionately about as you do. We've communicated quite a bit over the last few months about the subject."

"I'm surprised you've been so patient with her," I reply, truly meaning my words. I find it remarkable that a prince of Hell would take the time to woo anyone, much less a human. Considering Baal's history, it seems strange that he finally found someone to love more than he does himself. "Is Bianca your soul mate?" I have to ask.

Baal shakes his head. "No. She isn't. And before you ask, I can't explain why I have these feelings for her. I just do."

Ethan and Roan phase into the room. From their frantic expressions, I immediately know something is wrong and dread hearing what they have to report.

"It's... happened," Ethan tells me in a halting voice, looking shell-shocked. "She's implemented her plan."

"What has she done?" Lucifer is quick to ask.

"I think you all need to see it for yourselves in order to believe it," Ethan replies, coming to stand closer to Malcolm and me.

He pulls up the sleeve of his black War Angel jacket and runs his hand over his wrist to bring up the controls of his holographic display. After pressing a few buttons, a news report begins to play above his palm.

At first, I'm not sure what it is I'm looking at until the newscaster from Nacreous explains.

"The carnage is widespread," the woman explains in a tearful voice. "From the reports we're getting in, there are no survivors. The citizens of Virga have been massacred due to the explosion of a weapon most of us thought had been destroyed after the travesty of the Great War. Eyewitnesses on the ground have confirmed that they saw a nuclear device explode inside the cloud city of Virga. Parts of the Virga down-world city of Sydney have also been destroyed due to the debris field created as the cloud city disintegrated in the air. Citizens of Sydney, if you are able to see me, please evacuate the city as quickly as possible. The less exposure you have to the nuclear fallout the..."

The news broadcast is immediately cut off by another transmission. The face of a handsome young man stares back at us all. His cold, hard stare makes him look deadly even before he speaks.

I hear the scraping of Jered's chair as he stands. His eyes are fixed on the face in the display as he whispers, "Silas."

"Greetings," Silas says to the world watching him, "I'm sorry to interrupt, but I have an important message to relay to you all about what just happened in Virga."

Silas stops talking as another video begins to play. The shot was taken from a high vantage point and we can all see the cloud city of Virga as it once was. A blinding flash of light erupts from the center of the city. Even though it's only a video, I instinctively shield my eyes from the glare. Once it's passed, I lower my hand and watch as the city is filled with grey smoke that can't escape Virga's protective force field. Eventually, the force field fails and the proud city of Virga falls as a pile of rubble to the ground beneath it.

"As you can see," Silas says rather calmly when he comes back into view, "the cloud city of Virga has been destroyed. I know many of you are asking the same questions. Why has this happened and who is responsible? I'm here to give you the answers to both of those queries."

The angle of the video changes as it zooms out to show Silas dressed in a War Angel uniform, with four other men similarly dressed standing directly behind him. I gasp in surprise when I see the Cirrus palace in the backdrop of the shot. Out of the corner of my eye, I notice Jered phase to Cirrus.

"The Emperor of Virga was a staunch voice against uniting the peoples of the down-world and cloud cities. His unwillingness to join Empress Anna of Cirrus in her cause and blatant disrespect of her and her reign is what doomed him and his citizens to utter annihilation." Silas takes a menacing step closer to the camera as he stares directly into the lens. "To those of you who still remain on Earth, listen to me very carefully.

Anyone who opposes Empress Anna Devereaux will meet the same fate as Virga. Either bow to her will, or die. The choice is yours."

The video feed ends and returns to the original female news broadcaster, who now looks stunned and uncertain as to how to respond to what we all just witnessed.

I look away from the newscast when Jered phases back to the kitchen. He shakes his head at me, silently letting me know that Silas wasn't in Cirrus. The video we just saw was more than likely pre-recorded.

"Please forgive us for the interruption of that video feed from what looked like the interior of... Cirrus? Is that right?" The newscaster directs her question to someone off-camera. We all see her nod as if she's receiving confirmation. "We will be back with more information on this travesty as soon as it becomes available." The woman pauses again and her mouth goes slack with surprise. "This just in. Apparently, the cloud city of Stratus is also under attack."

A live video feed appears on the display, showing the remnants of what looks like a public transporter terminal within Stratus. There are people stumbling around with gashes all over them and dead bodies lay strewn across the area like broken dolls. We watch as people dressed in War Angel uniforms begin to fire into the crowd with plasma pistols, a weapon that has been outlawed since the Great War. The screams of those fleeing the area are quickly cut off as one of the attackers shoots directly at the camera filming the footage.

When the newscaster comes back on the display, you can tell that she's so traumatized by what she just saw that she isn't able to think of anything to say. The newsfeed ends as tears begin to stream down her face, mirroring the sadness of the world in that moment.

"I don't understand what's happening," she sobs. "Please, someone, help us."

Ethan closes his hand to end the transmission and lowers his arm.

Enduring

A weighty silence caused by shock settles over the room as we all try to absorb what we just witnessed.

"I knew she could be cruel," I finally say, attempting to wrap my mind around what Helena has done, "but I never imagined she would go this far." I look up at Malcolm. "We have to send people to Stratus to help. Those have to be rebellion angels that Helena is using to masquerade as War Angels."

"We'll go immediately to see what we can do to get rid of the rebels," Ethan offers.

"Take your jackets off," Malcolm orders. "Otherwise, people will think you're there to kill them, not help them."

Both Ethan and Roan quickly strip their jackets off and toss them onto the floor. They're bare-chested but that will have to do. Time is of the essence.

"We'll grab the others from the party," Ethan tells me. "As soon as things are under control in Stratus, we'll come back and report what we know."

Ethan and Roan phase out of the room to gather the other War Angels.

I turn my attention to Jered, who looks completely devastated after seeing his son accuse me of being the one who orchestrated the total annihilation of Virga. When his eyes meet my gaze, I can see the guilt he feels.

"I've failed you both," he says to me remorsefully.

"You haven't failed me," I tell him resolutely. "And Silas is simply following Helena's orders. You know that, Jered. Now is not the time for self-pity. We have to find a way to repair the damage she's caused."

"This can't be fixed," Lucifer says incredulously. "You don't have the power to bring five million people back to life, Anna! She murdered them in cold blood and has placed the blame of their extermination squarely on your shoulders. The humans were already wary of you and your War Angels. How do you think they're going to feel about you now?"

"We'll just have to explain what's really going on," I argue, trying to remain rational.

"The damage has been done!" Lucifer argues, throwing his hands up. "Even if you somehow convince people that you weren't behind all of this, the image of Silas and those others dressed as your personal guard will always remain in the back of their minds. You'll never be able to erase what everyone in the world just watched."

"There has to be a way to prove that Helena was behind all of this," I say.

"There is no proof," Lucifer states emphatically. "It'll just be your word against hers, and right now the video evidence proves that your War Angels are behind all of this."

"But they're not my War Angels."

"We know that, but the world doesn't. You have two thousand War Angels under your command. Very few people know what they all look like," Lucifer reasons.

"Then what are we going to do?" I ask, having a hard time coming up with a solution to solve our problem.

"Anna!" I hear Kyna yell out to me.

I turn around to find her and Olivia Ravensdale, Empress of Nacreous, walking down the hallway to the kitchen.

"Oh, my dear," Olivia says, giving me a much-needed hug as soon as she reaches me. "What can we do to help? Ethan told us what's happened to Virga and the chaos transpiring now in Stratus."

"I think sending help to those who need it should be our first priority," I say as Olivia pulls away.

"I could kill Lorcan, or Abaddon, whoever he is, for this mess," Kyna growls. "You and I both know he's allowing Helena to kill the people in my cloud city just so they can place all the blame on you and your War Angels."

I nod. "I know. Hopefully Ethan and the others can get them out of Stratus before they do any more harm."

Olivia lifts her left arm to look at something on her wrist. I presume it's a message on her personal holographic display. She lets out a heavy sigh after she reads it and then looks up at me.

"The Emperor and Empress of Nimbo have called for an emergency meeting to take place in the Mars pavilion first thing tomorrow morning," she tells us.

"Well, we knew that was coming," Malcolm grouses. "Helena's scheme to force Anna to step down as empress is playing out exactly like she planned."

"I'm afraid that's not all Helena can ask for from Anna. She will also be within her rights as a royal to ask for a trial," Olivia says, placing an even heavier burden on my heart.

"And if they convict me, what would happen?" I ask.

"At most, you would be exiled to an off-world planet to live out the rest of your life. She could ask for your execution, but it would never get that far. Bianca and I would vote against it."

"For what it's worth," Baal chimes in behind me, "so would I."

"For an execution of a royal to take place," Olivia explains, "it has to be a unanimous decision."

"That's good to know," I say, "but I can't be permanently exiled from Earth. If I am, Helena will have free rein here. We can't let that happen, Olivia."

"I completely agree," Olivia says. "Let's see how the meeting goes tomorrow. Maybe we can convince the others that you've been set up by a third party."

"Would it do any good for me to call Helena out?" I ask.

"And blame her for this?" Olivia questions skeptically. "No. If there's one thing you absolutely mustn't do it's that."

"But she's the one responsible for all this," I argue.

"I understand that, my dear, but the world will simply view it as you trying to push the blame on a woman who has done nothing but be courteous and benevolent to her people since she married Zuri Solarin and became empress. The people of Nimbo adore her because she seems so down to earth to them. She has played her role as a compassionate empress perfectly. If you try to lay the blame for this on her, everyone will view it as a lame attempt on your part to cast the guilt onto someone else."

"Can we at least say that the people in the broadcast are a rebel faction?" Malcolm suggests. "That's true."

"I think that's your only option," Olivia agrees. "You'll need to convince the others that you have no control over these people, and that they are acting of their own accord."

"But people will still doubt me, won't they?" I ask, knowing my standing among the other royals has been forever tarnished by acts that were beyond my control. "I was already having a reputation problem with the other cloud cities. This may just put the nail in the coffin of any reform to the down-world I wanted to accomplish."

"I wish I could find a way to kick Lorcan off the throne," Kyna says heatedly, placing a hand on her swollen abdomen, as if the action will calm her.

"We'll figure something out one of these days," I promise her. "You're the rightful ruler of Stratus. You always have been."

Brutus phases into the room and I immediately see Kyna's shoulders relax. I'm not even sure she was aware how stressed she was becoming over the situation.

Like a good husband, Brutus immediately walks over to his wife and takes her into his arms.

"Are you all right?" he asks worriedly, slowly rubbing one hand up and down her back in a soothing manner. "I just heard what happened."

"I want to kill Lorcan," she states, "but other than that I'm doing fine."

Brutus rests a cheek on top of Kyna's head as he continues to hold her close.

"Brutus," I say, "why don't you take Kyna home so she can get some rest? All of this stress can't be good for her or the baby."

"Are you sure you don't need me?" Brutus asks.

"We've got things handled," I assure him. It's not exactly the truth, but it's not a lie either.

"I'm afraid I need to be leaving as well," Olivia tells us regrettably. "I'm sure the people of my cloud city are worried they'll be attacked at any moment. I need to go and reassure them that they're safe."

"I understand," I say, leaning in to kiss Olivia on the cheek. "Thank you for coming today. I know Lucas appreciated you taking time out of your busy schedule to celebrate his birthday with us."

"It was my pleasure," she says with a weak smile. "I just wish the day could have ended on a better note than this."

"If you don't mind," my papa says, walking over to Olivia, "I would like to escort you home."

Olivia's smile instantly changes to a pleased one. "I don't mind at all, Andre. In fact, I would appreciate that a great deal."

As my papa and Olivia use their personal teleporters to travel to Nacreous, I return my attention to Jered. Of anyone else left in the room, he's the one I'm most worried about. It had to have been hard on him to see his son play the perfect pawn in Helena's strategy to disgrace me in front of the world. Lucifer had been right in his earlier assessment. Even if I'm able to find a way to prove my innocence, there will always be people in the world who will never fully trust me again. In the back of their minds they'll see the destruction of Virga and always believe that I was behind it, no matter what I say or do in the future.

"Jered," I say, "do you think there's any way you can find Silas and speak to him? Maybe if we could convince him to renounce Helena and tell the world that she put him up to bombing Virga, it will prove to everyone that I'm innocent."

"Even if I could find him, he won't listen to me, Anna," Jered replies sadly. "He hates me more than anyone else. I'm the last person to go to him and ask for a favor. Helena has warped his mind to a point where I'm not sure he can ever be saved."

I sigh, knowing Jered is probably right, but I had to ask.

Silas is now the face of this atrocity against humanity. If he came forward and told the truth, people just might believe him. Then again....

"It might be pointless anyway," I say, realizing a simple fact. "People would probably assume I asked him to take the fall to save myself and my crown. It's like I'm damned either way I turn."

"There's a way out of this," Malcolm assures me as he places a comforting hand on the small of my back. "We just have to figure out what it is."

"We need to kill Helena," Jered says in a cold, distant voice. "She needs to die for what she's done." He looks at me with a gaze as detached as his words. "The sword you brought back from alternate Earth. Where is it?"

"Why?" I ask, feeling a little frightened of Jered in that moment. I don't feel scared for my own safety, but I am fearful he'll do something reckless that will place his life in danger.

"It might be the only way to kill her," he says. "She has to be stopped before she ruins even more lives!"

"How is it going to look," Lucifer begins, "if you, one of Anna's most trusted friends, kills the Empress of Nimbo? Do you imagine people will just look the other way? Whether we like it or not, the world adores Helena because they believe she's on their side. In their eyes, Anna is the enemy. Anything you do against Helena right now will only serve her needs and prove to the world that Anna is the one they need to be frightened of. Is that what you want, Jered? To place Anna in a worse position than she's already in?"

"No," Jered says tersely, "of course it isn't. But how else do you expect us to get rid of Helena if it isn't in a coffin?"

"I don't have an answer for you," Lucifer admits. "But a resolution to this problem will present itself in time."

"How can you say that so confidently?" I have to ask.

"Because I don't believe my father would allow you to suffer like this for no good reason or for very long," Lucifer states as a matter of fact. "I'm sure He has a plan. We'll simply have to bide our time and handle things as best we can until He decides to share it with us."

It raises my spirits to see my father so full of faith in God's design for the future. I take heart in that fact and silently pray that God does indeed have a plan.

CHAPTER FIFTEEN

We do our best not to ruin the rest of Lucas' party. Malcolm and I decide against telling the children what happened to Virga or the reason the War Angels all had to leave so suddenly. They will learn the truth soon enough and now isn't the time to bring up such horrors. The short period of time that children are able to remain innocent of the world's troubles is precious. Once lost, a child is no longer a child and will have to face the fact that society is filled with dreadful acts of cruelty. I realize that Lucas has lost more of his innocence concerning the state of the world than most children, but I still feel as though I need to shield him from its terrors for as long as possible.

Brutus comes back near evening to take Bai and her brothers home with him. I have to admit that I'm slightly surprised Linn didn't ask him to fetch them earlier in the day when Virga was destroyed. I was, after all, the focus of Helena's diabolical plan. With me out of the picture, she will finally be able to absorb the Earth into her dominion. In a twisted sort of way, I can't help but admire her tenacity. She is at the precipice of having everything she wants, leaving me with nothing. Not even my good name.

While I nurse the babies in my bedroom, Malcolm and Mason decide to go to Stratus to see if there is anything they can do to help. We haven't received any reports from our War Angels since they left, and I fear the worst. Jess stays behind to lend me her support and help me deal with Liana. Jess has to hold the baby rattle Lilly gave me over my daughter's head in order to keep her calm enough to take milk from my breast. It seems to be a reluctant act on Liana's part, and the only reason she's allowing me to touch her is so she can fill her belly with milk. I suppose I should take comfort in knowing that she at least has basic survival instincts.

"Maybe you should let me try to kill Helena," Jess suggests. From the fire of hate in her eyes, I can tell she would do just that if I gave her my permission.

"It's a tempting proposal," I sigh, wishing I could take her up on the offer. "But we've already decided an attempted assassination would only help prove to the rest of the world that I can't be trusted."

"There has to be something we can do," Jess says in frustration, looking pensive as she continues to move the rattle above Liana's head. "And this little one, well, she's just as precious as they come. We have to figure out a way to change her attitude towards you. I absolutely refuse to leave before we think of something that will help the two of you have a real relationship. I adore my sons, but my daughter is my heart. It's like having a mini-me to pal around with all the time. I want you to have that connection with Liana, and I'm not going back to Heaven until we find a solution to this problem."

"Thank you," I say, unable to hold back a sob of relief. "You just don't know how much that means to me, Jess."

"Yes, I do," she replies, reaching out to cup one side of my face. "Listen to me very carefully, Anna Devereaux. We will find a way to break Helena's hold over your little girl. You have my promise on that, and I never go back on a promise. I'm too stubborn for my own good, which will most definitely work in your favor."

I nod my head and try to temper my volatile emotions into something I can control.

"I'm so grateful you're here," I tell her. "Malcolm's been wonderful about helping me deal with all of this, but it's nice to be able to talk to another woman who understands what it means to be a mother."

"Men can't fully grasp the bond that forms between a mother and her children while she's pregnant with them. Not to say that they love our children any less than we do. I think they love them just as fiercely but when you physically carry a baby inside you for so many months, there's a connection built during that time that can't be duplicated any other way."

"I know what you mean," I reply. I look down at Liam and Liana as they continue to suckle. No matter what might happen in the future, I know I will always love them and do everything within my power to make sure they have happy lives.

After the babies are through nursing, Jess helps me with changing their diapers. She has to continue to use the rattle with Liana as I handle her. In hindsight, I probably should have asked someone Helena doesn't hate to help me take care of Liana. As I'm tucking them into the middle of the bed I share with Malcolm, there's a soft knock on the door.

"Would you mind answering that?" I ask Jess while I finish up with the twins. "I told Lucas to come to me if he had trouble falling asleep."

Jess walks over to the door and opens it.

"Well," she says, as if the person who knocked should have been here before now. "I wondered how long it would take the three of you to show up."

"We were waiting until the situation down here calmed down a bit," I hear my mother tell Jess, "but that doesn't seem to be coming any time soon, and we simply couldn't make ourselves wait any longer."

I quickly stand up straight, rush towards the door, and readily accept my mother's awaiting embrace. Lilly and Caylin are standing directly behind her, looking happy to see me but also worried about my welfare.

"Oh, Anna," my mother says, holding me tightly to her. "I wish there was something I could do to solve all of your problems."

I pull away slightly to look into her eyes, and immediately see how my tribulations are causing her distress.

"If I could just find a way to stop Liana from hating me," I say on the verge of tears, "I would be doing a lot better."

"We may be able to help with that," Lilly tells me. Her words are hopeful, but her tone is cautious.

"How?" I ask, desperately wanting to believe that the miracle I need is at hand.

"I said 'may'," Lilly cautions, looking uncertain that the solution I crave will be an easy one to obtain.

"My mom pretty much told God He had better have planned ahead and given you a way to stop Liana from channeling Helena's hate," Caylin tells me, sounding proud that her mother took up for me with the Almighty Himself.

"And did He?" I ask, daring to hope for a positive answer.

"He says everything you need is right here on Earth," Lilly tells me, looking uncertain about how I will accept the information.

"It's already here?" After Lilly nods, I ask, "I don't suppose He gave you more of a hint than that."

"No," Lilly replies, but she doesn't look overly concerned about her answer. "I don't think it's something that's hidden from you, though. From the way He sounded, you have everything you need in your possession to make it happen."

"Well, did He give you a hint as to what it might be? Is it an object? A certain food? A place I need to take her to?" A thousand possibilities run through my mind, but which one is the correct one?

Lilly shrugs her shoulders helplessly. "I'm sorry, sweetie. I just don't know. I wish I could be of more help, but I can only do so much with the information He was willing to share with me."

I let out a low growl in frustration. "I don't see why He didn't just tell you what needs to be done. Why does He have to be so aggravating most of the time?"

"He likes for His creations to think for themselves," my mother answers.

"Amalie is right," Caylin tells me. "I think He feels a sense of pride when we figure problems out on our own."

"Still," Jess chimes in, "a hint every once in a while wouldn't kill Him."

We stand there together in a moment of mutual silence, each considering what the solution to my problem could be.

"I don't know about the rest of you, but I want to see my grandbabies," my mom says.

I escort my Heavenly visitors to the bed where Liam and Liana are still sleeping soundly.

My mom leans down and does the customary oohing and ahhing over her grandchildren.

"Oh my goodness," Lilly says as she looks at the babies. "I forgot how adorable newborns are. And twins, no less! I hope you and Malcolm are ready for a few sleepless nights when they start to teethe."

"I haven't even thought that far ahead," I tell her. "With everything that's going on, the furthest I can think into the future is tomorrow."

Just as I turn away from Lilly, I see my mother leaning over Liana and picking her up.

"Mom, no!" I yell, but the warning comes a second too late.

As soon as my mother touches Liana, my daughter's eyes fly open and she begins to wail at the top of her lungs.

"Oh dear," my mother says, quickly pulling her hands away from Liana. "She certainly has a set of lungs on her."

"And a complete hatred of people Dad loves," I tell her, grabbing for the baby rattle Lilly gave me as a wedding gift. I sit down on the edge of the bed and begin tilting the rattle back and forth above Liana's head to calm her down.

"I didn't realize my gift would be quite so useful," Lilly tells me, sounding pleased. "Thank goodness I had it made for you."

As I continue to sway the rattle back and forth and watch my daughter's eyes follow its calming movements, I hear Jess gasp.

"That's it!" she exclaims excitedly. "It's been here the whole freaking time!"

I look up at her and notice she's staring at the baby rattle in my hand. It suddenly dawns on what she's referring to as the solution.

"The rattle?" I ask.

"Of course!" Lilly says as if she should have thought of it herself. "I wondered why He didn't put up more of a fight when I asked for it to be made. He knew you would eventually need it to help her."

When I stop moving the rattle, Liana begins to wail again.

"How is the rattle going to help her?" I ask. "I can't keep rattling it above her head for the rest of her life."

"No, you most certainly can't do that," my mother agrees, looking thoughtful about the situation. "Have you tried just letting her hold the rattle without making the balls inside it chime?"

I shake my head, because doing something like that never even occurred to me. Since Liana is already upset, I tuck the rattle between her torso and right arm to test out our new theory. Almost instantly, she quiets. When she looks up at me, I no longer see pure hatred in her eyes. In fact, she begins to gurgle contentedly as if nothing is wrong and she's seeing me for the first time. She begins to reach a hand out in an attempt to touch my face. The movement causes the rattle to fall away from her and roll onto the bed. Liana immediately drops her arm back down and begins to wail again as she stares at me.

I quickly retrieve the rattle and place it underneath her arm again. Liana stops crying, but I think her previous exertion is just too much for her. Her eyelids droop, and she's soon fast asleep again.

"Okay," I say quickly, thinking through what we've just learned, "the rattle seems to act as a buffer between Liana and Helena, but I can't very well tie the rattle to Liana's body all the time."

"What if you could?" Jess says. "What if that's exactly what you're supposed to do?"

I shake my head. "I can't do that to her, Jess."

"No, you're not understanding what I'm saying," Jess replies with a small shake of her head. "All this time we've been thinking you were meant to bring the sword from alternate Earth back here to kill Helena with it, and maybe that's one of its purposes, I don't know for sure. But what if you were meant to bring it back to help with this problem, too?"

"I'm sorry," I say. "I'm not following what you're trying to tell me."

"I think I do," Caylin says excitedly, grinning from ear to ear as she looks at Jess. "The sword has Heaven's fire, right?"

Jess nods excitedly. "Exactly!"

"And how does that help me?" I ask, listening closely to what they say next.

"That particular type of fire is the only one that can melt the metal that was used to make the rattle," Caylin says. "It's just like when we made the daggers to place the princes of Hell in stasis. We used the fire Jess and Leah were able to produce to melt the princes of Hell's crown pieces. Since the rattle was made in Heaven, too, we can use the fire the sword produces to melt it down into something Liana can wear all the time."

"Like a bracelet or a necklace," Jess suggest enthusiastically. "I know this will work, Anna! Everything inside me says it will."

I gently slip the rattle out from under Liana's arm and hand it to Jess.

"So how do we use the fire of the sword to transform this into something she can wear?" I ask.

Jess winks at me. "Luckily for you I happen to know an excellent blacksmith. I've used him before, so I know he does good work."

"Brutus." I smile, remembering Malcolm tell me once that Brutus used to make weapons.

"I'll grab the sword and have Jered take me over to Brutus' house," she says, already heading for the door. "Do you have a preference about the type of jewelry?"

"Maybe a necklace he can add links to as she grows up," I suggest.

"Hmm, I think a bracelet would be better for a baby," Lilly says. "A necklace could become tangled and cause her problems. Plus, it could just slip off her head accidentally."

"You make some good points," I agree. "Ok, a bracelet then."

"A magical bracelet coming right up!" Jess walks out the door to complete her mission as quickly as possible. I silently urge her to move faster.

"Do you think this will work?" I ask my mother, desperately needing her to tell me exactly what I want to hear.

"I know it will," she replies with a confident smile. "And not a moment too soon, because I want to be able to hold that little girl one day without her crying when I touch her."

"You and me both," I say, unable to hold back my tears of joy at discovering a possible solution to the problem. "I wish Malcolm was here so I could tell him about this."

My mother begins to eye Liam surreptitiously. "Now that little one won't cry if I pick him up, will he?"

I shake my head. "No. I think Liam has to be the sweetest baby to ever exist."

My mother smiles. "That's exactly what I thought about you when you were born."

"I think every mother thinks that way about her babies," Lilly says as she watches my mom lift a still-slumbering Liam up into her arms, lovingly cradling him to her.

"I know I did when Kate was born," Caylin agrees. She smiles as if remembering the first time she held her baby girl. "At the time, I couldn't imagine holding anything more perfect in my arms."

"I was a little surprised you didn't come down with Aiden," I say to Caylin.

"I wanted to give him some time alone with Liam," she tells me. "Andel was such a big part of his life. I didn't want him to feel like he had to split his attention between us."

"I'm thankful that God has assigned Aiden to Liam, but the fact that He felt like He needed to scares me," I acknowledge.

"I know you and Malcolm will raise the twins to be strong enough to handle anything that happens next," Lilly tells me. I try to absorb as much of her conviction as I can. Considering the events of the last few days, my supply of self-confidence is sorely lacking.

"I don't want to fail them," I admit.

"Every parent has the same exact fear," she tells me. "All you can do is raise them the best way you know how and hope that you've done enough to prepare them for their future. And," she says, looking at Caylin standing by her side, "you have to realize you can't protect them from everything, even if that's all you want to do." Lilly looks back at me. "I think one of the hardest lessons to learn is that sometimes you have to let your children fall in order to prove to themselves how strong they can be without you."

"I'm not sure I can do that," I say.

"You don't always get a choice."

There's a moment of silence as I think about Lilly's words to me. Considering the chaotic life Malcolm and I lead, I know our children will eventually have to learn how to deal with conflict on their own. Whether it's right or not, I know I will always try to protect them. It's just the way I am.

The door to the bedroom opens and Malcolm strides in with Lucifer by his side.

"I heard we had some visitors," Malcolm says cheerfully as he walks directly up to Lilly, lifting her up in his arms and twirling her around like a child would a doll.

Lilly giggles and hugs Malcolm around the neck.

There was a time when I might feel jealous watching Malcolm with Lilly, but not now. All I feel is happiness for my husband as he's reunited with one of his best friends and the woman who helped show him how to find his true self again.

"Like we wouldn't want to meet your children," Lilly admonishes as Malcolm places her back on her feet. "We had to come see the miracle babies. Tara is probably having a fit in Heaven right now because we had to leave her behind."

Malcolm turns to Caylin and gives her a hug. "I sort of thought you would have come down with Aiden when he was here."

Caylin smiles. "That's what Anna said. Like I told her, I wanted him to have all the time he needed to bond with Liam. You know how devastated he was when he thought Andel died that day in the Guf. I can't tell you how overcome with emotion he became when God told him the truth. I just wanted him to concentrate on Liam while he was here and have some time to cope with the fact that Andel is still alive through him."

I see Lucifer walk over to my mother, who is still holding Liam. He gives her a kiss on the cheek and places an arm around her shoulders as they both gaze down at my son.

"He's perfection," my mother whispers to him.

"That he is," my dad agrees, smiling faintly.

"Malcolm," I say, unable to hold my tongue any longer, "since you knew we had guests, I assume you saw Jess before you came up here."

"Yes," he says, coming to stand by my side. "She told us she had to go see Brutus about something, but didn't say what exactly. She just told us that you would fill us in on the details."

I quickly explain what we learned about the rattle, and the reason Jess was going over to Brutus' house at such a late hour.

If one person could mirror the light of the sun on his face, Malcolm did in that moment. He quickly pulled me into his arms and held me tightly to him.

"I told you my father would have a solution," Malcolm whispers to me.

"I know," I say, feeling a pang of guilt for doubting his words. "I just hope He has a plan to handle Helena, too."

"I'm sure He does." Malcolm kisses me softly on the side of my neck before letting me go. "We just have to have a little faith in Him."

I nod, knowing he's right.

"How are things in Stratus?" I ask, wanting to know the answer to my question but at the same time dreading to hear it. "Were the War Angels able to help get things under control?"

"Yes," Malcolm says before letting me go, "but there were still a lot of civilian casualties. The War Angels are still there trying to help the wounded, and take care of the dead."

"I'm surprised Lorcan is allowing them to stay," I say, wondering why the Emperor of Stratus isn't pitching a fit over my men cleaning up the mess Helena has caused in his city.

"Kyna's father pretty much told him to get the hell out of the way so they can help people," Malcolm tells me, sounding amused.

I've only met Kyna's biological father once. His name is Barclay Stewart, general of the Stratus Imperial Army. Apparently, Kyna's mother had an affair with the Stratus general when she was younger. No one talked about her infidelity openly, and Kyna's mother never confirmed the rumor about her alleged affair with the handsome general. But considering the striking resemblance between Kyna and Barclay (most notably their red hair and green eyes), everyone in Stratus assumed the affair occurred. After Kyna left Stratus and married Brutus, she confided to me that she began corresponding with her real father on a regular basis. Now that she is no longer under Lorcan's tyrannical hold, she's free to acknowledge Barclay as her kin.

"So Barclay knows it was actually the rebellion angels who attacked Stratus and not our War Angels," I say.

"Yes. He knows that now, and he's offered to come to Mars tomorrow to testify on your behalf," Malcolm tells me. "If he does that, we might have a chance of convincing the world that you also had nothing to do with the bombing in Virga. Barclay's an impartial witness. We have no direct ties to him, so what he tells the others should be believed."

"Do you think Lorcan will even allow him to testify?" I have to ask.

"He isn't going to tell Lorcan what his plans are. He's just going to show up and do it."

"That's probably the smart way to go," I agree. "The less Lorcan knows the better."

"Exactly," Malcolm says.

We hear a gurgle come from the bed. Liana is waving her arms around like she doesn't want to be left out of the gathering. Malcolm leans down and picks her up, gingerly cradling her in his arms. For the first time, I don't envy how quiet she is with him.

I know I'll be able to hold my little girl soon and build a relationship with her that will last a lifetime and beyond.

Our heavenly guests stay with us for a little while longer, but eventually they have to leave. I hate to see them go, but I know Malcolm is right when he tells them I need to get a good night's rest. The gathering of the royals at the Mars pavilion the next day will be stressful, to say the least. I'm not totally convinced I will be able to sleep. To help me relax, Malcolm goes down to the kitchen and brings me back a cup of warm milk. I know he means well with his thoughtfulness, but the action makes me think of Cade. He's the one who always brought me warm milk at night, but now he's being forced to stay with Helena because of their bargain.

Or is he?

When we last saw Cade, before Lucifer attacked Helena at the party, he seemed happy. For me, finding joy around Helena seems like an impossibility, but I'm not her soul mate either.

After Malcolm hands me my cup of milk, he summarily lifts the cover off my body and begins to pull up my nightgown.

"Uh, what are you doing?" I ask him, finding his actions odd since the children are in the bed, too.

"Desmond gave me that miracle lotion to put on your belly," he explains, pulling out a small black plastic vial from the front pocket of his pants. "I know you've been wanting to use it."

"I could kiss you right now," I say, grinning from ear to ear.

Malcolm leans down until our noses are almost touching. "And what exactly is stopping you?"

After I kiss my husband for his consideration, he spreads a liberal amount of the lotion onto my still-swollen belly.

"How long will it take to work?" I ask eagerly.

"He said you should notice a significant difference by morning." Malcolm sets the now half-empty bottle on my nightstand.

As I continue to sip my milk, I look down at the babies lying on the bed. I long for the moment when I can hold Liana and show her just how much her mommy loves her.

"Do you think it will take Brutus very long to make the bracelet for Liana?" I ask.

"I don't think Brutus will sleep until after it's finished. In fact, I wager it will be complete before we leave for Mars tomorrow. I told Jess to bring it back as soon as it's made and to wake us up if she has to."

"Good," I say, feeling better knowing we'll get the bracelet as soon as it's available.

The milk seems to do the trick and relaxes me enough to yawn.

Malcolm takes the empty cup out of my hands and tucks me underneath the covers. After kissing me quickly on the lips, he says, "Go to sleep, my love. Get some rest."

As soon as I close my eyes, I drift off to the land of my own dreams. The next thing I know, Malcolm is gently shaking me awake.

"Anna, wake up. Jess is back."

I instantly sit up, which turns out to have been a very bad idea. I end up bumping heads with Malcolm, causing us both to say, "Ouch!"

"Good grief, woman," Malcolm complains, but I hear a touch of laughter in his voice over the incident. "I knew you had a hard head, but I didn't realize it was lethal."

As I'm rubbing the soreness from my forehead, I look around and see Jess standing a couple of feet away.

"Don't just stand there," I whisper urgently, not wanting to wake the babies. "Put it on her!"

Malcolm shifts down some to give Jess enough room to walk over to my side and lean over to put the little silver bracelet on Liana's right wrist. The bracelet isn't anything special. It's a simple thick band of pounded metal.

"Brutus asked me to tell you this bracelet is only temporary. He knew you wanted it as soon as possible and something plain was the easiest thing to do. He also told me to tell you that he can make you anything you want as she grows. He can melt down the metal at any time and make her new pieces of jewelry as she gets older."

Once Jess has the bracelet on Liana's wrist, I feel hesitant all of a sudden.

What if it doesn't work? What if she wakes up and begins to cry again?

I'm not sure my heart can take having my hopes and dreams dashed with such finality. This is my last chance at finding a solution to the problem Helena created.

"Pick her up, Anna," Malcolm encourages. When I look up at him, all I see is his confidence in our plan. "It'll work, my love. I know it will."

I take a deep breath, steeling myself against the possibility of Liana rejecting me yet again. I slide my hands underneath her and cautiously lift her into my arms. As I watch her face for any reaction, I see her little eyelids flutter open. She looks at me and proceeds to yawn. Her eyelids close again, and she falls back to sleep.

My eyes fill with tears as my dam of caution breaks down and a flood of relief courses through my body.

My daughter didn't reject me. She didn't cry or fuss. She simply trusted me enough to fall back to sleep in my arms, allowing me to hold her during her slumber.

"I don't think I can let her go," I say tearfully as I look up at Jess and Malcolm.

"Then don't," Malcolm tells me. "We have a few hours before we need to go to Mars and deal with the mess Helena has caused. Just enjoy the moment, my love. Enjoy your happiness."

I bend down and kiss Liana on the forehead. "I love you very much," I whisper to her. "Mommy won't let Helena take our home away. I refuse to let her win."

I'm not sure how I'll keep my promise to Liana, but I know I'll do everything within my power to make it come true.

CHAPTER SIXTEEN

I end up falling asleep with Liana still cradled in my arms. When I finally do wake up again, I find my daughter staring at me as if she's seeing me for the first time in her life. She reaches out with the arm that has the bracelet on it and presses her little open hand against my cheek. We stare into each other's eyes for a long time, simply getting to know one another in that moment. I watch in wonder as her little mouth twitches into a small smile.

"I wish I could tell you just how much that little smile means to me," I whisper to her. "One day, when you're a little older, I'll tell you about this moment and how happy you made me."

I feel Malcolm's weight make the bed dip slightly behind me. He reaches over and tickles Liana underneath her chin with his index finger, causing her to let out something like a laugh.

"I don't want to move," I tell him, completely captivated by my daughter. "I just want to stay in bed all day and cuddle our babies."

I hear Malcolm sigh and I know he wishes we could do just that, too.

I force myself to sit up to look at him. "How much time do I have before we need to leave?"

"Not long enough," he answers with a wan smile. "A couple of hours. You have plenty of time to get ready. Are you hungry? Would you like to eat something before we go?"

I shake my head. "I don't think that would be wise. I would hate to lose whatever is in my stomach if I get too nervous."

"I'll be there with you," Malcolm says, sliding his hand across the mattress to cover mine. "We'll make it through this together. Hopefully, with Barclay there to back us up, we'll be able to convince the others that you had nothing to do with the attacks on Virga and Stratus."

"I hope so," I say, not exactly feeling confident the word of the commander of the Stratus Imperial Army will be enough to exonerate me in the eyes of the world.

"I've prepared you a bath," Malcolm tells me. "Why don't you have a good soak before we have to start the day? I'll take care of the babies, so take your time in there."

I lean over and reward my husband with a kiss for his kindheartedness.

It's not until I begin to undress in the bathroom that I remember Malcolm said I should be able to see a difference in my figure from Desmond's miracle cream.

When I toss my nightgown to the floor and look down at myself, I can't help but exclaim, "Oh my God!"

Malcolm rushes into the room, looking ready to defeat whatever foe has caused me to call out his father's name.

I turn to him in profile and say, "Look at me! My stomach is almost back to normal. That cream does work miracles!"

Malcolm finds amusement in my excitement. "If bad things come in threes, do you think that means good things come in threes, too? If it does, I think that bodes well for the meeting on Mars today."

"From your lips to God's ears, I hope," I tell him.

I have to admit that I do feel a bit more confident now about attending the meeting with the other royals. Surely there has to be a way to make them listen to reason, even if the supposed facts seem stacked against me.

I take Malcolm's advice and allow myself to soak in the tub for a good half hour. I lie in the warm bubble-filled water, listening to Malcolm sing to the babies and tell them the story of how we met. Of course, he doesn't tell them how stubborn he was in refusing to admit that I was his soul mate. Oh no. He tells them that I was the one who played hard to get, but that he won me over with his irresistible charms.

"You may have been irresistible, but you were far from charming!" I call out to him from the tub.

"Anna, Anna, Anna," he says to me from the bedroom, as if he's disappointed in my rebuke, "I believe *I'm* the one telling this story, *not* you, my love."

"Well, at least tell a correct version of it!" I demand jokingly, unable to prevent myself from smiling.

"I'm telling it as I remember it," I hear him defend as his voice gets closer to the bathroom. I watch as he leans a shoulder against the doorway, crosses his arms in front of his chest, and gazes at me with a playful twinkle in his eyes. "And I remember a certain someone unable to stop throwing herself at me so, obviously, you found me irresistibly charming."

I squint at him, saying, "Then you're remembering it incorrectly. From what I recall, you were a stubborn brute who refused to admit he couldn't live without me."

"I'll have you know that I remember everything in exact detail," he says, leering at me with lasciviously as I lounge in the water. "I distinctly remember you unable to keep your hands off of me."

"Well look at you," I reply, eyeing him from the tip of his shoes to his long dark hair before meeting his eyes again. "How was I supposed to keep myself from wanting you?"

Malcolm pushes himself off the doorframe. "If we had more time, I would show you just how much I want you right now."

I smile. "Oh, I can see just how much you want me," I tell him, allowing my gaze to drop just below his waist. "Will you need to take a cold shower before we meet with Helena on Mars?"

"No," Malcolm says derisively as the passion dies in his eyes, "just the mention of her name is enough to do the trick. Besides, it's time you got ready. We don't want to be late. If we are, I'm sure she'll find some way to use that against you."

"You're probably right," I agree. When I stand in the tub, a blanket of bubbles covers my body, slowly sliding down my curves as they make their way back into the water.

"Really, Anna?" Malcolm moans as the heat of desire warms his expression again. "You couldn't wait a few seconds more for me to turn around and leave before tempting me?"

I shrug and give him a playful grin. "As you said, we don't have time for that right now."

Malcolm turns his head to look back into the bedroom towards the bed.

"The twins have fallen back to sleep," he informs me, taking a large enough step into the bathroom to close the door behind him. "I think we can find a little time."

I shake my head at Malcolm, but I also can't help but smile at him.

"Don't ever stop wanting me," I tell him. "I'm not sure my heart or my body could take that."

"You may have many things to fear in this world, but my desire for you should never be one of them," he declares as he walks over to me. In one swift motion, he wraps an arm around my waist and lifts me out of the tub.

"I'm getting you all wet," I tell him as our bodies press together. "You'll have to change your clothes again."

"I have plenty of clothes," he murmurs, lowering his head to kiss the side of my neck while he wedges his right hand between us to find the sensitive center that's throbbing for his attention. "But I only have one wife."

I wrap my arms around Malcolm's shoulders as he uses his mouth and fingers to give me pleasure.

"Malcolm," I moan, tilting my head slightly to give his lips better access to the tender flesh his lips are teasing, "this isn't our dream world. I don't think I'm supposed to make love so soon after giving birth."

"I know," he whispers. "That doesn't mean I can't bring your body pleasure. As you mentioned, I'll have to change my clothes anyway. I'll just take a quick cold shower before I do."

"I would argue," I say as I take an unsteady breath and close my eyes, selfishly enjoying the play of Malcolm fingers against me, "but I'm afraid I'm in no position to do that right now."

Malcolm chuckles softly at my confession as he playfully nibbles the skin along my right shoulder.

"Then hold onto me, my love," he urges huskily, "because we won't be leaving this bathroom for quite some time."

When we finally do emerge from our morning tryst, I have just enough time to feed the babies and prepare myself for the day ahead. For some reason, I don't feel as worried as I did earlier about the meeting. Having found a way for Liana to accept me is a large part of the reason. I've been so consumed by worry over her hatred of me that everything else took second place. Now that we've found a way to resolve that problem, the next hurdles we need to defeat are these baseless accusations that I'm the one responsible for the destruction of Virga and the attack on Stratus.

I have to hand it to Helena. She manipulated the situation masterfully. We knew she would use Silas and his cohorts to attack us, but I suppose we all thought it would be a frontal assault on us personally. I never dreamed she would come at me from behind by destroying a whole cloud city and placing the blame of its destruction squarely on my shoulders. Emperor Edgar Ellis had disrespected me at the previous meeting that was held at the Mars pavilion, unknowingly marking himself and his citizens for death in Helena's scheme.

Malcolm and I take the babies downstairs and find Jess, Mason, and Lucifer gathered in the living room, having a conversation with Ethan.

"Were you able to get things in Stratus under control?" Malcolm asks Ethan as he holds Liam in his arms.

"For the most part, yes," Ethan says, looking worried.

"What's wrong?" I ask him, sensing something is amiss.

"I can't find General Stewart," he informs us. "We made arrangements to meet up this morning so I could take him to the Mars pavilion. We've scoured the city, but he's nowhere to be found."

"Oh no," I say, unconsciously cradling Liana closer to me. "Do you think Lorcan found out he was going to help us?"

"That would be my guess," Ethan confirms. "I don't think anything else would have caused him to miss our meeting."

I look at Malcolm. "What can we do to help him?"

"I don't think we can," he replies. "At least, not right now. Let's work on clearing your name first. Then we can make a formal inquiry about Barclay's whereabouts."

"You don't think Lorcan killed him, do you?" I ask worriedly. "You and I both know Lorcan is a sadistic coward. I wouldn't put it past him to stab Barclay in the back for trying to help me."

"I don't think he would do that," Malcolm says thoughtfully. "No matter how powerful Lorcan believes he is in Stratus, Barclay is still general of the Imperial Army there. His men are loyal only to him. As you just pointed out, Lorcan is a coward. There's no way he would kill Barclay because he knows such an action would incite a riot among his soldiers."

I see the wisdom in Malcolm's words. If there is one thing I can count on from Lorcan, it's his need for self-preservation. He knows I can kill him with just one touch. If the world finds me guilty of the crimes I'm accused of, then I have nothing to lose by ending his life. Such a fate would be a kindness he doesn't deserve, though. There isn't a doubt in my mind that he colluded with Helena in her scheme to discredit me. He knowingly allowed the people of his cloud city to be attacked by the rebellion angel forces. After this is all over, I know I will have to find a way to take Lorcan off the Stratus throne and place Kyna there instead. The people of Stratus will never be safe if he's allowed to remain their emperor.

"Mommy, are you holding Liana?" I hear Lucas say as he walks into the living room, Vala and Luna on either side of him.

"Yes, I am," I say proudly to my son, unable to stop myself from smiling over the fact.

"Why isn't she crying?"

I untuck Liana's right arm from the blanket I have her swaddled in and show Lucas the bracelet.

"A little magic from Heaven helped us solve the problem. We made a bracelet from the baby rattle Lilly gave me."

"Ohhh," Lucas says, nodding his head sagely. "That was a smart idea. I wish I had thought of that."

"I was going to ask about her changed behavior towards you," Ethan tells me, looking a bit sheepish, "but I didn't want to be rude."

"It wouldn't have been rude of you to ask," I tell him, tucking Liana's arm back by her side and smoothing the blanket over her once again. She gurgles as she looks up at me, smiling.

"Can I hold her?" Jess asks. "You're not the only one who was getting tired of her crying all the time."

I place Liana in Jess' waiting arms.

"Hello, baby girl," Jess croons. "You and I have a lot to talk about while your mommy goes to fight the bad lady."

"Unfortunately, it won't be a physical duel," I grumble with disappointment. "At least with swords it would be a fair fight. I'm not sure I can do much with just words."

"You'll find a way," Mason tells me with a wink. "All of the women in your family have been strong-willed..."

"Nothing wrong with having that trait," Jess interjects.

"Did I say it was a bad trait to have?" Mason asks her. "No. I did not. It's one of the best inheritances you could have asked for from your ancestors. Just remember to choose your words wisely and don't let your temper get the better of you. I've been known to do that on occasion, and it never worked out in my favor. You'll need to keep a level head while they try to tear you down. If you can do that, I think you will come out of this relatively unscathed."

"I'll do my best to keep my temper in check," I promise.

Mason looks at Malcolm. "That goes for you, too," he tells my husband. "Take up for your wife, but don't start a war with your words or your fists. I know how protective you get when someone you love is being attacked."

"I'll try," is all Malcolm promises.

"I would offer to go with you," Lucifer says, "but I think that would only cause you more problems than my presence is worth."

"Sadly, I agree," I say.

"Don't worry," Malcolm tells my dad. "The other Watchers and I will be there to keep an eye on things."

"I assume you don't want any of us there," Ethan says, speaking for himself and the other War Angels.

"I don't think that would be wise, do you?" I reply. "The world believes the lie Helena has fed them. It's probably for the best if you all lay low for now and wait for today's outcome."

"I'll stay here in case you need us," Ethan says. "I can round up the others in a matter of minutes if something comes up that needs to be handled."

"Thank you," I tell him. "We'll get this worked out, Ethan. I promise."

"I know you'll try," he replies, not sounding as hopeful as I would have liked.

However, I understand his concern. If we're not able to convince the world that my War Angels were framed for a crime they didn't commit, God's plan for them to produce children with human women could be placed in jeopardy. What group of women would want to fall in love with, much less have the children of, mass murderers? Certainly not any women I would want my War Angels to marry.

"We should probably go," Malcolm advises me. "Jered and the others are supposed to meet us there." He turns to Ethan and hands Liam to him. Ethan looks perplexed, not understanding why Malcolm has chosen him to take care of our son.

"You need the practice," Malcolm explains, answering the bewildered expression on the other man's face.

"Great," Ethan mutters under his breath as he cradles my second son in his arms.

"We'll be back as soon as we can," I tell them all.

"And we'll be here waiting for your return," Vala assures me.

"Mommy," Lucas says, holding his arms up to me in the universal sign that a hug is desired.

I bend down on one knee and bring my son into my arms.

"Good luck," he tells me. "Helena can be a bully, but I think that's just because she's sad all the time."

I'm slightly taken aback by Lucas' words. He almost sounds like he's taking up for her behavior. He still doesn't know the extent of what she's done. I'm not even sure how to tell a seven-year-old that five million people lost their lives in one moment of blinding light.

I pull back from him and say, "Then she needs to find better ways to treat others."

"I'm not saying she's a good person," Lucas clarifies. "I know she isn't, but she's not all bad either. She protected me as much as she could on alternate Earth. If she had been completely heartless, she would have just left me on the streets to fend for myself. She didn't do that, though. She kept an eye on me. I'm just saying that maybe arguing with her isn't the only way to get what you want."

"I'll try to keep that in mind," I promise. After I kiss Lucas on the forehead and stand back up, I twine one of my arms around Malcolm's and say, "Let's go."

When we phase into the pavilion on Mars, people from each cloud city are slowly filling up the seats within the circular building. Malcolm phased us straight onto the dais for Cirrus, where two gold thrones have been set. Each of the seven cloud cities has their own designated section. Olivia has her back turned to us while she speaks to a man from her delegation. When I look over at the Virga section, I only see a handful of people present sitting behind the two throne chairs on its dais. One chair is empty, but one chair is not. Mammon, in his guise as Prince Callum Ellis, sits in the chair Edgar Ellis sat in during the previous meeting. It's a stark reminder that Callum is now the Emperor of Virga. I'm certain Helena warned him about the impending doom his city would have to suffer in order to perpetrate my downfall. Since he wasn't in the city when it was destroyed, I have to wonder if he watched the bomb go off and if he felt anything as he watched his city fall out of the sky. Odds are he didn't have the capacity to empathize with the dying. Otherwise, he would have come to us like Baal did, and told us what was happening so we could try to stop it. I don't pity him in the slightest even though almost everyone present does.

The once-great cloud city of Virga is gone, and its new emperor is partially to blame.

"Did the bracelet work?" I hear Brutus ask eagerly from behind us.

When we turn around, I see that Jered, Desmond, Brutus, and my papa are sitting in the row of seats directly behind our chairs. As an added surprise, Slade is with them to add his support. They all look worried, but there's really nothing I can do about that. As I look behind my line of Watcher protectors, I see row after row of lords and ladies from Cirrus who have decided to attend the meeting and act as witnesses to the proceedings. Low, nervous mutterings can be heard within the pavilion with our arrival. I'm not sure if those present are scared of me or hate me with every fiber of their being. It seems as though they've already condemned me even before I've had a chance to defend myself.

I return my attention to Brutus and try to focus on the happiness I felt before coming here.

"It works perfectly," I tell him. "Thank you so much for staying up last night to make it for us. You just don't know how much I needed something good to happen before we came here to face all of this."

"I'm just glad we came up with something that works," Brutus tells me.

I look at all my Watchers and have to wonder if they still feel like their thousand-year wait for me was worth it. In this moment, I don't feel worthy of the sacrifices they all made to stay on Earth and help me.

"We're here for you, lass," Desmond tells me, almost as if he knows where my thoughts have wandered. "We'll find a way to clear your name and make things right again."

"I think we're going to need a miracle," I reply.

"Then that's what we'll pray for," my papa tells me. "Just get through this day as best you can and remember that it won't last forever."

The atmosphere in the pavilion changes from one of uncomfortable nervousness to excitement. I follow the gazes of most everyone in the room to find that my arch-nemesis has arrived.

Helena stands proudly beside Levi on the Nimbo dais. Standing side by side, they look like the perfect couple. The polite smiles plastered on their faces make them appear as tranquility personified. Helena politely acknowledges all the gawkers with a slight nod of her head in greeting before she and Levi take their seats.

I keep a steady gaze on Helena until she finally looks over at me. She no longer has to pretend that she accepts me as her equal. I've been vilified in the eyes of the world, and no one in this room will consider her hostile reaction to me questionable. Almost everyone else believes I'm a mass murderer, so why shouldn't she?

Bianca Rossi teleports into the room on the Alto dais. She looks over at me and nods her head slightly, but it's all the confirmation I need to know she gives me her full support. Just as she takes her seat, Ryo Mori from Cirro teleports into the room. I still can't believe Baal is on our side. However, I know he's only doing what he has to in order to ensure Bianca's safety. Still, thinking about Baal caring for someone else more than himself is just odd to say the least. I never could have imagined him acting selfless, especially not for a human.

Olivia stops speaking to the man she was conversing with when we first arrived and turns around to face the rest of us.

"I see we are only missing the Emperor of Stratus," she notes, scanning the crowd. "Does anyone from his delegation know if he plans to attend this meeting?"

An elegantly-dressed blond woman sitting in the Stratus section stands. "He said he might be a little late, Empress," she tells us. "He also said to feel free to start the proceedings without him."

"Very well," Olivia says, not looking especially worried over Lorcan's tardiness. "Then I see no reason not to address the subject we are all here to discuss." Olivia directs her gaze to Callum Ellis. "I believe I speak for us all when I say how deeply sorry we are for the loss of your father and your city, Callum."

Callum snorts derisively and looks over at me, his eyes filled with unmitigated hatred. "I wouldn't say that you speak for *everyone* in this room, Olivia. Especially not that bitch sitting over there!" Callum points an accusing finger at me. If he had been closer, he probably would have spit in my face for good measure.

"My wife did not blow up your city!" Malcolm states heatedly. "And before you go pointing fingers and calling people names, perhaps you should consider all the facts first."

"Callum," Olivia says in a calm voice meant to bring reason to the proceedings before they get out of hand, "I believe we should allow the Empress of Cirrus to address the accusations about her involvement with the destruction of Virga and its inhabitants."

"She's just going to lie," Callum says scathingly. "What else do you expect her to do? Own up to her crimes?"

I see this as my opportunity to point out some common sense about my alleged guilt.

Feeling nervous, I stand from my chair and immediately draw the attention of every person in the room. If I'm going to clear my name, I have to speak up for myself.

I turn my head to look at Olivia and ask, "May I have the floor to address the allegations against me?"

"Please do, Empress Anna. I believe we would all like to hear what you have to say on the matter."

I clear my throat slightly before I begin.

"I would like to address what the Emperor of Virga just mentioned," I begin. "As he said, if I am guilty I certainly wouldn't be foolish enough to own up to the fact."

"See!" Callum shouts. "She's practically admitting she's responsible!"

"No," I tell him calmly as I attempt to keep my temper in check, "I'm trying to make a point. If I were the one responsible for orchestrating such a horrible crime, why in the world would I have my men make a video claiming that the atrocities they committed were by my order? Not only that but also to broadcast it for the whole world to see? That makes absolutely no sense."

"I beg to differ," Helena pipes up. "I think it makes perfect sense if you wanted to intimidate the world into following your lead. Doing something to make people fear you and bend to your will is a tactic that has been used by tyrants for centuries."

"If that was my intent," I reply, "why would I agree to come here today to defend my name and reputation?"

"Perhaps you're simply trying to make us all second-guess what we've seen and heard thus far," Helena counters reasonably. "Maybe you only came here today to mollify us into believing you're innocent of this crime just so we'll let our guard down to make it easier for you to attack one of us next time."

"I am not here to do that," I declare. "I'm here to set the record straight and assure all of you that I had nothing to do with the bombing of Virga or the subsequent attack on Stratus."

"What about your War Angel army?" Levi questions, spreading his stolen Zuri Solarin lips into a grim smile. "Do you deny they were the ones who set the bomb off in Virga and attacked Stratus? We all saw the video footage."

"The men in that video were not my War Angel contingent," I tell him, even though I know he's already aware of that fact. "I have personally never seen those men in my life."

"And we're just supposed to take your word that they don't work for you?" Levi scoffs derisively.

"If you want, I can have all two thousand of my War Angels come here right now and prove to you that none of them are the ones in that video," I offer.

"What good would that do?" Helena questions. "Who's to say that you haven't simply replaced the few that the world has already seen with stand-ins? In fact, I heard a rumor that your angels can actually force the souls of living men, women, and children out of their bodies in order to assume their forms. Is that true?"

"No," I say. "That is a lie."

"You say that," Helena says, sounding doubtful, "but how can we really trust anything that comes out of your mouth when your honor is in question here? In fact, you've already been accused of killing your own husband just so you could take the Cirrus throne for yourself and your lover. Genocide seems like a natural progression for your particular type of cruelty."

"As I have stated before, I did not kill Augustus Amador."

"Without any concrete evidence against Anna," Olivia states, "the video made by those responsible is simply hearsay. In fact, I put forth that it could have happened to any of us. They could have just as easily laid the blame on you, Empress Helena."

"Then why did they choose to use Anna as their patsy?" Levi questions, sounding doubtful about Olivia's suggestion.

"Everyone in the world knows that she has been accused of Augustus' death," Olivia reasons. "Perhaps they saw an opportunity with her weakened standing among us and decided to take advantage of it."

"To what end?" Helena asks.

"What better way to win Catherine Amador the election than to discredit and demonize her adversary?" Olivia says. "It could be that this rebel faction is actually working for someone else to ensure Catherine wins the throne."

An excited murmur ignites the crowd. I can see that her words have caused doubt in their minds about my guilt.

"And who exactly would do something so atrocious?" Helena asks. "I hope you're not suggesting it's one of us."

"I would never insinuate such a thing," Olivia says smoothly. "I only ask that you consider the possibility that Empress Anna is being set up to take the fall by an outside force that is beyond her control. Any of us could have been targeted by this group of radicals. I don't believe any of us is safe as long as they're still out there. Perhaps we should be focusing on finding the true identities of these rebels instead of accusing an innocent woman of genocide."

"Yet," Helena says, taking a long pause before continuing, "we don't *know* that she's innocent, do we?"

"Perhaps we should have a trial to determine whether or not the Empress of Cirrus is actually guilty of this crime," Callum suggests. "I, for one, need to know who is responsible, and if you believe she's innocent a trial should prove that."

"If a trial will put these rumors about me to rest once and for all," I say, "then I'm willing to do it, but I'm confident you won't be able to find any concrete evidence that I'm responsible for the travesties that have befallen Virga or Stratus."

As if he heard his cloud city mentioned, Lorcan Halloran teleports into the building onto the Stratus dais.

"I'm sorry I'm late," he apologizes, looking haggard. "I'm still trying to deal with the aftermath of the attack on my city. Have I missed anything important?" he asks Olivia.

"We were just discussing the possibility of a trial to determine the guilt or innocence of Empress Anna," Olivia tells him.

"I see," Lorcan says, looking my way. "I think a trial is just what we need. I fully support the idea."

"If she's found guilty, I want her publicly executed," Callum says, venom drenching his every word.

"Execution is not on the table," Bianca Rossi is quick to say, coming to my defense. "I will not vote for it."

"Neither will I," Olivia adds in.

"Since the execution of a royal has to be a unanimous decision," Baal says as Ryo Mori, "I believe exile to an off-world planet is the only other punishment that can be handed down."

"I accept the terms of exile," I say. I knew this was how today would go and am willing to do whatever it takes to prove my innocence. "However, I don't believe it will ever happen because I am not guilty of these crimes."

"We'll see," Lorcan says scornfully. "And we'll also see how you explain the evidence I found of your guilt."

The crowd in the room erupts with excitement. Several people shout out, "What proof?" and "Show us what you have!"

I turn my head to look at Malcolm but don't say anything to him. My husband knows the one question going through my mind. What proof does Lorcan believe he has to substantiate my guilt?

"Please, ladies and gentlemen," Olivia says, trying to bring the proceedings under control, "let's not get out of hand here. Everything will be brought out in the trial. Please, sit down and remain quiet until this meeting is adjourned."

People begin to quiet and retake their seats, but I can feel almost everyone gazing at me accusingly.

Once things have settled, Olivia turns to Lorcan and asks, "I presume you intend to act as the prosecutor in this case, Emperor Halloran, since you claim to have evidence of the crime?"

"I'm fine with that role," he says, holding his head up a notch. "I have no qualms about bringing a murderer to justice."

"Then it's settled," Olivia says with finality. "We shall reconvene here tomorrow morning to give each side a moment to gather evidence for their cases. I thank you all for coming and kindly ask that you vacate the pavilion as soon as it's convenient."

Malcolm doesn't waste any time. He takes hold of my hand and phases us to our bedroom in our New Orleans home.

He immediately brings me into his arms and doesn't say a word. I cling to him like my life depends on it.

After a while he says, "Well, that went about as well as we expected."

"I suppose," I reply, not feeling any better about the situation. "What kind of proof do you think Lorcan has against me?"

"I have no idea," Malcolm says, sounding as puzzled as I feel about the situation, "but I wouldn't credit him too quickly with finding something. He isn't that smart."

I lean back as far as I can in order to look at Malcolm's face without having to loosen my hold on him.

"He seemed confident he has something damning," I say.

"You need to listen to me very carefully," Malcolm tells me in a serious tone. "You will not be found guilty. We will not be moving to an off-world planet, and you will remain the Empress of Cirrus."

"You can't know all of that for sure," I say, still feeling the weight of all those accusing glares on me.

"You're being falsely accused for something you didn't do," he reminds me. "And the more people tell lies about it, the easier it is to prove they're lying. This will all work out in the end, Anna. You need to believe that. I do."

"Then I'll have to lean on your confidence for now," I say, laying my head back on his chest and listening to the steady beat of his heart.

Malcolm is a constant in my life that I can't live without. If his heart ever stopped beating before mine, I know I would be lost in a grief so fierce only death would be able to take it away. His faith in our future is the only thing keeping me together right now. I just hope he never loses it.

CHAPTER SEVENTEEN

(Helena's Point of View)

Watching Anna look so pathetic as she stands on the Cirrus dais makes my heart rejoice. My plan has worked perfectly so far, and now the people of Earth are asking for her to be exiled to an off-world. I would laugh but the Empress of Nimbo wouldn't react so cold-heartedly. The persona I've created for myself would be more empathetic towards the situation. Millions of lives have been destroyed but, even though I get to watch my sister take the fall for something I did myself, I don't need to gloat over the fact in public.

As soon as Olivia calls the meeting to an end, I feel a sense of relief that I can leave and go back to Cade. Perpetuating the pretense that we are a loving couple, Levi and I teleport out of the Mars pavilion together not long after Anna and Malcolm do.

"I think that went well, don't you?" Levi asks as we stand in my quarters in the Nimbo palace.

"Yes," I say. "It went as expected." I begin to walk to my bedroom. "I won't be back here until the trial, so don't come looking for me."

"Wouldn't it be wiser to stay here so your people at least think you care about their welfare? What am I supposed to say when they ask where you are?"

"Just tell them that the stress has been too much for me and I'm bed-ridden. Honestly, Levi, I don't understand how you've lasted this long. Why must I always be the one who thinks for you?"

Levi narrows his hazel eyes at me. "I just needed to know what you wanted me to say. Knowing you, if I chose to say something else, you'd get pissy with me like you are now."

"Just handle it!" I yell, slamming the door to my bedroom behind me after I enter. "He's such an idiot," I complain to myself as I begin to disrobe. I lay the dress I wore to the meeting on my bed and grab the black wool slacks in the same motion.

After I recovered from the initial absorption of souls from Virga, I quickly phased Cade and me to Sierra. I don't want him to know what I've done yet. I feel sure he'll leave me as soon as he does, even with our bargain still in place. He won't be able to understand my actions. His heart is too pure to fully realize that sometimes bad things have to happen to the innocent. Although, it's apparent to me now that not everyone in Virga was so innocent considering the deluge of new souls I received after its destruction. It was almost like re-experiencing the Great War all over again. I collected so many souls during that time that Hell became nirvana.

Intent on getting back to Cade as quickly as possible, I slip on my tight-fitting red cashmere sweater and black heeled boots. I had one of the servants here bring me the casual set of clothing while I was at the meeting. I needed something that was comfortable and warm, considering where I left Cade on Sierra.

When we got there yesterday, we went straight to The Grace House to find Evelyn. To say she wasn't pleased to see us again is an understatement. Nevertheless, after I told her what we needed, she took us directly to a remote cabin she had built in the mountains surrounding her city of Arcas. She told us that we could use it for as long as we wanted, and gave us money in case we needed to buy things in town. Personally, I think she just wanted to make sure we didn't bother her again. That was fine by me. I didn't like her attitude towards me anyway, and I knew if I had to spend any more time around Evelyn I might end up killing her in front of Cade. That certainly wouldn't perpetuate the intimacy I was trying to sustain between us.

I ended up leaving Cade in the cabin overnight. I needed to come back to Earth to make sure everything was running smoothly with my plan. I certainly couldn't trust Levi not to screw things up for me. He was an imbecile. I wouldn't trust him to pour me a glass of water correctly much less coordinate Anna's downfall. In fact, it was a good thing that I did come back. I was able to learn of General Stewart's plans to testify on my sister's behalf. If I hadn't discovered that fact, the meeting on Mars would not have gone as smoothly.

Now that I know things are going just as I planned, I can relax a little bit and work on figuring Cade out.

I grab my black wool coat from the bed and phase back to the living room in the cabin on Sierra. Evelyn's cabin is very modern in style. Many of the outside walls are made of glass held in place by iron beams. Stone and wood harvested from the mountain itself comprises the rest of the structure. Its design is clean and simplistic.

I don't see Cade or feel his presence in the house. I walk over to the center glass wall in the room and peer outside. I find him standing in the snow, swinging an ax as he splits a short log of wood into two pieces. He's shirtless, which I can appreciate, but considering how cold it is outside I'm not sure why he felt the need to shed his clothes.

As I turn around to locate the staircase that leads to the bottom floor, I slip my arms through the sleeves of my coat. It doesn't take me long to find the doorway leading out to the back porch. I walk over to the railing and lean my arms against the top of it. Just as Cade swings the ax above his head with both hands, he pauses as if sensing my presence and lowers his arms to turn his head to find me.

"Aren't you cold?" I ask him, unable to keep my eyes from darting down to his bare chest.

"I tried doing this with my shirt on, but I ended up tearing it down the back when I made my first swing."

I smile. "I'm definitely not complaining about your half-naked state. In fact, if you feel as though those jeans are a little too tight, feel free to dispose of them as well."

Cade chuckles and shakes his head at me in exasperation before continuing to cut the last log beside him.

"Was that wood already here and waiting to be cut?" I ask.

"No," he grunts, swinging the ax down towards the large stump he used to chop the small logs on. "I had to cut this tree down first."

"How resourceful of you," I reply, somewhat impressed. "A regular Paul Bunyan in our midst."

Cade places the head of the ax on the ground beside his right foot and looks up at me.

"Do you ever wonder what it would be like to just live off the land and not have to bother with the troubles of the world?" he ponders seriously, gazing up at me.

"Honestly? That sounds a little boring," I answer.

"Maybe," Cade concedes, looking at me contemplatively. "Or maybe it would be paradise."

"You shouldn't waste your time thinking about things that can never happen," I tell him. "Problems always have a way of finding the living eventually. It's just a part of life."

Cade does a one-arm swing of the ax in his hand and buries half the cutting edge into the stump. He then proceeds to lean over at the waist and gather up the pieces of wood he's split from the snow-covered ground. The angle of my vantage point allows me to admire his assets quite clearly. I sigh in slight disappointment when he stands straight again to turn around and make his way up the porch steps.

"I do believe this house has a heating system," I tell him as he comes to stand beside me on the porch. "It wasn't really necessary for you to cut up all that wood."

Cade smiles, lighting my heart with a fire that could keep me warm through any cold night.

"To be honest, I was getting bored here," he confesses. "I wasn't sure when you would be back from causing your chaos back on Earth."

"Chaos," I repeat with a roll of my eyes. "You make it sound like such a bad thing. I simply had matters that needed to be attended to, that's all."

"And have you gotten your wish yet?" Cade asks, all humor gone from his voice. "Have you found a way to force Anna off her throne?"

"Yes," I state, not seeing any reason to lie about my accomplishment. Cade has known my plans for Anna even before we ever set eyes on one another. "I believe I have. And before you ask, she and her family are safe and sound. Not a single hair on any of their heads has been set out of place, much less harmed."

"I wish you could find a reason to end this vendetta you have against Anna. She hasn't done anything to you. Why do you insist on making her pay for what Lucifer did?"

"It's not just that," I say, becoming irritable with the direction our conversation is going. "She represents hope to humanity, and that is something I have to get rid of."

"Why?" Cade asks, looking perplexed by my reasoning. "And what exactly do you mean by 'get rid of'?"

"I'm not talking about her death," I assure him. "Just an exile to an off-world planet."

"And how exactly did you manage that?" Cade thunders.

"I haven't yet," I snap back. "But it's only a matter of time before it happens."

Cade's shoulders instantly relax. "Oh, I thought it was a done deal. If you're still waiting for it to happen, it probably won't. Anna won't leave Earth unprotected from you. She doesn't run away from fights. I thought you knew her better than that."

"That may be the case, dear heart, but this isn't exactly a fight she can win by wielding her flaming sword. Things are far more complicated this time around."

Cade sighs and looks at me hard, like he can't quite understand what feeds my insatiable anger.

"Do you know what's sad about this situation, Helena?" he asks, looking at me as if he pities me for some reason.

"No, but I'm sure you're about to tell me," I quip.

"It's sad that you won't even try to get to know Anna. I think deep down you want someone to truly care about you. She's one of the few people in the world who might actually be able to do that. Why can't you at least try to befriend her instead of antagonizing her all the time?"

"I just told you why; weren't you listening?"

"Because she brings hope to the world?" Cade questions incredulously. "I don't think that's much of a reason, especially when she could help you grow as a person."

"I don't want to talk about this anymore," I say, storming back into the house and up the stairs to the living room.

I notice that he follows me inside, but I don't say anything to him. I don't even look in his general vicinity. I take my coat off and throw it onto the grey suede couch beside me. How dare he spout the virtues of my sister to me! I don't need to be lectured by him about 'growing as a person'. I like who I am just fine.

I hear him set the logs in the steel box by the fireplace in the room. The hearth is the centerpiece of the whole cabin, really. It acts as a separating wall between the living room and the dining room.

"Helena," I hear him say behind me, "don't do that."

"Do *what*?" I ask angrily, examining a non-existent piece of lint on my coat as it lays on the couch.

"Close yourself off to me," he explains. "You have to know that all I want is to find a way for us both to be happy."

Still, I don't turn around as I ask, "Then why do you insist on bringing Anna up every chance you get? If this is going to work between us I need to know that I come first, not her."

"And do I come first above everything else in your life?" he asks me in return.

I don't even have to think about the answer. "No—but you're not far off."

I hear him sigh in resignation of hearing the truth.

"When do you need to go back?" he asks.

"Tomorrow morning," I answer, finally turning around to face him. "Why?"

"I have a suggestion," he says, taking two strides forward to close the distance between us a little more. "Let's not talk about anything that's happening back on Earth. I think we need to continue what we were doing before we went to the party, and get to know each other better. We owe it to ourselves to see if there's a chance we can put one another first in our lives. Would you be willing to do that? To give us a real try?"

"What exactly do you want us to do until I have to leave?"

"There's still a lot I don't know about you," he says, "and there's a lot you don't know about me. You didn't know I could play the guitar until Lucas' birthday, right?"

"No, I didn't. I must have disregarded those memories as being unimportant while you were in Hell."

"Do you play an instrument?"

"I can play any instrument you give me," I inform him. "I've had centuries to absorb memories about a great many things from the souls who reside in my domain."

"I saw a piano upstairs in the study. Would you be willing to play something for me?"

"I suppose I could do that," I say hesitantly. "I've never actually played the piano before, but I believe I have enough knowledge to pull from to perform a piece of music for you."

"Come on then," he says, tilting this head to the staircase that leads to the upstairs. "Show me what you've got in those fingers of yours. Let's see how well you can tickle the ivories."

"Tickle the ivories," I say with a shake of my head. "As if I've ever tickled anything in my life."

"Then that implies you've never been tickled," Cade surmises with a twinkle of mischief in his eyes.

"Don't even think about it," I warn him in all seriousness. "I feel sure I wouldn't like it."

"How do you know if you don't give it a try?"

"I think I know myself quite well, thank you very much. Being tickled is not one of my life's ambitions, so keep your hands to yourself if that's your intent."

"Ok, I won't tickle you," he relents, "unless you ask me to."

"I don't see that happening anytime soon," I guarantee.

"If you change your mind," Cades raises his hands in the air and wiggles his fingers, "I've had a lot of tickling practice. Lucas loves it when I tickle him."

"Need I remind you that I'm not a seven-year-old child?"

As he lowers his hands, Cade replies, "No, you don't need to do that. I'm fully aware you're an old woman, because you act like one most of the time."

"Old am I?" I ask, finding his description of me amusing. "I do believe you're older than me, or have you forgotten Lucifer only made me after his father threw him out of Heaven? You were made well before that happened."

"I didn't say I was young. I'm old, too, which is one reason we should get along."

"Show me where the piano is before I get too old to play for you," I say, deciding to change the subject away from how ancient we both are.

"Come on," he says as he slowly begins to walk over to the stairs. "I'll show you."

I follow Cade up to the top floor and into the study. The black lacquered baby grand piano is the most prominent feature in the room. I vaguely take in the waist-high bookshelves filled with volumes against the walls and the desk in the corner. The piano has been strategically placed opposite the desk in the corner of the two glass walls in the room.

"I didn't realize Evelyn liked to play the piano," I say as I walk up to it and sit on the bench. Cade follows and rests his forearms on the lid, twining his fingers together as he leans against the baby grand.

"She told me her daughter is the one who likes to play," Cade informs me.

"And when did you talk to her about that?" I ask.

"She came here while you were gone. She wasn't sure I would know where to go in town if I needed some food. It's not a big deal, Helena. Evelyn was just trying to be nice."

"And poison you against me, too, I would wager."

"Not at all. She just wanted to make sure I was comfortable. You weren't even a part of our conversation."

"Which entailed what exactly?" I ask, still suspicious of Evelyn's motives to befriend Cade.

He shrugs. "Nothing important really. Like I said, she just wanted to make sure I was comfortable here."

I decide to drop the matter. It's not important enough get in a fight over. I'm tired of fighting with Cade. A little peace between us would be preferable.

I set my fingers into place on the piano keys. Their smooth surface feels cool against the tips of my fingers. I close my eyes and try to remember a piece of music to fit the occasion Cade and I find ourselves in.

As I begin to play the second movement of Mozart's Piano Concerto No. 23, I keep my eyes closed while my fingers begin to press the keys. The piece begins rather slowly, as if the composer was reminiscing about something sad he once experienced in his life. Then it changes, as if telling the listener that all hope isn't lost if you're willing to stretch out and touch the small ray of hope that is being offered. By the end of the concerto you're led to believe that the composer has finally found peace, even if it's only a fleeting moment in time.

When I'm through playing, I open my eyes and look up at Cade. He's staring at me as if he's seeing me for the first time. I notice an understanding in his eyes now that wasn't there before. It's almost as if he's glimpsed a part of my soul he didn't know existed and understands exactly who I am and where I've been.

"That was…beautiful," he whispers in awe. "I can't believe you've never actually played the piano before. It sounded as if you were the one who composed the piece."

"Mozart did," I tell him, not wanting to take credit for something I didn't do. "I've never written music."

"You should try it sometime," he encourages. "I think you would be good at it."

"I don't believe I could compose music that sounds quite as beautiful. It would probably be filled with too much anger."

"Still, I think you should attempt it one day. You never know what might happen until you try."

I consider his words and say, "I'll think about it."

I look around the room, hoping to see some more musical instruments lying around but I don't readily notice any.

"I don't suppose Evelyn has a guitar hiding around here somewhere?" I ask.

Cade shakes his head. "No. I should have brought mine along before we left Lucas' party."

"I didn't really give you a chance to do that," I say, remembering our hasty exit from the gathering. "All I wanted to do was get away from Lucifer."

I feel an unexpected melancholia at the thought of my father, but quickly brush it aside as an after-effect of the piece of music I just played.

"We could probably go to town and find you a guitar," I suggest. "It's not like we have anything better to do with our time here."

Cade's blue-grey eyes light up with excitement. "I would actually love to do that."

"Then grab that credit fob Evelyn left for us to use and let's go shopping."

Sierra doesn't actually have paper money. They use an electronic form of payment much like Earth utilizes. All you need is a credit fob and its password.

Cade walks over to the desk in the room and picks up a small rectangular piece of black plastic. I know from Lucifer's memories of visiting this planet that to make a purchase the buyer would have to pass the fob over a scanner and then manually enter the password into a keypad.

I stand from the piano bench and ask, "Do you happen to know where a music shop is in town?"

"Not offhand," Cade admits, "but I'm sure we can find one."

I lift a questioning eyebrow. "And do you intend to go shopping only half-clothed?"

"Would it bother you?" he teases.

"Not in the slightest," I assure him, "but a lot of stores won't allow you entry unless you're wearing a shirt."

Cade sighs exaggeratedly. "Then I suppose I'd better go put a shirt on. I wouldn't want to cause a ruckus."

"And I would hate to have to claw the eyes out of the women who stare at you for too long."

Cade shakes his head at me. "As if I would care if they did."

"You might not, but I certainly would. As you know, I don't play well with others."

"I'll be right back," Cade tells me, heading for the door. "Today is supposed to be a fun day for us, not one in which you kill someone to defend my honor."

I hear Cade walk down the hallway and open the door to a room. Within a couple of minutes he walks back into the study, buttoning up a maroon shirt.

"Is that new?" I ask him, not remembering him bringing extra clothing.

"Evelyn said I could wear the clothes that were left in the bedroom down the hall. I guess this place used to belong to her daughter and her husband, but after he died Julia left this cabin and hasn't been back since."

"So you're wearing a dead man's clothes?" I ask in disgust.

Cade shrugs. "It's all I have."

"Then we need to go buy you some new clothes first. I refuse to have you walking around in clothing that belonged to someone who's dead. It's a bit too morbid, even for my tastes."

"That sounds a little ironic coming from you."

"Perhaps it is, but it's the way I feel. I would rather you have new clothing anyway, not hand-me-downs from someone we don't even know."

"If it would make you feel better, that's fine with me," Cade relents. "I'll even let you dress me the way you want."

"That could be dangerous," I imply. "What if I want to dress you up in a pink tutu?"

"Well, if that's what turns you on, I say go for it," he jokes.

I let out a half-laugh at the picture that forms in my mind of Cade prancing around in a frilly tutu.

"That would most certainly do nothing for me in the carnal desire department." I walk over to Cade and take his arm. "Come along. I'm sure we can find something more suitable for you to wear."

CHAPTER EIGHTEEN

We phase to the center of town and begin searching for the two stores we need. The men's clothing store is the first one we locate. Cade is true to his word about giving me carte blanche when it comes to picking out his new outfits. I like Cade best when he dresses simply, so I opt for plain slacks, jeans, and shirts that can be layered to fend off the wintery cold on top of the mountain. However, when it comes to choosing his underwear I do seek his opinion.

"Are you a boxers or briefs kind of man?" I ask, holding up an example of each from a circular display of men's undergarments.

"Pick the one you think I would like, and I'll tell you if you're right or wrong," he challenges with a lopsided grin.

"Briefs," I say without much deliberation.

"You're right," he tells me, sounding impressed, "but I'm interested in knowing why you think I like them better."

"If I were a man, I wouldn't want to walk around with that thing hanging loose between my legs all the time. I would prefer to have it held securely in place."

"That's pretty spot-on," Cade says, looking surprised by my conclusion. "It sounds like you've given the subject a lot of thought."

"I have."

Cade looks puzzled by my answer. "Mind me asking why you would need to consider such a question?"

"When I realized I could make a body for myself in Hell, I knew I would need to decide whether or not I wanted to be a woman or a man. I deliberated a long time over the question about whether having a penis would annoy me."

Cade grins, finding my explanation humorous. "And I take it you decided it would bother you."

"Most definitely," I declare. "It's like a fifth appendage that has a mind of its own and I like being in full control, especially when it come to my own body. Honestly, I'm not sure why anyone would want to own one of those things."

As Cade begins to chuckle at my explanation, the female sales clerk who has been helping us walks over.

"I'm sorry to interrupt," she says, "but is there anything else you would like to buy? We have all of your other items bagged up for you."

I grab a handful of black briefs and toss them to the woman. Thankfully, her reflexes are quick and she doesn't drop a single pair.

"Add these," I tell her, "and that will be all for today."

The woman turns and walks back to the front of the store.

After we gather our purchases and walk out onto the street, I phase us back to the cabin.

"I thought we were going to look for a guitar," Cade says in disappointment.

"I need for you to change out of that shirt first," I say, eyeing the one he's wearing suspiciously. "I think it's bad luck to wear a dead man's clothing. We don't even know what Julia's husband died of. You could be wearing something diseased or teeming with germs. Besides, I would rather look at you and not be reminded that the previous owner is deceased."

"Do you have a preference in what I wear?" Cade asks, holding up the three bags of clothing.

"No. Anything will do."

Cade sets the bags down on the living room floor and begins to unbutton the shirt he's wearing.

"Why is it that you're not shy about being partially nude in front of me?" I ask, enjoying the show but curious to find out what his end game is all about. "In fact, it's almost like you do it on purpose. Is there a reason?"

Cade shrugs. "I didn't think you would mind."

"I didn't say I minded it. I just find the behavior odd."

Cade pulls out an off-white Henley from one of the bags and slips it on over his head. Without explaining his need to parade his body in front of me every chance he gets, he pulls out a brown leather jacket from one of the bags and puts that on as well.

"So you're not going to give me a reason?" I ask, finding his reluctance to answer my question even odder.

"If I did," he says, tugging on the cuffs of his shirtsleeves to pull them down, "the point of doing it would be lost. So, no, I'm not going to give you the answer you're looking for. Not unless I think my cause is a hopeless one."

Hopeless cause? What in the world is he talking about?

"Come on," he says, holding out his hand for me to take. "I asked the clerk at the store where we can buy a guitar. The music store isn't far from where we were."

I take his hand and he phases us back to the street where the store is located. A couple of blocks down, we find the music store. While Cade is browsing the collection of various acoustic guitars they have in stock, I look through the sheets of music they have in a display and find a song I haven't heard before. Obviously, being on a planet that isn't Earth means there are different people who compose different music, but since the souls here still end up in my domain, too, it's strange to find music that I don't recognize.

"Find something that you like?" Cade asks as he walks up, holding a black acoustic guitar. "Do you know that piece of music?"

"No," I say with a small shake of my head. "I was just thinking how odd it is that I've never heard this particular tune before."

"Can I see it?" he asks, holding out his hand to take it while setting the guitar he's chosen against the wall next to us.

After I pass it to him, he looks at the notes and begins to quietly hum the tune. Once he's gone through a few bars, he stops and looks up at me.

"If I buy this, will you play it with me?" he asks, as if he's asking me on a play date.

I hesitate for a moment. For some reason, performing a song together seems like an intimate act that I'm not sure I'm ready to do just yet. I almost want to laugh at myself for reacting so foolishly. Haven't I been the aggressor in this relationship with Cade? I've mentioned more than once that I want to have sex with him. Why would playing a piece of music together be any more intimate an act?

"We can try," I say, earning a smile from Cade that makes me have to swallow hard because my acquiescence seems to light him up on the inside with pure joy. I feel as if I've agreed to more than just a simple duet.

"Great," he replies, doing his best not to make a big deal out of my acceptance to his proposal, but he can't hide the fact that I've made him happy.

After we make our purchases, Cade suggests we go to a local grocery store and pick something up to cook for lunch.

"I've never cooked," I inform him bluntly as we walk down the street to the store.

"Just like you've never played the piano? Then you're probably a master chef," he jests, but I can tell he considers it to be the truth.

"Actually," I say, thinking through the memories I have accumulated from those who reside within my domain, "you might not be wrong."

As we walk down the aisles of the store, I instantly know what I want to cook for Cade.

"Leave," I order him, "but give me the credit fob before you go."

"Did I do something to upset you?" he asks, looking puzzled over my demand.

"Not at all," I assure him. "I just thought it might be more fun if I cooked you a surprise."

"That's...thoughtful of you, Helena," he says haltingly, looking somewhat amazed by my suggestion.

"Just give me the fob," I say impatiently, with my hand out. "I'll meet you back at the cabin once I have everything I need."

"Do you want me to do anything to help prep the kitchen for you?" he asks while sliding his right hand into the front pocket of his jeans to find the credit fob.

"I'll need a large pot," I tell him. "And a skillet. If you can find those and have them out for me, I would appreciate it."

"They'll be waiting for you," he promises, placing the credit fob in my palm as he leans in and kisses me on the cheek before phasing back to the cabin.

Thankfully, Sierra is similar to Earth as far as food items are concerned. I find all the ingredients I need to make tagliarelle pasta with truffle butter and sautéed chicken. Since most humans like to eat something sweet after their meals, I also buy all the ingredients required to bake a batch of sugar cookies.

It takes me less than fifteen minutes to shop and return to the cabin. Once I'm there I see that Cade is, again, shirtless. I find him sitting on the couch in the living room, fiddling with the tuners on the head of the guitar as he adjusts its strings. When he looks up at me, I raise my eyebrows at him and look pointedly at his naked chest.

"How would you like it if I ran around here not wearing a shirt all the time?" I ask him.

An amused smile stretches his lips. "I wouldn't be complaining like you are, that's for sure."

I roll my eyes at him and head for the kitchen area. Since the floorplan of the cabin is an open one, the kitchen is at the south end of the room. The area isn't huge, but it is well-equipped. The whole area is made from wood that's been stained to bring out the natural beauty of its lines. The counters along the wall are topped with a beige granite with brown veins and the kitchen island is simply topped with a butcher block. The pot and skillet I asked for are already sitting on the gas stove, waiting for me to use them.

"Do you need any help?" Cade asks as he sets his guitar on the couch and follows me into the kitchen area.

"Do you know how to cook?" I ask him. "I can't imagine there was much need for it in the palace."

"I cooked for myself and Lucas when we spent time together at my house."

"Then you can make the cookies while I prepare lunch."

"What kind of cookies?"

"Sugar cookies. Do you know how to make those?"

"I think I can manage that," he says with an easy grin.

I hand over the ingredients for the cookies and begin to concentrate on making the pasta entree for us.

As I'm chopping up the chicken breasts on the kitchen island, Cade rolls out the dough he made for the cookies. I notice him use a knife to cut the dough into shapes. When I glance over to see what shape he's making, all I can do is shake my head. He's cutting hearts out of the dough. I'm not even sure why I find that fact surprising. If there is one thing about Cade that's obvious, it's the fact that he wears his emotions on his sleeve. Well, that is if he wore sleeves. I allow my gaze to travel over the smooth, perfectly unblemished skin of his torso while I watch him work.

"So you chose that body to come to Earth in, correct?" I ask as I cup the chicken I just chopped with my hands and walk over to the skillet on the stove to dump it into.

"Yes," he answers, carefully placing his first heart-shaped cookie onto a baking sheet with a delicate hand.

"I approve of the choice you made," I tell him.

Cade smiles as he looks over at me with a gaze that sweeps me from head to toe.

"And I approve of the body you made for yourself," he replies. "It's perfect."

I shrug my shoulders and begin to sauté the chicken in the olive oil in the skillet.

"I saw no reason not to make it that way," I say. "Humans place special value on beauty. They seem to believe attractive people lead charmed lives."

"Would you call your life charmed?"

"No," I answer without having to think about it. "My life has not been charmed, but things are finally starting to look up. I feel as though I have more to live for now."

"Is it too much to hope that I'm one of the reasons you feel that way?" he asks uncertainly.

I glance his way and catch him watching me, waiting for my answer.

If I say yes, it gives him a hold over me, but if I lie and say no, he'll know I'm lying.

"It's not too much to hope for," I reply, leaving it at that as I return my attention to the chicken in the skillet.

Cade doesn't force the matter any further, but from the corner of my eye I can see him grinning happily.

By the time I have our pasta lunch prepared, Cade is pulling out the first batch of sugar cookies. The smell fills the cabin with a homey aroma. Everything feels so normal and perfect, making me wonder if this is the way Anna lives on a daily basis. As I told Cade, my life has been anything but charmed. I was never given the advantages that my sister has had, but it doesn't stop me from hoping for a better future for myself.

While the second batch of cookies bakes in the oven, we sit down at the dining room table together and begin to eat the meal I prepared.

"Wow," Cade says after finishing his first bite. "This is the best pasta I've ever tasted."

"I'm not sure that's saying much," I say, even though I'm secretly gratified that he likes my first attempt to cook a proper meal. "You've only been on Earth for a few months."

"Even if I had lived my whole life there, I don't think my opinion would be any different."

"Well, eat it before it gets cold," I tell him. "If you wait too long, the butter sauce will solidify and make it inedible."

Cade doesn't waste any time eating his bowl of pasta, and even goes back for a second helping. Once he's through gorging himself, he sits back in his chair at the dining table and rubs his full belly.

"That was the most delicious thing I've ever eaten," he proclaims, looking completely satisfied.

I don't admit how delighted I am by his declaration. As I look at him smiling at me happily, I notice a spot of sauce at the corner of his mouth and reach out to wipe it off with my index finger. Just as I'm sliding my finger to wipe it away Cade turns his head, causing the tip of my finger to slide into the warm wetness of his mouth. While he stares straight at me, he gently uses his teeth to trap my finger while his tongue licks away the sauce.

My breathing become shallow and my heart begins to pump so fast I feel myself begin to become flushed.

"Do you realize you're being cruel?" I whisper to him as I pull my hand away from his face.

Cade looks puzzled. "How was that an act of cruelty?"

"You know how much I want you," I say, feeling my temper rise, "and yet you blatantly tease me like that. How can you not consider that being cruel?"

"I want you, too, Helena," Cade says ardently.

"Then why do you keep making us wait? What are we waiting for?"

"I can't tell you that," he says, his voice filled with regret.

"Then, what *can* you tell me?"

"That I'm not sure I can wait for what I want before taking you," he admits, looking me straight in the eyes. His desire for me is so naked in his gaze, yet he continues to hold it in check. "You're not the only one having a hard time waiting, and I'm not sure how strong my resolve will remain because every time I look at you a large part of it gets chipped away."

I sigh, feeling both aggravated and disappointed. I wish I could speed up the process of breaking down his wall, so he finally gives in to what we both want to happen.

I stand from my seat, picking up my empty bowl and walking over to the kitchen sink to wash it. I hear Cade get up and follow me. In silence, we clean up the mess we made in the kitchen. Cade stays behind to finish baking the rest of the dough for the cookies while I go into the living room to study the sheet of music we bought earlier in the day.

The tune looks simple enough. In fact, it's very similar to an ancient Earth song called "Falling Slowly".

"Follow me."

I look up and see Cade standing in front of me with his hand held out.

"Let's go practice the song," he suggests when I don't move right away. "I would like to hear how it sounds with the both of us playing it."

I stand from my seat and take his hand, allowing him to lead me upstairs to the study. Once I'm settled on the piano bench, Cade brings over a small chair so he can sit beside me with his guitar propped up on his lap. I open the sheet music and place it on the piano's music rack.

I look over at Cade and ask, "Are you ready?"

Cade reads the first few bars of notes before nodding his head. "It looks simple enough." He strums the strings of his guitar with his fingers, as if warming them up.

"Don't you need a pick to play with?" I ask, remembering clearly that he used one at Lucas' party with his own guitar.

"The strings on this guitar are nylon," he explains. "The one I have on Earth has steel ones. I use the pick with that one because if I don't the music ends up sounding too oft. I'm fine with using my fingers on nylon because there isn't much of a difference in he sound."

"Ahh," I say, finding that interesting. "Then shall we begin?"

"Let's go on three," he suggests. "One…two…three…"

We begin to play the music in unison, but I find it hard to slow myself down enough to keep in time with Cade's slower, more melancholy, version of the song. We start over three times, but each time I always end up playing faster than he does.

"Can't you speed up your tempo a bit?" I ask him, becoming irritated.

"I don't think this song is meant to be played fast," he explains. "Besides, why are you trying to rush through it?"

"I just like to get things done, and I personally believe it should be performed faster than the way you're playing it."

Cade sighs as if he's disappointed with my answer, and sets his guitar down beside his chair before coming to sit next to me on the bench.

"Sometimes you're meant to take things slow so you can enjoy them," he begins to explain. "This song is supposed to start out slow, almost like a lullaby, but by the time we reach the end the pace should be picked up, like you're suggesting, because it becomes more jubilant. It's like falling in love," he says, looking into my eyes. "You have to take it slow in the beginning, otherwise you'll miss all the small first moments."

"Haven't we had enough first moments for you yet?" I ask him, sensing he's talking about more than just the music we're playing.

"I'm still waiting for one more," he whispers, searching my eyes for some intangible sign.

"Can I at least get a kiss?" I ask.

Cade smiles and leans in, gently pressing his lips against mine.

"Do you really consider that a proper kiss?" I breathe as he holds his head only an inch away from me.

"I thought it was very proper," he replies, his warm breath caressing my lips, "just not as satisfying as this."

He lowers his lips to mine again, but this time I feel the heat of his desire to lay claim to me. As his lips and tongue tease my own to play with him, I can sense a certain desperation inside his soul for something I haven't given to him yet. What this something is, I have no idea, but I desperately want to figure it out so we can move past the invisible barrier keeping us apart. What is it that he needs from me to finally break down the last block holding him back?

When Cade ends our kiss, I almost feel as if he's taking a part of me with him. Strangely enough, I don't mind. I want him to keep the little piece of me that he's stolen and treasure the fact that he's the only person I would ever let have it in the first place.

"I think we should try again," he tells me as his eyes keep searching mine.

"All right," I agree, not feeling as vexed as I usually do when he refuses to give in to what we both desire.

Cade returns to his chair and picks up his guitar again. I turn to face the keys and take a deep, shuddering breath. This time I close my eyes because I know the song now and don't need to read the notes anymore. I let my mind drift back to the first moment I saw Cade as I softly press the correct keys with a light touch of my fingers.

With the first notes we play together, I'm reminded of how surprised I was to find out I had a soul mate. At first I wanted to deny that our connection was real, but the more I tried to reject it the stronger our bond to one another became. I've tried to play if off as just a sexual attraction, but even I know that isn't the truth. No. It goes much deeper than that, and I secretly love the fact that Cade is trying so hard to get to know me. I don't believe there are a lot of men out there who would deny themselves the physical pleasure of being with their soul mate. For Cade, getting to know who I am on the inside seems more important to him than frolicking between the sheets. I can't say I've ever had anyone care about me enough to take the time to figure out what I like and don't like. Cade is so different from the only other man in my life who ever meant something to me. He doesn't seem to have a personal agenda to use me for his own purposes, unlike Lucifer.

The tempo of the music picks up, as if allowing an unexpected joy to push aside the melancholia of the tune. I suddenly realize what it is that Cade has been waiting to see in my eyes all this time. He wants to know that I truly care for him and don't simply want to use him for my own needs. If our relationship is ever going to survive the trials we're bound to face in the future, he wants to know that I'm willing to do whatever it takes to make that happen.

I'm honestly not sure I can go that far yet. All I do know is that I care for him more than anyone else in my life. That's all I can offer him right now, and I don't know if that will be enough. He seems like an 'all in' kind of man, and I don't think I'm ready to give everything of myself to him.

When the music crescendos and comes to a slow conclusion, I allow myself a quiet moment before I open my eyes. I turn on the bench and look at Cade with a new sense of purpose. Just before I speak, I notice something strange.

"Have you always had that tattoo on your arm?" I ask him, finding it odd that I haven't seen it before now.

Cade becomes deathly quiet and still. I'm not even sure he's breathing as he stares at me, looking slightly stunned.

"You can see it?" he asks, sounding amazed by the fact for some reason.

"Yes," I say, not completely sure why he seems so astounded by the fact. I tilt my head as I study the odd version of a yin and yang symbol with a black feather and a red dragon. "In fact, I can't believe I haven't noticed it before now. It's not like it's small."

Cade smiles and says, "It took you long enough."

I still feel confused.

"I'm usually more observant than this," I tell him, feeling as if I need to apologize for not noticing it earlier. I stand from the bench and walk over to him to take a closer look at the tattoo on his left bicep. "I still don't understand how I've missed seeing it all this time."

Unexpectedly, Cade stands from his chair and roughly pulls me fully up against him. His lips are covering mine before I can even put forth my next query. Far be it from me to question the change in his behavior. I wrap my arms around his waist and allow him to continue his pleasurable assault on my lips. For the first time since we acknowledged we are soul mates, I feel as though Cade is allowing himself to let go of a part of himself with me. He isn't holding anything back physically, and it's as if he's offering his heart to me completely. What exactly did I do to bring about this change in him? I don't want to stop the kiss, but I have to know if the difference in his attitude is a one-time thing or if it's permanent.

Reluctantly, I pull my head back enough to look into his eyes.

"Wait," I beg, because I see him leaning down to continue the kiss. "I need to know something."

"What do you need to know?" he asks huskily.

"Why the change?" I question. "I feel like I could ask you to do anything right now and you would do it. Why?"

"Because you saw my tattoo," he says with pleased smile, one filled with the promise of more pleasurable delights to come.

"What does that have to do with anything?" I ask, still not understanding.

"Only someone who truly cares about me and doesn't mean me any harm can see t," he explains. "That's why I kept walking around you without a shirt on. I needed to know if you could see it and now you do."

"So it's some kind of magical tattoo?" I ask.

"In a way. If you can see it, it means you're finally allowing yourself to admit that you care for me, and that's all I ever wanted from you, Helena. I needed to know you were willing to share your heart with me, even it's just a small piece of it. You're not trying to shut me out anymore. You're letting me in now. I'm not asking you to profess your undying love to me. I know how hard that would be for you to do, but as long as you allow for the possibility of it happening sometime in the future that's all the hope I need."

I honestly don't know what to say, so I say nothing. I just lean in and kiss Cade unreservedly. He wraps his arms around me, holding on tight. I feel like the veil separating us has been lifted, and we're finally able to show one another how much we care. Cade phases us to another room. I have my eyes closed, so I don't know what room it is until he ends our kiss and takes a step back from me, causing me to open my eyes. I look down and see that we're standing beside a bed. The implications of being here aren't lost on me.

"Does this mean what I think it does?" I ask, looking back at him.

"What do you think it means?" he asks in a quiet voice.

I give in a little since he is, too. "I think it means you're finally going to make love to me, Cade."

He smiles. "Then it means exactly what you think."

Cade reaches out and slides his hands underneath my sweater, deftly lifting it up and over my head. I didn't wear a bra today, so my breasts are immediately naked to his eyes. As he lets my sweater slip from his hand and onto the floor, he pulls on the waistband of my slacks until the magnetic closure opens, allowing them to fall unhindered to the floor. I quickly slip my shoes off and step out of my pants, standing before Cade only dressed in my panties.

"You're almost there," I say hoarsely, impatiently waiting for Cade to finish what he started.

Cade bends down on one knee in front of me and places both hands on my hips. He slides his fingers on the inside of my last garment and slowly tugs them down my legs until they reach my ankles. As I step out of them, he stands back up. In one fluid motion, he lifts me in his arms and gently places me on top of the bed's beige comforter.

I look down at his jeans and ask, "Do you need my help taking those off?"

Cade grins as he begins to undo the top button. "No. I think I can handle it."

And handle it he does. In barely two heartbeats Cade stands naked in front of me, making me thankful that we're doing this in the middle of the day instead of at night. I would have hated to miss the sight of him completely nude in front of me for the first time. It's a picture I never intend to forget.

I hold my hand out to him. "Touch me, Cade," I practically beg.

Cade lies down beside me on the bed and pulls me into his arms until our bodies are firmly pressed together. The warmth of his body lulls me into a place of complete compliance. The smell of sugar cookies lingers on his skin like nectar, making him taste that much sweeter on my tongue. My mind drifts on a wave of ecstasy as he presses me back onto the mattress and begins to slide his mouth down my body to explore what else it has to offer him. When he touches the center of my being for the first time, I feel as though I'm drifting on a cloud made of pure bliss, and he's a warm, gentle breeze pushing me through the sky, coaxing me higher and higher until I can almost touch the stratosphere. I end up begging him to stop when the pleasure becomes more than I can handle.

Cade kisses his way back up my body, stopping for a moment to pay special attention to my breasts, allowing me time to recover even though I know my body needs more. There's a ravenous hunger deep down inside me that only he will be able to satisfy.

Never being shy about letting him know exactly what I want, I reach down between us as soon as Cade's mouth reaches mine again. I grab hold of the root of him, causing Cade to grunt slightly in pleasure as I position him between my legs. Thankfully, I don't have to prod him any more than that. As he presses himself inside me for the first time, I feel a sharp, unexpected jolt of pain and involuntarily gasp from the feeling of being torn apart.

"Helena?" Cade asks urgently, placing his hands on either side of my head as he looks down at me with worry. "Am I hurting you? Do you want me to stop?"

I shake my head as the pain begins to subside in waves. "No. Don't you dare stop. Don't ever stop."

Slowly, Cade begins to thrust himself inside me. I know he's moving slowly because he wants to make sure he isn't hurting me. I do still feel a little bit of pain, but the faster he moves the more the pain is pushed to the side by a build-up of pleasure. I lift my legs and place them around his waist, allowing him to go even deeper. There comes a point when the pleasure is too much for me to take, and a hot rush of blood courses through my body. I call out Cade's name as he pushes faster and faster, finding his own release within the warm folds of my body.

Afterwards, Cade lies down beside me, bringing me into his arms and kissing my face as if I'm the most precious thing in the world to him.

"If I didn't like you so much, I could kill you for making me wait so long for that to happen," I joke, unable to stop myself from smiling as I look at him. For the first time in my life, I know what it feels like to be happy and content.

"And if I didn't love you so much, I could never have held myself back until you were ready for this to happen," he states.

I don't make a reply. I don't want to ruin the moment by pointing out the fact that he just said the L-word to me. Is he testing to see if I will say it back to him? I'm not prepared to delve into my true feeling for him just yet. The simple fact that I even said I like him seems enough of a commitment to me for the moment. Honestly, I'm not sure he realizes he said it aloud. I choose to ignore the word and snuggle up to Cade to bask in the afterglow of our lovemaking.

Good grief. Now he has me thinking of it as *making love*, too. Oh well, I guess I can give in that much. After all, they're just words.

"Did I hurt you?" he asks, kissing my forehead as we cuddle.

"A little," I admit because there's no point in lying to him about it. "I really didn't think about the whole virginity thing, to be honest."

"Neither did I. I guess I assumed you would have left that part out when you made your body."

"Apparently, I didn't plan ahead well enough."

"Was it that bad?" he asks, sounding concerned over my welfare.

"It was worth it," I tell him, not wanting him to worry over something that doesn't matter. "It was *well* worth it in fact, but..."

Cade raises his head off the pillow slightly to look at my face as I continue to rest my head on his chest.

"But what?" he asks, sounding a little worried that our first time together was disappointing to me in some way.

I lift my head up to look him in the eyes.

"But," I say, then pause for dramatic effect, "I hope you realize that now that I've had my way with you, I'm going to want more of the same in the very near future."

Cade smiles as he places his right hand behind my head, urging me to come closer or a kiss. Who am I to say no to such a tempting invitation?

Besides, who knows where it all might lead...

CHAPTER NINETEEN

If I could make Heaven exist in the land of the living, I would make it a cabin on top of a snow-capped mountain with a roaring fireplace and a warm body lying next to me.

"What are you thinking about?" Cade asks, tightening his arms around my waist as we lay on a makeshift pallet of comforters and pillows in front of the fireplace in the living room.

"My idea of Heaven," I answer truthfully, turning in his arms so I can face him. "I was just thinking that this is exactly the way I would want mine to be like."

My honesty earns me a sweet kiss on the lips.

"It would be nice if we could just stay here forever," Cade says as he rests his head back on the mound of pillows and looks at me with more tenderness than I deserve. "I wish we could."

I don't make a reply because we both know I'll have to leave soon. Anna's trial starts today, and I want to be there to watch my sister's downfall. Of course, I can't tell Cade any of this. Besides, I don't think it's necessary for me to say the words aloud. Cade already knows about my plans to force Anna into exile, finally leaving the Earth vulnerable to my rule. Everything I've worked towards will come to fruition today. Even though I would love nothing more than to stay naked underneath the covers with Cade all day, there are things that need to be done.

"When do you need to go?" Cade asks me, being smart enough to know that he can't change my mind about leaving.

"Soon," I say, feeling my heart sink at the realization that our paradise will have to be put on hold for a little while. "But I'll come right back after I'm through on Earth."

Cade's brows furrow, but he does the smart thing by not trying to dissuade me from my goal. He doesn't have to put his disapproval of my actions into words. I know just how much he detests what I'm about to do.

Cade stands up, allowing me a full view of his perfect naked form as he walks away.

"Where are you going?" I ask as I sit up and pull the comforter towards my chest.

"I'll be right back," he calls over his shoulder as he heads toward the kitchen area.

A few seconds later he returns, holding the plate of cookies we've been snacking on all night long. He hands me the small white plate that has the last remaining cookie on it. I think we were both eating around it because it was the ugliest of the bunch. The heart-shaped cookie is slightly burnt around the edges and not perfectly shaped.

"Do I get to eat the last one?" I ask as Cade retakes his place on the pallet next to me.

"I want you to keep it," he tells me. "And when you look at it, I want you to remember that there is someone in this universe who loves you."

"I appreciate the romantic gesture," I say, finding his request an odd one, "but why didn't you pick one of the perfect cookies before we ate them all up?"

"Because I'm not perfect."

"I would beg to differ on that point, dear heart."

"No one is perfect, Helena," he says as he looks down at the cookie. "You seem to think that I am, but I'm not. If I was perfect, I would be able to help you find a way to let go of your anger towards Anna."

"You're not a miracle worker," I tell him, trying to ease his guilt over such an insignificant shortcoming. "And that's what letting go of my anger would take, a small miracle."

"Finally lowered yourself to sleep with the enemy I see…" we hear an unexpected visitor say to us scornfully.

Cade and I both look up to see Lucifer standing in the middle of the living room, Evelyn by his side.

"That was a very bad move, Evelyn," I tell her menacingly, feeling my temper rise with her betrayal. "I'm surprised you're taking Lucifer's side in this matter."

"I'm not taking anyone's side, except for maybe his," Evelyn says, nodding her head towards Cade. "I think he deserves to know what you've done."

"Leave, Evelyn," Lucifer tells her. "I don't want you to get hurt, and Helena has that look in her eyes."

"What look?" I ask disdainfully.

"The murderous one," my father replies.

Evelyn phases, leaving me alone with my father and lover.

Lucifer looks at Cade and begins to shake his head in disappointment.

"You're more of a fool than I thought you were," Lucifer tells him. "How can you stay with her after what she's done?"

"Keep your mouth shut," I snap at Lucifer.

Realization dawns on my father's face. "He doesn't know what you've done, does he? I don't know why I'm surprised by that. Of course you wouldn't tell him about the genocide you committed."

My heart sinks.

"Genocide?" Cade questions, looking at me with a startled expression on his face. "What's he talking about, Helena? Does it have to do with what you wanted to hide from me?"

"Of course it does, you fool," Lucifer scolds condescendingly. "She used her henchmen to blow Virga out of the sky and frame Anna for it."

Cade's face goes slack with shock.

"Helena, is that true?" he whispers, as if he's frightened to hear the truth. "Did you kill a whole cloud city full of people?"

"Yes," I answer because I know I can't lie my way out of the situation. Cade would know if I tried to lie to him. "It was a means to Anna's end."

Cade looks over at Lucifer. "How can anyone on Earth believe Anna would do such a thing?"

"Helena had Jered's son, Silas, and his cronies do a broadcast announcing that they did the deed in Anna's name. Now, my daughter has to go on trial for something she didn't do."

Cade looks back at me. "That's how you plan to force her into exile?"

"Yes," I reply. Strangely, I don't feel as proud of the fact as I did yesterday, not with the way Cade is looking at me now.

Cade begins to shake his head in dismay. "I can't believe you would go so far just to exact your revenge on Anna. There were children in that city, Helena! Innocent people died just because you want to make Anna pay for merely existing."

"All humans die eventually. The only thing I changed was the amount of time they ending up spending on Earth. And before you get too judgmental, I can tell you many of the people in Virga don't deserve your pity. What do you think made me fall to my knees the other day in the graveyard? I'll tell you. It was a surge of new souls entering my domain. So before you get too weepy over their loss, remember that fact."

"Nothing you say can justify what you did," Cade tells me bitterly.

"I don't need to justify myself to you," I tell him.

"No, you don't," Cade agrees, standing up in all his naked glory. "You'll always do exactly what you want, no matter who gets hurt. I guess I've always known that fact deep down inside. I was foolish to think you might want to change for me, even if it was just a little bit."

"I am who I am," I tell him unapologetically. "Take it or leave it."

"Then I'm going to have to leave," Cade announces. I don't have to be a human lie- detector to know he's telling me the truth. "I can't stay with you, Helena, even though I want to. I can't be with you, knowing that you're framing Anna for something so horrific. I need to know you can change just a little bit because you care about me. I refuse to be with someone who isn't concerned about what I think or how their actions will affect me and the people I love."

"I'm a creature of habit, not change," I inform him tersely. "If you can't stand being around me, then go ahead and leave. I won't stop you."

"What you do today will affect us both," Cade tells me. "You need to decide what's more important to you: your hate for Anna or what we have together. I hope you choose the latter, but I won't be counting on it. I know how deep your hatred for her goes." Cade turns to look at Lucifer. "And you're to blame for it."

"I've never forced Helena to do anything she didn't want to do," Lucifer defends.

"That's probably true because I don't think anyone can force her to do anything, but you're the reason she hates Anna so much. You need to own up to that fact or Helena will never be able to get past it. You made her, Lucifer! You made her just like you made Seraphina, yet you keep trying to deny they're the same. I thought being in Heaven all this time would have made you realize all your failings, but it seems to have just made you more stubborn in denying any of this is your fault. Be a father to Helena. Be a person worthy of calling Heaven his home again and tell her how sorry you are for treating her like dirt. You need to own the mistakes you made while you were alive and fix them. Why else do you believe God sent you back down here?"

"To help Anna," Lucifer says obstinately.

"I don't believe that's the only reason, and from the look in your eyes, I think you're realizing that I'm right. You need to fix the problems you caused while you were still alive, Lucifer."

"I'm not a problem that needs to be fixed," I snap at Cade.

When he looks down, I'm surprised to see pity in his eyes.

"No, you're a daughter who needs to know her father doesn't hate her," Cade tells me, with more compassion than I deserve. "Everything you've done to Anna is just your way of acting out towards Lucifer. She represents what you want for yourself, and you're determined to make her as miserable as you are, Helena. Can't you see that? The sad thing is that I could help you build a life like Anna's, if that's what you really want. I could give you everything your heart desires, but you're not willing to let go of your rage long enough to accept me into your heart. There's no room in there for me, Helena. Not until you stop hating Anna, and I won't play second fiddle to your anger. You either have to stop this vendetta you have against her or let me go. The choice is yours."

Cade phases, and I see that he's returned to his beach house on Earth.

I look over at Lucifer. When our eyes meet, I can tell what Cade just said to him is making him think about all the time we spent together and how he shaped who I am.

"You can leave now," I tell him, detesting the fact that he's so close. "I don't need you to act like you care about me. We both know that would be a lie. You and I have been through a lot together over the years. I've lived with you hating me for a long time. There's no reason for you to change how you feel about me now. You have everything you've ever wanted. You don't need me anymore."

"Do you feel like I abandoned you?" Lucifer asks in a low voice as he continues to stare at me.

"Does it matter if I do?" I ask derisively. "You left, and I found out that I don't need you. In fact, I'm happier without you always trying to be in charge. Look what I've achieved in your absence! You had thousands of years to find a way to rule the Earth, and yet you never quite took that final step to make it happen. I think it's because you never wanted to go completely against your father. I always knew you loved the old bastard, and it was that weakness that stopped you from becoming who you were meant to be."

"And can your love for Cade do the same thing?" he questions.

"I've never said I love him," I'm quick to correct.

"You don't have to say it," Lucifer says. "I could see it in your eyes when he was talking to you. Are you really going to let the one person in the world who can truly love you the way you want to be loved slip through your fingers so easily? And for what? Just so you can exile Anna and her family to some distant off-world planet? Don't you know how rare it is for creatures like us to feel love, much less find someone who can love us in return after all the bad things we've done to others? Destroying Virga doesn't even compare to what I did to the world while I was still alive. Amalie was able to look past my sins and still find a way to love me for who she knew I could be. It took me a long time to see past my hate. I don't want that to be your fate as well, Helena. I know I haven't been a good...*father*... to you, but you need to know that wasn't your fault. None of this is your fault. It's mine, and I think my own father sent me here to finally realize that fact. If I hadn't rebelled and hated Him so much for sending me to Earth, I wouldn't have felt the need to make you."

"Why *did* you make me?" I ask, needing to know the reason for my existence.

"I didn't want to be alone," Lucifer confesses, not only to me but also to himself for what might be the first time. "I needed someone with me who could hate as much and as deeply as me. I used you like a crutch to lean on because I had no one else to help me shoulder the burden of what I had become. I wanted someone who could make me feel good about myself and who could share my hatred for humanity. What I did to you wasn't right, and I know that now."

"Yet, you still hate me."

"No," Lucifer says, "it was never you that I hated. I detested what I made myself into, and I needed someone who would accept me for who I had become. I'm sorry I made you hate the world as much as I did. Doing that to you is one of my greatest sins, Helena."

"Is that supposed to make it all better, Father?" I ask scathingly. "Do you want my forgiveness for making me feel lacking in your eyes all these years? Well, guess what: I don't forgive you. If you want amnesty for your sins, maybe you should go ask your own father for absolution."

"I wish I could have loved you," Lucifer says, sounding remorseful, "but I couldn't even love myself back then. You became a repository for all of my hate, and I don't think there's anything I can do now that will resolve that for you."

"I'm fine just the way I am," I state proudly.

"I used to think that way, too," he tells me. "I can't change what I did to you, but I can try to help you open your eyes and see what it is you can have now. You can have love, Helena, and I think that's all you've ever wanted. I was just too blinded by my own feelings to see how I was hurting you. All I cared about was myself, and that was wrong. It took the love of two extraordinary women to make me face my shortcomings, and realize how foolish I was being to refuse not only their love but my father's love as well. I don't want you to throw away what might be your only opportunity to be loved by someone else."

"It's a little too late to start caring for me now."

"It's never too late, and it isn't too late for you to change your life. All you have to do is find a way to show Cade how much you care for him. You need to prove to him that he means more than your need for revenge against a person whose only crime against you was being my daughter. Stop punishing Anna for my sins, Helena. Prove to yourself that you can be more than what I created you for."

"I need you to leave," I tell him. "Just go."

Lucifer opens his mouth like he wants to say something else to me, but thinks better of it. He phases, leaving me alone with my thoughts.

For the first time in my existence, I'm not sure what my next move will be. If I go through with my plans, I risk losing Cade forever. Yes, I told him I could live without him, but is that the truth? The thought of living a life without him in it makes me feel physically ill. My life would be empty to the point of being worthless. Yet, if I give in and end my vendetta against Anna when I'm on the cusp of winning, what does that say about me? What will I become if I grant her mercy?

Which is more important to me?

What am I going to do now?

CHAPTER TWENTY

(Anna's Point of View)

"Anna, stop pacing," Malcolm begs. "You're not going to be exiled today. I won't allow it to happen."

"I can't help but consider the possibility that it could happen, Malcolm," I say as I keep walking back and forth in front of the fireplace in the living room. "We still don't know what Lorcan's supposed proof is. He could have anything!"

"He can't have much," Malcolm reasons. "You're innocent of the crime you're being accused of committing. No proof exists that can show you are the one responsible for what took place in Virga or Stratus."

"Then he's manufactured something that places the blame on me," I reason. "But what?"

Malcolm suddenly phases in my path, causing me to come to an abrupt halt.

"You have to stop stressing over this," Malcolm says, placing his hands on the balls of my shoulders in an attempt to calm me down. "Lorcan Halloran isn't smart enough to find a way to prove your guilt."

"But Helena is," I say. "She's outsmarted us at every turn. Whatever Lorcan has as proof was given to him by her. You and I both know that."

"And we'll deal with whatever it is during the trial."

"Uh-hmm," we hear from the entry to the room.

We both look over and see Jered standing there.

"I hate to be the bearer of bad news, but it's time for us to head over to the pavilion," he informs us. "Almost everyone is already there waiting."

"I guess you and the others didn't have any luck," Malcolm says in a resigned voice.

Jered, the other Watchers, and my War Angels spent the previous night trying to discover what proof Lorcan Halloran is planning to present at the trial this morning. They were also supposed to search for Kyna's father, General Barclay Stewart. He made a promise to Malcolm that he would testify on my behalf and tell the world that the people who attacked Stratus were not a part of my War Angel guard. As it is, my only defense today is the testimony of Bianca Rossi and Olivia Ravensdale, but they are only character witnesses. Without knowing what Lorcan has in his possession, we have no idea what we'll have to defend against at the trial.

Jered shakes his head. "None, I'm afraid."

"I don't like going into this blind, Jered," Malcolm says.

"None of us do," our friend acknowledges, "but we'll make it through this just like we have throughout the last thousand years. There's a way for us to come out of this victorious today. We just have to wait for our opening and take it."

I wish I could have as much faith in the outcome of today's events as Jered seems to have, but worry for my family and the world prevents me from doing that.

"Where are the children?" Jered asks, peering into the room looking for the kids.

"Jess and Mason are looking after them for us," I reply. "I didn't want them around me this morning. It would just worry them too much, especially Lucas. He doesn't need to see me like this."

"And Lucifer?" Jered asks.

I shrug my shoulders. "I haven't seen him this morning. Jess and Mason don't know where he is, either."

"Well, I'm sure he'll turn back up," Jered says. "Right now, we need to go. We don't want to be late. It wouldn't look good."

Malcolm takes hold of my hand and phases us to the Mars pavilion. A few people are still finding their seats, but I see that almost all of the other cloud city leaders are already present and sitting in their thrones. There's only one chair that's empty: Helena's.

"Why isn't she here yet?" I ask Malcolm, finding the lack of her presence suspicious. "I would have thought she would be one of the first to arrive."

"Let's not question small miracles," Malcolm suggests. "If she doesn't come, that just makes one less person we have to worry about arguing with here."

As Malcolm and I take our seats, I say, "I'm not sure if her absence is such a good thing for us. She might be plotting something else to blame me for."

"Emperor Zuri," Olivia addresses Levi, "will the empress be attending these proceedings today?"

Levi looks uncomfortable having to answer Olivia's question.

"I'm not sure where she is this morning," Levi confesses uneasily. "I'm sure if she can make it here, she will."

"Very well," Olivia says, turning her attention to Lorcan Halloran. "Emperor Lorcan, yesterday you claimed to have irrefutable proof of Empress Anna's guilt in the Virga explosion and the attack on your own cloud city. Are you prepared to tell us what it is you believe you have?"

Lorcan, dressed in a solid black suit that contrasts dramatically against his thin, pale face, stands from his throne.

"Thank you, Empress Olivia," he says graciously before turning to address the assemblage. "Yesterday I did claim to have proof, and I would like to present it now."

The double doors on the ground floor straight across from our dais open. Two men dressed in uniforms of the Stratus Imperial Army walk in, pushing an oblong metal object on a cart.

I lean over to Malcolm and whisper, "What is that thing?"

Malcolm narrows his eyes on the object, and I can tell he immediately recognizes it.

"It's a nuclear bomb," he tells me, sounding worried.

"Emperor Lorcan," Olivia says in distress as she stares at the object, "have you just wheeled a bomb into these proceedings?"

"Yes," Lorcan confirms.

Panicked voices fill the pavilion.

"It's been disarmed," Lorcan says loudly. "Please everyone, I wouldn't be stupid enough to bring a live bomb into this building. I simply needed to show you what we found in our city. We were lucky enough to find it before it was detonated, or my city would have suffered the same fate as Virga."

"And how, exactly, does this prove Empress Anna was responsible for Virga's demise?" Olivia asks, sounding unconvinced that it proves anything at all.

"As you know," Lorcan begins, "every nuclear device and weapon that was left over from the Great War was catalogued before they were supposed to be destroyed. If you look at the serial number on this bomb, you'll find it in the catalogue as belonging to Cirrus' arsenal. Yet, as you can see, it was never destroyed." Lorcan looks over at me accusingly. "Who knows how many of these weapons the empress has stored away? It's possible she has enough to annihilate us all. Even the plasma pistols we were able to retrieve during the attack on Stratus can be traced back to Cirrus. It's concrete evidence of Empress Anna's guilt!"

Malcolm stands up. "All it proves is that the weapons once belonged to Cirrus, Lorcan," my husband defends. "It's been hundreds of years since anyone has seen a nuclear weapon. For all we know your cloud city could have some hidden away, too. In fact, how do we know these weapons didn't come from a Stratus facility? It doesn't take much to change numbers on a piece of metal and make it appear that they belonged to Cirrus. Your evidence doesn't prove anything about Anna's guilt. If anything, it should place doubt on your innocence in all of this."

Lorcan's pale face turns blood-red with anger.

"Your wife is the one responsible, Emperor Malcolm," Lorcan spits out, calling into question the validity of Malcolm's title with his sarcastic tone. "If you could get your head out from between Anna's legs for long enough, you might be able to see the truth."

I see Malcolm's hands tighten into fists. I reach out for him to stop what he's about to do, but I'm too late. Before I can even turn my head in the direction of the Stratus dais, Malcolm has already punched Lorcan square underneath the jaw, causing the Stratus emperor to go flying off his dais and onto the floor next to the bomb.

"Emperor Malcolm," Olivia admonishes as she tries her best to hide a pleased smile, "I will kindly ask you to return to your seat and remain quiet during the rest of these proceedings, or I will have to ask you to leave."

"That's all you're going to do?" Lorcan asks incredulously, holding his jaw like he's not sure it will remain attached to his face as he looks at Olivia accusingly. "He assaulted me! He should be thrown into jail!"

"Emperor Lorcan," Olivia says, like she's indulging a child's tantrum, "considering your crude statement I think you should consider yourself lucky to still be alive, much less walking and talking. Now, please retake your seat so we can continue these proceedings in an orderly manner."

Lorcan looks up at Malcolm, who is still standing on the Stratus dais as if he's daring Lorcan to come back up.

"I will as soon as he moves," Lorcan whines.

"Emperor Malcolm," Olivia says calmly, looking straight at my husband, "please retake your seat now."

Malcolm looks down at Lorcan. "Watch your mouth," Malcolm threatens, pointing a menacing finger, "or I won't leave you with one next time."

Malcolm phases back to my side and retakes his seat next to me.

"Did that make you feel better?" I ask him, doing my best not to look amused.

"Actually, it did," Malcolm replies. "He had it coming anyway, the sniveling little rat. He's lucky I didn't do more."

I try to keep my face expressionless and trap my laughter on the inside as I look at Malcolm's satisfied face, but I find it impossible. Instead, I cover up a small laugh by pretending to cough.

"Good job," I hear Desmond say behind us. "If you hadn't done it, one of us would have."

"He had it coming," Brutus agrees. "It just shows how ignorant he is to insult Anna in front of us."

"I suggest you aim lower next time, Malcolm," Jered proposes smoothly.

"I just might do that," Malcolm says, looking at Lorcan threateningly to keep him in check.

Lorcan seems to notice the death stare my husband is giving him and wisely chooses to avert his gaze from our general vicinity.

"Emperor Lorcan," Olivia says, "did you have any other evidence to present to us oday?"

"No," Lorcan says, still massaging his sore jaw. "That's all I have, but I think it's enough to cast doubt on Empress Anna's innocence. Considering the weapons and the broadcast of those men, I don't see how any of you can doubt she was the mastermind behind everything!"

"And you would know everything there is to know about being a mastermind," we all hear Helena say.

It takes me a few seconds, but I finally locate her position. She's standing at the op of the Nimbo section on the upper level walkway. It's the same exact spot where Catherine made her grand entrance to accuse me of murdering Auggie.

"Empress Helena," Olivia says, unable to keep surprise out of her voice by Helena's sudden appearance, "we weren't sure you would be attending the trial today."

"Please excuse my tardiness," Helena says apologetically. "I would have been here sooner, but I was having some trouble locating someone who can shed the light of truth on these proceedings."

"Are you saying you have a witness to present to us?" Olivia asks, sounding as nervous as I feel about such a prospect.

Helena smiles. "Yes, I do. I have two, in fact, who should be able to tell us what really transpired in both Virga and Stratus."

The door directly behind Helena opens up, and we all watch as General Stewart pushes in a handcuffed Silas. I sense Jered stand up behind me as his son is forced into the room.

Several gasps of surprise can be heard from the gathering. By now, everyone in the world has seen the broadcast Silas made to take responsibility for the attacks on Virga and Stratus and to accuse me of being the one who coordinated it all.

"Silence please!" Olivia says to the assemblage. "Silence so we can hear the testimony of this young man!"

Once people finally settle down, Olivia returns her attention to Helena and the two men standing beside her.

"General Stewart of Stratus," Olivia says, sounding like she finds it as odd as I do that Barclay is with Helena. "Why exactly are you here with Empress Helena and a supposed terrorist?"

"I wouldn't be here if it hadn't been for Empress Helena coming to rescue me from a jail cell in Stratus," Barclay tells us.

"And why were you being detained in a cell?" Olivia asks in surprise.

Barclay looks down and points an accusing finger directly at Lorcan. "He put me in one because I wanted to come here and tell the truth about what happened in my cloud city."

"And what truth would that be?" Olivia asks.

"Empress Anna's War Angels weren't the ones who attacked Stratus," Barclay declares. "In fact, if it wasn't for her sending them to us, I'm not sure we would have been able to stop the people who did attack us."

"Really?" Olivia says, sounding extremely pleased by Barclay's testimony. "Well, that's certainly good to hear, General Stewart. And how exactly did you apprehend the terrorist in front of you?"

"Apparently he was in the jail cell right beside mine, Empress," Barclay answers. I think you should ask him who was really behind the destruction of Virga and the attack on my city."

"Do tell?" Olivia says, sounding intrigued. "Young man, what is your name, and what information can you give us on the attacks?"

"My name is Silas," Jered's son answers, "and I was hired by Emperor Lorcan Halloran to blow up Virga and attack his own city to divert suspicion away from him. He also told me to place all of the blame on the Empress of Cirrus. He was concerned her proposal to give cloud city technology to the down-world would take hold, and he doesn't want to lose control over his people."

"That's a lie!" Lorcan shouts, standing up from his seat to hotly protest the accusations. "You can't believe a word he says! He's actually working for Empress Helena if you want to know the truth of the matter. She's the one who's really responsible for this mess!"

Helena looks down at Lorcan as if she pities him.

"First you try to lay the blame for this catastrophe on Empress Anna, and now when the truth is finally told your plan is to try and accuse me?" Helena questions. "All I can say is that you're acting like a desperate man who has been caught in his own lies. If I can make a suggestion to my fellow royals, I think Emperor Halloran should be stripped of his title and immediately imprisoned. Perhaps it's time for the rightful ruler of Stratus, his sister Kyna, to take the throne and fix all of the problems Stratus has been struggling with since her brother became emperor."

"You can't do that!" Lorcan storms like a petulant child. "I'm the emperor! The Stratus throne is mine!"

"Oh dear," Helena says, looking at Lorcan as if he's completely lost the ability to think rationally. "Perhaps it would be best if the emperor was also evaluated for mental instability. I think we can all agree that he's acting a bit on the insane side."

"I don't have to stand here and take this," Lorcan proclaims, phasing away before anything else can be said.

"Well," Olivia says, looking shocked by Lorcan's sudden disappearance. She looks up at Barclay and says, "General Stewart, by the will of the other royals here, I would kindly ask you to track your emperor down so he can be brought to justice for his crimes."

"It would be my pleasure," Barclay says, bowing to Olivia.

"Considering everything that has been presented here today," Olivia says to us all, "I believe sufficient evidence has been presented to clear Empress Anna's name and place the blame on the correct party, Emperor Lorcan Halloran of Stratus. I suggest we reconvene here once the emperor is captured to determine his punishment. Until that time, I officially adjourn this meeting and ask Empress Anna to forgive us for placing her on trial for a crime she obviously had no part in committing. Good day, ladies and gentlemen, and thank you for coming."

I breathe out a sigh of relief as I sit further back in my chair.

"What just happened?" I ask Malcolm, still stunned by the events.

"Helena saved you," Malcolm says, equally shocked.

"Why would she do that?" I ask in confusion.

"I have no idea," Malcolm admits, "but it looks like she might be coming over to tell us."

Malcolm and I stand from our chairs as Helena walks down the steps from the upper level to our dais.

"I suppose you have some questions for me," she says knowingly. The small, pleased smile on her face tells me she's enjoying our bewilderment.

"Why did you help me?" I whisper, not wanting to be overheard.

"I didn't do it for you," she tells me in a low voice. "I did it for Cade...and for myself to an extent. I just came over here to tell you that, for now at least, I won't be finding ways to attack you anymore. I've decided I want to try a different life, and I'm hoping Cade will be able to help me find a way to have it. I may not deserve his forgiveness after what I did to Virga and to you, but I hope he loves me enough to give me a second chance to prove myself."

"I hope so, too," I tell her, truly meaning it. Selfishly, I assume that if she's happy with Cade she won't have time to cause any more havoc in my life.

"Anna, you still have the rebellion angels to look out for," she warns me. "They won't be happy that I helped you today. The possibility of you being disgraced and exiled off Earth is the only thing that was keeping them at bay. You'll need to figure out a way to deal with them."

"Thank you for the warning," I say. "I'm sure we'll be able to figure out a way to deal with them."

"Well, I should be going," Helena says. "Hopefully, you won't be seeing me for quite some time. It all depends on if I can talk Cade into leaving with me and starting over somewhere else."

"Where will you go?" I ask.

Helena shrugs. "I don't know yet, and it's probably better if you don't either."

Helena phases away, leaving me stunned and hopeful of a brighter future without her in it.

CHAPTER TWENTY-ONE

"She's right," Malcolm tells me, "we need to get back to the house and tell the others what's going on." Malcolm turns to my Watcher protectors who are standing behind us. "I need for you to gather all the War Angels and bring them to the house. I bet you anything Lorcan just went to inform them that Helena betrayed them all. They're going to be livid and see Anna as their only target."

"We're on it," Jered says as they all phase away.

"Come on," Malcolm says, phasing us to our New Orleans home.

When we phase into the living room, Lucifer is there speaking with one guest I'm not surprised to see and one guest who is very unexpected.

Christopher, the rebellion angel who was acting as a go-between for us and our mole within the rebellion angel ranks, is standing beside Cleo. The last time I saw Cleo, she had brought a group of rebellion angels to this very house to attack my Watchers and me. I can still remember that fight. Jered had his arm cut off. Luna was just a puppy at the time, but she defended me and ended up being thrown against a wall, which injured her head. It was a horrible fight and one I would rather not relive today.

"So you're our mole?" I ask Cleo as Malcolm and I walk up to the others.

Cleo tosses her beautiful long blond hair as she considers me appraisingly.

"I felt like I owed Lucifer one for old time's sake," she says. "You look good, by the way. I can barely tell you just gave birth to twins. If your breasts weren't so huge, I'd hardly even notice."

"Thank you, I think," I reply uncertainly. It may have been an oddly stated compliment, but at least she wasn't here to attack us. "Why are you here? I thought information was supposed to go through Christopher to keep your identity unknown to us."

Cleo shrugs her slim shoulders. "I didn't see the point. Hale and the others will be ere shortly, and you're going to need all the protection you can get. They won't be oming here to make threats. They're coming here to kill you and anyone who might get n their way."

"Lorcan certainly didn't waste any time," Malcolm grumbles. "I should have illed him when I had the chance."

"Yeah, I was with Hale when he showed up to complain about Helena saving Anna."

"Did you have a chance to speak with her?" Lucifer asks me.

"Yes. She came to Malcolm and me before she left. I think it's the first time I've een Helena look content. She said she was going to take Cade somewhere else for a resh start. I assume she meant to an off-world."

"Good for her," Lucifer says, sounding pleased by the outcome. "Maybe the talk I ad with her this morning helped some."

"Talk?" I ask, realizing that's why no one knew where my dad was this morning. "What did you talk about?"

"I told her how sorry I was for what I did to her," he tells me. "I should have done it a long time ago, but I was just too stubborn to admit that how she turned out was my fault."

"That must have been hard for you," I say.

Lucifer shrugs. "It was long overdue. I think it finally gave us both some closure."

I turn to Malcolm, clutching his right forearm. "If the rebellion angels are coming, we need to take the children somewhere safe. We have to get them out of here."

Malcolm phases us to the kitchen where we find Jess, Mason, and my papa with the kids and dogs.

S. J. West

"Rebellion scum are on their way here," Malcolm tells them. "The kids will need to be taken somewhere else."

"Where is a safe place?" Mason asks as he picks up Liam.

"Let's take them to my grandfather," I suggest. "They may not know he's still alive."

"I like Grandpa Rory," Lucas tells me as he comes to place a comforting arm around my waist. "Great idea, Mommy."

"Helena may know about Rory," my papa points out. "She could have told Hale and the others that he's on Mars."

"It doesn't really seem like something Helena would bother telling them about," I say. "Plus, only a handful of people even know who or where he is right now. I think it's the safest place for them."

"Anna," I hear Zane say, drawing my attention as he and Marcus enter the kitchen behind me. "Ethan told us to get you and the kids to a safer location."

"I need for you to take the children to Mars and stay there with my grandfather," I tell my War Angels.

"And you," Zane says, noticing that I didn't include myself in the bubble of safety.

"I'm not leaving," I inform them. "All I would do is draw attention if I left. It's me they're after, and it's me they will meet when they get here. Right now, the well-being of my children takes top priority."

As we gather up all the items we think the children will need while they're in hiding, I can't help but tear up as I pack the twins' diaper bag.

"They'll be okay," Malcolm tells me. I look across the kitchen table to meet my husband's reassuring gaze. He's placing the snacks Lucas picked from the cupboards into a backpack for him to take.

296

"I know," I say with a sniffle, "I just don't like being forced to hide them away like this. I'm tired of our family being in constant danger, Malcolm."

"I know," he sympathizes. "I am, too, but let's try to focus on the positives right now. Helena is going away, so we don't have to worry about her for a while. You've been found innocent of being a terrorist, and we found a way to break Helena's connection to Liana. I would say we're doing pretty well, wouldn't you?"

"I don't think Liana's connection to Helena is broken. I think all the bracelet does is counteract her influence enough not to affect how Liana feels."

"Whatever it does, I'm just glad it works."

"Me too," I admit.

"We haven't met anything that we couldn't handle together," Malcolm reminds me. "We'll make it through this like we make it through everything else."

"I know you're right."

"Then don't look so sad, my love. I have a feeling we're close to ending all of this animosity towards our family. Plus, this will give Lucifer the chance to talk to his angels and possibly put right what he got so wrong in Heaven."

"I hope it does," I say. "They can't all be bad, right? Some of them have to want to return to God's side."

"I would think so," Malcolm says cautiously, "but some of them will carry their hate around with them until the day they die. Some people live for strife."

"Anna, I don't know where your grandfather's home is," Zane says, walking up to me with Liam in his arms. "I haven't been there before."

"I'll phase you over," Malcolm tells him, handing Lucas his full backpack. "Don't eat all of that food at once."

"You know me, Dad. I just like to be prepared," Lucas replies, securing his pack on his back.

Malcolm ruffles Lucas' hair. "Just like a Boy Scout. Always prepared."

I walk over to Zane and gaze down at Liam.

"I love you," I tell my baby boy, kissing him on the forehead. "We won't be separated for very long. I promise."

Marcus walks over to me, knowing without having to be told that I want to say farewell to my little girl, too.

"You take care of your little brother," I tell my girl. "And when you get back, we're going to have a big party with all the citizens in Cirrus to celebrate the birth of their new prince and princess."

After I kiss Liana on the cheek, I pull Lucas into my arms.

"Take care of them for me, okay?" I say.

"I will, Mommy. I promise."

"Don't worry about the children, Anna," Vala says. "Luna and I will protect them if it comes to that."

"I know you will," I tell one of my best friends. "Hopefully by moving you all to Mars, we won't have to worry about anything happening. As soon as things have settled down here, we'll come and get all of you."

"Be back in a minute," Malcolm says, kissing me on the cheek. "You might want to change before Hale and the others get here, though."

I nod, agreeing with his assessment of my wardrobe. If the rebellion angels make us fight them, the dress I'm wearing isn't exactly conducive to free, unobstructed movement.

I phase up to our bedroom and pull out my leather outfit. Unfortunately, it doesn't quite fit like it used to. The pregnancy has changed my body too much, and its tightness is restricting my movement. I opt for a pair of black pants, white shirt, and boots. I'm not sure where my sword is, so I phase downstairs to ask Jess since she was the last one to use it.

I don't see anyone in the kitchen so I phase to the living room, but I don't see anyone there either. Just as I'm about to leave to search the dining room, I happen to glance out one of the front windows and see where everyone has gone.

"The children are safely with your grandfather," I hear Malcolm announce, apparently just arriving back from Mars.

"Come on," I tell him, walking towards the front entry. "We have visitors outside."

When we step into the foyer, we see that the front door has been left wide open.

As soon as we step over the threshold and onto the stoop, we're standing directly behind Lucifer, Jess, and Mason. Standing in a line on a step below us are my Watchers. Out in the front courtyard, staring each other down, are the War Angels and the rebellion angels.

"Stay behind us, Anna," Lucifer instructs me. "Apparently, we're waiting on their fearless leader to arrive. I guess he intends to make a dramatic entrance."

"Who?" I ask. "This Hale person Cleo mentioned?"

"Yes," Lucifer answers, keeping a steady gaze on the rebellion angels he once commanded.

"He's a bit of a drama queen," Cleo complains from her position beside Jess. "He thinks of himself as Lucifer 2.0."

Lucifer snorts. "There can only be one me in existence."

"Yeah, another ego as big as yours can't possibly exist in this reality."

"I see you still think you're witty, Jessica," Lucifer grumbles.

Jess shrugs. "I can't help it. I make myself laugh. Plus, you've always been an easy target."

"Dad," I say from behind him, "have you tried to talk to them?"

"It won't do any good until Hale comes," he answers. "Rebellion angels are followers by nature. How do you think I was able to convince them to rebel in the first place?"

"I sort of resent that remark," Cleo says.

"At least you've shown some initiative by joining our side," Lucifer tells her. "That's more than I can say for those fools out there."

"You might want to curb your insults," Jess tells him. "You're supposed to be making a mea culpa with them, not pissing them off."

Lucifer sighs. "Old habits are hard to change. I'm more used to just giving them orders, not asking them to reexamine their lives and choose a different path."

"Well," I say, thinking about what's been said so far, "you did just say that they're followers. Maybe you just need to persuade them to follow you one more time."

"It wouldn't hurt to try," Jess agrees. "That *is* one of the reasons you came back here."

"I suppose I can try," Lucifer says, just as a new rebellion angel phases in front of the others.

He's a handsome black man with striking hazel eyes. This has to be Hale, the new leader of the rebellion angels that we've all been waiting for. When he meets my gaze, all I see is hate. It's obvious by the way he's looking at me that he detests the mere fact that I xist. Now that I've seen Hale, I seriously doubt my father will be able to change his mind, but who would have thought Lucifer would ever ask for forgiveness. Miracles were known to happen.

"I can't believe you had the audacity to come back here," Hale says to my father. "We don't need you anymore, Lucifer. Go back to Heaven and leave us alone."

"You know I can't do that," Lucifer tells him. "Not when so many of you are trying to kill my daughter. Helena is gone, Hale. She won't be helping you anymore. She's moving on with her life. I suggest you do the same."

"Moving on?" Hale asks incredulously. "What exactly are we supposed to move on to?"

Lucifer walks down the steps to stand a little closer to the crowd of rebellion angels.

"If our father can forgive me, don't you believe He can forgive the rest of you?" Lucifer asks them. "I know for a fact that some of you want to return to Heaven more than anything, and I'm here to tell you that you can. All you have to do is ask for His forgiveness and it will be granted, no questions asked."

"Do you really think anyone here believes you came back for us? You came back to protect your daughter. Not act as our father's go-between to try to convince us that all our sins will be forgiven if we just *ask*."

"If you don't believe Lucifer's words, will you believe mine, Hale?" I hear God say.

I don't see Him right away, but the gathering of angels in front of my house do.

The rebellion angels part as if God was a pebble thrown into their midst. As they all back away from Him, I can't help but feel comforted by His presence. With Him here, I know there won't be a fight.

God stares at Hale, patiently waiting for an answer to his question.

"How could you forgive any of us after what we've done here?" Hale questions.

"I forgave Lucifer, didn't I?" God points out. "What makes your sins any greater than his?"

Hale doesn't answer. I can only presume it's because he doesn't have one to give.

God considers all the rebellion angels around Him. Most of them look like they're in shock. A few even begin to cry. Could this be the first time some of them have seen their father since the Fall?

"When I exiled you all from Heaven," God begins, "it was with the hope that you would someday find your way back to Me. I don't ask for much from you. All I need is for you to truly repent for betraying Me and for the sins you have committed against humanity. If any of you can do those two things right this second, you can return home...return to Me.

"And that's all You want from us?" Hale asks doubtfully. "For us to bow down to You again and obey Your every command?"

"I'm not asking you to bow down to Me," God patiently explains. "I'm asking you to accept My love again and rejoin Me in Heaven where you all belong. Sending you here to Earth wasn't a punishment. It was simply the only way to make some of you find yourselves again."

An angel I don't know steps closer to God.

"I want to go home, Father," he says tearfully.

"I know you do, Jessop," God says, smiling benevolently at him. He looks at the gathering of angels and says, "I know many of you want to return with Me but that you feel unworthy to ask for My forgiveness just yet. There is a simple solution to your dilemma." God finds me with His eyes. "If you feel as though you need to prove ourselves to Me, stay here and protect Anna and her family. There are still those among you who hold her personally responsible for Lucifer's salvation and subsequent return to Heaven." God looks directly at Hale. "Whether you hate her because of that fact or because you are jealous his love for her was so absolute, I know it will take more time for you to finally come back to Me. I've waited this long for you. I can be patient and wait a little longer. Those of you who wish to stay and help Anna should phase to the front of the house and stand with her War Angels so the rest of your brethren know where your loyalties lie."

Well over half of the rebellion angels phase to join us.

"You're nothing but a bunch of hypocrites and cowards!" Hale shouts at them angrily.

"No," Cleo tells him, "many of us are thinking for ourselves for the first time in our lives. Just because you don't agree with our decision doesn't make your choice the only right one. I think you and the others should leave now, Hale. Your numbers are too few to defeat us and Anna's War Angels, not that you ever had much of a real chance against them anyway."

I didn't think it was possible, but when Hale looks at me again his eyes are filled with even more hate than before, and I know he'll find a way to retaliate. It may not be now, tomorrow, or even next year, but sometime in the future he'll do something that may force me to kill him.

"Let's go," Hale tells the few rebellion angels still loyal to him.

They phase from the courtyard, leaving only God and those who have chosen to protect me. God walks closer to us.

"Hello, Anna," He says, smiling benevolently. "I'm glad to see you looking so well."

"Thank You for coming," I reply. "And thank You for helping us solve this problem."

"Well, I wouldn't give all the credit to Me." God looks at the rebellion angels who have decided to side with us. "I believe their decision is what turned the tide in your favor."

"Yes, but it was Your presence that reminded them of home."

God grins and nods His head once in agreement with my assessment. He turns His attention to Lucifer.

"I know this was one of the missions you set for yourself before returning home," He says to my father. "Are you ready to come back with Me now?"

"I believe so," Lucifer answers. "I've done what I came to do."

My father turns to me, spreading his arms wide, silently asking for a hug. How could I deny him something I also want?

"Thank you for coming to help me," I tell him, tightening my arms around his waist as he holds me firmly around my shoulders.

"There is nothing in this world that I wouldn't do for you, Anna," he says. "I'll be watching to see what Hale and the others do next, but I don't believe you'll be hearing from them for quite some time. Enjoy this moment of peace while you have it. There's no way of knowing how long it will last or what will happen to disrupt it next. If I see that you need my help again, I'll return."

I nod my head against his shoulder, silently letting him know that I understand his words of caution. Happiness can make you complacent at times because you can't imagine anything being able to interrupt it. I'll need to remain vigilant against the remaining rebellion angels who hate me, and for the possible return of Helena if things don't work out how she plans with Cade. I can well imagine she would blame me for such a failure.

I pull back from my father. "Thank you for talking with Helena earlier. I know it must have been hard for you, but at least she's decided to end her vendetta against me. Well, at least for now."

"I would like to believe that I played a role in her decision, but if she didn't have a good man who loved and believed in her I'm not sure my words would have been as effective."

"She just needed to know that you care about her. Every daughter does."

My father kisses me on the forehead and hugs me tight one more time before letting me go. I know he needs to return to Heaven. It must have been hard for him to be away from my mother for so long, but I am eternally grateful that he returned to help me. Without him, I fear what might have happened.

"We should probably be going back, too," Jess says before turning to my papa. "Unless you're marrying the Empress of Nacreous soon. We could probably stay long enough to attend the wedding."

"What?" I immediately ask, looking at my papa. "When did you have time to ask Olivia to marry you?"

"I haven't," he replies, sounding as surprised as I am about his upcoming nuptials. "Not yet at least. I was planning to wait until things settled down before I even asked her out on a proper first date. I swear to you, Anna, I have not asked her to marry me yet. You would be the first to know if I was even thinking about doing it."

"Oh, come on, Andre," Jess says. "It's so obvious by the way you talk about her and look at her when she's around that you'll be popping the question soon."

"Can I at least decide that for myself first?" my papa asks in exasperation. "Besides, we need to all focus on the upcoming election."

"Oh, yeah, the election," I say with a grimace. "With everything that's been going on, I completely forgot about that."

"I wouldn't worry too much," God tells me. "I have a feeling you'll remain the Empress of Cirrus for a very long time to come."

With His words, my worry instantly melts away.

"Thank You."

As we finish saying our goodbyes to everyone, my mind drifts off as I wonder how Helena and Cade are doing. I'll miss Cade dearly, and I hope he comes to say goodbye to us before he leaves with Helena. I truly hope they can find happiness togethe and live a long, long time treasuring every moment.

CHAPTER TWENTY-TWO

(Helena's Point of View)

After I leave the Mars pavilion, I phase onto the porch of Cade's beach house on Earth. It was the place his phase trail led to when he left Lucifer and me to talk on Sierra. I feel hesitant to enter his private sanctuary. Mostly I'm worried he'll tell me to leave him alone, unable to forgive me for what I did to Virga. Yet Amalie was able to forgive Lucifer for far worse than that. He had, after all, prodded the Great War along, which resulted in almost a hundred times more deaths than the destruction of Virga.

A part of me wishes I could feel guilt for what I did, but I would only be lying to myself and to Cade if I said I was sorry. All I can do is hope he can overlook what he views as a character flaw. Hopefully, clearing Anna's name of all charges will be enough to prove to him that I do place value on his feelings. I need him to forgive me and try to find a way to give me a second chance.

I hate feeling as though I need him in my life, but that's exactly the way I feel. There's no getting around the fact that he is the single-most important person to me right now. If I had to exist without him it would only be a half-life, at best.

I take a deep breath and place my hand on the front door's brass knob. I turn it and step inside, ready to do whatever it takes to make Cade understand how much he means to me.

I find him sitting on one of the stools at the kitchen island. He has his hands folded in front of him, looking contemplative as he sits in the mostly silent room. The only sound I hear is the rushing of the ocean waves behind me as they crash against the shoreline.

Slowly, Cade turns his head to look at me. He stands from his seat and takes two steps toward me, but stops as if he's waiting for me to come the rest of the way to him.

"I cleared Anna's name," I tell him. "And you need to know that I did that for you not her. She won't be exiled now, and I see no reason why she won't win the election in Cirrus to remain in power there."

"Thank you for doing that," he says, looking relieved. "And did you get things straightened out with Lucifer after I left?"

"As well as could be expected, considering our history together," I reply. "I think we both got what we needed out of our conversation." I clear my throat as I let go of the doorknob and take another step into the room. "I'm a creature of habit," I tell him. "I don't see myself changing overnight, and I hope you don't expect that of me."

"I don't expect you to change who you are," Cade says, taking another step towards me as we slowly close the gap between us. "I only expect you to think about me when you make decisions that affect those I love. What you tried to do to Anna is beneath you, Helena. On Sierra, you gave me a glimpse of the person I want to be with for the rest of my life. I won't take less than the woman I held in my arms and made love to."

"Are you willing to forget what I did?"

"I can't forget it," he says. "I can't even comprehend it fully, but just knowing that you helped Anna gives me hope that someday you won't feel the need to hurt others for your own personal gain. If you're here that means you're willing to change, even if it's just a small bit."

"Right now," I say, taking another step forward so that we're only two steps away from each other, "all I want is to take you somewhere else and never come back to his planet again. I want us to have a chance at a real life together. A place where I don't feel the need to watch Anna's every move and figure out a way to cause trouble in her life. If I can learn to let go of my hatred towards her, maybe I can finally live."

Cade takes another step and holds his hand out to me.

"Then let's go, Helena. Let's find a planet where no one knows who we are and we can have a fresh start."

I take the last step and place my hand into his.

"As long as you don't force me to live off the land," I say jokingly, remembering his musings when he was chopping wood on Sierra. "I have certain standards of cleanliness that I won't change for anyone; even for you, dear heart."

Cade chuckles. "I think we can work with that."

"Then you'll go with me?" I ask, just to confirm that he's agreeing to my suggestion.

"Will you let me come back here to see Anna, Lucas, and the others?"

"If you must," I acquiesce, knowing that if I say no he might change his mind. I'm so close to having what I want, I can't even conceive of having it snatched away from me now.

"Then, yes, I'll go with you, Helena. Lead and I will follow you to the end of the galaxy."

I quickly phase us to the Nexus in Hell.

"It's about time you came back here so I can talk some sense into you," my alter ego says as soon as I enter my domain. "Have you lost your mind?" she demands hotly. "Why did you help Anna? And why are you planning to hide on some other planet with this piece of meat?"

I leave Cade's side and stride up to my mirror image, even though I know he can't see her. She's simply a manifestation of my subconscious that I can't control while I'm in my domain.

"Go away," I say through gritted teeth, determined to shut down this part of my brain once and for all. "I don't need you anymore. I have everything I want right in front of me. All I have to do is take it."

"You mean you had everything you wanted until you decided to clear Anna's name!"

"She doesn't matter to me anymore!"

"Helena?" Cade says behind me, sounding worried since he sees me talking to nothing but empty space. "Are you okay?"

I turn my head and tell him, "Let me handle this first and then we can go."

I whip back around and stare into the eyes of my own id.

"I'm happy for the first time in my life, and I won't allow you to take it away. Do you hear me?" I shout. "You," I say, pointing to my phantom, "can stay here and run things. I don't need this place anymore."

"Place?" she questions incredulously. "This place *is* you! It's like you don't even remember that anymore since you found a way to split yourself into two. You will never be able to leave here because it will always be inside you. You are Hell and Hell is you. I'm just the rational part of you that remembers that fact. You're not meant to live a happy life. You're meant to torment those who end up here, because they were bad people who died with sins so great this is where they were sent to spend their eternity. You're deluding yourself if you think that meat- suit over there is going to change your life for the better. You are what you are, and the sooner you accept that fact the better off we'll both be."

I shake my head. "You're wrong. I can have happiness because he's standing right there," I say, pointing to Cade. "Not even you can stop me from loving him."

"Love?" I hear Cade say behind me. "Did you just say you love me, Helena?"

310

It takes me a moment, but I suddenly realize what I just said. I turn to face Cade, drinking in the sight of him as I allow myself a moment to work through my feelings. When Lucifer fell in love with Amalie, I thought him the worst type of fool. And while I watched Anna fawn all over Malcolm, I decided then and there that love had to be a drug that made you lose all reasonable thought. They both acted so foolishly in my eyes that I associated love with insanity.

Yet, as I look into Cade's eyes, all I see is his love for me. Maybe love is a drug, but it has to be the best kind. In this moment, all I want to do is accept what he's offering me and lavish him with my own feelings in return. I begin to feel a burning sensation build up inside my chest, urging me to follow what's within my heart and tell the man in front of me exactly how I feel about him.

"I do love you," I say far more easily than I could have ever imagined. "I love you," I tell him again, feeling even freer of the bonds trying to keep me shackled to reason. "I…"

Cade doesn't allow me to finish because he phases over, wraps me inside his embrace, and kisses me as if the world is about to end when the complete opposite is true for us. We're about to embark on an adventure without knowing exactly what awaits us. It's the first time in my life that I don't know what will happen next, and I couldn't be happier about that fact.

I feel myself lose all of my inhibitions, allowing the love I feel for Cade to course through my veins like molten lava. Pure happiness consumes me, setting my body on fire.

And then I realize Cade isn't holding me anymore. His mouth is no longer pressed against mine, and I can't feel the frantic beating of his heart against my breast.

What I do hear is maniacal laughter coming from behind me.

"Smooth move, Cinderella. You just killed your Prince Charming."

My alter ego's taunt forces me to open my eyes. Cade is nowhere to be seen. When I look down at my hands, I see that they are now covered with sparkling black ash As I let my eyes fall to the floor in front of my feet, I see that a pile of ash lays where Cade once stood.

"No," I say with a shake of my head, unwilling to comprehend what I'm seeing, "this can't be happening." I take a step back but can't seem to make myself stop staring a the pile of ash on the floor. "This isn't happening!"

"Poor Helena," my alter ego croons. "You found love but, unfortunately for Cade, your kind of love kills."

I swiftly turn around. "You did this!" I accuse "I don't know how, but you killed him because I wanted to leave this place!"

"I am you, silly. Yes, *we* killed him, but only because you loved him too much."

"I didn't kill him!" I protest.

"Your undying love for him did, though. Do you remember when Anna got so angry after Levi killed Millie that she went searching for him?"

"Yes," I say, not seeing where this is leading. "What does that have to do with this?"

"Anna was so angry at Levi that she lost control of her powers and accidentally killed one of her own Watchers. The one they called Daniel."

"What does that have to do with this?" I yell again, hysterically.

"Anna's uncontrollable anger killed Daniel just like your uncontrollable love for Cade ending up killing him," my phantom explains.

"No!" I shout. "No, this is some sort of twisted game that you're playing with my mind. I know how you work. You twist reality and make people believe their worst ightmares have come true." I place my face in front of hers and demand, "Where is ade? What have you done to him?"

"He's right there on the floor behind you," she replies calmly. "I'm not lying."

In a growl of rage, I phase myself to my bedroom in Hell.

"Cade?" I call out, quickly looking around the room for any sign of him. When I on't see him, I run out of the room and into the dimly-lit hallway of my dark fortress.

"Cade?" I call out again, but more urgently. I know the mind games my domain an play, and I refuse to be a victim of one of them. "Cade! Answer me!" I demand again, picking up my pace as I run down the hall, checking each room as I go. As I ontinue to search, realization slowly begins to sink into my heart.

I come to a complete stop in the middle of the hallway and look down at my ands. The black glittering ash still covers them like a permanent stain. I take in a deep reath. And then another. And another, each time filling my lungs to capacity. All I can ear is my heavy breathing and the roar of blood in my ears as the truth of what I've done inally becomes real.

I've killed Cade.

I've killed the only person in all of existence that I loved and who could love me in return. Giving him all of my love wasn't a moment in some fairytale. It was the very thing nightmares are made of, crumbling everything in its path to black, glittering ash. My love was poison, and it killed the only person who mattered to me.

I hear horrible, heart-wrenching sobs, but they sound so far away at first. It takes me a moment to realize that they're coming from me.

In that moment, I realize Lucas' prophecy has come true. This is why I was crying so uncontrollably in his vision. I should have known then that only the loss of Cade would make me lose control over my emotions and cause me so much grief all I can do is cry out my sorrow and wish I could join him in death.

I don't know what to do. I don't know where to go. All I can feel is this raw, gaping hole inside my chest, making it almost impossible for me to breathe. There's a chasm now that no amount of time or wishing will allow me to breech. I know without having to be told that Cade is in Heaven. It's the one place I can't reach. If I could die I would take my own life to be with him, but how can a thing like me find peace in death?

I can't. I'm doomed to live an eternity yearning for someone I will never be able to see again no matter what I do.

"Cade," I cry out in a whimper as I drop to my knees in misery, wishing he could hear me. Wishing he could come back to me.

I lie down on the floor and curl up into a ball, sobbing until no more tears come. After a long while I finally calm down enough to start breathing normally again, but I can't seem to find the will to move. I'm barely breathing. I'm barely there.

I'm not sure how long I stay on that floor, but eventually I find enough energy to sit up. I begin to cry again when I realize all I want is for Cade to hold me and tell me everything will be all right, but he can't do that. He's dead. Gone forever, and I'll never see him again. I'll never feel his hands touching my face. I'll never feel his lips pressed against mine or hear him tell me he loves me. All of that has been stripped away from me forever, leaving me with nothing but pain.

I look around the hallway, realizing I can't stand to be here anymore. I have to leave. I have to get away before my shadow finds me to taunt me over my loss. I phase to the Nexus, being careful not to look at the floor. If I see Cade's ashes, I might break down again and never leave this place.

I have to get out before my grief weakens me again. I look at the universe of planets, knowing that running away won't work forever, but right now it's my only alternative. I can't stay on Earth or go back to Sierra. I have to find a new place to call home.

Nothing takes your mind off your own problems like conquering a new world.

CHAPTER TWENTY-THREE

(Anna's Point of View)

That evening, after everyone leaves, Malcolm and I go to Mars to bring our children back home. I haven't spent much time with my mother's father, but that was partially my fault. I didn't want to rush a relationship with him. The few times we have been together, I've felt an awkwardness between us that makes me uncomfortable. He hasn't said as much, but I don't believe he blames me for my mother's early death anymore, yet when he looks at me there's a sadness in his eyes that I know will never go away. I'm sure it's because he sees a lot of my mother in my face. It's not exactly something I can change or would even want to for that matter. So I limit the time we spend together for both our sakes.

When we return home, I practically have to tell Marcus that I want him to leave. I can appreciate his desire to be around Liana because of her connection to Arel, but all I want is a quiet moment with my family where we can just be together and shut the world out for one night.

"I will build a barricade against this door to keep people out if I have to," Malcolm declares as he closes the door to the study.

"Just come here and look at our beautiful babies," I urge him from my place on the floor in front of the fireplace.

"They are pretty cute," Lucas agrees from his seat beside me on the makeshift pallet of blankets we made so we could all sit together.

Malcolm sits down on the other side of me with his legs crossed.

"Yes, I do believe your mother and I did a fine job making you a little brother and sister to play with. Maybe we should get started on making you some more siblings."

"Oh no," I say. "We're not making any more babies for quite a while. Let me recover from this pregnancy first. Then, we can talk about having more children."

"Well, if my opinion matters at all," Vala tells us from her position beside Malcolm, "I vote for sooner rather than later."

Luna walks over to me and starts to lick my left cheek, as if she sympathizes with my plight.

"At least you understand, girl," I say, ruffling the white flaming fur on the side of her neck.

She licks me one more time and goes back to lay on the other side of Lucas.

Both Liam and Liana are lying in front of us on the pallet, gurgling as they try to look at us all around them.

"If I have my wish," I tell them both, leaning forward until my head is over them, and I have their complete attention, "the two of you will have charmed, happy lives."

As I gaze at my babies, I notice Liana's bluer than blue eyes watching me closely. To me, it's proof that the connection between her and Helena is still present and that the bracelet does nothing more than act as a temporary dam. Yet maybe Helena didn't hate me as much as she once did now that she's trying to build a life with Cade. It would solve so many of my worries for Liana if that turns out to be the case.

Someone softly knocks on the study door. It's a hesitant knock, and I immediately know something is wrong.

I stand from my place with my family and go to the door, even though Malcolm urges me to ignore the plea for our attention.

When I open the door, I find Lucifer standing in the hallway with a troubled frown on his face.

"You wouldn't be back here this soon if something wasn't wrong," I immediately say, feeling panicked. "What's happened?"

Lucifer looks further into the room to find Malcolm.

"I need to take you and Malcolm somewhere," he tells me cryptically. "There's something the two of you need to know about."

"Can we bring the children and the dogs?" I ask, not wanting to leave them behind.

"It would be better if you didn't," Lucifer says, glancing back into the room. It seems like he's looking directly at Lucas. "It might be too upsetting," he whispers to me.

"I'll go get Jered to come up here to look after them," Malcolm says before phasing to the stables.

"You're scaring me," I whisper back to my father. "What's wrong?"

Lucifer shakes his head. "I would rather show you, so you can fully understand what's taken place."

It only takes a minute for Malcolm to return with Jered. Once the children are secure, Malcolm and I step into the hallway in front of my father, holding hands. Lucifer touches my shoulder and phases us without informing us beforehand where we're going.

He doesn't even have to tell us where we are once we arrive.

We're in Hell, yet the room he's brought us to is beautiful. As I stare at the plethora of soft, glowing balls of light floating in the room, I have to ask, "Are these planets?"

"Yes. They're ones I've been to over the years," Lucifer tells us. "I call this place the Nexus, and almost every inhabitable world in the universe is represented here."

"And why did you bring us here?" Malcolm asks.

"Because I need to tell you what happened here today," my father begins, even though he looks reluctant to weave his tale. "Anna, I hate to be the bearer of bad news, especially today when you have so much to celebrate, but I thought the sooner I told you the better it would be for you."

"What bad news?" I ask breathlessly, wondering what terrible tragedy could have happened to make my dad return from Heaven so soon.

"Cade is dead," he tells us quickly, as if saying it fast will make it hurt me less.

I don't need to ask who killed Cade. Besides myself, there should only be one other person in existence who has the power to kill an angel protected by one of Bai's tattoos.

"That doesn't make any sense, Dad. I saw Helena's love for Cade in her eyes. Why would she kill him?" I ask as feelings of rage and sorrow fight for control over my body.

"She didn't mean to," Lucifer says as he kneels down on one knee in front of us. It's only then that I see the pile of ash on the floor. I gasp, covering my mouth with both hands as I stare at what's left of Cade. "Helena was never made to love someone," Lucifer tells us, seeming to be unable to take his eyes off Cade's sparkling black ashes either. "The fact that she found a way to do it still baffles me, but she did love Cade. She loved him so much that every part of her being became electrified with it. I talked with my father, and He basically confirmed my theory about what transpired here."

When Lucifer doesn't continue right away, Malcolm says, "Well, don't leave us hanging. What happened?"

Lucifer stands back up. "She allowed herself to feel the love she has for Cade while they were here in Hell. It was the worst possible place she could have brought him to share her feelings."

"Why?" I ask.

"I think Helena believed that by leaving her domain she could have a life separate from it. What she doesn't seem to grasp is that everything that happens here affects her. With the arrival of new souls from Virga, Hell became filled with an overload of energy. I'm sure she felt it when it happened, but it was only when she came back here that she absorbed it all. Her body became the physical manifestation of an old-fashioned powder keg; her love for Cade acted like a spark, triggering the explosion. Opening her heart to him caused a tremendous release of energy all at once and resulted in this," Lucifer says returning his gaze to Cade's ashes.

I feel a sorrow for Helena that I never thought I could feel. To finally find the one person in the universe she could truly love, only to kill him with it.

"Where is Helena now?" I ask, feeling a need to go to her. I don't know if she'll talk to me, but I can't just ignore the pain she's in right now.

Lucifer lifts his eyes to look at the miniature planets surrounding us.

"She's gone to one of these worlds," he tells us.

"Which one?" I ask impatiently.

"I don't know," he says, standing back up, "and my father won't tell me."

"Wait," Malcolm says, looking around us, "are you saying that from here, we can go to any of these planets?"

"Yes," Lucifer confirms. "I left permanent phase trails to all of them."

"Permanent?" Malcolm questions, looking confused. "Our trails always fade over time."

"Yes, but you didn't have the power of Hell behind you to keep them open. I did."

I sigh heavily because I know finding Helena will be an impossible task.

"There's no way we can find her," I say. "Not unless she wants to be found."

"I'm not sure you want to find her right now anyway," my father says, sounding as : finding Helena might lead to dire consequences. "After she works through her grief, he's going to be mad. Madder than you or I have ever seen her. I think it would be better or everyone involved if you left her alone for a while. There may come a time when you an reach out to her, but I don't believe that time is now, Anna."

"Lucifer is right," Malcolm tells me. "I know you want to help her because that's ust the kind of person you are, but you need to let her cool down first. Let her go through .er grieving period. If she was able to kill Cade with her love, she might be able to kill ou with her anger. I think we should feel lucky that she's left Earth. I pity the planet he's gone to now."

I know Malcolm is right, but my heart still goes out to Helena and Cade. To find ɔne another in this world full of people, only to have the love they felt for one another be he reason Cade was snatched away.

"Have you seen Cade?" I ask my father.

"Yes. He's dealing with what happened."

"Should I go to him?"

"I think you need to give him some time, too. Loss is a horrible thing, and when hat loss will last an eternity it's not an easy idea to comprehend."

"I understand." I want to go to Cade, but I do understand his need for privacy right 10w. I can remember feeling the sadness of my mother when she thought she would be separated from Lucifer forever. I can only assume Cade is experiencing that same sense of loss.

"We'll have to tell Lucas," Malcolm says to me with a great deal of dread.

"I know," I reply, tearing up at the thought of having to tell our little boy that his best friend is dead.

"I'll do it," Malcolm offers, placing a comforting arm around my shoulders. "You've been through enough."

"It's not like you haven't been through everything with me," I tell him, loving the thoughtfulness but knowing I can't take it. "We'll both tell him."

Malcolm nods his agreement, knowing he won't be able to change my mind.

"Thank you for coming back to explain everything to us," I tell my father, walking over to give him a hug.

"I felt you needed to know the truth," he says, patting me on the back. "I should return to your mother. Apparently she missed me while I was gone."

I pull back. "I'm sure she did."

"Good luck with telling Lucas and your friends," my father wishes us just before he phases. However, I can see by his phase trail that he's gone to a city I don't recognize. It seems strange that he wouldn't return to Heaven right away, but I assume he has his reasons.

I look at the planets in the Nexus, wondering which one will have to feel the wrath of Helena's loss. All I know is that I pity them greatly, and my heart aches for Helena. She was so close to having everything she wanted. Now, it's lost forever.

When we return home, we ask Jered to stay so he can hear the news and deliver the unhappy tidings to everyone else for us.

Lucas' sorrow over Cade's death makes everything feel real and final. He crawls into Malcolm's arms and cries his heart out. We sit there with him, trying to bring him comfort, and I know a part of Lucas' childhood has come to a tragic end. It wasn't something I could protect him from, and unfortunately death is simply a lesson that everyone has to learn to deal with at some point in his or her lives. I just wish he could have been older before having to face it, and that his first experience with it hadn't been with his best friend.

I think about the wall of seashells Cade has at his beach house and make a mental note to have it moved to the palace. I know how much pride Lucas felt every time they added a new shell to their collection. When he gets older, I know my son will appreciate having it in memory of his first best friend.

Lucas ends up crying himself to sleep. After we tuck him into bed, I ask Vala to stay with him through the night and to let us know when he wakes up. Luna, of course, doesn't leave our son's side and crawls onto this bed to sleep beside him.

After I feed the babies and we have them tucked into our bed, I follow my son's lead and crawl onto my husband's lap to finally cry out my own sorrow over losing Cade. Malcolm tries to urge me to go see him in Heaven, but I refuse. I want to respect Cade's feelings and allow him time to heal.

He had won the love of someone who wasn't supposed to be able to feel such an emotion. We all knew Helena loved Cade but she refused to admit it, even to herself. When she finally did, all was lost, and that kind of love story was worthy of my tears.

EPILOGUE

"Empress Anna, would you like pancakes or waffles for breakfast this morning? 'Cause, those are my two specialties."

I smile as I look at Lucas standing by his father at the stove.

"Hmm, that's a very difficult decision, Prince Lucas. I hereby decree that you should cook whatever you think I might want this morning."

Lucas giggles, not because of my answer but because I called him a prince.

Three months have passed since the night Lucifer came to tell us the circumstances surrounding Cade's death. For days afterwards, I worried Helena would come back to Earth and find a way to blame us for what happened to him. Yet, we haven't heard from or seen her since the trial on Mars. I pray she's made peace with her beloved's death, but I know if I were in her shoes I would never truly be able to forgive myself. At the very least, I hope she finds a way to go on with her life.

The election to determine whether Catherine or I would be Empress of Cirrus happened only a month ago. It took longer than expected to repair the infrastructure of Cirrus enough for people to return to their homes. Malcolm kept telling me not to worry about being elected, but worry I did until the ballots were counted. As usual, my husband was right.

I ended up with eighty percent of the votes, a landslide win. It turned out that having my citizens live in the down-world for a while gave them first-hand knowledge of how difficult it is to live on the surface. They were able to fully understand how sharing cloud city technology could change the lives of those on the ground. Since Catherine was part of the old regime and stagnant in her beliefs about sharing technology with the down-worlders, the people decided to vote for change. I represented a future they all wanted to live in.

Now that we all live in the palace again, life is back to normal and the only problems we have to face are the small, everyday ones.

"I bet Liana would like to gnaw on a waffle," Marcus says from his position at the kitchen table as he holds my daughter. "It might massage her gums and stop her from being so cranky."

"I'm all for trying that trick," Zane says from his seat right beside Marcus as he cradles Liam in his arms. "Though, I'm thinking we might need to pray to our father for back-up."

I can't help but laugh at my two War Angels and their predicament.

"Waffles it is then," Malcolm declares, settling the age-old argument between the two tasty pastries.

"So are you two in charge of the babies today?" I ask Marcus and Zane.

For the past two months, the War Angels have been taking turns caring for the twins. Malcolm and I felt it was important for them to learn the basics of childcare so that they were prepared when it came time for them to have children of their own. We weren't about to have them become fathers and expect their wives to do all the work. As far as I know, none of my War Angels have found loves of their own yet. I thought for sure that, out of the two thousand of them, at least one would have found someone they want to marry. Yet, none of them have. Sometimes, I get the feeling they're waiting because they fear something bad is about to happen. I don't know if it's the uncertainty of Helena's whereabouts and what she's doing that's causing them to hold back, or something else.

"Yes," Zane tells me, "we'll be the ones staying behind while the rest of you go to the wedding."

"I'll come get you when it's over," Malcolm tells them as he watches Lucas flip the old-fashioned waffle-maker open. Even though we have a machine that can make waffles with the push of a single button, my husband refuses to use it. He claims that waffles need to be made in a waffle iron to taste good. "I'm sure people at the reception will want to see the babies."

"Speaking of the wedding," I say, "I should probably pop over to Papa's house and see if he's eaten anything this morning."

"Knowing Andre as well as I do," Malcolm says, "I'll bet you can find him in his office, pacing back and forth nervously. That's probably where you learned that bad habit."

"Do you think he's that nervous about marrying Olivia?" I ask, not remembering my father ever being nervous about too much in his life.

"Of course he's nervous," Malcolm says as if I should know better. "Weren't you on our wedding day?"

"I think I was more anxious than nervous. Either way, I should go check on him."

"Tell him I'm making my special waffles," Lucas says. "He'll come back with you for those."

I smile at Lucas. "I'll be sure to pass the good news along."

I phase to my papa's study in his house and find him doing exactly what Malcolm predicted.

"Papa," I say, gaining his attention since he didn't notice me phase into the room.

My papa looks up with a troubled frown on his face.

"Have I made a terrible decision?" he asks me earnestly. "You can tell me the truth, Anna. I can take it. Am I making a monumental mistake by marrying Olivia?"

I walk up to him saying, "Only if you don't love her, Papa. Do you doubt your feelings for her?"

He immediately shakes his head. "No. My love for her isn't in question here. It's the fact that I'll be ruling Nacreous by her side. What if her people don't like me? What if they think I'm only marrying her so I can share her power?"

"No one is going to think that," I assure him.

"I have nothing of value to bring into this marriage," he declares despondently.

"You're bringing yourself," I adamantly remind him. "And if you ask me, that's worth more than a world made out of gold. You have years of knowledge to pull from, and even if you didn't you're the only one who makes Olivia happy. She loves you, Papa, and you love her. That's all that matters."

"Of course, you're right," he says, shaking his head at how he's acting. "I'm just being foolish and paranoid."

"You're not a fool. You're just a human."

My papa smiles and opens his arms. "I could really use a hug right now from my daughter. I think that will fortify me for the day to come."

I walk into his arms and rest my head on his chest.

"I'm going to miss having you live in my city," I tell him, tightening my arms around him to accentuate my statement.

"I'm still only a teleport away," he reminds me. "If you call, I'll be here."

"I know, but it's still not quite the same."

"Nothing stays the same in life. If it did, none of us would ever go anywhere or experience new adventures."

"Well, this is definitely a new adventure for you, and one I'm looking forward to seeing you take with Olivia by your side. Have the two of you talked about having children?"

"She already has two sons, but we have discussed having one of our own together Olivia worries that she's too old to go through another pregnancy."

"That might have been true a hundred years ago, but with today's medical technology, she isn't too old to carry a baby to full-term. I think you should do it. Any child the two of you bring into this world would be lucky to have you both as parents. I know I always feel like the luckiest girl on Earth to have you as my papa."

He hugs me tighter, letting me know how much my words mean to him.

I pull back and tell him, "Lucas is making his special waffles for us. I think you should come home with me and be with your family this morning. Then we can all go to Nacreous together."

"That sounds wonderful, actually. I don't suppose Jered has returned to the palace?"

Unfortunately, I have to shake my head. "We haven't seen him in a couple of weeks, actually. Ever since Silas disappeared from his jail cell in Stratus, Jered's been searching for him."

"He has to know Helena probably has him with her. Odds are she was the one who rescued him."

"We've tried to tell him that, but I think he needs to prove to himself that there's nothing else he can do to help his son. You know as well as anyone that he can't let go of his guilt where Silas is concerned. I know he's been back to Hell to look for him, but he hasn't seen any sign of him there."

"I still believe Silas is wherever Helena is right now." my papa sighs. "He's too good a soldier for her to leave behind."

"Then Jered definitely won't find his son until Helena wants him to."

"I fear all we can do is wait."

"I just hope Jered figures that out soon." I loop an arm around one of my papa's. Let's not think about that right now, though. Today is supposed to be a happy day for you. I would rather concentrate on making sure you get married and have the best day of your life."

After we finish breakfast, we have just enough time to get ready for the wedding. Since I'm Olivia's Matron of Honor, I put on the dress she picked out for me. It's an aubergine- colored floor-length chiffon dress with one ruffled shoulder. A slim, diamond-incrusted belt encircles the waist.

"I thought no one was supposed to look more beautiful than the bride," my husband teases as he grabs his black suit jacket off his side of the bed.

"Well, you haven't seen the bride yet either," I point out.

As Malcolm walks around the bed to my side, he says, "I don't have to see her to know you'll be the most beautiful woman at the wedding."

I smile as I turn to face him, adjusting the dangling diamond earring in my left ear.

"I do believe you are buttering me up for something with all that flattery, Emperor Malcolm. What is it that you want?"

"You make me sound so devious." From the devilish way Malcolm smiles at me, I know I've guessed right about him. "I want nothing more than your promise that I can rip that dress away from your body later and pleasure you for at least a little while."

"A little while?" I ask, aghast, placing my hands on my hips, feeling somewhat offended. "I'll have you know I expect it to last more than those words suggest."

"Then a very long while," Malcolm promises, yanking me into his arms.

I place the index finger of my right hand over his pursed lips as he dips his head down to kiss me.

"Don't," I tell him. "If you kiss me, we may end up missing my papa's wedding, and I refuse to be even a second late for it. You can rein in your passion for me until this evening. I have faith that you have enough willpower to do that."

Malcolm groans in disappointment. "I believe you give me too much credit. Where making love to you is concerned, the only willpower I possess is making sure you're fully satisfied before I find my own satisfaction."

"And I do appreciate that thoughtfulness," I say, wiggling out of his embrace. "But today is for my papa and Olivia. We're going to make sure everything runs smoothly, and that they are happy. Your happiness will just have to wait."

"As you wish," Malcolm says, but not sounding even slightly happy about my declaration.

I laugh and hold my hand out to him. "Come on, love of my life and father of my wonderful children. Let's go find Lucas and head to Nacreous so we're not late."

When the three of us phase to Nacreous, we discover that we're early. Only the servants are bustling about the ballroom of the palace where everything has been set up for the wedding.

"Empress Anna," one of the female servants says as she walks up to us, "Empress Olivia asked me to watch for your arrival and to bring you directly to her chambers."

"Go on," Malcolm tells me before kissing me on the cheek. "Lucas and I will stay here. The others should be arriving soon."

"I guess I'll see you at the altar then," I tell him. I turn to the servant. "Lead the way."

When I get to Olivia's chambers, I find her in a state similar to the one my papa was in earlier. However, unlike him, she notices my presence in the room right away and ceases her pacing.

"Am I making a mistake?" she asks me worriedly. "Am I forcing Andre to live the life of a royal?"

I smile and proceed to calm her wedding jitters just as I did for my father. I then help Olivia get dressed and do everything a dutiful future daughter-in-law should do. Bianca Rossi and Kyna come to Olivia's rooms just before the ceremony is set to begin. Since the Empress of Alto is presiding over the ceremony, she comes to confirm that Olivia isn't having any second thoughts about the marriage before we proceed.

"Oh, good grief, no," Olivia assures her. "I am not stupid enough to let a good man like him go. Is he having second thoughts?"

Bianca smiles. "Absolutely not. In fact, he asked me if I could speed things along little faster."

Olivia breathes out a sigh of relief and I know then that everything will go smoothly.

"Have you had any luck finding Lorcan?" I ask Kyna. I know for the past three months the world has been on the lookout for the wayward ex-Emperor of Stratus. After being accused of the atrocities that befell Virga and Stratus, Lorcan has remained in hiding. Although most of us believe Abaddon, the demon that possessed the real Lorcan Halloran, has probably ditched the body and found a new host by now.

"No, we haven't seen him," Kyna confirms.

"I've heard the down-world people of Stratus threw you a party when you became Empress," Bianca says.

"They did!" Kyna says happily. "It was one of the best days of my life. Brutus and I have been able to do so much to help them since we took over."

"From what Brutus has told us," I say, "he's never been happier."

"I wish I could have taken a picture of his face when Cara was born," Kyna says with a smile. "Between her birth and finally putting things right in Stratus, our lives couldn't be more perfect."

Having Kyna in control of Stratus meant there were now five cloud cities willing to share their technology with their down-worlders. All we needed now was for Levi and Mammon to admit defeat and join us. Levi was finding it increasingly difficult to come up with plausible excuses for Helena's absence in Nimbo. I understood his conundrum. He didn't know if Helena would ever return to retake her throne. He had to perpetuate the illusion that they were still together in case she did.

The wedding ceremony is quiet by royal standards. There are only about five hundred people in attendance because Olivia was afraid anything bigger might frighten my father away or make him ask for an elopement.

As I stand beside Olivia, holding her bouquet, I suddenly feel the hairs on the back of my neck prickle. I can feel someone in the crowd of guests watching me. When I turn my head away from the proceedings, I immediately find the person whose gaze has alerted me to their presence.

She's an older blond woman who stills possess the beauty of her youth even though a few wrinkles at the corners of her eyes mark her age at being somewhere around sixty. She is staring at me, but not unkindly. There is an urgency in the stiffness of her shoulders that tells me she wants to speak with me as soon as possible.

After the ceremony is over and my papa is walking proudly down the aisle with his wife holding onto his arm, I pull Malcolm aside and tell him about the woman. I have no idea if she's a friend or a foe. For all I know, she could be someone Helena has sent to spy on me. To what end I have no idea, but I feel being overly cautious is the best course of action.

Malcolm looks out at the crowd to find the woman in question so he can judge her for himself, but she's already walking over to us as we continue to stand by the altar.

than and Roan also approach, since they were assigned to join us at the wedding in case
e needed extra protection.

"Excuse me," the woman says to me, "I'm Evelyn Grace. I know your father."

"Which one?" I ask, getting the feeling from her that she's not as human as she
ppears.

"Lucifer," she clarifies.

I feel Ethan and Roan come to stand just behind Malcolm and me.

"And what is your business here?" Malcolm asks. "I assume this isn't a social
all."

"No, it isn't," Evelyn replies. "I have something in my purse I believe you should
oth see."

"What is this about?" I ask.

"It concerns Helena," she answers in a conspiratorial voice.

"Give me your hand," I tell her, holding mine out for her to take. "I would rather
ot disrupt my father's happiness with any business that pertains to her."

Evelyn seems to understand why I'm making my request and doesn't argue. She
places her hand in mine, and I grab hold of one of Malcolm's arms. I phase us to the
allroom in my own palace on Cirrus. Ethan and Roan phase in right behind us.

"What do you have to show us?" I ask her, feeling my heart race inside my chest.

Whatever Evelyn is about to reveal to us, it can't be good. People you don't know
arely seek you out to deliver good news.

"I should preface this," she says, raising the small white beaded clutch purse in her
hand, "by saying that I don't live on Earth. I live on a planet called Sierra. Helena and
Cade spent some time there in a cabin I own. Did Lucifer tell you about it?"

"No," I say. I can only assume that it's where my father had his talk with Helena about their relationship.

"After she left my planet, I had a security system installed because I wasn't sure if she would ever show up there again. I didn't want to have a surprise waiting for me if I decided to use it for my own purposes."

Evelyn opens her purse and pulls out a black rectangular object.

"I haven't seen one of those in a long time," Malcolm comments. "Your planet must not be as developed as Earth."

"No, we're not. We're still using cellphones to communicate with one another."

Evelyn slides her finger across the screen before handing it to me.

"You need to watch this video footage my security cameras recorded last night. I think you'll find it very interesting. Just touch the screen when you're ready for it to begin."

I look at the screen in my hand and see a still picture of Helena. She has her back to the camera, but I can still tell it's her. No one else has such gorgeous long blond hair. Though, I find it strange that she's dressed all in black instead of her signature red. She appears to be wearing a black turtleneck sweater and pants. Perhaps the change in the color of her wardrobe shows that she's still in mourning over Cade.

I tap the screen with my index finger to start the video. Helena is sitting on a piano bench in what appears to be a study. She places her fingers on the keys and begins to play a piece of music. It's a sad song and I can only imagine she's thinking about Cade as she plays it. I can see her shoulders shake slightly, and I know she's crying without having to see her face. When the song comes to an end Helena slides to the edge of the bench and turns to stand up, providing us with a side view of her face and body.

All four of us involuntarily gasp. I immediately tap the screen to freeze the video.

There, for all of us to see, is a pregnant Helena.

"Is that Cade's baby?" I hear Ethan ask from behind us, in total shock.

"If I were to guess the answer to your question," Evelyn says, "I would have to say 's his. When I took Lucifer to confront Helena, we found her and Cade in a ompromising position."

"I didn't even know she could become pregnant," I say, feeling like the world has addenly started to spin out of control again.

"Apparently she can," Evelyn says. "Unless she's started stuffing pillows nderneath her shirts, I would say she definitely has a bun in the oven and that Cade is the baby's father."

"But what will it look like when it comes out?" Roan questions. "Helena looks uman, but will the baby?"

I shake my head. "I have no idea."

"You should watch the rest of the video," Evelyn encourages me.

I tap the screen again to pick up where we left off. I can't see Helena's face learly, but her expression makes her look dead inside. She stands from the bench, but urns back towards the piano. In one swift, super-human movement, she stretches her rms out, pushing the baby grand piano so hard it breaks through the iron and glass walls t's set in front of, causing it to fall outside the cabin. Helena lets out a scream mixed with ooth anger and pain just before she phases away.

"Did you follow her phase trail?" I ask, feeling an urgent need to know where he's gone.

"No," Evelyn tells me. "I didn't see this video until this morning. By then, all races of her had disappeared."

I hand her back her phone. "Thank you for coming to us and letting us know about her condition."

"I knew you cared about Cade and that he loved your family like it was his own. I didn't know him for very long, but I could tell what a good person he was. I'm just sorry he got involved with Helena. From the looks of it I think she's sorry now, too."

"How did you know Cade was dead?" Malcolm asks.

"Lucifer came and told me what happened before he returned to Heaven. He wanted me to be wary and watch my back in case Helena came looking for me. She and I don't see eye to eye, as you can imagine. I don't think she got along well with anyone besides Cade."

"Anna," Ethan says to draw my attention to him. I turn around to face him. "We can't let Helena keep Cade's child. We owe him more than that."

"I'm not arguing against that point, but you need to remember that it's her child, too," I say. "She's not going to just let you take her baby away."

"Maybe if we can find her," Roan says, "she'll listen to us and understand the baby deserves to grow up in a normal home. Nothing she can provide would be normal. You know that, Anna. Even if she has the best of intentions towards the child, she'll corrupt the baby with all of her hate just like Lucifer corrupted her. Cade would never want that for his child. I know that for a fact without even having to ask him."

"Helena could be on any planet in the universe," Malcolm points out. "The odds of us finding her are astronomical at best. At worst they're non-existent."

"We have to try!" Ethan practically roars. "I refuse to just stand here and not make an attempt to save Cade's child!"

"Okay," I say, holding up my hands to try to calm Ethan down. "First we need to come up with a viable plan for finding Helena. If we can't do that, we'll at least have a starting place."

Ethan still looks upset, but he nods his agreement.

"I have a suggestion," Evelyn says. "If I were you, I would post people in places elena might visit. I assume she came back to the cabin to feel closer to Cade. Maybe at's what she's doing right now. If you station people in places that Cade or Helena ked to go, you might just be able to catch her."

"We should probably have someone watching your cabin," Ethan says. "She might o back there again."

"I'll have one of my people keep an eye on the video surveillance 24/7. If we see er, we'll contact you immediately."

"Roan," I say, "go with Evelyn back to her world so at least one of us can phase ere in case we need her help."

Roan stands next to Evelyn. She places her hand on his arm and phases back to her lanet.

"I should go tell the others what we've learned," Ethan says to us. "We'll start tationing people in any place we can think of that she might go."

"Okay, Ethan," I say, knowing he feels as though he has to do whatever he can to ind Helena.

Ethan phases, leaving Malcolm and me alone.

"Do you think I should phase to Heaven and tell Cade what's happening?" I ask Malcolm.

"I don't think that would be wise until we know we can find Helena. If we can't, it will only cause him more worry."

"You're right," I say despondently. "I just wish there was something we could do ow."

Malcolm pulls me into his arms, instantly bringing me comfort.

"The War Angels will find her," Malcolm says confidently. "I've never known them to fail in something they set their minds to."

"I'm not sure what I'm more worried about," I confess. "Them finding her or not finding her. She won't give that baby up easily, Malcolm. I can tell you that much."

"Let's not worry about that until we have to," my husband suggests. "Let's just try to find joy in the day again and worry about tomorrow when it comes."

I hug Malcolm even tighter, knowing that he's right. There's no point in worrying about something that may or may not happen. All that would do is drive me crazy.

I do worry about the baby, though. I know how fierce my own love is for my children. What if Helena's feelings are just as strong with her own when it's born? If she touches the child, will she kill her own baby like she did Cade? His death was unintentional, but it doesn't mean the same thing won't happen again.

Ethan's right. We have to protect Cade's descendant. We can't let Helena harm the child with either her hate or her love.

And I refuse to fail Cade a second time...

Author's Note

Thank you so much for reading the Dominion Saga!

For the first time ever, I am going to let everyone vote on which Watcher book I should write next. Your choices will be the following:

1) Sweet Devotion – Mae and Tristan's story, which will be a single book.

2) War Angel Contingent – To be honest, I'm not sure if this will be one or more books. I really need to think about it some more before I can say for sure. It will deal with the War Angels finding Helena and Cade's child.

You will be able to vote on which book you would like me to write next at my website (www.sjwest.com) between November 15 – December 31, 2016. I will look at the poll on January 1, 2017 and announce which book has won.

The next book I plan to publish is entitled *Moonshade (Vampire Conclave, Book)*, which is a vampire romance series with a unique twist. After this letter, you will find the first chapter of the first book. I hope you enjoy it and join me on a new adventure that should be a lot of fun to read. I hope to have the first installment of this series out in December 2016. As always, I will keep you posted and let you know when the pre-order is available. Those of you who pre-order the book, will be able to purchase it at a slightly reduced price. This series will also be available to those of you using Kindle Unlimited.

Once again, thank you for reading Enduring!

Until next time…

Moonshade: Chapter One

It all started about two weeks ago. I woke up one morning feeling anxious about something. It's just like the feeling I used to get when I was a kid on Christmas mornings. I would want to rush downstairs as soon as I woke up to see what jolly old Saint Nick had left me underneath the Christmas tree, but I knew I had to wait for my parents to wake up or Santa might not be as generous the next year. That's the exact same feeling I have right now. Like there's a present somewhere just waiting for me to discover it. The only obstacles are: one, I have no idea what it is and two, I have no clue where to start looking for it. My heart literally feels like it will shrivel up inside my chest if I don't discover the whereabouts of my secret gift, but my mind is a complete blank as to where I should begin my search.

I decide to tell my best friend, Kaylee, how I'm feeling. I always thought Kaylee and I could pass for sisters. We have the same oval face and high cheekbones. Her hair is a bright shade of red cut in a cute short, layered style; whereas mine is long and a dark auburn color. She has green eyes, and I have brown eyes. She's a cute petite 5' 4" and I'm almost 5' 7". Well, on second thought, maybe we don't look that much alike, but we were raised as sisters, that should count for something.

When I was ten years old, Kaylee and I had a sleep over at her house. The next morning I learned the home I shared with my parents caught on fire, destroying not only the house I grew up in but also my life. After the death of my parents, Kaylee's folks went through the legal hassle of adopting me. Since I have no living relatives, they saved me from being swallowed up by the foster care system and raised me in a loving home where I was truly a part of the family. The Hughes weren't rich by any standards, but they always made sure Kaylee and I never wanted for anything important. We lived in a quaint neighborhood at the end of a cul-de-sac in a nice ranch style home with the obligatory minivan parked in the driveway.

The first year after the loss of my parents was a tough one for me. If it hadn't been for the unconditional love the Hughes supported me with, I'm not sure how my life would have turned out. It's quite possible I could have ended up living on the street if the state had tried to shuffle me around between different foster homes. I count my lucky stars every day that I was blessed with the perfect people to help me cope with my grief.

Enduring

After Kaylee and I graduated from college with our degrees in education, she married her high school sweetheart. Ever since we were children, Kaylee has always written stories and dabbled in poetry. With her love of the English language, she decided to be a high school English teacher. I, on the other hand, was always drawn to science and the logic behind how things work, so I decided to be a biology teacher. We were lucky enough to both find jobs at the Pecan Acres Junior High School. Yesterday was our last day of the spring term, which ended up being perfect timing for me. I'm not sure I could have concentrated on my classes considering my current state of mind.

Kaylee's gained a lot of weight in the past seven months, but I guess she has a good excuse. She *is* growing a little Emma Louise inside her after all. The only problem with trying to discuss things with a pregnant woman is that all of her responses seem completely driven by the set of raging hormones running rampant inside her body.

"Maybe this anxious feeling you're having means you're about to find the love of your life," she beams excitedly while we sit at her kitchen table. "You know, your horoscope for this month said you would meet new and interesting people."

"I don't believe in that mumbo jumbo. You know that," I tell her, absently playing with my cup of tea on the table. Even though this is supposed to be a relaxing Saturday morning breakfast with my bestie, I'm unable to shake the uneasy feeling that I'm supposed to be somewhere else.

"Sarah, you need a man in your life," she sighs.

Kaylee and I have had this discussion at least twice a month since she became the poster woman for marital bliss. She is determined to have me engaged by my twenty-forth birthday. Luckily, that means I have exactly a year before she goes into psycho matchmaker mode.

"I wish you could find someone like my Ben," she says with a dreamy look on her face.

Ben Whitaker is Kaylee's husband. We all went to high school and college together. Ben and I never really hit it off. We only tolerate one other because we have to share Kaylee, but I have to give him props. He does make my sister extremely happy, and that's all that matters in the long run.

"You got lucky," I tell her, feeling a small pang of jealousy. "Not everyone can find the person they're meant to marry when their sixteen."

Kaylee places a comforting hand over the one I have resting on the table beside my cup. "There's someone out there meant just for you, Sis. I know it."

"Ever the optimist." I try to smile but my facial expression doesn't quite make it that far.

"One of us has to be where your love life is concerned."

I finish my tea and make up an excuse about needing to restock my kitchen with groceries.

"Hey, would you mind telling me how Emma is feeling today before you leave?"

I can't help but smile at Kaylee's constant desire to be reassured her baby is emotionally well adjusted. However, I guess if I had access to that sort of information about my own unborn child, I would want to know too.

Ever since I can remember, I've always been able to sense what other people are feeling. I'm sort of like Deanna Troi on Star Trek, an empath. Sometimes it's a real pain in the ass sensing the emotional states of strangers, but the certainty of knowing the people you love the most love you back just as fiercely is priceless. I've learned how to dampen my ability when I need to, if for no other reason than to just keep my sanity intact. There are some real weirdos out in the general population. The world is a much happier place when I don't know they're out there.

I put my hand on Kaylee's bulging belly. Normally, I don't have to touch someone to know what they're feeling, but since little Emma is still safely snuggled inside her mother's womb, I need the extra closeness to distinguish Em's feelings from Kaylee's.

"She's happy," I report, cherishing the pure, innocent emotions emanating from my little niece. "And she loves her mommy very much."

Kaylee smiles and places her hand over the one I still have on her bump. "Thank you."

I bend over and kiss Kaylee on the cheek before turning back around to grab my purse off the table.

"Don't forget we're taking you out for your birthday tonight. So don't eat a big lunch," Kaylee orders.

I roll my eyes at her. "How could I forget? You've been reminding me every day for a month now about our big secret adventure. What exactly *do* you have planned?"

"If I wanted you to know, I would have told you a month ago. Just make sure you wear that dress you wore to the faculty dinner."

"So we're going somewhere fancy?" I ask, doing my best to glean some tidbit of information about her plans.

"Stop trying to make me tell you anything, birthday girl. Just do what the pregnant woman says so you make her happy."

"As you wish Princess Butterball," I bow in Kaylee's direction to which I get hit in the head with a wadded up paper towel.

"Ohhh, just you wait, Sarah Marcel," Kaylee promises, narrowing her eyes and pointing her index finger at me. "When you're as big as a house with your first child, I'll remember you called me that."

I laugh and wink at her before heading down the hallway to the front door.

"And try to take a nap this afternoon!" she yells at my back. "We're going to be out late!"

I wave my hand over my head as I head out the door so she knows I heard her. After I get into my newly purchased silver Toyota Camry, I crank the engine and end up sitting in Kaylee's driveway for a good five minutes trying to decide where I want to go. I don't really need groceries. I haven't been able to eat that much in the past two weeks. In fact, I haven't slept that much either. If I can just figure out why I have this feeling that I'm supposed to be somewhere specific, maybe I can get back on track and start living normally again.

I put my car into drive and take off down the road, not really having a plan, which is so unlike me. I always plan things out before I do them. Kaylee often picks on me for my obsessive compulsive disorder, but I know she appreciates my organizational skills, especially when it comes to planning parties and vacations. She doesn't have to think about anything when we're traveling together. All she has to do is enjoy all my hard work. But, it really isn't work to me. I feel happier when I know exactly what it is I need to do. I suppose that's why I feel so unhappy right now. I don't know what to do, and I don't know how to plan for something I can't figure out.

I decide to drive around town for a bit to take my mind off my problem. Pecan Acres is a small town in Louisiana, no more than eighteen-thousand people live within its city limits. If we want to go to a big city, New Orleans is only an hour away. My town has the basic necessities: restaurants, a mall, a movie theater and of course, every small town's staple of survival, a Super Wal-Mart.

I find myself driving down Bayou Road where the new and old moneyed families live. Some of the houses are old style antebellum era homes built in the Greek revival style and some are newer more up to date versions trying to imitate them but failing miserably. Personally, I prefer the older mansions. They have a sense of history locked into every nook and cranny unlike the new construction, which just seem like expensive wannabe knock offs.

I feel an unexplainable urge to pull off to the side of the road in front of one of the older homes. It's a custom-built red brick mansion with grand Georgian scroll molding over the front door and four large Greek Corinthian white columns lining the front porch. My anxious feeling seems to subside somewhat as I continue to study the manor. I'm not sure why, but I feel a violent urge to run up to the front door and barge inside. There's something in there pulling at me, compelling me to throw common sense out the window and simply follow my instincts. Before I completely lose my mind and do something I'll regret later, I shift my car into drive and head back to my apartment.

When I finally make it home that afternoon, I try to do what Kaylee suggested and take a nap. I end up tossing and turning in bed until it's time for me to get ready for my big night out with her and Ben. I pull out the dress she wants me to wear from my closet to see if it needs to be ironed. Luckily it doesn't. If there is one thing I hate doing in this world, it's ironing clothes. It's a little black knit dress with a twisted halter empire bodice and short skirt that comes to just above my knees. It's a simple outfit but formal enough to wear to a nice restaurant.

Enduring

As usual, Kaylee and Ben are late picking me up. Ben knocks on my apartment door most thirty minutes after the time Kaylee said they would be there.

When I open the door, I smile politely at Ben who is dressed in a nice baby blue button own shirt and khaki slacks.

"Better late than never, right?" I joke.

"You know how she can get," Ben grins. "We can't leave the house if she has a hair out place. Are you ready?"

I grab my small black purse from the coat tree and lock the front door before I step out. I ollow Ben back to the new family vehicle he and Kaylee just purchased in expectation of Em's rival, a silver Dodge Durango.

"I'm pregnant," Kaylee uses as an excuse for their tardiness as I slip into the back seat ehind Ben's chair. "I move a lot slower now."

"You know that excuse isn't going to work after you have the baby," I tease her buckling y seat belt.

"By then she'll have moved on to 'It's the baby's fault'." Ben chuckles as Kaylee layfully slaps him on the arm.

"You two need to be nicer to me." Kaylee sticks her bottom lip out to garner our ympathy. "I'm doing the best I can."

"We both love you more than anyone else in the world," I tell her. "So stop pouting."

Kaylee sticks her tongue out at me, but I know she isn't offended by our teasing. Plus, he likes being reminded how important she is to both Ben and I.

"So can you tell me what my birthday surprise is now?" I ask.

Kaylee turns her head to look back at me. "We're going to New Orleans and eating at Wolfgang Puck's restaurant. Then we're takin' you dancing on Bourbon Street!"

"Seriously?" I must have heard her wrong, right? "You're actually taking me dancing in your condition?"

345

"My doctor said it would be ok as long as I took it easy. So don't worry, mother hen. Little Em and I will be just fine. Who knows, maybe you'll meet somebody while we're out."

I shake my head in exasperation but remain mute on the subject. I turn my head to watch the passing scenery outside the window. Unfortunately, there's not much to keep my eyes busy on the highway besides pine trees and the occasional swamp. I don't want to argue with Kaylee when she's trying to do something nice for me on my birthday. Although, I can already tell she' going to be in full matchmaker mode that evening. I just can't believe she's actually thinking about pawning me off to some random stranger at a bar! I hang my head and silently pray for divine intervention. I would like to be spared any embarrassment on my birthday, but the odds o that happening don't seem to be in my favor.

The food at the restaurant is probably wonderful. To be honest, I can't really tell. I haven't been able to taste food for two weeks. I almost feel guilty for not being able to enjoy my meal since I know the entrees are slightly on the expensive side at this restaurant. In fact, you have to make reservation months in advance to even get a table. I hate not being able to enjoy th filet mignon I ordered. I'm sure if things were normal it would have tasted like a little slice of heaven in my mouth. To be totally honest, I'm relieved when dinner is finally over.

By the time we leave the restaurant, it's already ten o'clock.

"Shouldn't we just head home?" I ask them as we stroll down a crowded Bourbon Street. Saturday night in New Orleans probably isn't the best time to come with a pregnant woman. I try to play offense and walk in front of Kaylee so people who aren't paying attention to where they're going or simply drunk run into me first.

"No, we're going dancing," Kaylee states in her 'don't you dare argue with me' voice.

We end up at a nightclub called the Voodoo Lounge. Kaylee knows I'm not much of a dancer. It's not that I can't dance. I just don't like to dance in public. From the way the people inside the club are acting, you would think it was everyone's birthday and not just mine. There is a raised wood dance floor in the middle of the room. It's so full of gyrating bodies I don't see how Kaylee expects to survive within the crush of people. There's a DJ playing music on his own platform against a sidewall. A full bar made out of mirrors is located at the backend of the

om and is swarming with patrons trying to purchase beverages. Kaylee and I sit at one of the
mall, stool high tables near the dance floor while Ben fights the crowd to get us some drinks.

I'm not much for imbibing in alcohol, but I do enjoy the occasional Crown and Coke.
en brings one back for me, a Corona for himself, and a ginger ale for our Kaylee.

I'm about halfway through my drink when I feel the hairs on the back of my neck stand
1 end. Someone is staring at me. Usually when I'm in a crowd of people, I block my empathic
bility so I'm not bombarded by a multitude of mixed emotions all at once. For some reason, I'm
ot able to block out the emotions of this particular person. Their feelings are a jumbled mess,
ut the one that stands out the most is hunger. It's not a sexual hunger either. No, this is more
rimal than even that. It's almost as if this person wants to eat me alive, literally. What in the
orld is that supposed to mean?

Kaylee crooks her index finger at me silently beckoning me to come closer to her. I lean
orward so I can hear what she wants to say over the loud music reverberating against the walls
f the nightclub.

"There is a gorgeous guy behind you who hasn't been able to take his eyes off you since
ve got here," she informs me, lifting her eyebrows suggestively, attempting to play her role as
upid.

I lean back on my stool and turn a little in my seat so I can take a sneak peek at the man
Kaylee is eyeing as a potential suitor for me. Before I even locate him, I know without a shadow
of a doubt that he will be the same person whose emotions I can't keep out of my mind.

The room is dark, only lit by the multi-colored lights flashing chaotically across the
lance floor. The rhythm of the music seems to beat in time with the hammering of my heart as I
lowly turn my head to look where I know he's standing.

I see him leaning against one of the concrete pillars in the room with his arms crossed
oosely in front of him. He's wearing a dark grey button down shirt and black jeans. If I were to
say he's just handsome, I feel like it would be an insult to his beauty. The confident way he holds
imself gives him an air of royalty. He reminds me of an Eastern European prince with his dark
short-cropped hair and perfectly pale skin. He has a strong face with a full bow shaped mouth

and hauntingly dark deep-set eyes. His forehead is slightly wrinkled in a troubled frown as he continues to meet my steadfast gaze. The longer I stare at him the stronger his disapproval with me grows. I instantly feel like a kid who has done something wrong. For some inexplicable reason, I don't like feeling as if I've disappointed him.

Most people will give you some sign to acknowledge your presence when you catch them staring at you, but this man doesn't even flinch or try to look away. He just continues to stare at me without any hint of apology or embarrassment. The longer we gaze at one another, the stronger his need to be closer to me becomes. His emotions are so raw and open they almost overwhelm me. There is something familiar about him, yet strange and mysterious at the same time. The rapid beating of my heart causes a tightness to form in my chest, making it difficult for me to take in a full breath. I'm the one who ends up looking away first, trembling slightly from the encounter.

Kaylee touches my arm, breaking the spell the stranger just cast by forcing me to look up at her.

"Are you ok?" she asks, obviously worried about my reaction to the man.

I nod my head and try to smile reassuringly. The doubt in her eyes tells me I'm not fooling her for one second.

"Well try to pull yourself together because Mr. Gorgeous is heading this way."

I didn't think my heart could hammer against my chest any faster than it is, but somehow it finds a way to add an extra beat. I can physically feel him get closer to me. With every step he takes, the connection between us becomes more solid, like there's an invisible string tethering us together, growing more taunt the closer we come to one another. Oddly enough, I feel myself begin to relax and instantly feel the anxious feeling I've been living with for the past two weeks slowly dissipate.

I know the exact second he's standing behind me and can't stop myself from automatically turning around to face him.

He leans forward and whispers into my ear, "Come."

He holds out his hand to me not worried in the least bit that I will refuse his order.

Normally, I would have just laughed in a guy's face if he had said such a thing to me. But ith him, it's like I don't have a will of my own. I find myself placing my hand into his, eager to ollow him wherever he wants to go. I can only imagine this is what it must feel like when eople are hypnotized.

His skin is cold to the touch, like he's been standing inside a walk-in freezer for hours. et, I don't flinch away from his frigid caress. In fact, I feel myself wanting to melt into him, roviding him all the warmth my body has to offer.

Without saying another word to me but keeping his dark brown eyes fixed on mine, he ads me onto the dance floor where the music instantly changes to a slow song. He wraps his rms around my waist, and I drape mine over his shoulders, clasping my hands loosely around is neck. We sway to the music for a while just staring into each other's eyes. There's a soft rotectiveness in his gaze that makes me feel inexplicably safe. For some reason I can't nderstand, I know I can completely trust the stranger.

He slowly pulls me in closer to him. His cold cheek brushes against mine as he whispers n my ear once again.

"You need me as much as I need you," he says with a husky yearning, making my body hiver with anticipation of his next words. His voice sounds so familiar and yet completely oreign to me. He has a slight European accent I can't quite place. It sounds like a mixture of arious dialects. "I know you've been feeling like there's something you need to find. As if a iece of you is missing. I *am* that piece. I'm what you've been searching for these past two veeks. Don't try to fight it, Sarah," he murmurs before kissing the tender flesh just below my ar. He proceeds to kiss his way down the side of my neck, resting his lips on the pulsating artery ust below the thin layer of skin. His breathing becomes labored as he opens his mouth and ightens his lips around my throat. The sharp edges of his teeth gently graze my skin, as if he's esting how tender the flesh is in that spot. I feel slightly drunk on the intoxicating aroma urrounding him, a mixture of chocolate and cinnamon. I want him to do something to me, but 'm not exactly sure what that something is supposed to be.

Finally, he raises his head and looks into my eyes.

"You know where to find me."

He pulls away and leaves me standing on the dance floor feeling completely bereft by h sudden departure. I feel light headed from the encounter, almost like his touch was a drug. I don't want him to leave without me but am unable to make my feet move to follow him. Every cell in my body yearns to chase after him and demand to know who he is and why he means something to me. Maybe if I at least had his name I *could* find him again. What he said to me was the complete truth, not a boast.

I do need him.

I just don't know why.

Made in the USA
Middletown, DE
09 April 2017